STAR TREK®
VULCAN'S SOUL
BOOK III

EPIPHANY

JOSEPHA SHERMAN
& SUSAN SHWARTZ

BASED UPON *STAR TREK*
CREATED BY GENE RODDENBERRY

POCKET BOOKS
New York   London   Toronto   Sydney   Remus

Pocket Books
A Division of Simon & Schuster, Inc.
1230 Avenue of the Americas
New York, NY 10020

This book is a work of fiction. Names, characters, places, and incidents either are products of the authors' imagination or are used fictitiously. Any resemblance to actual events or locales or persons, living or dead, is entirely coincidental.

First Pocket Books paperback edition March 2008

Cover art and design by John Vairo Jr.

Manufactured in the United States of America

10   9   8   7   6   5   4   3   2   1

ISBN-13: 978-0-7434-6363-8
ISBN-10:   0-7434-6363-3

To Elly Brinkley and Peter Morphos, because every
godchild needs a trilogy.

With thanks to Keith R.A. DeCandido for service
above and beyond.

And our respects and thanks to Leonard Nimoy
and Joanne Linville, for the logical reasons.

ARCHIVIST'S NOTE

Not since the Vulcan matriarch T'Pau and Captain Jonathan Archer of Earth discovered the Kir'Shara has any artifact shaken our "knowledge" of Vulcan history as the coronet whose story the Vulcan Science Academy now releases to the United Federation of Planets for the first time. Presented to Surak upon Mount Seleya and subsequently bestowed upon Karatek, scientist of the former Vulcan Space Institute, the records contained in its crystals provide new information about the so-called Sundering from Vulcan. It is a story more complex, with more ambiguities of courage and honor, than any of the peoples involved had previously "known."

Experience has taught me that the lessons an eaglet, or aspiring officer, learns in the Imperial War College at Ki Baratan are different from the history learned by cadets such as my eldest daughter T'Savia, who, after the end of the Dominion War, has returned to Starfleet Academy. These lessons differ in content and orientation from the formal debates at the Vulcan Science Academy or from the harsh training in survival taught in the mines of Remus.

Inevitably, new events alter both history and the context in which we view it: as examples, consider Shinzon's revolution and the Watraii incursion.

My first human friend, Admiral Leonard McCoy, told me that on Earth, these refractions of history were once called "spin." But just as light that has been broken into colors can be reunified, the various "spins" put on historical events can be resolved by additional evidence.

For the new evidence we have now, the Vulcan Science Academy, the United Federation of Planets, the Romulan Star Empire, the Watraii Hegemony, and the Klingon Protectorate of Remus acknowledge their debt to the groundbreaking research of field exo-sociologist Commodore Terise Haleakala-LoBrutto (retired) as well as the efforts of Imperial Commander Charvanek (believed missing in action) and former Vice Proconsul M'ret, now in exile. More recently, these efforts have been supplemented by the mission of Healer and Adept T'Selis of Vulcan to wage peace with the Watraii. Finally, in this as in all things, we must acknowledge the unflagging efforts of Ambassador Spock of Vulcan toward reunification of a race that was not sundered into only two parts, as had been believed, but into four.

Just as a lens can break white light into color, then restore it to its original form, the lens of accurate and unsparing perception reveals the truth—at least until additional information is found. May we live to perceive and appreciate it.

—Ruanek
Research Fellow, Vulcan Science Academy
Formerly Commander, Fleet of the Romulan
Star Empire and son of Stavenek
House Minor Strevon, the Hearth of Romulus

EPIPHANY

ONE

MEMORY

Karatek, his wife T'Vysse, his surviving children, and the exiles who had pledged to spend a six-month rotation on this world of fire and ice to earn their fair share of the glowing planet now snatched from their grasp, stared at the viewscreen as if hoping that their enemy might say something different just this once.

"You will expand your current habitat. You will harden the landing field to receive ore transports, and you will keep yourselves fit so you can work.

"You will work, or you will die."

They had heard him correctly the first time.

On Vulcan, Karatek's people had weathered sand-fire storms. They had learned how to deal with predators that ran on two legs or four. They had survived raids, pillaging, and radiation as a result of tribal or planetary war. During their journey away from the Mother World, they had survived black holes, pirates, and even betrayals. But they had never before been confronted with abandonment on a barely habitable world with orders from their own blood kin to work or die!

1

Was life still worth it at this price?

The gale sleeting down outside the sealed mining colony's main viewscreen was cold beyond any known life-form's ability to survive. Air and water pulsed fast and loud in the tunnels they had hollowed out, as if their habitat was a living Vulcan heart struggling to withstand what could well be a mortal blow. Despite the painstaking seals of their airlocks, cold seeped in.

Cold was as much an enemy to a desert people as betrayal. It slowed them, weakened them, and made them sick at heart as well as in body. On the surface, the ruins of their shuttles and explorer ships were already icing over. They had no way off this planet now. As the storm rose, visibility plunged to zero. When they would finally dare to venture out to repair the landing field, they would find their ships' wreckage already entombed in frozen nitrogen.

"Avarak!" Karatek shouted. "Avarak! Do you hear me?"

"Never mind him," Solor spoke urgently into Karatek's ear. "Try to reach Vorealt, back on the ship. Use the backup system."

Solor hurled himself at the controls as his sister, Sarissa, pointed out, "Backup power is limited."

Her husband, Serevan, nodded. The habitat grew perceptibly colder as the engineer channeled power from life support to communications. The light dimmed to a deeper red, a color that was, ironically enough, an almost comforting reminder of Vulcan.

Healer T'Olryn huddled beside the airlock as it unlocked, bringing a gust of cold. Two more people trudged in, bearing a body so damaged it seemed too small to be a person.

"The wind is so strong we almost couldn't get the outer door unsealed," one of the newcomers said.

2

"We will not open it again until the storm subsides," Karatek replied.

"But there may be more people out there!" T'Olryn protested.

"I grieve with thee," Karatek said. "With all of us. Nevertheless, you will lock and seal the hatches. Am I understood? I will post a guard if I must."

The last thing that anyone trapped on the surface would see as his eyes froze would be the receding ships that had once held friends and brothers but now held traitors.

Perhaps, once the storm subsided, they could go out to retrieve and identify the bodies. And secure their envirosuits, which had suddenly become more valuable than their wearers, for recycling.

"This man is dead," T'Olryn's voice reverted to its earlier softness. Kneeling over the last body brought in, she set her hands over the place where its head should have been and closed her eyes. There was no *katra* left for her to find. She rose unsteadily, swaying, and flung out an arm. Solor grasped her hand and drew her in against him, a violation of privacy that, under the circumstances, was understandable.

"Vorealt!" Karatek cried. "Do you hear us?"

Static rose as if warring with the storm.

"They're jamming us," Sarissa observed. "It was to be expected."

"If we continue to divert backup power to communications," Serevan warned Karatek, "our shield generator will stall, and ambient radiation will penetrate the habitat. I estimate 3.7 days until it reaches lethal levels."

"I imagine that you've learned, right about now, that you're running out of time, Karatek," came Avarak's voice, startling them. *"I wouldn't waste it trying to appeal to Vore-*

alt or the others who've remained on board the ships. Some of them may be taking possession of Shavokh, your old home, right about now. They are talking about a complete refit, but they also need the raw and processed materials that we have promised them—and that you are going to provide if you expect to outlast your current food supplies."

They had perhaps two hundred days at full rations. Perhaps fifty more, if they stinted themselves. In this cold, to go hungry was to die.

"*The landing field will have to be repaired as well,*" Avarak said again. He allowed himself a sharp grin. "*In addition to fulfilling your initial mining quotas and expanding that kennel of yours.*" He turned his head as if listening to someone speaking out of range of the viewscreen.

"*Further communications waste my time and your power. You will hear from us again once the field is cleared and your output is ready for pickup.*"

Avarak's face disappeared. Karatek took a deep breath, wishing it had been he who had blotted it from existence. What recourse did he have? His conclusion: not much.

S'task, the fleet's leader, could not know of this betrayal. Obviously, sick as he still was, he would not be told. Vorealt and the ship clans could not be reached, at least not until the storm subsided and Karatek's engineers could repair the main generators.

Karatek met T'Vysse's eyes. For the first time in their very long lives, he regretted marrying her. With another mate, she might have stayed safe on Vulcan. Or she might have fallen to a biocide, like their eldest child, been trampled in a riot, or blasted to charred, radioactive bones.

T'Vysse touched his temple with her joined fingers.

"It is as it is, husband," she said. "For now, we have no

4

choice 'for we lived as slaves until we made ourselves free.'"
Her voice rose slightly as she quoted one of the last lines of
the te-Vikram prophecy. Thousands of years ago, those words
had forced the tribes out of Vulcan's cities, sending them out
across the Forge, and into the Womb of Fire.

"'We will remember; we will avenge; we will walk the
desert free.'"

The chanted response rumbled out from all of the te-
Vikram. Dissidents and terrorists they might be; they were
now their fellow laborers, except for one man. Flinging
back his head, he began to wail a death chant. Drawing his
knife, he poised it above his throat where the blood beat
most strongly.

An envirosuited figure brought a gauntleted fist down
across his neck, clubbing him to the deck. The figure unhelmed and faced T'Vysse: N'Evran, first woman to head a
te-Vikram clan.

Back on what they had dreamed would be their new home,
she had asked for all the desert land in the south continent.
To win it, she had pledged her own people to join Karatek's
clan on Remus. The world possessed minerals and hazards
enough to test even her tribe. But it had no air people could
breathe or land they could walk on without mortal peril. And
now, her people were trapped here.

How would she respond?

Slipping out of her envirosuit, N'Evran drew a dagger
from her belt and slashed it across her palm. In the reddish
light, the blood gleamed black.

T'Vysse reached for the knife and drew it across her own
hand, letting the blood flow onto the stone of this world.

"I speak for my family," T'Vysse whispered. "You speak
for your clan. We are one."

The two women joined palms. Blood trickled from their joined hands before the wounds closed in the quick healing that was part of their heritage from lost Vulcan. For a moment, the bleak little habitat did not seem quite so cold, nor their people quite so abandoned.

Karatek drew a deep breath, thankful that his control enabled him to keep it steady.

"What is our current status?" he asked.

"Redirecting power to life support," Serevan reported. Light and some faint warmth rose in the module, scarcely larger than the lost *Shavokh*'s main assembly hall. "I recommend we keep ambient temperature at 40 percent less than Vulcan optimal to conserve energy. The habitat module is undamaged, and field stabilizers appear to be intact. I don't think repairing the landing field is beyond our capabilities. Once the storm subsides, we can blast the ice smooth and allow it to superharden. That should sustain a landing while we contrive something longer-term."

"What if a ship did crash through into liquid nitrogen?" Solor's eyes flashed. "Would it be so bad? They've sentenced *us* to death."

"We still live, brother," said Serevan. "We still have a chance. I will not be responsible for reprisals."

T'Olryn leaned close to Solor. Her mate lowered his eyes.

"I want an inventory of our supplies," Karatek said. "We have to conserve in case we run into . . . additional unforeseen difficulties in mining. "

One of the te-Vikram laughed bitterly. "Avarak and his clan might be late with the next shipment. They might enjoy cracking the whip." He clenched a fist.

The ice overhead shuddered in response to a sharp quake followed by aftershocks. Overhead raged the storm. It was only the first of many they must survive until they took back what was theirs.

How could I have failed to notice Avarak's brutality or how many clients he amassed? Karatek demanded of himself.

He had always known Avarak was ambitious, that his logic was faulty when it was a matter of pride or property. At the very least, he should have remembered that the man held a grudge against Solor, against their entire family, because Karatek's son had won T'Olryn. What did it matter that Avarak was long married and the father of a highly unusual five children that he would easily be able to sustain on that other world? His pride had been injured, and he had fanned grievance into hatred for all these years.

How could I have led my family this far wrong?

If only Karatek could talk to S'task. The few times they had been able to converse quietly by themselves, their minds had followed much the same logic.

As well hope to bask in the warmth of the firefalls on the homeworld that had been stolen from them. As well hope to see Mount Seleya again. As well hope to have time now for meditation and even to record this staggering betrayal on the crystals of the coronet that had been one of the few personal items Karatek had brought with him into what were supposed to be temporary quarters.

"Father?" Sarissa was looking at him.

Karatek could not fail her, not again. He made a supreme effort, met her eyes openly, and nodded.

"We had better get started," Karatek's daughter said.

He heard people counting off, forming shifts.

"I suggest you make it four shifts, not three," Serevan said. "We are unlikely to have the endurance, at least at first, to work for long periods in the cold. If you lead the first shift, I

7

will have created production tables by the time you come off duty."

"Why four shifts?" demanded N'Evran.

To Karatek's surprise, Serevan grinned, a humorless stretch of white teeth that looked feral in the ruddy light of the habitat.

"I want us to exceed production quotas," he said. "More minerals. More crystals. More effort in expanding the habitat and getting manufacturing under way. We will give them what they demand."

Sarissa nodded. "The rest, we will keep for ourselves. We will yet be free once more."

People began to get up, to start moving in the light, still that comforting red, not the blue white of actinic radiation or the whirling darkness of the storm outside.

The first shift trudged down into the mines in the certain knowledge that they would have to make the ice turn productive or be buried in it.

TWO

MEMORY

"When beginnings are flawed, the enterprise itself is marred. I grieve, not just for the harm done to us, but for the harm that Avarak and his allies, with whom we journeyed out from Vulcan into the dark, have done to themselves. I do not think, as I have been told, that I am being needlessly kind.

"How could I have overlooked Avarak's growing malice and ambition? This much I understand: his clan tired of their hardships. Nevertheless, we have spent too many years with them, shared too many ordeals to abandon them to their misdeeds by saying only: they are our enemies.

"When next the supply ships land, I shall attempt to reason with them yet again, as much for their sakes as for our own."

For all the good that would do!

Karatek removed the coronet that contained his memories and stored it in its silk-lined box. It was generous of his people to allow him use of this storage room as a meditation chamber. His meditations might bring him no solace. But history must be preserved. And so, each day, Karatek donned the coronet and recalled for whatever posterity might survive the story of how Vulcans had betrayed Vulcans and forced them to labor beneath the ice.

Each time the ships had landed to take away what store of processed metals and crystals Karatek's people had been able to wrest from the ore beneath the ice, he had tried and failed to reason with the people Avarak had sent.

He ran his hand across his brow. It came away green. He checked his radiation badge: not time, yet, to go to the dispensary that T'Olryn and her volunteers had established for radiation treatments.

He let his hand slip to touch the warmth that the memory crystals, the color of a healthy man's blood, still generated. As they cooled, he shivered. Although Serevan had restored full power to the habitat, his team of engineers and the volunteers working four shifts to the day had expanded it, too. Their priceless generators wheezed like an old man whose lungs were losing the fight against water-sickness. As the exiles whom treachery had turned into slave labor drilled farther through the ice and into the rock, the habitat became even colder than *Shavokh* at the worst of its equipment breakdowns.

Last time the supply ships had touched down, Karatek thought, one officer was careful to let slip in his hearing that the settlers on what should have been their homeworld, too, had had to break up one ship for readily accessible metal. In one last petty vengeance, they had chosen to destroy *Shavokh*. It was illogical to pity what was, after all, a disintegrating ship, he mused, but if it had not been betrayal to give away some of their own hard-won reserves, he almost thought that some of his people might have done so to preserve their former home. He sighed. What was, was; *Shavokh* was gone.

Now that they had managed to craft one additional generator, Serevan had promised more heat in their living quarters. As they began to process more tritanium and duranium, the ion furnaces would make it even warmer and provide them with ample supplies of fresh water. Soon, they could expand their gardens. Best yet, the projected completion date for the duranium door cores that would seal in precious warmth from the surface had been pushed back.

With that superhardened metal concealed within their old airlocks so the cargo ships' sharp-eyed crews would not see the improvement and boost their demands, Karatek's people would be safe from the nitrogen and methane storms that constantly threatened to blast their way in, freezing them all as they huddled together for warmth.

The warmth came at a grave price. As his people delved deeper and deeper, radiation would begin to be even more of a problem than injuries and despair. Wounds were already slower to heal, and T'Olryn had reissued the sorts of stringent radiation protocols Karatek remembered after nuclear strikes back on Vulcan.

If they had wanted to die of radiation sickness, why had they bothered leaving the Mother World? N'Evran had asked.

Karatek had observed that she asked an odd question for one who had grown up in the Womb of Fire. That, she said, was natural radiation. So was this, but the place was not of their choosing.

He heard the quick, light tap of heels on the frost-slicked floor and identified the step: T'Olryn, bringing him the latest casualty reports and supply lists. As the labor colony's needs grew, demands for medical supplies had become requests and, Karatek suspected, would deteriorate into pleas as T'Olryn's lists lengthened.

"Father?" came her voice. "May I speak with thee?"

11

"Always, daughter." Sarissa had been dear to him from the minute he had met her on the Forge. His care for T'Olryn had developed over time, but was no less heart-deep.

"I have two cases where I have had to amputate fingers and toes," T'Olryn told him. Her eyes flicked to the minute wounds on his brow, evaluating, triaging, and dismissing the injuries before she went on.

"More serious: I think I shall have to remove Ovatri's arm below the elbow. We shall have to ask for additional prosthetics when the cargo ships return 4.1 days from now."

"I shall do my best," said Karatek.

His daughter-in-law glanced away, as if abashed.

Night and day, it was not as if she were an extravagant, cloistered girl out of the oldest erotic verses of Vulcan's First Dynasty, wheedling lavish fire-gems or silks out of her lover's father! T'Olryn was a healer, and she had—her patients had—a right to the tools that would enable her to practice her arts.

It hurt that Karatek could not simply hand over what she required. Both his daughters and, for that matter, his own consort could use some gentleness in their lives.

Karatek saw in T'Olryn's face his own awareness of the cold equations that governed their lives: basic supplies were provided only after their quotas were met. For anything else, demands in terms of increased productivity and specialized output were very high. The advanced regeneration therapy and gene resequencing techniques T'Olryn had asked for a year ago had cost them a third of their reserve of crystals, although not their best ones. When the painfully acquired supplies had been landed, at least half of them had been found to be defective.

Prostheses, along with the additional food and agricultural

supplies he had requested, might require them to add a fifth labor shift. As his people tired, the rate of accidents would increase, and people would begin to die more quickly than they were already doing. At some point, their population would drop to the point where they could not meet Romulus's demands or reproduce themselves.

She said, "Solor believes we have hit the point of diminishing returns."

"Solor's view is unnecessarily bleak," Karatek tried to tell her. And it had grown bleaker after T'Lysia, the surviving daughter of the two born in space to T'Vysse, had died, unable to thrive beneath the ice. T'Vysse had mourned her other children deeply. She spoke not at all of this one.

"I believe he misunderstands: those on the other world want us strong enough to labor, but not strong enough to resist."

"And we continue to labor why?" T'Olryn asked.

"It is life," Karatek said.

"Is it? Is it still life?" T'Olryn demanded. Behind her pale, composed face, Karatek thought he could see the anguish of a girl-child whose pet *sehlat* had failed to return from a foray into the desert. His eldest daughter—not the two little girls who had died since then—how she had wept when I-Rayna disappeared! Karatek had not thought of I-Rayna's loss for more than one hundred years. And then, his strong, healthy girl had gone out with her class and never returned herself after that sneak biogenic attack.

He met T'Olryn's eyes and tried to will his own conviction into them. If she, a healer, were beginning to despair, how could the rest of them endure?

She sighed, and then looked down.

"We are what remain of Vulcan," she conceded.

It was sufficient for now.

Karatek suppressed the elation he felt that, once again, she agreed with him. One day, she might not, and then where would they be?

"You must do the best you can with what you have," Karatek heard himself say. He sounded like a stranger to himself.

T'Olryn's eyes blazed. Then, she looked down, mastering what he knew was a completely logical outrage. He wanted to tell her he understood, but he had vowed to master his passions, and master them he would. Besides, if he gave way to hatred, that way lay despair.

"I ask pardon," she murmured.

"In the family, all is silence."

"Then I ask permission to withdraw."

He had nodded. "You are a good woman, daughter, and I wish I had more to give you." He reached out to touch her wrist with two fingers, a caress permissible between father and daughter, and sensed, heartbreakingly, her forgiveness.

Sighing again, Karatek left the meditation chamber. His miners were beginning to chip away crystals that rivaled his coronet's gems for size, if not functionality. If there was ever time, those of the exiles with the strongest mental gifts would begin to test them. If they could amplify the gifts of the mind, they might be able to improve the terrible living and working conditions here—to say nothing of replacing increasingly uncertain communications systems.

"T'Olryn!" came a shout from the communicator grid set into the corridor.

For a moment, Karatek froze. Who would he lose this time? His son-in-law? His son? His daughter?

What manner of man are you? he demanded of himself.

The ice was no respecter of persons, nor should he be. Each of his people was of inestimable value.

But as he recognized his son Solor's voice, his heart subsided to its normal pounding.

"It's Refas!" Solor's voice boomed into the habitat, drawing people away from their tasks. *"Refas has gone out into the ice!"*

THREE

WATRAII HOMEWORLD

2377

The *U.S.S. Alliance* screamed out of its orbit above the Watraii homeworld, soaring out into open space, all the while dodging the continuing flashes of garish green ground-to-air fire from Watraii outposts but deliberately not retaliating.

We do not want to risk killing Watraii civilians, Ambassador Spock thought.

Originally, the *Alliance* had been commissioned as a science vessel. But from the start of the Dominion War until now, a year after the war's end, the vessel had been serving primarily as a warship.

Right now, though, Spock thought, sitting in the seat next to the command chair of his wife, Captain Saavik, it might be more accurate to call it a rescue ship. Or even, considering that a theft—or recovery—of a Romulan artifact had also been part of that rescue, perhaps it could be called a privateer like their two Klingon allies, *Dragon's Wrath* and *Demon Justice,* who were closely following them.

16

Spock recalled the Federation's first encounter with the Watraii as an eerie apparition on a viewscreen:

The alien wore some form of ceremonial mask, a perfect, featureless oval of so dark a green that it was almost black, and ornamented with etched zigzags from top to bottom like so many lightning bolts. The mask covered the alien's face so completely that only the occasional hints of dark blue eyes could be seen.

A voice boomed out, cold and without emotion. "I am a Watraii. You do not know this name yet, but you shall. You will come to learn it and to fear and respect it as well. For we are a wronged people, a race denied its rightful home. Hear me, you who watch. My people lay claim to the homeworlds of our kind. We lay claim to nothing less than the worlds you call Romulus and Remus."

Yes, Spock thought, and in the process of making that incredible claim they had destroyed a defenseless Romulan colony world and killed all those upon it, and then, in a second attack on the Romulans, had stolen away an artifact that Admiral Uhura had described as vital enough to be considered a "secular Grail." They had also taken a human prisoner, Admiral Pavel Chekov.

Now both Chekov and the artifact had been recovered. Spock, a captive on the planet's surface, had spoken with the Watraii commander, and in the process of trying to negotiate with him, had also, as the humans might have put it, broken Chekov out of jail. Meanwhile, the unlikely team of Ruanek, who had been born a Romulan but was now living as a citizen on Vulcan, and the android Lieutenant Commander Data, on leave from the *U.S.S. Enterprise,* had stolen the artifact out of a Watraii stronghold.

But what would come from that double rescue and from

Josepha Sherman & Susan Shwartz

the Watraii claims and attacks, no one could logically predict.

Once out of orbit, Captain Saavik ordered, "Bring shields and cloak online." The cloaking device had been an unofficial gift from the Romulans. "I assume that we *do* have cloaking again?" she added. Thanks to equipment incompatibilities, they hadn't had it for most of the perilous trip toward the Watraii homeworld. "Yes? Excellent."

"Watraii ships approaching from the surface," Lieutenant Abrams said.

Not surprising.

The *Alliance* sped away for the system perimeter, *Dragon's Wrath* and *Demon Justice* keeping pace with them and the Watraii ships in pursuit.

"We are clear of the system," Abrams said.

Saavik nodded. "Very good. Go to warp three. Get us out of here."

Once in interstellar space, the *Alliance* received simultaneous messages from the captains of the two Klingon ships, who had clearly been waiting with anticipation for the chance to rejoice. Their faces appeared side by side on the viewscreen.

"*Captain Saavik,*" JuB-Chal, captain of the *Dragon's Wrath,* announced with glee, "*you have given us a glorious fight.*"

Tor'Ka of the *Demon Justice* added, "*And it will be joyous to join you in battle yet again.*"

"If need be," Saavik said carefully. Her quick glance at Spock said without words, *Let there not be a battle.*

Even though they seemed to have outpaced the Watraii ships for the moment, no one aboard the *Alliance* would have been foolish enough to believe they were out of danger. Not when they were carrying so precious a cargo as they were.

Chekov was part of it, of course. But one human life, no

matter which life, was not the major issue at the moment. There was also the Romulan artifact. The object was vital to Romulan culture and, just possibly, also vital to that people's continued existence.

But what is it? Spock mused. *Why would two cultures claim it so fiercely and be willing to fight and kill to possess it?*

Oh yes, the artifact was, without doubt, a rare and beautiful thing. A mysterious object, it looked most like an elegant, intricately engraved metal crown such as a priest might have worn on Vulcan in the long-past days before Surak. Wrought with all the bold artistry of ancient Vulcan, set with green gems wound with bright wire, it was a true work of art.

But that was hardly the reason for its importance. The artifact was so much more than a mere relic, no matter how old or valuable, and its beauty was only incidental to its actual purpose. Neither Romulan nor Watraii had yet been able to decipher its secrets.

Spock had, of course, many years ago, though that was a closely guarded secret. The question now was, what did the Watraii want with it?

But that issue lay in the future. For now, the more important concern was deciding what to do with it and where to take it.

"I have considered the problem at length," Spock murmured to his wife. "It seems only logical that the artifact will be safest on Vulcan."

"Logical, indeed," Saavik agreed, just as softly. "Set course for the Eridani system," Saavik said to the conn officer.

"Aye aye, Captain."

She who had recently been Ensign Tara Keel, a new human assignee to the *Alliance,* looked warily about the hallway as

Josepha Sherman & Susan Shwartz

she walked, pretending to be merely checking a reading on the small padd she held as she went.

No one noticed her. But that wasn't surprising, after all. She seemed, she knew very well by this point, like nothing more than just another one of the several new ensigns on board the *Alliance,* in this case a young, blonde human, ever so slightly awestruck and naïve.

No one would ever have believed the truth, either. Bah, they would have no reason to even suspect it. Her true name wasn't Tara Keel but T'Gara, and her homeworld was not Earth but Korak, a Romulan colony planet. Of course, until very recently even she hadn't known the truth about herself—who she was and what she was—thanks to the checks and balances that had been carefully placed in her brain by her Tal Shiar superiors before the mission had begun.

T'Gara had, until now, been merely an observer, a passenger in her own body waiting for awakening, in the meantime performing the normal duties of an ensign without complaint. But the retrieval of the missing artifact by the *Alliance* had, as had been planned by her superiors, removed the alterations in her brain that had kept her seemingly human and docile, and allowed her to remember who and what she was and why she was here.

Oh, there actually had once been a Tara Keel, but the young human woman had met with an unfortunate fate shortly before she was to board the *Alliance.* This disguised version of that unlucky human was, T'Gara knew, perfect enough to fool a genetic scan. She was, to all intents and purposes, exactly who she seemed to be, rather than what she really was: a deep-cover operative.

Ah, perfect. No one was anywhere near her. Tapping into the *Alliance*'s communications system, the agent sent her

20

message in one efficient microburst. The contents—that the artifact had been recovered, that their course had just been so significantly altered—would quickly be received by the proper sources and forwarded to Chairman Koval—always assuming, of course, that the sickly chairman was well enough to acknowledge them.

But T'Gara ignored that moment of doubt. *Someone* in the Tal Shiar would receive her message. It would be delivered to the proper recipients.

And yes, even if someone here aboard the *Alliance* noted the sudden tiny surge of energy, there would hardly be time just now even for someone as efficient as Spock to investigate, let alone to discover the agent on board and to learn that the Tal Shiar, and the Praetor behind them, now knew that Captain Saavik had just diverted the ship to Vulcan.

"—and perhaps the Vulcan Science Academy would be the most logical place for the—"

Lieutenant Abrams cut in urgently, "Sorry to interrupt, Captain. We're not alone anymore. What looks like the entire Watraii fleet is coming after us."

"Not surprising," Ruanek muttered. "In their place, I'd be sending everything after us, too."

"Indeed," Spock agreed. "We have what might be called their main bargaining chip."

Saavik opened the intercom. "Engineering, I need to go to warp six."

From the engine room came a familiar voice that held a Scottish burr and a definite touch of humor. *"'Tis not a problem, Captain."* Captain Montgomery Scott said with relish. *"The engines can easily stand the strain."*

Turning to her husband, the corners of her lips turned up

oh-so-slightly, Saavik asked rhetorically, "And how many years has he been waiting to say that, I wonder?"

"The Watraii are keeping pace with us," Abrams said. "Not gaining, but not falling back, either."

"Time until reentering Federation space?"

"Three hours, forty-five minutes."

Too long. "Warp seven."

"They're still keeping pace with us," Abrams said after a moment.

The *Alliance*'s unlikely allies, *Dragon's Wrath* and *Demon Justice,* suddenly decloaked.

"This chase is ridiculous!" Captain Tor'Ka snapped over the com system. *"We shall even the odds a little."*

The two Klingon ships turned back to the Watraii in two perfectly synchronized arcs that spoke of previous teamed experiences. The neatly assembled, carefully organized Watraii fleet fell into sudden disarray as the lead ships took evasive action and their captains tried to fire at the swift, maneuverable privateers without hitting their own vessels.

Saavik raised an eyebrow at Spock. Useless to tell those two to stand down: They were neither part of her fleet nor under her orders.

"They've taken out two Watraii ships," Lieutenant Abrams said almost calmly, "and damaged two others. The Watraii fleet is reassembling but dropping back to warp . . . six point seven."

"Those pirates can't be planning to take on the whole fleet," Ruanek said. "Unless they've decided that this really *is* a good day to die."

They hadn't. In another perfectly synchronized move, the two Klingons arced away from the Watraii and sped back to rejoin the *Alliance.*

"You give us the chance for glorious battles!" Captain JuB-Chal announced.

"I'll take that as a compliment," Saavik said dryly.

"Didn't do much good," Abrams said with somewhat less calm. Twin explosions on the viewscreen told them all that the Watraii, cold-bloodedly practical as ever, had simply destroyed the two damaged ships. "They're back at warp seven."

Saavik let out a small sigh. "Warp eight."

The *Alliance* sped into Federation space, but so—their speed undiminished—did the Watraii.

FOUR

MEMORY

"Keep Refas talking. If he shows any signs of opening his envirosuit, stop him!" T'Olryn's voice arched up. "Sir, he's not listening to the workers on shift! He's moving out past the excavation area."

"Refas!" Solor shouted until Karatek could hear the strain in it, *"You keep those gauntlets on! I'm coming out to join you!"*

Don't you dare *die.* Karatek could practically hear the words his son had not spoken.

The thought was illogical, but the desire to preserve life was an imperative.

"Tell him *I* am coming," T'Olryn called up at the com. She hurried toward the lockers by the hatches, where the few spare envirosuits were stored. "I shall join you as soon as I can suit up!"

The ground shook slightly. Karatek glanced at the monitors set into the rock walls. T'Olryn was the only fully qualified healer they had.

"Not you, daughter!" Karatek ordered. "Of all of us, we can't spare you."

24

Refas, he thought. *Why him, of all the Vulcans now doubly exiled?* He had been one of the people who had been rescued from that planet where three disembodied brains forced them to fight and gambled on the waste of Vulcan life. Karatek's old teacher Rovalat had died to recover them.

In carrying Rovalat's *katra,* Karatek had learned just how much each of his students had meant to the old explorer, from the moment that they first entered his *kahs-wan* survival classes to the instant when Rovalat had left with Karatek all that he had ever been so he could sacrifice himself to preserve his students. The old teacher had tracked each one of his pupils lifelong. Losing any of them had been a cause of tremendous personal pain. Losing this one— Rovalat's *katra* had long released itself, but Karatek found himself unwilling for Rovalat to lose yet another student.

Rovalat had died to save Refas. What perversion of logic would motivate him to throw away what remained of his life? The man was not ill, he was not injured, he was not alone. He had survived the parasites who had wagered on Vulcans' deaths. He had survived the long, long journey. Refas had always supported *Shavokh*'s people, because they had saved him. And for that, he had been sentenced to the ice.

He must be reminded that life is worth living!

Even if he knows that is a lie?

It is no lie!

Karatek reeled from the onslaught of T'Olryn's mind. Her eyes blazed at him like the fires he had seen flickering where the ice thinned. One day, the planet's core might yet break through to the surface, yellow and red magma freezing as it fell back onto the ice.

But not today.

T'Olryn had always been a powerful telepath. Now, her

thoughts struck his consciousness without touch to direct them or apology for transgressing his privacy.

Or was what Karatek felt just another quake, more powerful than the ones that came before?

T'Olryn shook her head.

"I have just demonstrated to you the logic of allowing me to go. I have the best chance of retrieving him," she said. "If I can get into his line of sight . . ."

"Would you coerce him?" Karatek demanded. *"Can* you?"

Even for the man's own good, was the mental control T'Olryn proposed ethical?

His daughter-in-law tossed her head. A braid, pinned close against the nape of her neck so she could work unimpeded, came loose.

Preserve all life as if it were your own, but let the unwilling katra flee! That was one of the greatest of their ethical laws.

Father, there are so very few of us left!

Clearly, T'Olryn had decided to expand the guidelines set down for adepts and healers. From where had she gained this additional strength?

Shame colored her thought. She broke contact.

I ask forgiveness for my loss of control.

"Think, my daughter," Karatek demanded. "Regardless of the ethics of what you plan, Refas is one man. What of the needs of your other patients? Think of Ovatri, who will lose an arm if you cannot heal him. Think of your obligation to the rest of the colony!

"I shall go," he said. "In your place and in your service. I am too old to work a shift in the mines. For once, let me do something more meaningful than bandy words with Avarak's tame slave masters."

The corrugated metal of the new flooring shook for an

instant. *Worse than the usual tremor,* Karatek thought. The stresses of a planet that was half furnace, half ice often jolted the fragile colony. *Note: Make the development of new and better stabilizers a priority.* They had lost six people when one floor segment snapped open during a quake, then closed before the injured could be extricated. Engineers were still repairing a web of cracks in the landing field between the habitats and the place where ships usually touched down.

Let the ice gape and swallow them! Karatek thought with a level of rage that he had not felt for many years even before he left Vulcan. His hatred shamed him.

They had suffered a major quake 3.2 days ago. As Remus shuddered, racked by fire and ice, aftershocks shattered fragile equipment and threw the unwary off balance.

Karatek would have to take increasing care as he descended past the zone of ice into the newest excavation areas. A severe quake could bring the cave roof down on everyone working in the area.

If he did not come back, the task of negotiating with their captors would fall to Serevan or Sarissa, or even T'Vysse.

Who knew? Considering how spectacularly Karatek had failed, blind to the plots that had trapped his people into ice and slavery, almost anyone else could guide his people more wisely.

T'Olryn's eyes widened, growing very soft and bright. She stared at him as if she had not truly seen him for a long, long time. Then, she inclined her head, hiding her expression as if, this time at least, she regretted intruding on the privacy of his thoughts.

"I do not agree with your self-assessment," she said in a soft voice. "If you survive, we must discuss that. But I will help you suit up. And I will monitor your progress."

Karatek knew a moment's triumph—so there was still some use in being an elder—before realizing T'Olryn had probably decided that he, too, needed a purpose in life or he, too, would walk out onto the ice. Well enough, he decided, as long as that conclusion kept the colony's chief healer safe. He raced after the smaller, faster woman toward the storage lockers. They passed one set of obsolete airlocks, then another.

How much ground our people have already covered! he thought with a moment's pride. *Even in a prison, we can still build.*

But a larger prison was still only a prison.

Suicide, however, was no way for Refas to escape imprisonment.

By the time Karatek reached the lockers near the sealed doors leading to the most recent excavations, T'Olryn had pulled out an envirosuit and had laid it out, ready for him to put on. With exaggerated precision, Karatek hung up his padded overrobe, tugged off the cumbersome indoor boots, and stepped into the suit. Once encased, he began to assemble boots and gauntlets, sealing them against cold, radiation, and toxic gases.

Since their kinsmen had turned into their jailers, how many Vulcans had walked out to die? Even when they had left Vulcan, some people still preserved the custom of going out into the desert. A person who was blind, halt, or unable to keep up gave his or her flesh to the sand that had birthed all Vulcan, freeing the *katra* to drift on the wind and seek rebirth with the next child to draw breath.

The custom was condemned as barbarous, and rightly so. Probably, it dated from the predynastic, even the primitive, times, when to be Vulcan was to be nomad, except for the few

28

at the oasis in Gol or at Mount Seleya. Though it was mostly the te-Vikram who adhered to the old practice, every year a few of ShiKahr's oldest old hobbled out of the gates. If Vulcan had survived, probably, even now, they were not stopped.

In the ancient days, *kalifee v'rekor,* or battle with the desert, had been a way of winning a quick death without burdening one's clan. Was this colony's new custom to be a revival of barbarous old ways? Would those who lost heart or health simply walk out into the eternal cold rather than consume resources? It had happened. Some of the men and women who had died actually had endured long enough to strip off some of their gear, that it might be preserved and recycled for those who still lived. Their bodies were preserved in the ice.

As the settlement pushed outward, establishing new airlocks to mark their expanded territory, they had been able to retrieve some of those bodies and, with the terrible practicality forced upon them by their environment, use them for reaction mass.

Can we truly do no better than this? Karatek demanded of himself. His hands, in the heavy, articulated gauntlets, shook.

"Kneel," T'Olryn said. "Otherwise, I cannot reach your head."

He knelt, and the healer fitted the helmet of his envirosuit carefully onto his head. For an instant, her hands rested on the helm above his temples.

He calculated a 1 in 9.8 probability that she could read him even through the heavy protective layers of his helm. He pulled away, but not before he had received sensations of calm, acceptance, devotion.

She studied him, and then, with a tug, secured a latch he had forgotten. On this world, forgetfulness could kill.

He nodded his thanks.

The ground shuddered again: a reminder. He remembered the time T'Aria had forgotten that Remus could be even more treacherous than the people who had banished them. Her body had been buried under so much ice it could never be reclaimed.

Karatek checked the remainder of the fastenings with renewed concentration. If he had not taken proper care with his envirosuit, he would only be throwing another life away. If *he* died, no one would ever believe it was an accident. They would think he had abandoned them. They might lose heart and wish to die. And they had to live.

"Attach the telemetry hookups," T'Olryn said. "Maybe I can help you persuade Refas to come back to us."

Attaching the telecommunications links and securing the medical scans would add 2.8 minutes to the time before Karatek could head out in pursuit. A man could die in those moments. Still, if T'Olryn could appeal to Refas, their chances of saving him improved.

They had not left Vulcan just to die as slaves! Karatek had to believe some good purpose yet remained, or he would go out onto the ice himself. He nodded and powered up the circuits.

T'Olryn raced over to the nearest com unit.

"He's coming!" she cried. "Refas! Wait for us! Don't leave us!"

Her voice broke.

Did she know she had lost emotional control?

She was a healer. Her response was only logical.

When all the scans and gauges had been checked and rechecked, each ready light glowed. A new radiation badge gleamed surgically clean upon the breast of Karatek's envirosuit. Steadying himself against another aftershock, he inclined his head to the healer and lumbered toward the airlock. He stepped in, heard the slam as the door sealed, followed by the hiss as the outer door opened and precious, warmed air rushed out into the annihilating cold. Then he stepped outside, following the beacons of greenish white light that engineers had drilled into the walls of ice as he moved into the caves that they had been drilling for their very lives, in order to hunt his lost kinsman.

The thick walls gave way to striated, icy stone, opening into a wide bay in which triangular structural elements buttressed the thick walls. Drills bit deep into the veins of ore as suited workers, their faces invisible under sealed helms, the visors darkened against the sparks their drills provoked, pried at the glittering crystals embedded in the stubborn rock.

Recently, some of the dilithium crystals that had been mined were different, containing radioactive nanoblocs that could produce more power than the ones with which they had been familiar. Enough power, perhaps, to send ships soaring beyond the speed of light? If *Shavokh* had survived, Karatek would have exulted. He had ordered that those crystals be studied by their own physicists and, no matter their need, *never* be turned over to the slave masters on the hearth world that beckoned and frustrated them every time they looked out the viewscreens. He would order them destroyed or dropped into nitrogen or a lava pool first.

Another quake halted Karatek in his tracks. Throwing one arm up to protect his helm, he braced himself between two triangular structural supports until the tremors subsided. Ice and rock clattered down, smashing against his suit. For a long moment, he retreated within his consciousness, mastering his fear.

The ground steadied, allowing Karatek to recover his composure. If he did not hurry, a life would be lost unnecessarily.

Making what haste he dared on the slippery slope, he moved deeper into the pit. In the glare of the actinic lamps sunk into the frigid rock, he could see veins of ore shimmering in blood-greens and purples, phosphorescent as decaying vegetation, as he raced past.

"Do you have a fix on Refas?" Karatek called.

His voice echoed in his helm, like words in an empty barrel. Communications crackled with conflicting signals, distorted by heavy veins of metallic ore and the ambient radiation of the belowground.

Here, the main excavation didn't just narrow, it divided into a number of narrow channels that had been either carved out by drills or, in the tightest areas where the crystal deposits were too rich to be risked by machinery, chipped out by the labor of individual workers.

"Refas!"

Illogical egotism on his part to think that his voice might matter to a person planning to abandon his life on the ice, but he had to try.

"I saw a figure without drilling equipment heading toward coordinates 39X by 42Y by—"

The ground shook again. A few rocks fell.

"Say again? I missed your Z axis," Karatek called. He flung up a plated gauntlet to fend off a few last, tiny rocks. It was not nearly as bad as he had expected. But then, they had shored up this portion of the excavation with metal whose greater tensile strength enabled it to withstand more shocks.

"52Z, T'Kehr! I have him in visual range," came the voice. *"Shall I try to make contact?"*

"Keep him engaged!" came T'Olryn's command. *"Do not try to restrain him. It might provoke him."*

The Z coordinate indicated a steep descent down what was

32

still more a heap of rubble than an inclined plane. Handholds had been welded into the rock, cables strung between them to prevent falls severe enough to crack a faceplate.

Karatek paused, taking the instant he spared from his footing to check his radiation badge. The red meant his exposure was creeping toward the danger level: while it was nowhere near lethal, concentrated exposure . . .

"T'Olryn!" he called. "Tell Serevan I want shift times shortened for workers in this area. Tell him now!"

He heard her voice, fainter, as if she had turned away and was speaking off-line.

"Refas!" Karatek called again. "Where are you? I need to talk to you."

Static erupted, physically painful in the close confines of the helm.

"We've got a fix on him, T'Kehr!"

"Refas, don't move!"

"We're coming out to you!"

Voices erupted in Karatek's earphones. It was all he could do not to cry out in protest or press both gloved hands against his helm. Another aftershock struck then. He staggered, falling against a support. He clung to it with one hand and fended off rocks with another. If that ceiling caved in . . .

He should order it shored up. He would, assuming he survived. If he died, they would find him and do so anyway, he reassured himself.

Shouts of orders, warnings, and alarm and the rumbling and clattering of small cave-ins all around him created an exquisitely painful combination through which Karatek could still hear T'Olryn's voice.

"Kroykah!" Her command was almost as shrill as the alarms.

33

When all the noise had subsided, all Karatek could hear was his own breathing. Too rapid, he told himself: at this rate, he would consume all his oxygen so quickly that he, too, might require rescue.

"Refas?" he ventured to call.

"T'Kehr, *they've sent you out here on a fool's errand.*"

Success: Refas felt sufficiently engaged to speak up.

"No one sent me, Refas. I came of my own free will. Send me your position. I'm coming out to join you."

"Don't!" The younger man's voice became almost a scream of anguish. *"If anyone comes out here, I swear, I'll crack open my helmet!"*

"Why?" Karatek made himself ask. "Why would you do anything that illogical?"

He heard a gulp, then rapid breathing as if a Vulcan of mature age fought not to weep. *"T'Kehr? I appreciate the gesture, I truly do. But don't waste your own life coming after me. That last quake opened up a crack in the rock. It's 'hot.' I think I've found a lode of those nanobloc crystals. They're glowing. More: I'm seeing a kind of mist."*

"Radiation?" came T'Olryn's voice. Despite her control, Karatek could hear how worried she was, yes, and grieved, too.

"Elevated," Refas reported. *"In eight point five minutes, I will have reached terminal exposure."*

Over cries of *"Come back now!"* Refas continued. *"At least, I can be of some use now. Let me report. There's a kind of outgassing here, a pool of liquid . . . nitrogen, and . . ."* there was a long pause, during which Karatek held his breath and tried to subdue his heart rate to a more sustainable two hundred beats per minute. *"I can see them."*

Refas's voice changed. *"You know those extremophiles*

34

that the first missions down here sighted? There seems to be a whole colony of them by the pool here. They're tiny. This is going to sound illogical, but it's as if they're basking in the radiation. Their colors are changing, becoming deeper, more luminescent. They are actually quite aesthetically appealing."

"Father," came T'Olryn's voice in an urgent whisper on Karatek's private channel. *"I'm sending you a fix on Refas's position. See if you can approach him carefully. He might respond to you, even if not to the younger workers. But you'll have to be quick. The radiation levels are rising. If you can't convince him in ten minutes, you must leave. Do you hear me? I won't be able to heal you if you wait any longer."*

"I'm moving toward him," Karatek whispered.

"This is fascinating," came Refas's voice. His anguish seemed to have dissipated, replaced by rapt intellectual curiosity. *"In the three point two minutes since I spotted the extremophile colony, it has grown approximately 35 percent. I'm seeing different colors now, as if they're mutating under my very eyes. Some of the creatures are larger now . . . no, that's not correct; they seem to be combining . . ."* Refas yawned. *"It must be the radiation. Because it's getting warmer where I am. And it's so beautiful."*

"T'Kehr, *I think he's hallucinating,"* one of the miners called out to Karatek.

"He is not," T'Olryn said. *"I would like to observe these phenomena for myself."*

"You said there wasn't time!" Karatek protested.

"We're getting tremor spikes; this one's going to be big; take hold, take hold!"

Seeing no structural supports within reach, Karatek hurled himself at a natural rock arch as the ground vibrated so hard he fell to his knees. A chunk of what was practically solid hyponeutronium ore toppled from the cave face less than half a meter from Karatek's head. A crack opened in the rough-cut floor, and dust rose from the depths.

Refas cried out as if he'd fallen hard. For an instant, there was silence, then hard breathing.

"I told you, don't come for me! It doesn't matter now. I fell. One hand's in the pool. I can't feel it, and my helmet's cracked. The radiation's coming through. Don't grieve for me, and don't *retrieve my suit. It's too contaminated for you to recycle. Just let the creatures . . . they're glowing . . . changing . . . Such beautiful patterns, I almost think . . ."*

Refas's breathing grew rougher and shallower. Just as Karatek squeezed between two stalactites that sensors told him were almost pure dilithium, it stopped. Karatek halted. He saw the haze that Refas had mentioned. He saw the younger man's suited body lying facedown, half in, half out of the pool, and edged closer to it. Now he could see light glowing in the depth, a shivering rainbow of fire reflected in the dilithium crystals overhead.

Ice had begun to form on the suit. So had, Karatek realized, a population of what Refas had called extremophiles. Refas had told them, practically with his last words, how quickly they could mutate. For now, he was looking at a colony of teal-blue creatures with flagella of blood-green, glowing, crimson vacuoles, and odd fringes in the same colors as the fire trapped in the pools, far, far below. Their numbers were increasing fast, forming rainbow patterns that looped down the back and sleeves of Refas's envirosuit. As the colony grew, the ice that had begun to form a thin slick on sleeves, back, and helm began to melt.

Karatek forced himself forward, calling to the two miners he saw.

"We've got to get him out of there," he said.

Even though he was at least one hundred years older than the others, he reached Refas first and was engulfed in the vapor from the pit.

"Father!" came T'Olryn's cry of warning.

Seeing that he had one boot planted in what had been frozen gas, Karatek moved so fast he almost overbalanced. Now, he could see the corrugated tracks of his boot sole. Again, the nitrogen began to freeze—until what seemed like an entire loop of the extremophiles broke free of Refas's suit to populate the footprint. They spread out fast, then began to rise several centimeters, as if the liquid nitrogen engorged their vacuoles, or as if they had begun to multiply exponentially.

No time to make the calculations. He hoped his helmet cam was recording this.

Karatek cast a fast, desperate glance at Refas's boots. No damage there, and no extremophiles. He bent, grabbed the boots, and pulled the still figure away from the pool.

"Get out of there! You don't know what they'll do!" came T'Olryn's voice.

"Bad enough we're trapped here!" he said. "I won't take responsibility for wiping out a species native to this world."

He gasped. He was having trouble getting enough air now.

"Not even if we die for it!" he gasped. "They were here first!" He felt his knees weaken and sank onto the ice.

The two miners hastened toward him at a stumbling run. Grabbing him by the arms, they dragged him away from the pool, away from the pulsating colonies of extremophiles, and away from the body that was now almost totally covered by them.

Then Refas stirred.

FIVE

MEMORY

"He's alive!" whispered one of the miners.

Karatek recognized him: S'laron, a tall, thin man, emotionless even for a follower of Surak.

"Abomination," whispered his comrade. Shorter than S'laron, the figure was stocky. The voice whispering from the helmet com unit carried a heavy te-Vikram accent.

"Creature of the waste! We have to kill it before it devours our souls." The miner reached down to his belt and pulled out a serrated blade encrusted with cabochon gems that glinted amber and blood-green.

"No!" Karatek stepped in front of him. He got a look at his radiation badge and wished that he had not. Soon, the damage would be irreversible. If he returned too soon after that, T'Olryn would only be able to prolong his death. Unacceptable. And exquisitely painful.

The shimmering loops of tiny life-forms that wreathed about Refas's suit began to slough off, sliding down toward the freezing nitrogen slurry as the figure struggled first to its knees, then to its feet.

"Kroykah!" snarled T'Olryn. *"There is neither time for this terror nor logic in it. The radiation is too high for my remotes to work. Would you rather terrify yourselves, or will someone kindly get a medscanner out of emergency supplies and use it as it is meant to be used, please? Tell me what you see.*"

"I ask pardon," Karatek muttered. He fumbled out his scanner, activated it, and—greatly daring—stepped closer to Refas, or whatever it was standing there now.

"We have two point five minutes in which to evacuate the area," S'laron whispered. *"Can he walk?"*

Through the tinted visors of their helms, Karatek saw the primal dread in the eyes of the te-Vikram, the apprehension in S'laron's eyes at the idea of carrying Refas, of touching him at all.

If Karatek did not take immediate steps, he could have a panic on his hands. He glanced at the monitors T'Olryn had been so wise in insisting that he put on.

"Telemetry says Refas is alive," Karatek said. "What's more, his radiation levels aren't just nonlethal, they're optimal. Your fears are illogical."

He only hoped his voice was steady enough to hide his own misgivings.

"How can that be? His helm was cracked. He fell into that pool," whispered the te-Vikram.

The man would be screaming "Abomination!" again soon, if no one did anything.

Refas took the decision out of Karatek's hands.

Slowly, painstakingly, he turned to face them. Now, all the extremophiles were sliding free, dropping back down to coil about the nitrogen pool. All the extremophiles except for the ones that covered the cracked faceplate of the helm with a radiant mask that was slick as ice, but more brilliant.

"They're protecting him," whispered T'Olryn. *"Some-*

39

how, when he fell and the faceplate cracked, they must have touched him. . . ."

"How could they have survived contact with a living Vulcan's body temperature?" Karatek asked.

Or even the temperature of one who had just died.

"T'Kehr!" cried the te-Vikram. *"The Eater of Souls is coming for us! Shall I kill him?"*

Karatek shut his eyes as much in frustration as to block the sight of coils of living creatures, fringed and glittering, that came looping out of the nitrogen, edging toward the Vulcans' heavy boots.

"T'Olryn, are you getting all this?" Karatek asked.

"I'll be right down!"

"We're out of time," cried S'laron.

"Check your air as well as your radiation badges," T'Olryn's voice ordered. Her breath came fast, and Karatek knew she was suiting up as fast as she dared.

"Nominal," said the te-Vikram. The shift from terror to the language of science made Karatek bite back a laugh. *"What sorcery is this?"*

His voice rose in a scream as Refas's heavy glove came up, its fingers parted in the ancient greeting of peace. If not for that slick mask of alien life covering his helm, Refas would have looked like just one more tired miner relieving another of duty.

Karatek brought up his own hand, returning the greeting. "I grieve with thee," he whispered.

The words seemed appropriate. After all, the extremophiles that had first touched Refas were all dead, long dead. It seemed, however, as if the hardiest had survived to fission off and mutate, generation after generation, until those that formed this living, protective faceplate had evolved to cope

40

with what would have been the intolerable warmth of Vulcan physiology.

"Serevan's initial report noted extremophiles near volcanic vents as well," came T'Olryn's whisper. *"Apparently, they can handle radiation as well as extremes of heat and cold. My working hypothesis: they also appear able to decrypt our very genetic code."*

"Refas?" Karatek asked.

"I . . . I live again. I must live now," came a soft, astonished voice. The newness, the wonder, of the sound brought Karatek almost to tears. *"Too many lives were spent to restore me."*

Refas drew a deep, sighing breath.

"They are alive. They are intelligent. They are curious. But they are not merciful, or they would have let me die."

"But now that they did not, can you scorn the gift? Can you refuse the sacrifice of those who died to keep you alive?" Karatek asked.

He heard a quick, rhythmic crunch behind him but dared not turn to see who approached.

"Healer," said the te-Vikram, inclining his head as T'Olryn ran toward them.

She had spent less time suited up than most of the other prisoners, yet she scarcely faltered as she hastened over the rough ground.

Karatek stepped between her and Refas, if the figure whose face was masked behind that glowing faceplate was indeed still Refas. It turned, as if seeking to meet her eyes behind her own faceplate.

"Let me pass, please."

That was not the voice of a much-cherished daughter-in-law, the mother of Karatek's grandchildren. That was not even the voice of a skilled healer. It was the voice of the priestess that T'Olryn had been trained to be so long ago, and it had the power to command instant obedience.

Karatek stepped back, bowing slightly. He would tell Solor, T'Olryn's mate, that he had been compelled to yield to the logic of the situation. He had married the woman; he had to know what she was like.

T'Olryn drew a long, wondering breath. Slowly, cautiously, she moved forward, one gloved hand going out in the formal split-fingered gesture of greeting.

Don't touch it! Karatek wanted to warn her. He had no idea how quickly any of those minute, radiant creatures that swarmed on Refas's faceplate could dart from it and contaminate T'Olryn's own envirosuit. Decontamination would probably kill them, but what if they could penetrate the suit's heavy, composite layers? And what of his earlier scruples about exterminating native life?

No: T'Olryn and Refas had placed him in a complicated situation. And he suspected that at least one of them knew it.

Very slowly, Refas's glowing helm bowed. So, whatever lived inside that suit retained awareness that respect must be shown—or the appearance of respect. But that, too, could still be a trap.

T'Olryn's fingers brushed Refas's gauntlet, then clasped it. With the greater telepathic sensitivities she had shown in the time they had spent trapped here, perhaps she did not need to be in actual physical contact with her—could you really call this a patient?

"Not precisely," came T'Olryn's voice, low and fascinated. *"Refas is here. And more than Refas: ambassadors. A composite organism. It speaks for its people, but it is very young."*

42

"We have no wish to trap you. But you live, you move . . . we want to live!"

T'Olryn's voice and another, deeper voice spoke simultaneously. It was Refas's voice, and yet not, as if some other intelligence spoke through his mind and body, unsure, frightened, but as determined as any Vulcan in exile had ever been.

"We're running out of air," came S'laron's voice. *"If we don't head back in ten point eight minutes, we won't make it. T'Kehr, should we go and send the next shift, maybe some guards?"*

"Do you understand?" T'Olryn's voice had lost its earlier imperious quality. Now it was soft, deeply compassionate, as if she indeed spoke to someone—or to many someones—who were very young. *"Conditions will be very harsh. You will suffer; you will mutate; but your descendants will be strong."*

The figure inclined its helm again. The creatures glittering on its faceplate shifted, forming iridescent patterns. Did they mean anything? If they did not all die in the next minute, Karatek suspected he would have the opportunity to learn.

"There is always risk, always death. Always growth. So much to learn. Already . . ."

"Since Refas rose, I calculate that approximately eight hundred generations of these creatures' lifespans have passed," T'Olryn said, her voice abstracted, as if she were in a deep, therapeutic meld. *"One further condition: once we are within our own environment, you must release your host. We will arrange life support for you as best we can. Let me acquaint you with a tradition we brought with us from the Mother World throughout our exile: guest-friendship."*

She turned toward S'laron. *"Contact my medcenter. I want a full mobile isolation unit. They are tracking me; telemetry will tell them the environment they must create."*

She stepped closer. Taking Refas's arm, she led him up toward the habitat.

"The Eater of Souls has found us!" cried the te-Vikram. *"This is abomination."*

"No," whispered T'Olryn and the Refas-figure. Simultaneously, they turned to look at the Vulcans who followed them back up to the habitat, toward warmth, predictability, and what safety they had managed to create.

"This is salvation," they said. *"For both our peoples."*

SIX

PACIFICA

2377

He was Neral, Praetor of the Romulan Star Empire, a lean, grim leader who had been aged beyond his years by the trials of war and the perils of simply being a Praetor. Neral sat straight-backed in his command chair, looking, in his silver-gray uniform, as cold and keen and quietly dangerous as the edge of an honor blade.

All around him on the bridge of his flagship, *Conqueror,* there was wary silence. There was silence from the two escort ships as well. The officers and crew alike were all very well aware of their Praetor's dark mood, his growing anger and frustration.

How should I not be frustrated?

He had seized the praetorship after the assassination of Praetor Narviat—Narviat, who'd been too idealistic, at the end, to survive a cabal of jealous senators. He had led the Romulan Star Empire through the intricacies and seemingly endless perils of the Dominion War. He had even, when there seemed no other way to move, made alliances with the thrice-cursed Federation. And now, now after all that, they would dare put him off with *platitudes?*

Neral eyed the blue globe growing on the viewscreen skeptically. Pacifica, he'd learned the Federation called this quiet, pretty world of rippling turquoise seas, white sand-rimmed islands and equally pretty resorts all nicely designed to blend in with their surroundings. Scans had shown the temperature planetside to be predictably mild, and the winds—the breezes, rather—to be equally mild. Predictable, because "pacifica," he'd been told, was another Federation word for "peaceful," from some archaic Earth language.

Peaceful. Tranquil. Placid. The Federation had a hundred synonyms for "passive," the Praetor thought with distaste.

Akhh, "stagnant" is more like it.

Or perhaps that thought should more correctly be "deliberately maddening." That would seem to fit the situation more accurately.

Neral's hands tightened on the armrests of his command chair at the thought of the communications he'd already received from Min Zife, that blue-skinned lying idiot of a Federation President with that flow of smooth, useless words: "We understand your issues, but surely you see our own difficulties . . ." and ". . . so soon after the Dominion War . . ." and "Federation resources are still so stressed . . ." and "Please understand, of course we're concerned for you and your people, but surely you understand how matters stand."

Of course I do, Neral thought. *They stand against the Romulan Star Empire and our problems, even after we helped them win that damned war. And that is what underlies all*

46

those platitudes and that false show of concern and smiles that mean nothing.

For a few moments, Neral allowed himself the luxury of regretting that Narviat was no longer alive. Whatever his flaws, he was someone who was perfect for dealing with bureaucrats and smoothly smiling politicians.

And were Narviat still alive, this ridiculous voyage would have been *his* mission to undertake. Instead, Neral had to do so rather than stay at home where he was more greatly needed and, yes, where he could more efficiently watch his back.

But dwelling on what might have been was utter foolishness. The past could not be changed, not without changing the present and future as well.

And Neral had to make this trip himself, and not some less skeptical underling who might be fobbed off by smooth words or even bought by sly, false promises of power. He was Praetor Neral of the Romulan Star Empire. He had survived the administrations of two prior Praetors, one of them a perilous tyrant and the other an even more perilous idealist. He had led the Empire through that nearly devastating war. And he was not now, not ever, going to be fooled, bribed, or, above all, simply ignored.

SEVEN

MEMORY

"'The body is flesh to which the mind gives meaning and into which the katra *breathes life,' Surak wrote in his* Third Analects. *I myself saw Surak receive and release a* katra: *he understood spirit cannot be restrained, or denied. I fear, however, that the guest-friends who preserved Refas's life and whom T'Olryn now preserves have created a crisis of morality for my people. Certainly, my own family is painfully divided on the subject."*

The extremophiles evolving in their sealed bubble under watch in the medcenter never seemed to rest. T'Olryn's monitors showed them to be reproducing and mutating throughout their short lives at rates that were, if not exponential, extremely rapid. The "colony" in the medcenter's chilled isolation unit changed as he watched.

Most of it was now the glittering blood-green of the crystals in his memory device. The central loop of creatures that wreathed about Refas's helm, however, twining in and out of it through the crack in its faceplate, glimmered in the same translucent array of rainbow pastels as the sundweller Karatek had seen on Vulcan the day he had met Surak.

Because the extremophiles in T'Olryn's medcenter required so much attention, she could not attend to the health of the Vulcans in the mines and conduct research simultaneously. Karatek had released a bioscientist, a geneticist, and a skilled technician from their shifts in the mines to work with their new guest-friends. It was not, after all, as if they had been such competent miners. A deep-green keloid still marked the brow of the technician; the geneticist limped; and the bioscientist hoped to study regeneration to see if she could regrow the fingers she had lost.

All of those injuries looked fresh and acutely painful, but "There is no pain," Vyorin, the young technician, told him. Karatek suspected that the idea of working in their chosen professions, rather than as high-risk slave labor, had a great deal to do with that statement.

Nevertheless, Vyorin refused time to meditate, pain medication, or attention from T'Olryn in favor of continuing to adjust the climate-controlled chamber in which Refas had been living under nearly constant observation. That period was ending today, after T'Olryn completed a final examination of Refas.

Repeated mind-melds had assured her that he no longer wanted to die. And scanners indicated that he was free of the physical presence of the extremophiles that had preserved his life. It was equally clear, however, that he would never be free of their consequences.

Now, Refas's eyes glowed with the same light that radiated from every place where extremophiles had been found. The examination room was cold. T'Olryn had wrapped herself in every robe she possessed, but Refas wore only a light tunic and trousers, such as Vulcans wore in the heat of the day. The atmosphere in the isolation unit was even thinner than at the peak of Mount Seleya. T'Olryn wore a breathing mask, but

Refas showed no discomfort. Somehow, the extremophiles that had preserved his life seemed to have adapted him to live more efficiently on their native world.

There were, T'Olryn had reported to Karatek, logical conclusions to be drawn from Refas's acclimatization. And numerous vials of blood to be drawn from Refas himself. That blood glowed strangely, although it gave little indication of increased radiation. T'Olryn's new staff had been working to isolate the new factors that gave his blood the glow. They had even developed the radical, if logical, theory that it might be possible to develop a treatment that would render Vulcans more tolerant of Remus's extreme cold and radiation.

After T'Olryn's announcement, Sarissa and Solor had asked to confer with Karatek in the medcenter. Solor's face was expressionless. That struck Karatek as unusual because he had always been the most volatile member of the family. By contrast, Sarissa looked worn.

"Are you quite well, daughter? Do you require treatment?"

Had she brought Solor with her to support Karatek as she told him bad news?

His fear was not logical, he thought. If Sarissa had serious news to share, Serevan would be here, too. Nevertheless, Karatek felt his face change, his blood chill.

"I am quite well," Sarissa reassured her father swiftly. "Only tired."

That was an understatement. She and Serevan now led different shifts in the mines, attempting to create a surplus that might tide them over in case of accidents, or even allow them to experiment with the materials they mined, refined, and fabricated. Karatek himself had been working with Serevan on a prototype engine.

There was never enough time! Not for research, not for

life, especially not when the grinding discipline of simply enduring this planet was added. But apparently, that was a burden Sarissa did not wish to shed, at least, not in the way that her sister-in-law was suggesting.

"I wanted to make sure that T'Olryn isn't suggesting . . . she can't suggest that we all submit ourselves to this . . . this violation!" Sarissa told him.

His eldest surviving child seemed reluctant to look at the blood samples, which glowed a deeper emerald than any of the blood he had seen shed in more than a hundred years. Refas's blood was more efficient, T'Olryn had declared, at processing oxygen and nutrients. Already he was hardier than any other Vulcan on this world, including men and women fifty years younger than he.

Solor turned away from the clear panel that divided his wife and her patient from his elder sister. "Sister, you insult my consort if you think she would impose any such solution on unwilling subjects."

"Subjects!" Sarissa exploded. Her hand tightened into a fist and battered on the panel, drawing the attention of healer and patient.

"I ask pardon," she added, relaxing as Solor nodded, granting it.

T'Olryn raised an ironic eyebrow. Refas—was that a grin Karatek saw on his face?

It did seem as if he had regained his earlier interest in life, his actual desire to live, as if the creatures he hosted had infused him with their own ferocious survival imperative. For that, Karatek thought, he owed these tiny, improbable collections of flagella, wisps, and tubules his thanks. Aesthetically, they were actually quite pleasing; intellectually, they fascinated him, although his own academic interests lay outside, in the building of engines and the study of the dilithium crystals that had caused these . . . these astonishing guest-friends to mutate so rapidly.

What passed in the extremophiles for DNA and RNA, T'Olryn had already told him, was immensely adaptive.

"These creatures are biological impossibilities. The idea of real-time genetic adaptation to environment— T'Lyrey's fallacy was disproved two hundred fifty years before the Exile!" Sarissa argued.

"Then, it may be that we must regard Vulcan as a special case," came T'Olryn's voice through a microphone. *"Or we must concede that our knowledge of the Mother World's biology was almost as incomplete as our knowledge of the biology here in our new home."*

That brought Solor around. This prison world was, he had said often enough, no home of his, although if T'Olryn's preposterous new research program had brought her contentment, he had already admitted he was pleased.

At length, T'Olryn turned away from her patient.

"I can find nothing wrong with you," T'Olryn told Refas. *"Except, of course, your ability to withstand conditions on this planet. I have, however, found one anomaly: preliminary scans at the genetic level show that your telomeres have been shortened. You will be hearty throughout your life. You may not, however, be long-lived."*

"Longer-lived than I'd have been if our little friends hadn't rescued me," Refas told her. *"They gave me back my life, and now I know what I want to do with it. I'm heading back outside. I want to make arrangements to work out on the edge of habitable territory. I can be useful again. And I can keep our people from destroying the habitats of the creatures that saved my life."*

"What about the colony here?" asked Karatek.

T'Olryn emerged from the examination chamber, followed by Refas. His complexion darkened in what was apparently, for him, great heat. Instantly, Vyorin brought him water.

Saluting the others with the water flask, its metal dulled with frost, Refas drank deeply before walking over to look at the glowing colony of extremophiles. Mostly, the creatures were deep red now, darkening to violet. But, even as he watched, those vibrant tones appeared to be fading to an unpleasant brown, interspersed with streaks of blackish green. Although it was illogical to use Vulcan aesthetics to gauge the health of an alien species, Karatek wondered if some blight had struck these most recent generations of the creatures.

T'Olryn seemed to read his thoughts.

"They cannot live much longer in this habitat," she said, sorrow in her voice. "We have attempted to replicate their environment, but our work has proved inadequate."

"I'll take them back outside," Refas said. "You seal them in whatever sort of container you think gives them the best chance to survive, and I'll get them back to where we found them. We can seal off the area and direct mining operations in other directions."

"Didn't the mining assay say that the area in which we found them had the finest crystals found to date?" asked Sarissa.

"There are other sources of crystals," said Refas. His eyes went even stranger as they focused on T'Olryn. "I shall work with the mineralogists. We will find them. We will make our quotas, *if we have not already done so,*" he added emphatically, "and we will protect our guest-friends, in accordance with our oldest laws."

Karatek widened his eyes at Refas's animation as well as

53

the conclusion that he had drawn. Only the few people involved in his own very private research product should have known about the crystals and metals diverted from production quotas now that they were, indeed, running a surplus.

Sarissa raised an eyebrow minutely at him. No doubt, she was calculating a new threat assessment. In response, Solor tilted his head toward his consort before focusing once more on his elder sister.

He, too, had reached a conclusion, Karatek decided. Interesting: he had reached an age at which mental processes might well be expected to slow. Since being trapped on Remus, however, his powers of reasoning appeared to have improved.

He saw, however, that he had lost Refas's attention. The man was not focusing on mining quotas, but on the extremophiles and—Karatek's eyes narrowed—on T'Olryn herself. Their tiny allies had given him new purpose, and a strength that T'Olryn could spend the rest of her life researching and probably would.

"Will we be safe from these creatures?" asked N'Evran. She came around from behind a screen, fastening a heavy outerrobe about her. A tiny graft of a darker green stood out on her face; she had been in the medcenter for removal of a tiny skin cancer.

"Why would we not?" asked T'Olryn, turning to inspect N'Evran's face. "I will clear you for light duty. When you leave the sealed environment, be certain to use this cream and renew the plasm on the graft." She exchanged polite nods with the te-Vikram elder before turning back to the colony. The globe into which the creatures had formed themselves was beginning to dissipate into wreaths again.

"We had best move them quickly," she said. "I regret the

loss of the opportunity to observe them closely because I suspect that study of Refas's DNA will enable us to synthesize the proteins that make them so hardy. . . ."

N'Evran came back around, her eyes blazing. "Are you saying that—"

"They will not take us over!" Refas protested. "They have been in contact with my mind now, and the healer's. When they saw me fall, all they could think of was that here was help for their . . . well, they have no hands, have they? They may not be what we could call an advanced culture, but they saw in us a way of preserving their kind. And now, they have learned from us how not to violate the living mind—and to let the dying spirit go, even if I am profoundly thankful now that my own life was spared."

Karatek watched his daughter-in-law store the glowing vials of Refas's blood. As clearly as if he himself were in the grips of a rapport such as T'Olryn and Refas said the creatures could project, he could anticipate the arguments for and against creation of a hybrid race, the outcry in favor of, and against, racial purity. The extremophiles were not just primitive, they were innocent.

It must be a matter of honor to make certain they remained that way. And to protect them against the Vulcans who had imprisoned Karatek and the people of *Shavokh* here on the ice and demanded their quota of this world's riches.

What about their quotas? Karatek stiffened. Just a few moments ago, he had concluded that, while he was growing old, his wits had, if anything, sharpened. Perhaps it was that he had finally learned to trust his deputies as, logically, they had earned.

He glanced at the nearest status monitor. At this very moment, the shifts were changing. Shift 1 was lugging out onto the now-stabilized landing field the structural components, processed metals, and crystals that constituted their quota.

Karatek had meant to be present when the ships arrived. The prior month's food supply had been even less palatable than he had assumed. It was time to have words with the commander of the supply ships. Or with whatever under-officer would deign to speak with him.

It was time for him to go, but, he had to admit, Refas's rebirth fascinated him. The man was on the move again. His hand opened the throat of his shirt. His face glowed as if he were in the throes of the Fires, and Karatek looked instantly away.

"I would recommend haste," Refas told T'Olryn. "It is unpleasantly warm here and must be even worse for our guests."

The healer looked up into his face, then away. Solor stepped forward protectively, and Sarissa watched every one of Refas's moves as her sister-in-law attached grips onto the isolation bubble containing the extremophiles and Refas's helmet.

"Contaminated past repair," she said. "Even if it could be decontaminated and recycled, I cannot imagine that anyone would be willing to wear it."

Solor looked relieved. At least his consort's enthusiasm for this new species had not interfered with her understanding of her own.

"I will take the helmet," said Refas. "Consider disposing of it to be my problem. You will have sufficient challenge in keeping the people who have decided I'm an incarnation of the Eater of Souls away from me."

He paused for a moment. "Be sure that you do." His voice changed, deepened.

Karatek controlled a shiver as menace filled the cold air of the medcenter. *"We will defend ourselves."*

"Let me help you return our friends to their home," T'Olryn suggested.

"I see no logical reason for you to endure the cold—until you must," said Refas. "All I need is a breathing mask and a few supplies. I think I'll make myself a sort of camp out there, use it as a base for explorations in between the times when you don't want me for tests. After all, I have to heal sometimes from all the needles!

"Besides," he added, "I want a few words with my friends here."

T'Olryn had shown Refas's medical records to Karatek. Although he had had the training in the disciplines that all sons and daughters of Vulcan received, he had shown little psionic ability. Now, however . . . *"If I need anything, you will know it,"* he told them.

But not in actual words.

The extremophile colonies were strongly telepathic. What passed for thought impulses with them, as well as sensations, were amplified by the crystals embedded in the living rock of the planet. Now that their curiosity had been gratified—and their evolution greatly advanced—the two species would be able to avoid each other. Unless, of course, at times of mutual need, they chose to ally once more.

Wrapping his hand around one of the grips fastened to the isolation bubble, Refas lifted it. Instantly, the creatures within scattered away from the helm with its cracked faceplate. They divided and subdivided into intricate new braids and patterns until, finally, they coated the entire bubble and the helmet with metallic rainbows in a farewell gift that consisted of one last rainbow. As Karatek watched, its colors changed, becoming more and more ethereal until, once again, he remembered the sundweller that had been such a creature of good omen on Vulcan.

They see it, too!

Karatek drew in a breath of sheer wonder.

Refas nodded agreement. "They find your presence . . . satisfying," he told Karatek.

Karatek blinked, then bowed slightly. "I am honored."

Courtesy seemed only reasonable. At Karatek's words, the emotional climate in the medcenter lightened. The creatures were relying on him now to redirect mining operations; to control those who would, inevitably, come to fear and hate them; to act as a voice of reason.

I promise, he thought, and knew that he was understood.

Raising his free hand in salute, Refas started down toward the ice.

"Unseal inner hatches," Karatek ordered.

The new doors were jagged, multileaved hatches with duranium cores. They unlocked and swung aside without a sound, revealing another, even heavier pair that separated the colony's living quarters from the mines.

"Seal integrity at 99.8 percent," came a recorded announcement.

Serevan would probably take that missing 0.2 percent as a personal affront.

Carrying the clear containers that held extremophiles, Refas stepped into the compartment between the doors. The creatures' glow was much dimmer now.

"Activating viewer," Solor said as the inner doors slid closed once again.

"Hatches sealed," came the announcement. *"Proceed."*

"Open outer doors," Karatek ordered, and watched as the heavy doors unsealed. Refas strode out toward the mines. Already, the extremophiles' color had improved. Once again, they mimicked the colors of the sundweller they had seen in Karatek's mind. Even as he watched, the colors grew richer and deeper than any he had ever seen.

"Closing doors."

Refas disappeared from sight.

"Sir, we could track him in the mines, if you wish," Solor offered.

Karatek nodded assent.

What was Refas now? Vulcan, or some blend of Vulcan and the creatures that had preserved his life? It no longer mattered. They were bound together now, Karatek thought, and with them, the fate of all the Vulcans on this world.

A tremor shook the habitat. Solor frowned minutely as he glanced at the panels on the walls. "Three point five," he said. "No further weakening of the door seals."

A touch of his hand activated a viewscreen within the mines. Refas had stopped, his head bent over the container of extremophiles, as if listening.

"Communing" might be a better word. That, too, was only logical. He and the creatures he bore home were bound together.

"I suggest we install secondary stabilizers by all of the locks," Solor said.

"How many projects do you think Serevan can work on?" Sarissa demanded.

"You saw that seal integrity dropped from 100 percent. We're going to need the security as the project . . ."

"Kroykah!"

Karatek glanced at the scanners set into bulkhead by the

59

Josepha Sherman & Susan Shwartz

doors. Zenite levels were nominal for this world, though in the first days of their acculturation, they would have sufficed to throw Vulcans into a rage almost as violent as *Plak-tow*.

Coping with zenite contamination was yet another daily challenge to master: even Vulcans whose study of Surak's disciplines was long advanced had become subject to a higher degree of irritability—or decreased ability to conceal or control it. The very thought annoyed Karatek, a sign of its validity.

Perhaps increased time spent in deep meditation might improve the situation. But where were the hours to be found, given that each able-bodied adult and the oldest children worked two to three of the four daily shifts?

Another alarm went off.

Karatek restrained himself from pounding the wall with a fist. Why did crises and earthquakes have to occur just when he was trying to *think*?

"T'Kehr *Karatek, to controls. Cargo ships have appeared in orbital perimeter.* T'Kehr *Karatek, please report.*"

"It appears our lords and masters have arrived to claim their tribute," Solor said.

Sarcasm? How very interesting.

"You've been reading the old epics again," Sarissa said. "You would do better sleeping. Or trying to discuss the repercussions of T'Olryn's research with her."

Solor eyed Karatek, then his sister.

I was not meant to hear that, Karatek realized. Best to change the subject quickly.

"Have you hidden . . ." Karatek began. T'Olryn was not the only one of his family to have a private research project that might mean death for all of them if their captors learned of it.

60

Unless we have succeeded in making them totally dependent on us . . .

Unlikely. They might be cruel; they were not fools.

If only Karatek had been able to convince Vorealt to accept raw crystals in trade for even one processed gem! But the Vulcans who remained in the great ships didn't just remain in orbit; they maintained a very precarious balance between captors and captives, jealously preserving neutrality regardless of either world's attempt to win them as allies.

The great ships in orbit required the minerals extracted from this world, true. They also required supplies that could be provided only by the new homeworld from which both the ship clans and Karatek's people were barred. An overflight, much less a landing, by one of Vorealt's shuttles would be noted. Karatek's own encrypted communications with the ship clans were painstakingly timed for the periods when the major settlements were out of range.

"We never moved the crystals offsite, and the components are still in the fabrication units," Sarissa said. "Even if they send search teams, they will see a minuscule surplus of 2 percent. The actual surplus is 15 percent. You will be pleased, Father. We have processed enough duranium to build engine containment now."

Karatek nodded. This world's metals were stronger, more resistant than those he had worked with on Vulcan. The ship he planned would be small, only a prototype: but he thought it would fly, and fly well.

"On my way," Karatek spoke directly to the scanners. He strode ahead of his son and daughter, taking in the reports that each com panel emitted as he approached the command center.

On the bulkheads of each compartment, screens lit, showing real-time simulations of the cargo ship now in orbit and projected shuttle trajectories.

"Ordnance check!" ordered Solor from behind him.

"Ship's weapons activated, but not locked. Shuttle's weapons are hot."

The shuttles preferred to minimize their time downworld. They would not offload supplies until every last crystal, ingot, and chemical had been loaded, inspected, and logged in. If the miners were late in delivery, reprisals in the form of decreased supplies, increased quotas, or even an attack on the landing field were a distinct possibility. Karatek had already lost the argument that those punishments were counterproductive. Past a certain point, productivity was not the point: intimidation was.

"Approaching controls," Karatek spoke up again, although he knew that the watch there could track him by his radiation badge. "Report when cargo is ready for transport outside."

"Transit under way, T'Kehr. Estimated completion time: three point nine hours. Shall we contact the ship?"

The ships were probably monitoring cargo transport from orbit, Karatek thought. To think he had helped the engineers who had designed those scanners. Self-reproach, however, was as illogical . . . as what? Turning kinfolk into slave labor?

"I will make contact when I arrive." He turned to Solor and Sarissa. "You two, emergency stations. Now."

Karatek's command crew, which now included anyone in a responsible position, had standing orders to disperse throughout the habitat when ships approached. In case of a preemptive strike, the miners would not be left leaderless.

"I wonder what that crew would do if it knew the kinds of guests we've been harboring," Solor's voice faded as he disappeared into the corridors. "I'd like to introduce them. . . . "

"One day," Sarissa said. "Just not this one."

Solor's voice had been cold, cold as the ice to which Refas was returning their controversial guest-friends. Karatek hoped he would succeed in getting them into an environment in which, once again, they could thrive. At least some beings on this world should find a home to welcome them.

They are the key, something whispered in his mind. He dismissed the thought as an illusion. Vulcans were touch telepaths, not precognitives. Granted, Vulcans had prophesied before: the Forge and the Womb of Fire had always had the unpleasant habit of producing the occasional odd, violent religious cult like te-Vikram. The last such prophet of which Karatek had personal knowledge had been Surak himself.

Had Karatek himself been a prophet, he would have listened to his own fears and never have left the Mother World.

You would probably not have survived, he told himself. After all, Surak had not.

It is logical to be skeptical. Therefore, it is logical to distrust even skepticism. But, nevertheless, you believe.

He would definitely need additional time to meditate. Possibly, he should speak to T'Olryn, not as his daughter-in-law, but as his healer.

She had been preoccupied with the extremophiles and with healing Refas. Perhaps, now that they were gone, she would return to whatever behavior was normal for a healer, even one whom he thought he knew so well.

What he needed, he knew, was more information because, truly, he did not have enough data to believe or disbelieve. The lack of information exposed him—exposed the entire colony—to risks that were unacceptable even for life on Remus.

Control, he urged himself. He paused, drew three breaths,

and subvocalized a mantra that he had not used nearly often enough these ice-bound days.

Drawing himself up, Karatek made the final turn into the command center. As the men and women on watch rose to greet him, he waved them back into their seats.

His heads-up display showed him the status of his mining crews, his research projects, and the cargo being stacked onto the landing field. All satisfactory. Or at least, appropriately concealed.

"Karatek to approaching shuttle," he spoke as he gazed out into the darkness. From here, he could not even see the planet that oppressed them: just plumes of frozen nitrogen, streams of liquefied gases, and the eternal ice. "Conditions are clear for landing."

The shuttles would not land in a storm. Would not dare to, which told him something about transportation availability on the world he could not see. Well enough: the colony was still valuable. He was completely convinced that should the day come when their oppressors no longer needed them, they would be turned loose to starve or freeze.

We will manage on our own, he told himself.

That too had the sense of prophecy. Of truth.

Somehow.

"Incoming message, T'Kehr."

"Put it through," he said, forcing himself back to the here and now. Cargo transfers were as dangerous as storms or quakes: the weapons carried by that orbiting ship could wipe them all out.

"Karatek?" The transmission came from the cargo ship still in orbit, not from the shuttle. There was no visual, but he thought he could recognize the voice. So, Avarak could not deny himself the pleasure, could he? Good. If Karatek

could not strike him, let his own self-indulgence weaken him.

"Speaking."

"We require you to take delivery of this cargo in person."

"T'Kehr, no!" Serevan's voice spoke from the entryway. Though his helm rested in the crook of his arm, the engineer still wore his envirosuit. It was covered with frost, and waves of cold radiated from it. "Let me go. In your name, and in your honor."

"We cannot risk disobedience," said Karatek. The last word was sour in his mouth. Who were these people, that he should obey them?

The answer was obvious. They were the ones who trained weapons on Karatek's people from space, the ones who controlled delivery of foods and medications they still could not produce for themselves. Perhaps, if their population were larger, he could make other plans. But Karatek could not possibly wish more people to share his imprisonment, could he?

He could not.

Serevan strode forward, but Karatek held up one hand. "Take command here."

And if I do not return, preserve my son and daughter from their worst impulses.

"I am suiting up," he told the cargo ship. "I will report when I reach the surface."

Flakes of frozen gas whipped past Karatek as he stepped out of the habitat. In the reddish glow of his helm's light, they glittered pale blue and the green of frozen blood as they swirled past. Awkward in heavy boots and liners, he searched out the track left by the motorized cargo pallets and followed it onto the landing field. He slipped, then caught himself against a transport that had had to be abandoned when the metal of its treads cracked asunder in the cold.

It was hard to imagine that on the far side of this world, it was hot enough that there were pools of liquid metal, not liquefied gases, and blazing eternal sunlight rather than the darkness of space, broken only by distant, uncaring stars.

Suited figures turned to acknowledge him, thick, almost stubby in bulky protective suits. Above them in the darkness he could make out the landing lights of the shuttle as it descended. The ground shuddered. No fear of damage from a quake that slight here, of all places. The landing field had been more carefully stabilized even than the habitat.

From the jagged escarpment that lay beyond the landing field poured an avalanche of ice and rock, disappearing into a crack outside the range of the stabilizers that, one day, they would have to explore.

The shuttle leveled off.

Night and day, if the shuttle's crew lost its nerve and returned to Avarak's ship, someone would have to remain until it decided, finally, to land. And if it did not . . .

I would plead to preserve the lives of my people, Karatek thought. *I would* beg.

"Karatek to ship. I am in position. Where is your shuttle? Landing conditions are optimal. Or," he added grimly, "as good as they will get. I would suggest haste. Storms can strike quickly."

"Making final approach. Touchdown in fifteen point three minutes. Your presence will be required at the landing ramp."

"Understood."

If no storm erupted, if no icefall trapped him, Karatek would have more than enough time to complete whatever task their jailers had in mind and return to the habitat with an acceptable reserve of air. Behind him came footsteps that his now-heightened awareness sensed, rather than heard, as shifts changed, and the men and women who had loaded the supplies onto the landing field were dismissed to warm themselves in what limited comfort they could find in the habitat.

He could not see their faces, but with that strength that was still new to him, he sensed their presence, their support. Their stubborn Vulcan loyalty.

"Stay back," he said. "They want me at the landing ramp. Let us give them no encouragement to act illogically."

He heard mutters of assent, even a chuckle or two from crew members who had not followed Surak's teachings, or who had renounced them.

Now, he could see the tiny lights, a trio of red and white glows, and the fires of the shuttle's engines as it made its final approach. It touched down on the landing field, which shuddered again, then steadied. A fog of ice melt puffed up around the ship, veiling it until a light wind, barely gale force, shredded the clouds of vapor that refroze, then tumbled into the rapidly freezing pools.

Karatek waited. He heard his suit's heaters whine, struggling to compensate for the cold that he could feel even through the heavy composite layers of his boots.

Finally, he could see light as the shuttle's hatch opened, extruding its jointed, copper-colored ramp onto the ice.

"Karatek?"

"Present," he said. "Unarmed, as you can see." He held his arms out at his sides. "We are prepared to load at your order."

"Proceed."

Suited figures from the shuttle started down the ramp. They were heavily laden with containers that Karatek recognized as the medical supplies and foodstuffs of the exiles' "bargain" with the Vulcans who held them hostage.

Pairs of suited figures reached down, lifting the pallets of minerals and fabricated components, the sealed chests of crystals. Moving slowly, carefully in the cold, they trudged toward the ramp. Would they actually be allowed on board? On prior missions, their captors had always taken steps to prevent boarding, fearing an attempt to take over the shuttle.

This time, however, crew members emerged. They were armed with what looked like a thoroughly vicious combination of a *lirpa* and an energy weapon. A single blow could crush a suit joint or shatter a visor; a single blast could reduce a Vulcan to char and ice melt.

"You will load now," came the order.

"Do what they say," Karatek confirmed.

Damn them to the ice! They had turned him from leader to overseer of his own people's oppression. He drew deep breaths to compose himself, regardless of the drain on his air supply. He could always renew it; but if he flew into a killing rage, he was gone forever, and his people needed him. His family would need him in the troubled days to come.

And why would those days be more troubled than today?

You know. You just have not admitted it.

He watched as his people, under constant guard, bore their tribute into the shuttle, always under guard. One guard remained, his weapon trained on Karatek himself.

Finally, all of the supplies were unloaded.

"We have fulfilled our obligation," Karatek said.

Now, it was the shuttle's turn to produce the medical and food supplies that the miners desperately needed. The shuttles always made them wait for a moment or two, as if tormenting them with the thought that they might take off, leaving the miners with nothing.

This time was no exception.

"Do you want us to offload our supplies, too?" he asked, goading them.

"No need. Stand by to receive cargo."

Once again the guards appeared. This time, they formed a double row down the landing ramp through which moved a slow file of suited figures. They were heavily laden and moved slowly, awkwardly in what looked like substandard suits. He thought he could even see ice crystals forming on one of them from moisture seeping out through a tiny leak.

One by one, they trudged down the ramp. As one touched ground, he stumbled and went sprawling. Instantly, a guard loomed over him, holding his weapon like a club over the figure's faceplate.

"Stop!" Karatek cried. Over the helmet com, he heard the guard laugh.

The suited laborer struggled to his feet. He could not pick up the container, but he pushed and shoved it toward the others before he stumbled down onto his knees. This time, the guards allowed him to remain there.

"T'Kehr?" one of his crew spoke into his com.

Why would they abuse one of their own? Karatek thought. *Unless, of course . . .*

"Third man from the end," Karatek said. "He's got a leak at the left elbow joint. Someone get an emergency seal on him. Now."

One of his crew started forward, to be stopped by a guard, *lirpa* raised, ready to smash in his faceplate.

The frost on the elbow joint grew deeper. Now, he could see a plume as air escaped. The man toppled to the ground as the suit tore. The guard shoved him off the ramp with the toe of his boot.

Karatek felt it as his people tensed, poised to leap forward, appalled at this callous waste of a life, even an enemy life.

"*Kroykah,*" he cried.

Hands up, Karatek moved forward to the foot of the ramp.

"Explain," he ordered.

Two guards started forward to punish the defiance that was his only weapon.

"*Specify.*"

The voice came from a figure standing at the top of the ramp. He wore a fine suit, not just customized, but bearing ornaments of rank that Karatek did not recognize, but that glowed blue and green in the spectral light cast by the helms of his guards.

"Why you murdered one of your own."

The man laughed. "*Always the idealist, Karatek. Always looking for easy answers. Consider the possibility that he was not one of ours, but one of* yours."

A terrible surmise chilled Karatek as much as the frozen nitrogen mounding around his feet. "*Aren't you always complaining that you haven't enough people to meet your quotas? We've brought you some help. May they use better judgment here than they did on the homeworld—or die fast. On the whole, I would think death would be preferable, except that we need their labor as well as yours. So you will do your utmost to preserve their lives. Unacceptable casualty levels will—let us simply say that we would have to take steps, in that case.*"

Karatek looked over at the medical supplies, then at the men and women who had offloaded them and who stood, knelt, or leaned against their former burdens. There was never enough to go around. And with newcomers, untrained, traumatized newcomers, some possibly injured . . .

"We don't have enough to go around," he heard himself say. "Will you increase food deliveries?"

"When you increase production." The constant answer. *"You have a choice, Karatek. We have exiled these people."*

"But why?" he demanded.

"Their logic was defective. Why else? Now, sensors indicate a storm is coming. We have no desire to ride it out either on board ship or in your kennel. So, this conversation is over. We could order you, but we will not. The choice is yours. Take charge of them, or let them freeze.

"Or," the voice turned very pleased with itself, *"if you ask politely, if you plead, my guards will see that they die quickly."*

The guards had been marching back up the ramp. Now they turned and paused. Their weapons were poised, always poised to attack the prisoners—both the new ones and the ones already trapped on the ice.

The needs of the many outweigh the needs of the few.

Karatek knew the maxim.

Overriding it was a most uncharacteristic rage. Night and day, those zenite sensors had to be malfunctioning! He would have to speak—and sharply, too!—to Serevan about his engineering staff's diligence. To say nothing of its competence.

I will not have these people's lives on my hands! Karatek vowed. They were Vulcan. They were strong. Somehow, they must be convinced to live, rather than die on the ice.

The ramp drew back in. The ship's warning lights kindled.

Clearly, it was nothing to the shuttle's commander if his takeoff burnt not just his political castoffs, but all the prisoners where they stood.

Karatek's own people, used to the hazards and as healthy as possible under the circumstances, could make it back, with time to spare. The newcomers, however, could barely move from shock, exhaustion, and, probably, injuries that needed attention.

"Move!" Karatek shouted.

He had the satisfaction of seeing fifteen of the prisoners stagger to their feet, starting toward his own people. He started toward the ones who could not summon the strength to rise and pulled the nearest one to his feet. The other colonists followed. Strong from their work in the mines, they grabbed the newcomers and dragged them away from the landing field just as the shuttle ascended in a plume of fire and freezing vapor.

"I wish they would crash!" came a mutter across the open communications system.

"Kroykah!"

Karatek was not the only one to utter that rebuke. He pulled a second exile to her feet. He knew this one. Why, it was T'Zora. She had been a botanist; her teacher had even been a colleague of his back on Vulcan. Peaceful, inoffensive: what had she done to merit this life in death?

A red warning light blinked. His air supply had reached critical levels. He shut his eyes for an instant, trying to invoke the slower breathing techniques he had learned during meditation.

He achieved partial success; there was no time for more.

His scanners showed the wind building up toward gale force. He flung an arm awkwardly across her armored back and urged her toward the people trudging toward the habitat.

"Follow them," he told her, trying to make his voice gentle. "You will be safe."

The assurance was already a lie.

He took a deep breath, then spoke the words that would risk the entire colony's life.

"These newcomers are our guests," said Karatek. "Get them inside first. Tell command center I want everyone off-shift to suit up and help. First, the people. Then, the supplies. Attach hand lights to them to mark their location and help us spot them when the storm hits."

They would know to string lights and ropes from the habitat's seals to the landing field. As the storm built, people would be drawn toward the ropes. If they could reach them before the blizzard annihilated all visibility, they could struggle, hand over hand, toward safety. They might not be lost.

Might.

Right now, however, he was too cold, too tired, and, he had to admit it, too afraid to calculate the odds.

A second warning light kindled within his suit, this one blood-green. If he turned back immediately, he might have enough air to return. If he raced, he would consume it faster; if he conserved energy, his supply would run out.

Not only couldn't he help the newcomers, he would have to ask for help!

A wave of dizziness swept over him. If he fell, he might never rise, and his children needed him!

With a hand that felt twice as thick and awkward as the envirosuit's gauntlet, Karatek triggered the distress beacon on his suit. The figure nearest him pushed a captive into the arms of a teammate. Stumbling toward Karatek in the thickening swirls of nitrogen "snow," the man reached him.

It was Serevan, probably the strongest of them all. He glanced down at Karatek's suit readings, bit off an expression that probably would have been as improper as it would have been logical, and reached behind him to his air supply. With a quick twist, he detached the tube from his backup cylinder. Karatek felt himself sagging.

"A moment longer, Father," Serevan reassured him. Strong arms caught him, supporting him and half turning him.

He felt a jolt as Serevan attached the tube to his own emptied oxygen tank, then gasped as air flooded his lungs. It was like finding water on the Forge as the sun hammered down. No, it was better.

Tethered to his rescuer, Karatek struggled to match footsteps with him as they headed inside. "Sand fire," he gasped at Serevan. "Must get under cover . . . leave me . . . you go on . . . run!"

"We are not on Vulcan," Serevan reminded him. *"Breathe, Father. Deep, steady breaths. The hallucinations should stop as the oxygen reaches your brain. There is no desert here."*

As they stumbled toward what safety this world held for them, Karatek felt his wits return, and with them a deep shame. Not only had he been unable to help the newcomers, he had had to accept help himself.

The shame, he decided, was logical. His punishment would be to live with it.

EIGHT

ROMULUS

2377

Proconsul Hiren of Romulus stole careful glances around him as he walked with seeming calm down the hallways of the Romulan Senate in Ki Baratan. He'd long ago mastered the art of looking purposeful wherever he went to avoid any awkward questions. Even so: no watchers, no overt signs of spy eyes, but one could never be too careful about ambitious Tal Shiar operatives or, more probably and dangerously, that cursed Charvanek.

Akhh, yes. Charvanek, who didn't have the good taste to fade into obscurity as the widow of the so sadly deceased Praetor Narviat, but who had stubbornly remained in office during Praetor Neral's administration as well. Charvanek, who handled Romulan Security with a grim tenacity and maddening incorruptibility that could teach even the Tal Shiar a few lessons.

Hiren reached the agreed-upon corridor, smaller than the main way and less well lit, downright shadowy in places, and headed down it with the air of someone taking a familiar shortcut, still looking, he knew from practice, perfectly calm. It was a façade on which he'd been working for years. Hiren knew perfectly well that he looked like any ordinary Romulan bureaucrat, solid and middle-aged, his dark hair thickly streaked with gray. There was, deliberately, nothing flashy about him. As honorable, staunchly middle of the line Senator Hiren of the Romulan Star Empire, there was nothing overtly dangerous about him. He had a decent record of political activity, nothing too outstanding, nothing that could be criticized. Nothing to arouse suspicion.

There was no hint of the steel under the mild veneer. And so far only one other knew of his ambition.

Two figures were coming purposefully toward him out of the shadows. For a moment, Hiren's heart lurched in alarm as he thought, *assassins,* no unlikely menace in these uncertain days. But then it settled back into its normal rhythm as he recognized them. That slender, black-clad figure was definitely Rehaek, yes, with that smirk of a smile that hid the diabolically clever brain behind the young, narrow, sharp-featured face, and with his bulky bodyguard-aide Torath looming over him. Not a surprise: Rehaek, either paranoid or amazingly self-protective, never went anywhere without that muscular shadow.

That Rehaek, with his sly and casual air about dispatching annoyances, might be paranoid or perhaps even a bit of a sociopath and as such, far more dangerous than any assassin—Hiren shrugged mentally. One never advanced without taking risks.

"Rehaek."

"Senator."

But when Hiren would have said something more, Rehaek

muttered, almost too softly for him to hear, "Not here. Not now. Torath."

The hulking figure brushed by Hiren so closely he nearly knocked the senator over. Before Hiren could even start to complain, he felt Torath's large hand force something small and hard into his palm. Hiren reflexively closed his fingers about what felt like a tiny padd.

"Directions," Rehaek said. "A less . . . obvious place and time for . . . allies to talk. Be there."

It was not a request.

With that, Rehaek, Torath at his back, strode on down the corridor, never glancing back.

Hiren stood looking after them. *Was that meant to frighten me?* he thought. *Rehaek, swagger all you want. You are my tool, you and that muscular lout at your side as well. And when I am finished with you, when I have what I want, then you shall be discarded.*

He had the most uncomfortable feeling, though, that Rehaek, still smiling, was thinking the same thing.

A sound at the door of her office brought Charvanek, seated at her desk, to full alert, although she showed no sign of alarm other than to let one hand slip down to the grip of her disruptor pistol. She hadn't managed to survive two Praetors by being careless.

"Enter." Her voice was absolutely calm, but her glance shot to the scan over the door.

The Romulan who entered was tall, wiry, sharp-featured, and still young. But despite his youth, he held himself proudly straight-backed. His dark blue tunic and trousers were severe in cut, almost military fashion, and his narrow face and cold gave away nothing of his thoughts. "Commander."

It was the title she preferred even after all this time, though few knew that. "Levak."

Even though she'd just made a visual ID, even knowing that an automatic scan had also revealed him as truly being Levak rather than some clever imposter, her hand never moved from the pistol's grip. Charvanek trusted Levak . . . about as much as she trusted anyone just now.

Particularly in this case. With a touch of wry humor, Charvanek thought that it was not at all unusual for an agent of the Tal Shiar to be meeting with the head of Romulan Security. What was unusual, of course, was that this stern-faced young man was actually first and foremost in her employ. That the opposite could surely be said of some of *her* staff—akhh, almost certainly true. That was, after all, how one played the game.

There are times, Charvanek thought almost wearily, *when I could easily give this all up, go off to some peaceful colony world to live in rural comfort . . .*

And quietly fade away like some farmer's widow? she promptly answered herself. No, that was not the way to honor the Empire, or the late Narviat's memory.

Her office was tucked away into a quiet corner of the Ki Baratan government buildings, as though it was nothing more important than just another room in the Romulan government bureaucracy. Actually, it hardly looked like an office at all, let alone a dangerous place. The room was, instead, almost ironically tranquil, with its walls painted a soothing pale blue. In addition to her desk and chair of pale golden *shera*-wood, the room also contained a softly cushioned beige chair of elegantly curved Irlani design, and a finely woven historic tapestry of Estrak and Thuraka, the colors only slightly faded by time, that would not have been out of place in a noble lady's mansion.

It had, actually, come from a noble lady's mansion: her own.

Only the viewscreen and piles of printouts cluttering the desk spoiled the illusion of luxury—that, and the war trophies hanging on one wall. They were Charvanek's, all of them earned by her in battle.

And do you realize that, my young agent? she silently asked Levak. *Do you even* understand *that kind of battle?*

"Report," she said.

He straightened. "In the matter of Chairman Koval, there has been no change in his condition, either for better or for worse."

"I already knew that," Charvanek all but drawled, and saw Levak wince at the sarcasm. *A fine head of security I'd be if I didn't know something so basic.* "Continue. Tal Shiar information."

Levak went down the list of Tal Shiar activities, at least those known to him, with an agent's flawless recall. Charvanek listened, her memory just as finely trained. Interesting, but hardly useful, at least for now. Nothing overtly suspicious . . . although there seemed no doubt that ambitious Tal Shiar operatives were already jockeying for position, not waiting for Chairman Koval to actually do anything as useful as die. His guards had better be on full alert day and night if they wished to continue watching over a living chairman. But there was nothing to affect Romulan Security or the Empire's safety, not yet at any rate.

"Continue," she said. "Senators."

Without more than a blink of his eyes, Levak went down the list of senators and their activities, and Charvanek listened just as intently, her mind making comparisons and drawing possible links.

"Well done, Levak," she said when he had finished. "Nothing more? Then you are dismissed."

After Levak had left, Charvanek sat back in her chair with the smallest sigh of frustration. Far simpler to be a warbird commander, even during times of war, than to play this game and be in constant conflict with the Tal Shiar and that damned Koval. That he was slowly dying didn't bring her any joy: As the humans put it so dramatically, "Better the devil you know." But why could he not see that their two agencies should complement, not fight, each other?

Charvanek leaned forward again, running her fingers over a small console, and a viewscreen that had till that moment masqueraded as an archaic painting of the firefalls facing her desk sparked into life, showing her instead the Senate chamber and those who were meeting within it. She caught a quick glimpse of her reflection in the screen, but then ignored it. Perhaps her eyes were a little harder than they'd been before Narviat's assassination and the war, but as she stared at the senators, Charvanek was fierce and elegant as a warbird itself. She studied the senators, identifying and mentally cataloging each one as to potential for treason or other trouble. Nothing outstanding: The meeting was one of those dealing with food production, with no suspicious undercurrents and a minimal amount of shouting. Boring, but reassuring.

Neral, for all his ambition and devious mind, had been innocent of any involvement in Narviat's death, which, Charvanek thought, was why he was still alive. She didn't actually like or personally trust the Praetor, and knew that the feelings were mutual, but despite her personal opinion, he was, at least so far, good for the Empire, and as such, worthy of her protection. First and foremost, he had gotten the Romulan

Star Empire through the Dominion War, a conflict that might otherwise have destroyed them.

But curse it, Neral, how can I protect you if you go flying off on these insane missions?

Charvanek had, of course, surrounded him with her operatives, and she had reason to know the Federation's relative trustworthiness better than most, having been their "guest" for a time back when she was still Commander Charvanek. But there were still too many chances for "accidents" to happen to him, and too many chances for ambitious senators to plot in his absence.

Senator Hiren, now . . . that meeting with Rehaek, brief though it had been, could have been perfectly innocent—but if she was a gambler, she wouldn't have taken odds on it. And Hiren wasn't the only one needing monitoring. Charvanek could name a good dozen who would have thought nothing of stabbing Neral in the back, or of smothering Koval in his sickbed and taking over the Tal Shiar.

Get back here, Neral, and swiftly—or there just might not be a praetorship to which you can return.

NINE

MEMORY

His arm around Karatek's shoulder, Serevan half led, half dragged him, boots scraping in the melting ice, toward the emergency air tanks always kept at the airlocks. As Karatek sagged against the rock, Serevan equipped each of them with a fresh cylinder. Then he headed back into the blizzard. His massive form disappeared within seconds.

Gusts of frozen vapor piled drifts in the airlocks as more and more suited figures, newcomers and colonists alike, staggered in. In the darkness, reddish helmet lights bobbed in all directions, distorting the lights on sensors and control panels.

"Is that the last of the prisoners?" came the question from the command center. Sarissa's voice.

"Where is Serevan?" Karatek asked.

A shadow, covered with rime, formed in the airlock and stamped inside. Suited figures collapsed onto the floor and rolled out of Serevan's path.

"There's no one out there," Serevan's voice boomed through Karatek's helmet. *"No one alive. Yes, I'm certain. I'm going to seal up now."*

"Medical team ready, as soon as you release the inner seals." The relief in Sarissa's voice was palpable.

"Closing now!"

With a clash they felt, rather than heard, through their suits, the doors sealed. Karatek had a brief, nightmarish memory of the man who had collapsed and died, lying out there all alone. So, there were indeed worse fates than exile to the ice. The habitat, though bleak, had finally assumed the semblance of home.

All helms in the crowded airlocks turned to watch the sensors as air flooded into the entryway. Even before pressure equalized fully, Serevan had overridden the locks so T'Olryn and her medics, swathed against the chill, could dash into the crowd of tumbled, suited figures. Some of them were already removing their helms. Others struggled to sit up. But far too many others lay motionless. Some had drawn their legs up to their chests in rejection of this new environment.

As a medic approached him, Karatek motioned him away. His wits were restored. He was neither injured nor ancient. He could remove his own helm, he decided, and did so.

"They brought us convicts!" he gasped at T'Olryn. His daughter-in-law knelt beside another woman whom Karatek remembered from the exile. She had been a technician who kept close to her computers, a quiet woman who tended to vote with the majority. She had tugged her helmet off on her own—a good sign, but she was moaning slightly, which was not good at all.

For a moment, the green of blood rage flashed before Karatek's eyes. Slave labor. As the te-Vikram were altogether too fond of saying, abomination.

"Night and day, what's going on down there?" he cried. Illogical to demand a briefing of the injured, the catatonic, or the dying. Perhaps he had taken more damage from oxygen deprivation than he thought.

"Fighting," wheezed a man's voice as he struggled to free himself from his gauntlets. "I can help," he told T'Olryn. "Zebed son of Orivar son of Bardati. Geneticist. Used to be a physician. They wanted me . . . cloning experiments. Forced multiple births. I refused."

T'Olryn thrust a medkit at him. "Is that why they sent you here? What's going on down there? Don't they have everything they could possibly need?"

"Need, yes; want, no. They're fighting," said the quiet woman. It troubled Karatek that he could not remember her name. That was what happened when you made yourself a cipher: people forgot you. But they remembered you soon enough when they wanted someone to abuse.

"Always fighting," she muttered. "My mother T'Ralya . . . spoke out before the councillory was disbanded . . . she called Avarak a slave driver. She disappeared. One of our family . . . was sentenced, chosen by lot. . . . I lost."

She rolled over onto her side and met Karatek's eyes. "When they abandoned you, we did not fight. We did not speak. We were frightened. Some of us are sorry now," she said, letting her pallid face fall into the frigid rock. "You should have let us die."

"Where is S'task in all this?" Karatek demanded. Green blurred before his eyes again, and he flung out an arm to balance himself.

"Stay where you are," ordered a medic. The young man knelt before him, holding a flask of water to his lips. Karatek drank thirstily. The water was recycled, heavy with chemicals that were probably slow environmental poisons, but never had he tasted anything so fine.

"Turned inward," a man almost old enough to retreat and teach his grandchildren snarled. "Oh, the old man has a seat in the councillory when he chooses to warm it, but I think he is just waiting to die. Wants to die. Just as they keep him alive because, well, because he's S'task, and one day, some petty tyrant or other may find a use for him."

How could S'task have deteriorated so far?

"Isn't it enough that they stole our new homeworld from us?" came a shout of pure outrage. "Must they destroy it, too? Is this what we left Vulcan for?"

Karatek could feel the rage building behind his eyes. It was like weather sensitivity. On Vulcan, you knew when the sand fires would erupt. Here, you could sense blizzards on the surface. T'Olryn had explained it as pressure on one's sinuses or a response to a change in ionization levels.

More likely, it was instinct. He brought both hands up to his temples. The emotions he sensed around him threatened to drive him to his knees, retching. He had never been a particularly strong telepath. What was happening to all of them?

"Maybe they'll all die!" There was grim pleasure in that outburst from one of the medics, of all people, a woman almost as small as T'Olryn, her long eyes burning with rage.

"Kroykah!" T'Olryn shot the word at her.

"If they die, we die," Serevan observed. "We are not yet self-sufficient." He turned to T'Olryn. "My sister, as soon as our . . ."

What were the newcomers to be called? Serevan was an engineer, not a lawmaker, and he swung back to Karatek, clearly wanting him to resume control.

He could not collapse, could not consume medical resources when so many people might die. His people, the newcomers as well as those who had become his family here in this second exile, needed him.

A shaft of memory struck him, so incongruous he would

have laughed if he had been so lost to the control he had begun to acquire on that very day.

"I name thee guest-friends!" he shouted.

Of all the people who had witnessed how Surak and his two disciples had come to the Gates of ShiKahr, he was the only one still alive. His action then had set all this in motion: the exile, the arrival at the Two Worlds, even this second betrayal. Now, the thing must take its course, and Karatek must move with it.

"Like the extremophiles, these must be our guest-friends," he looked at each of his friends, his family, his fellow exiles in turn. "We are all exiles together now."

Serevan had been systematically stripping suits off the newcomers. "There's almost no logic in repairing these suits. Substandard, certainly never intended for conditions on the surface. As matters stand, if they'd been out in that blizzard five more minutes, we'd have lost half the . . . guest-friends. Some of the components may be worth recycling for use in the caverns, but I wouldn't want to trust my life to them."

Now that Serevan had a definition, guest-friend, assigned to the people he had helped rescue and a technical problem to solve, he could swing back into action. It was this certainty, this solidity of his, that had helped draw Sarissa to his side. Karatek did not know how he knew that, but he knew he was right.

"Some of these people may be spies," that was Solor's voice. He must have run all the way from his emergency station. To Karatek's displeasure, he was armed.

"They can barely walk." Karatek glanced at the weapon as he rebuked his son.

"I ask forgiveness." Solor returned the weapon to his belt with a singular lack of contrition.

"There are tests to learn whether our guest-friends are

friends indeed, or secret traitors," T'Olryn's voice was detached, with a coldness Karatek had never heard from her.

"Such tests require consent," Solor replied. "You would not force an unwilling mind."

Would she? Karatek wondered. T'Olryn had changed so much in the time since her discovery of the changes that the extremophiles had made in Refas.

Solor walked over to stand beside T'Olryn as she worked over one of the catatonics who remained curled up, rejecting this world or any other.

"I will not have to," she said. Solor looked closely at her. He reached out to brush a strand of hair away from her brow. She moved away from his touch. "Can you help? We need to get the worst injured into medcenter. This one needs warmth. They all do. We're going to have to examine all of them for frostbite before we do anything else." She looked up at her husband, at his extended hand, the one that had held the weapon. She did not offer to touch his fingers.

In all the years that Karatek had known her, she had never failed to welcome Solor, regardless of how busy she was.

She turned her attention to Karatek. "I wish all the newcomers brought to the medcenter. You, too, *T'Kehr.* I monitored your suit readings, and I want you under observation. And prophylactic radiation treatment."

Karatek opened his mouth to protest.

"Sir," T'Olryn interrupted him. "Consider this: while you are in the medcenter with these . . . guest-friends of ours, you will be the first to learn everything they can tell. Surely you see the desirability of that."

Karatek closed his mouth and did as T'Olryn had requested.

TEN

MEMORY

"The homeworld that was taken from us has sought to burden us still further by shipping us its 'undesirables' as convict labor. By dealing peace with them, however, as Surak taught us, we have succeeded in turning potential enemies into friends. A small percentage of our new guest-friends have, unfortunately, failed to thrive. We have taken their katras into our minds, as we do for our own friends and families.

"True, the newcomers have included several criminals. But they have been set to hard labor and reeducation. Thus far, they are too exhausted to show signs of violence. Besides, they have nowhere to flee but the ice, on which they are ill-equipped to survive.

"I have observed, however, that by far the greatest percentage of the newcomers were dissidents strong enough of mind, will, and body to pose a threat to the existing regime. Or the many regimes on that sunlit world from which we are barred. It will be . . . intriguing to find out if the people who banished us survive. That offers possibilities. Perhaps we can wage peace more successfully with the next regimes to seize power. I suspect we will learn more with the next ship."

It would be simple justice if Avarak became prisoner, not slave master, Karatek thought as he removed the coronet. For an instant, he touched the crystals, savoring the warmth imparted to them by his thoughts. These days, it took slightly longer for the infinitesimal wounds on his brow to cease bleeding. T'Olryn had assured him that was not due to radiation poisoning. Nevertheless, he did not have to be a healer to know that continued exposure to heavy minerals and irradiated dilithium crystals meant that injuries healed more slowly, and he was always tired, weakened. They all were, except, perhaps, Refas.

As Karatek heard from everyone, with varying degrees of insistence, he was working too hard for a man his age. He spent three out of four shifts performing some sort of more or less strenuous physical activities, even if he was not a miner. He stood watches in the command center and put in extra time helping to design and build what might one day be the first of a fleet of ships. On Vulcan, he could have looked forward to retiring to the comfort of his own courtyard; here, he would work until he died.

Many had been unable to adapt and had already died. Some had been very young. Others had simply rejected this world and lay in an isolated, quiet medcenter ward, tenderly cared for by family members or those who wished to serve.

When had they come to assume that if the physical dangers of wresting survival from rock, ice, and glowing crystal did not kill them, radiation exposure would change them permanently? Generations from now, they would not recognize their descendants.

Just as had happened to the extremophiles.

T'Olryn and the geneticist, Zebed, who had refused to help breed soldiers for bloodthirsty oligarchs, had already extracted samples of genetic material from the population. The shortened telomeres T'Olryn had found in Refas's genetic material were common. None of them were likely to live as long as Vulcans on the Mother World or on the planet they were forbidden to share.

Logically, Karatek had to face the fact that the coronet must pass from his hands into those of an heir, probably sooner than he would have expected. A historian would have been the best choice, but T'Vysse was his agemate. Solor, the younger of his two surviving children, had always been more volatile than Sarissa, quicker to act than to think. That left her as the appropriate choice.

He would have to speak with her about it. Soon. And ask her to designate an heir of her own. It was not, after all, as if any of them had so many people to choose among.

Karatek sighed. In a desert world, a low birthrate was a survival advantage. Here beneath the ice, it was a disadvantage. They badly needed a strong second generation of colonists, but miscarriages were on the rise and the number of conceptions had declined. It was logical not to wish to give birth to children who would be laborers and slaves.

Zebed had proved a great asset in T'Olryn's research. T'Zora, too, had recovered and demanded to repay the colony for her life. Convalescents or those too weak to work in the mines now labored with her to construct greenhouses that would enable the colony to grow more of its own food.

It was a sensible precaution. Cargo deliveries were long on equipment, short on food. And there was no guarantee that the mining outpost wouldn't be thrown upon their own resources due to war or whim or deliberate cruelty. It was possible that the orbiting ships might help them, but not likely, or they might have intervened when Karatek's people were marooned.

He calculated that T'Zora's work would enable them to achieve self-sufficiency in terms of food production in 8.6 years and to break even in terms of an oxygen–carbon dioxide balance throughout even an expanded habitat in 15.9 years. The colony owed her its thanks, even if her efforts were only a logical outgrowth of her own struggle to survive.

Wrapping the coronet in its usual silks, faded now and starting to perish with age, Karatek put it away before heading to the medcenter. T'Olryn, who had never been satisfied with his recovery from oxygen deprivation, insisted on monitoring him. And disregarding her instructions generally tended to be as unpleasant as it proved to be counterproductive. T'Olryn was nothing if not emphatic about the health of her charges.

If this world really had an oligarch, Karatek decided, it was his daughter-in-law.

He shook his head slightly. In these days of their second exile, he seemed to have grown more fanciful as well as more telepathically sensitive. That his bond with T'Vysse had intensified was scarcely a hardship, even if he found it difficult to believe after all these years that it could have deepened further. Now, at times, he thought he could see what she saw or hear her thoughts. His entire family bond had grown stronger, too. A kind of constant, very low-level awareness of everyone in the colony possessed his waking thoughts.

He was not the only one to perceive this enhanced mental response. In the times when they were not mining or refining minerals for masters who had once been brothers, some of their artists were experimenting with the arts of the mind, as they might with music, paintings, or mosaic. Karatek had witnessed one such "concert" generated by a collective meld and found it fascinating, not so much for what it was, but for what, in years to come, it might be. They would have to test the strength and the range of these new gifts and whether they could be preserved and passed on. Inevitably, too, the privacy codes would have to be adapted to protect these new talents from abuse.

However, there was one person in whom the links with family and community seemed to have eroded: T'Olryn. Well, she was a healer, one of the strongest telepaths remaining to them. It was logical she would seek to protect her mental "privacy."

But it was more than that. Even within the family, the privacy of individual family members was sacrosanct. But this wasn't privacy T'Olryn sought. She was keeping secrets. The instincts Karatek had come to trust told him that the blank wall where once there had been a responsive, vibrant intelligence represented a problem he would have to confront. Solor, he suspected, was already struggling with it.

Karatek entered the habitat's medcenter. Instantly, he wished he had not. He took a step forward, making his footsteps louder. If his son and daughter-in-law had to acknowledge his presence, perhaps they might cease what every instinct told him was a quarrel that might well strain their bond past bearing. The anguish he sensed between his son and his son's wife made him suppress a wince.

"Why didn't you tell me?" Solor's voice rose. Karatek had not heard it that angry since he, Surak, and Surak's disciples had had to restrain a boy willing to fight to the death to protect his sister.

"Did I or did I not tell you," T'Olryn asked with exaggerated patience, "that Zebed was teaching his techniques for performing genetic splices? You know we were working on an inoculation, drawn from Refas's blood serum. If it succeeds, we can use it to help the newcomers adapt more efficiently."

Solor looked down and away.

T'Olryn's hand came up, grasped his chin, and made him look at her. "You had to know. Now, of all times, is no time to begin to lie to me."

"I thought your experiments would stop with helping the newcomers," Solor finally said. "You also told me that Zebed was sent here because he refused to consent to . . . how did he describe it? Mass-producing children. Cloning. Forced multiple conceptions. In vitro fertilizations. So I hoped."

"I still refuse," Zebed replied, coming out of a sealed laboratory and pulling off his hood. "I will not create fodder for tyrants' armies. However"—he met Solor's eyes without flinching—"helping people adapt to a world that would otherwise kill them is a different matter. It may still be morally ambiguous, but—"

"Don't you dare rationalize these genetic experiments under the 'needs of the many' principle!" snarled Solor.

He sounded ready to offer a death challenge like the young te-Vikram in the throes of blood madness who had stolen and crashed a shuttle, almost destroying *Shavokh*.

Time, and past time, to stop this display of illogic.

"My son," Karatek said.

All three people in the medcenter turned to stare at him.

"I ask pardon for the intrusion," he continued, "but I was due to report for examination. You yourself were quite firm on the subject," he added to T'Olryn.

Magic words weren't even a game for children, but he hoped that if he hit on the right thing to say, he might see a faint hint of relaxation around her long, thoughtful eyes, the even fainter curl of humor about her mouth that had made her a prize men had fought over.

Did she ever remember that Avarak had threatened to challenge Solor? It would be illogical to blame herself for their current exile, but she was a healer, and healers, like leaders, assumed responsibility for the people whose welfare they safeguarded.

T'Olryn looked away, shielding herself and her thoughts from Karatek. He suppressed a sigh.

"I ask forgiveness," he said again, looking down to try to hide his sorrow. Even if she had sensed it, the courtesy was deserved.

"May I ask," he began cautiously, "why a genetic experiment has incited this degree of illogical dispute?"

"Zebed and I spliced genetic material from the extremophiles into Refas's DNA," T'Olryn said.

Night and day, if she had done that to him, what had she done to herself? His suspicions chilled him more than the medlab.

T'Olryn wore only the lightest of medical robes, though the medcenter, like the rest of the habitat, was cold. So, she had been spending a good deal of time in the area where life support was rudimentary: the area where Refas lived, a short distance from the nearest colonies of those small, rapidly mutating creatures that had saved his life.

"We wanted to see if his system would mutate further, yet remain Vulcan. Or," Zebed added with what Karatek considered unnecessary candor, "at least, Vulcanoid."

"You took skin samples?" Karatek asked. "Not just skin? What else did you do?"

T'Olryn looked down.

That explained Solor's anger. Not physical infidelity, but

a level of, at least, medical intimacy that a man who prized action over experimentation could never approve of. Or consent to.

"Once we saw that extremophile gene plasm, to use an oversimplified term, worked on the male, it seemed logical to ascertain whether it would work on female reproductive material."

Now T'Olryn met his eyes and her husband's eyes fearlessly. "I usurped no one's consent by experimenting on samples that Zebed drew from me."

Solor whirled, bringing a fist down on a table so hard that a beaker shattered.

Get back, Karatek mouthed at Zebed. *Far, far back.*

Solor was wearing his te-Vikram blade.

All he could do was to warn the physician to behave with his son as if he were going into *Plak-tow*. If that were true, Solor could attack at any moment. He might lash out at his father, too, but Karatek hoped that the bonds of the family still held in their case.

As, clearly, they had frayed the bond between Solor and his wife.

Solor bent to pick up the shattered fragments of the beaker. "I am quite sane," he told T'Olryn. "My blood is cool. My eyes are cool. And will remain so."

He set the fragments down on the table. Blood ran down his hand and dripped onto it, green upon sterile white, staining the transparent glass shards.

"Let me see that," T'Olryn ordered, stepping forward and taking his hand. The bond between them flared into passion. He tugged her closer, almost into his arms, despite Karatek's presence.

"What have you done?" Solor whispered. His face was greenish white, as if he sensed horror through their bond.

Her face went remote. Stepping out of his grasp, she reached for a bandage spray, to apply it to the jagged cut that scored her mate's palm.

She was not, Karatek noticed, wearing the bloodstone ring that had been one of his House's few surviving heirlooms. She had never removed it before.

Solor too stepped back. His gaze flicked to her bare hand, then away.

"As you wish," she said. She set the spray upon the table for him to use upon himself, or not.

"You know I am correct," she said to Karatek and Solor. "You know that we, too, are going to have to increase our population if we are to survive, much less become self-sufficient. We are going to have to adapt. I can show you the medical records. We are changing already. Deteriorating. We are going to die younger. If we do not replace the people we lose, this colony will be lost. My experiments simply accelerate the process of adaptation."

"Then let it!" shouted Solor. "Free creatures die in imprisonment."

"Wise creatures learn to survive within it, to adapt cunningly, so once again they can seek to gain their freedom," Zebed dared inject. "Your wife has given you an unprecedented opportunity to adapt to this world. Here where you are, it is cold, but she is warm. Already, your minds reach out to one another with more freedom than I have ever seen. Physiologically, you can adapt to conditions here, if you will.

"Or you can die. Healer T'Olryn has chosen to try to find a way to help you adapt. Do you think so little of her gift?"

"What *gift?*" Solor whispered. He looked around the quiet medcenter, then strode toward the laboratory that Zebed had just left. "What's in there?"

"Don't go in; there's a sterile field!" Zebed cried. "You could kill them."

"Them?"

"The next logical step," said T'Olryn. "To combine the modified gametes. To watch the blastocysts divide."

"To see if they mutate true. If they are viable. There were six, at varying stages of development," Zebed added, with more enthusiasm than discretion.

It wasn't just his refusal to create disposable warriors for his masters that had gotten him exiled, Karatek decided. It was his abysmal lack of tact. "And then, finally, to implant one . . ."

As T'Olryn folded her small hands, well-tended even now, over her abdomen, Karatek kept his face impassive with an effort that made him feel physically ill.

"Get out of here," Solor whispered at Zebed. "I will not tell you again. I cannot."

His eyes began to roll back in his head. His hands curled into claws.

Zebed left. Fast.

Two quick steps brought Solor to T'Olryn's side. This time, he did take her in his arms.

"You did not tell me. You did not ask me. If you wanted another child, why did you not ask *me?*"

"I did not want," she said precisely, *"a* child. Or even *our* child. What I wanted, what we all need here, is *this* child. Refas's DNA was adapted for the purpose. And available to me."

When Solor's arms loosened and dropped, T'Olryn stepped back. Her face was shadowed, but only briefly.

"The child will be male," she said. "I should have preferred to begin with a female. In many ways, we are more resilient before birth and during the first year of life. A male, however, can have many children with many females. Assuming, of course, other women agree with the step I have taken, as I project that they will."

The veils flicked over Solor's eyes, giving him a blinded, anguished look. Again, Karatek remembered that night in the desert and a lost, terrified child fighting for adulthood.

"I cannot ask you for forgiveness," she said. "Because I have done only what the logic of our survival demands."

"And the logic of our bond?" Solor's voice was so sad that Karatek blinked fast to repress tears.

Would this new creature—this new type of child—whom T'Olryn now bore have the same sort of eyes? Would it have keener night sight? In that case, generations from now, would this world hold Vulcans for whom night was as bright as day? Karatek was relieved that he would not live to know it.

T'Olryn met her bondmate's eyes for a long, long moment. She held up two fingers, as if asking him to touch them, to accept her and the decision she made.

Minutely, Solor shook his head.

"I cannot. Not now. Perhaps, if you had told me before you acted," he said.

"You would have stopped me. You were the only one who might have done so, and I could not allow it, husband. Not if we are to survive. It is worth the sacrifice of all we were." Her voice went husky. "It must be."

"At least our children are grown," Solor said. "Your *other* children."

T'Olryn looked down. "I grant the provocation to be great, but I see no need to be gratuitously cruel," she said,

"Forgive me," Solor said. But he kept his hand at his side, balled into a fist. Blood seeped from it onto the floor.

"One day," she replied, "perhaps you will forgive me. I shall not, however, hope. Given the wound I have dealt you, hope would be illogical."

Solor strode from the room.

Karatek felt their bond end as cleanly as a blade severs a newborn from its mother.

As Karatek cleared his throat, T'Olryn held up a hand, forestalling him.

"Sir," she said to Karatek. Not "father-in-law." No longer. "I think we had best reschedule your examination. Tomorrow, perhaps, at this same time?"

Karatek nodded.

T'Olryn turned to fit a sterile hood over the braided coils she had never cut because Solor had always told her how aesthetically appealing he found them. That she retained that innocent, loving vanity even now . . .

There is no pain, Karatek told himself.

And knew he lied.

Dismissing him with a courteous inclination of her head, T'Olryn stepped into the sterile field that divided the familiar medcenter from the future she was creating.

Karatek fled.

He would have to tell T'Vysse. And then he would have to think of how he could comfort his son for a wound from which he saw no healing.

ELEVEN

U.S.S. ALLIANCE

2377

"The Watraii have just slowed to sublight," Lieutenant Abrams announced abruptly.

"Interesting. Do the same," Saavik ordered.

"Are they having trouble?" Ruanek murmured to Spock. "Or is it some kind of a trap?"

Spock returned, "Let us see what has happened to them before we pass any judgments."

"Captain Saavik," Lieutenant Suhur said suddenly from his communications post. Young though he was, the dark-skinned Vulcan officer still managed to express both excitement and tension without betraying so much as a hint of unseemly emotion. "The Watraii have just opened a communications channel."

That split-second of hesitation was telling. "Not to us, I assume," Saavik said.

"No, Captain—to the Federation."

"Interesting," she repeated, glancing quickly at Spock.

"And they do seem to have forgotten all about trying to pursue us. Patch us in, Lieutenant, but do not let the Watraii know that we're eavesdropping."

The Vulcan was busy at his console for a few moments, fingers flying over the controls, and then said, "I have the frequency."

Spock listened in silence for a time to the exchange taking place between Watraii and Federation speakers.

"Fascinating," the ambassador murmured at last. "It would seem that the Watraii are making a formal diplomatic protest to the Federation."

But there was something about the Watraii speaker's voice . . . something almost familiar. . . . An eyebrow raised, he fell silent, analyzing that voice. There was some distortion due to the patched-in link . . . but there were certain similarities in the pitch . . . the tone. . . .

"Rushing things a little, aren't they?" Ruanek commented. "Making a diplomatic protest before even trying to establish diplomatic relations."

Spock ignored him. "I know that voice," he said suddenly. "That is the Watraii commander."

Ruanek turned sharply to him. "The one you met on the planet? The one you nearly won over to your side?"

A flash of memory reminded Spock what he had said to that very Watraii commander: *Your fight is not with the Federation. Hear me out. I know that you are concerned for your people. I saw that when the shuttle crashed. I know that you ache for your children. I heard that in your voice. For the sake of your people, for the sake above all of your children, believe me. Take your quarrel to the Federation.*

"That is somewhat of an exaggeration, Ruanek," Spock finally said, "though he did, indeed, seem willing to at least open preliminary negotiations with me." *And it was I who told him about the Federation, and the opportunity to air grievances.* "He did, indeed, also seem to care about the welfare of his people, not merely their warrior status. And now, the fact that he should take so open a risk as this, leaving his homeworld, exposing himself to attack, must mean that he is feeling a high degree of desperation about his people, indeed."

"Or has a true gambler's heart," Ruanek said.

"Even so," Saavik cut in, "our Klingon allies are not going to begin any more 'glorious battles'—are they?"

She didn't need to add that if, when the two privateers had attacked the Watraii ships, they had taken out the Watraii leader, they would have ended all hope for peaceful negotiations there and then. Whether or not the Klingons agreed with that view or not, it was impossible to tell from their lack of reaction, but both captains rather grudgingly did finally agree:

"We will hold back."

"We give you the honor of letting you make the first strike."

All the while, that same cold Watraii voice was continuing to the Federation official at the other end of the communication. *"Above all, we make formal protest about the unwarranted and utterly illegal sneak attack on our sovereign nation, our homeworld. We make formal protest as well about the wanton destruction of Watraii ships as the invaders withdrew and this most recent destruction of three Watraii ships by Klingon pirates."*

There was a concerted roar of laughter and raucous cheering from the Klingon ships at that.

"Typical," Ruanek muttered.

The Federation voice replying to the Watraii also sounded familiar to Spock. He suspected from its professional smoothness and self-control that it belonged to Koll Azernal, President Min Zife's shrewd Zakdorn chief of staff. Logically, the Watraii leader would, indeed, have been passed up the official ladder to him.

In a diplomatically calm tone, Azernal assured, *"We will take your protests under advisement."*

"Advisement!" the Watraii screamed. *"Do you not believe me?"*

"Of course I do, we all do, but—"

"This isn't a matter for polite words. What happened to us was nothing less than a blatant act of aggression! We were attacked without warning or provocation!"

"As were the Romulans," Ruanek muttered. "Forgotten about that little unpleasantness, have we?"

The first Watraii attack on the Romulans had, indeed, come without warning or provocation, and had taken out an unarmed colony world.

"We understand that an unfortunate event occurred." Azernal's voice was still professionally smooth and soothing, giving no clue as to *which* "unfortunate event" he referred. *"And I assure you, sir, that the matter will be thoroughly investigated."*

"Do you try to trip me up with your diplomatic clichés?" The Watraii leader's voice could have cut xenosteel.

"No insult or trick is meant, I assure you."

"Very well, then, I shall answer you in proper diplomatic form—at least for now: We of the Watraii make two demands, which as an invaded and attacked sovereign nation we may certainly do."

"Of course."

"We make the demands and insist that they be answered! One: We demand that our attackers be severely punished. Two: We demand that the artifact that was stolen away by those dishonorable thieves, the artifact that is sacred to us, not to the Romulan murderers—we demand that it be returned to us!"

Ruanek snorted. "Listen to that. They lie very skillfully."

"Truth or lies," Spock murmured, "I find it fascinating that they are making formal complaints at all rather than simply attacking us or anyone else. This could still lead to war—but it could, instead, lead to the start of genuine negotiations."

"Assuming," Ruanek said, "that you could trust the Watraii. Which you can't."

Spock raised an eyebrow. "Generalizations are never logical."

"Oh, I agree, of course they aren't, but in this case, Spock, you have to admit that—"

"And negotiations," Spock continued calmly, "are often possible just when they seem the least likely."

Ruanek started to reply, but then, as if aware it was a losing cause, sighed ever so softly and satisfied himself with nothing more than a shrug.

As Saavik's fleet approached the Eridani system, Lieutenant Abrams stiffened in sudden alarm. "Captain," she said, "looks like we're not alone any longer."

Saavik raised an eyebrow. "Continue."

"There are"—a quick tally—"ten ships out there, blocking our way. Make that ten Romulan warbirds, with weapons online."

"On-screen," Saavik commanded.

"There," Spock said after a moment as they viewed the

Romulan fleet. "That is their flagship. It is the only warbird to bear a definite insignia."

Ruanek straightened with a startled hiss, staring at the viewscreen, then moved in one fluid leap almost to Lieutenant Abrams's side. "That image—I need to see it more clearly."

The urgency in his voice left no room for questions. At Saavik's command, the image of the insignia was enlarged and clarified, revealing a symbol arrogantly close to that of the Romulan Star Empire itself, this warbird in profile though, and lacking the double worlds clutched in the imperial warbird's talons.

"Yes," Ruanek all but snarled, all his Vulcan-learned self-control gone for the moment. "I do know that insignia. It hasn't changed over the years. That warbird, and the rest of those ships, are being led by Commander Tomalak."

The barely suppressed anger in his voice made Spock glance sharply at him in surprise. Ruanek explained with a touch more restraint, forcing his face back into proper Vulcan calmness, "Let us merely say that he is someone I remember without any fondness from the 'bad old days' on Romulus."

"The commander has a history with Starfleet as well," Saavik said succinctly. "The *Enterprise* and the *Grissom* are but two of the ships he has clashed with over the years."

Spock had to silently agree with that. Commander Tomalak had definitely been one of the most visible of the Romulan leaders along the Neutral Zone before the Dominion War, and had, indeed, had several encounters with Starfleet throughout the 2360s. Most notably, it had been Tomalak in command of the warbird that had so blatantly violated the Neutral Zone back in 2366, and it had also been Commander Tomalak behind the elaborate deception surrounding the unfortunate Alidar Jarok's defection.

And it was, as Saavik indicated, the Enterprise *that had forced Tomalak to back down both times.*

But since those pre–Dominion War days when each side warily tested the other and neither side trusted the other, the commander had been far less visible, at least as far as the Federation was concerned.

He was barely more visible on Romulus. I don't recall seeing him more than once in all that time. Has Tomalak been planning a quiet seizure of power on the homeworlds all this while? Spock wondered.

There had been no clear evidence of any such intrigues in the time that Spock had spent on Romulus, particularly not in the capital of Ki Baratan. But that didn't mean such intrigues hadn't been there, below the surface, since he could hardly have been aware of everything taking place in a city so full of plots, particularly if they hadn't directly affected Spock's mission there. Given Tomalak's excellent military record and his solid history of cunning maneuverings, a grab for power on his part should hardly be difficult if he had, indeed, developed a hunger for power.

Then for him to be here, now, at the head of this Romulan fleet when he could be more safely consolidating power back home meant that he was taking a definite gamble, risking all that had come so far in his career against the hope of one more triumph over Starfleet. To regain the Romulan artifact and return it to the Empire would be an astounding triumph, indeed, and would mean that his political ambitions would be all but fulfilled.

But Tomalak must surely be aware that in the cold, fierce Romulan way, one defeat here would negate all his prior successes in the minds of Romulus's citizens, politicians, and military.

He is a gambler, then, in true Romulan fashion.

Spock could almost read Saavik's thoughts about the situation: *So much for Spock's hopes for unification.*

That was not necessarily the case. But it was undeniably true that if Romulus and Vulcan fought, they, and their allies with them, would lose all the gains made over the centuries.

They would be cast back to the vicious days of the Sundering.

TWELVE

MEMORY

"Now that the newcomers who survived are finally adapting to life beneath the ice, we have had . . . not quite leisure, but enough workers to meet our quotas. Now, not everyone needs to work three out of four daily shifts at all times.

"Effective immediately, I have reduced the schedules of the disabled who are able to work at all and those over one hundred fifty years of age to two shifts out of four. I qualify for the exemption, but I have spent my 'free' shift fine-tuning the engine of the one ship we have managed to construct. I am pleased to find that my son Solor shares my zeal for the project. The severance of his marriage bond to T'Olryn has left him understandably distraught, and I have found that where meditation does not avail, hard work may."

SOLOR'S STORY

Solor watched his father walk out to join the engineers and technicians hovering by the remote control panel. Those seated rose; those talking in quiet voices hushed.

108

His father's quiet authority was a gift. The first time Solor had seen Karatek was with Surak two nights after their parents had been killed in a raid on their desert settlement. They had stolen Sarissa! They carried her away, and controlled him—and somehow, even after all that, he had learned to respect Karatek, to care for him, even to trust someone again. Karatek would make things right. As a boy, when the dreams were bad, Solor had been able to sleep after telling himself that.

Solor was adult now, the father of two grown children. Illogical as the wish might be, he wanted that boyhood faith back.

"You know, you should be resting," Karatek was telling Solor's associates.

"We prefer this," Stalat, a stocky engineer who, Solor knew, often worked on his brother-in-law's shifts, told Karatek.

Solor backed against the wall of the sealed launch bay, welcoming the cold of the roughly smoothed, mottled dark stone. Once it had held a rich vein of pergium ore. The lode had been exhausted more than a year ago. Nevertheless, miners had gone on hollowing out the rock until they had created a vast chamber that could be converted to other uses—such as this first full test of the ship's experimental engines that had been Karatek's own special project.

He glanced away from his father. If the old man looked into his eyes, he would see far too much that Solor was not ready to let him see. He did not understand much of it himself. But he was an adult. He could resolve his own confusions.

If the engines worked, Solor thought, the prototype would be one more step closer to flight. He already had a name for it: *Vengeance*. First of its class.

Did he have a purpose in that name? It was too early to think of purpose. Karatek could simply decide that it was illogical to create a ship that would be used only for destruction.

It would not be just a warship! Solor protested silently. That was a rationalization. He wanted *Vengeance* to be a warship *first.*

"Shall we begin?" Karatek asked. Eager nods answered him.

In that moment, he seemed as centered, as serene, as Solor had ever seen him back on Vulcan. How strong his control was. It was not envy Solor felt; envy was unproductive. It was respect where respect was due.

Karatek adjusted his headset. "Assume goggles. Begin test burn."

It was a sign of his father's excitement that he had ordered, not requested.

With a roar, flame erupted from ignition tubes into a pit that not only caught the terrible heat, but was lined with energy cells to catch and transform it into power that would benefit the habitat.

Inner eyelids flicked down as, despite the protective goggles that they wore, the work team averted their eyes from the engine's fire. From the blue-white at its core to the yellows and reds, it was mirrored on the prototype's sleek raked sides and the curved triangular supports and telemetry struts that restrained it.

Despite the stabilizers carefully installed throughout the cavern turned launch bay, the ground rumbled. Sensors showed ice cracking on the surface beneath hatches that, in a true flight test, would open and release the ship.

May I be chosen as one of our first ship's first crew! Solor wished.

He forced himself to stare through tear-filled eyes at the prototype. It reminded him of himself: it too struggled to be free, to be more than it was.

What is the point? whispered a dark voice in his head. Even if they could build a fleet of ships, this second exile could last as long as the flight from Vulcan—or even longer. And he would still have nothing.

"Surface telemetry, please report," Karatek ordered.

"Surface ice cracked to a depth of fifteen meters, T'Kehr. Rock stresses within acceptable parameters," came Serevan's voice. With characteristic thoroughness, he had suited up and gone outside to measure the impact on the launch bay and the habitat itself of this first test fire. He had calculated a 1 in 256.9 chance that the ship's engines might collapse the launch bay. Reason enough for him to risk his life monitoring stresses from outside.

Serevan, too, had all the composure that Solor lacked. He had not spoken to his brother-in-law, knowing that whatever he might say would, inevitably, find its way back to Sarissa. She had been eyeing him, and when Sarissa got *that* look, it meant she was on the trail of a puzzle that concerned her. In all their years together, she had been as much mother as sister to him.

That had never concerned him until now.

"Merely acceptable?" Karatek asked.

"I'll get volunteers out here with stabilizers. We can get the number down by 10 percent within five hours."

"That must wait until your crew has had a chance to rest," Karatek said. "Others deserve a chance to share the work."

"Yes, sir." Serevan, despite his unfailing composure, sounded discontented.

"If you don't rest, you will hear it from Sarissa," Karatek

retorted with mild humor. "Worse, it might come to T'Olryn's attention."

"We're coming in!" Serevan replied, deliberately speaking too quickly.

This time, Solor really did flinch. He flicked a glance across the gallery. No one had noticed. It was illogical to feel aggrieved at the success of his acting, more illogical still to recoil just from thinking the name of the woman who had been his wife for so many years.

These days, her name was as intolerable to Solor as focusing on the psychic wound that replaced the reassurance that had once been their marriage bond. It was not like the fire and fury of the ship's engines. He had no headset to put on and protect himself against the torment of that one name.

Names, like beginnings, were important, Solor thought. Now that the prototype's engines showed they could achieve and sustain ignition, it needed a name. His father might argue that naming prototypes was so premature it was illogical, but Solor disagreed. *Vengeance.*

Metal-poor as Vulcan had been, it had taken years merely to mine sufficient ore to produce the great ships such as *Shavokh*. Here, at least, metals stronger than anything they had ever been able to smelt on Vulcan were plentiful. Once this ship passed its flight tests, they could build more.

If they stayed out of line of sight of their captors, they could even refine its engines in space. Karatek had ambitions of achieving 98.5 percent light speed. He thought of the ship as a way of bargaining with their oppressors. Serevan thought of it as a technical challenge, while Sarissa—Sarissa opposed T'Olryn's plans to adapt their people to their prison. Opposed, but, thus far, had been able to come up with no acceptable alternative.

For that, they would need to build a much bigger ship. First, they would have to convince the colony that a second exile, with no assurance that they would find a viable world, was preferable to life doing forced labor. Even if all could be brought to agree, to build such a ship they would need more space, more refined metal, and larger equipment.

The undertaking—Solor did not delude himself—would be prodigious, all the more so because it would have to be done in addition to the quotas imposed upon them. The work would have to be done in secret, concealed from their masters' overflights. And it would have to justify the expense and labor of design, mining, construction, and testing to the people who devoted their exceedingly brief leisure times and risked their lives to build and test it.

I will not see it in my lifetime, Solor realized. *Refas has given people one reason to hope, hideous as I believe it to be. But I cannot simply oppose him. I cannot simply say, "Hold firm; one day, we will be able to flee this place." People cannot always be living for tomorrow, the next day, the next generation. What can I offer them that can make life here worth living?*

Families, certainly. He flinched from the idea, although he knew perfectly well that it had been he who had avoided his and T'Olryn's children, not the other way around. Tracing their close resemblance to her in their feaures, once a pleasure, had become unbearable. The long, dark eyes, full of thought, the seeming delicacy that masked more power than was commanded by any other woman in his generation—he saw them replicated in his children, and they tore at him.

She had sent back the ring that had been their pledge. The ancient, faceted bloodstone glittered on his hand as if he had cut it, a wound that would not heal, a constant reminder of their failure.

You have become a slave to your emotions. You will need more control, less passion if you are to achieve your goals. Can you manage that?

He did not know. Another failure, this one his alone.

In the launch bay beneath the gallery, the ignition test raved on. Solor stared at it through his tears.

"Terminate test burn," Karatek said. "Please."

The fire died. The light subsided. The ground ceased to rumble underfoot. In the silence, they could hear ice falling onto the immense hatches they had cut into the rock above the launch bay.

"Power capture?" he inquired.

"Four days' supply." Serevan said with immense satisfaction.

From just a five-minute burn! Serevan would be able to take their main generator off-line for servicing, with no risk to life support.

"Satisfactory," said Karatek. "Highly satisfactory indeed."

He removed his headset.

"Vent the launch bay," he ordered. Instantly, the thrum of life support intensified as small generators worked to restore a breathable atmosphere in the immense docking bay that had been solid rock before the captive Vulcans burrowed into it. If they were forced to live here long enough, a veritable world would be hollowed out beneath the ice. And not one meter of it would be free, safe, or healthy.

But Solor could no longer think that far in advance. Even though he knew that his interest in the prototype had pleased and reassured his father, he was just as restless as ever. The person best qualified to help him restrain himself was the one person he could not bear to see. She did not, he realized, wish him ill. But her research, her goals, even her desires, had taken her down another path that he could not bring himself to walk.

Think of something else!

It could be months before they were ready to conduct final flight tests, years before a larger ship could be completed, perhaps a generation before all were ready to leave. That was too long to wait.

There must be another solution, Solor thought. Or, at least, an outlet for his restlessness. And the heartache that threatened to overpower his control.

"You're planning to do *what?*" Sarissa's voice rose as Solor unsealed his door. Behind her loomed Serevan, his face lit with curiosity, courteously restrained.

"Come in," Solor invited his sister and brother-in-law. "You do not need to announce my plans to the entire corridor."

When his marriage had dissolved, Solor had moved out of what had been his family's quarters to a small chamber, barely larger than an adept's cell. It held a narrow bed, a workstation, storage for a few garments, plus a table and four seats, two of them pulled down from a wall installation. Table, work stand, and the other two seats were carved from black stone. Veins of ore too fine to be worth processing glinted in the rock. A metallic green thermal blanket lay across the table; others provided scant padding for the stone chairs. The only ornament, if a weapon could be called an ornament, was the triangular ceremonial blade Solor had taken from N'Keth after he had helped the old warrior die. Light played on the cabochon gems of green and gold and blue that studded its hilt.

Solor caught Sarissa's glance at her mate, then back at him.

"I find the resemblance to the shelter in our home on the Forge attractive," he told her.

"Morbid nostalgia," Sarissa muttered.

Solor pretended not to hear.

Long before the exile was ever thought of, their family had been killed in a raid on the Forge. Only he and Sarissa (they had been Kovar and Tu'Pari then) had survived, to be found by Karatek. He had been traveling with Surak and his two disciples—Skamandros, Solor remembered, who had frightened the boy he'd been at the time; and Varen, who had admired Sarissa far more than Solor approved of. Once the two of them realized that these newcomers weren't going to kill them, they had taken their newly found "guest-friends" to a hidden emergency shelter almost as bare as these new quarters of his.

These days, everything had changed in Solor's life—and nothing. Once again, he fell back on the basics of shelter and security. There was reassurance in it, and potential for yet another start.

"Here," Solor said. "I believe this is the first time you have honored my quarters. Permit me to offer you water."

He reached for a set of stone goblets that had been old even before the exile. A bonding gift, one of the few he had retained.

"Permit me," said Sarissa.

She poured water from a pitcher wrought from the metal of the shuttles shot down by their captors.

In the shelter on the Forge, Sarissa had offered their guests water. They had knelt to her as to a great lady, then. That had been ritual, peace-making; this was simply hospitality within the family.

As her eyes met his, Sarissa's face softened. Solor hissed a quick warning at her. He did not require pity; he required a hearing, preferably followed by swift agreement.

"The surface?" asked Serevan. "You want to explore the surface?"

"Why not?"

"I consider it a gratuitous risk. The last time I was on the surface, supervising the installation of stabilizers for the new sector we're opening, I was caught in an ice tremor. You know that. I would have been preserved for all time in a nitrogen pool if you hadn't pulled me back. I see no logic at all in exploring a surface so inimical."

"Do you realize what an interesting part of the dark side our habitat occupies?" Solor demanded.

Swinging a chair around, Solor seated himself at his workstation and called up a hologlobe. Almost half of the translucent, rotating image seemed a smooth, glowing thing.

"Considerable volcanic activity on the sun side," said Solor. "We have only the initial scans showing molten pools of metal, gas plumes, bare rock. I've marked the principal features, but except for that massive range"—he highlighted a plateau several kilometers above what looked like a sea of molten metal—"we have little specific survey data."

"There seemed no reason to go there," said Serevan. "We were not equipped to explore it. We suffered unacceptable casualty levels just in landing here."

"You made the appropriate decisions," Solor assured his sister and her mate.

The globe rotated, showing them a representation of the ice, in some areas blue and green, in others orange and the deep red of lost Vulcan, only cold, so very cold. Solor touched a control, showing constant motion from ice storms, avalanches, and rock falls. He highlighted geological features, like the escarpment that bounded their landing field and the active volcanic fields.

117

Serevan leaned forward, his face lighting in the glow from Solor's model. "I had no idea you could build models this detailed. From what sources do you derive your data?" he asked.

"I aggregated data from all the ships' scans from when the fleet entered this system and we were still sharing information," Solor told him. "I refined it using data from the initial survey missions."

"You realize that data could be flawed," Serevan warned.

"The zenite exposure?" Solor said. "I know it deranged your crew. I assume that if it damaged instrumentation, you would have reported it once you recovered."

Serevan inclined his head.

Solor made the globe revolve again. "We are locked with one side facing this system's star and the world we should have been living on . . ."

"Trapped between fire and ice," Sarissa interrupted.

"There is sufficient perturbation in this world's orbit to create a band of twilight," Solor said, indicating a shadowed band that ate into the hemispheres of fire and ice. "It has atmosphere. Surprisingly enough, there appears to be somewhat of a warmer spot near the northern pole. If we could reach it, perhaps we could build an outpost where people could live aboveground, secured from the worst of the radiation in the ores we mine."

Sarissa flashed him a look, then turned to Serevan. Solor kept his face impassive.

"Do you have any idea of the drain on our resources a secondary habitat would represent?" she asked.

"Rhetorical question. I have not even performed a first approximation," Solor assured her. "What I am thinking of is a hope. Somewhere to go that is not this burrow we have made

118

in rock and ice just to survive and serve the people who cast us out of what should have been our home. It may take years, years in which we have to learn to be a people, a culture, not a race of slaves that were once Vulcans or a race of"—his voice broke, and he glanced away—"whatever hybrid creatures that my . . . that Healer T'Olryn is helping to raise. On board *Shavokh,* we had a species of *kahs-wan,* uniting us with our past."

Solor remembered his own ordeal, how many died, how old Rovalat had scoured the desert to bring out as many youths as he could find.

Rovalat had died rescuing other young Vulcans, Refas among them. If only that good old man had failed in that attempt. But Solor was unjust; Rovalat had rescued others besides Refas. Besides, if the man had not helped steal what he prized most . . .

"The journey would be something of our own," Solor said, his voice deliberately toneless. "Just as the *kahs-wan* has always been: a test of strength, skill, craft, and will to live, going into the waste places and surviving in them."

"By that reasoning, our entire life here is just such an ordeal," said Serevan.

"But not by our choice," Solor told him. "This journey would be."

Serevan nodded. He saw too much, Solor thought. So did Sarissa, whose face gentled as it rarely did, these days. Orphaned on the Forge, she had tried to mother him, girl that she was, afraid and grieving for the loss of her betrothed as well as their parents. What was his name? Sivanon, that was right. He had died defending them. Karatek and Surak had left memorials at his grave. Even now, something in Sarissa, fierce as she had become, ached to protect him.

"Permit me, please," asked Serevan, gesturing at the workstation.

At Solor's nod, the engineer took over operations of the hologlobe. Instantly it shifted, assuming more granular detail under his expert manipulations.

"Calling this area a twilight zone makes it sound unduly inviting. Yes, I hypothesize it will be warmer than our current habitat. Yes, radiation levels will be lower on the surface than in the mines. But perturbations in the area are likely to be terrible. As gas currents sweep across the ice and the zone of fire, they might create winds so powerful you could not stand."

"But there might be air we could make breathable," Solor said. "And we might not have to claw a habitat out of the rock. We will not know until we go there. And we have . . ."

"You want to take the prototype?" Sarissa asked. "It could be detected."

"Once it neared the twilight region, yes. I propose using it to drop caches of supplies. One, two, as many trips as need be. There is room in the prototype for at least two people. One could pilot while the other scanned. This would test the ship fully in hazardous conditions, and we would be learning more about our world."

Serevan made a faint sound of protest.

"And the last phase of the journey?"

"I plan to make it on foot. And in the doing, learn more about my will, my ability to survive and, therefore, our people's. I would be reminding us that we are Vulcans!"

Solor knew that passion rang out in his voice. He no longer cared. After all, was survival not an instinct, and following it one of the most logical actions a being could perform?

"What T'Olryn is doing," he argued, his words coming

fast, "is making people over in this world's image. Do you think I would have broken with her if I could have reached any kind of agreement? I know you do not agree with her either. So here is what I propose. I propose that we make this world *ours*. In spirit, if not in flesh.

"We cannot simply be prisoners. How many generations before we simply die out because Vulcans are not meant to live as slaves? Are you willing to leave it to the extremophiles and hybrids?"

Sarissa's eyes were blazing. That gave Solor hope. His sister had perhaps the strongest will of anyone who had survived thus far. Profoundly devoted to Serevan, she had refused to bear children during the journey from Vulcan. She refused now to bear children into captivity. But if her life had taught her strength, it had taught her pragmatism. She knew that she neared a time when, even if she could still conceive, she would lack the physical strength to carry a child in a hostile environment. She would have to make a decision, or her age would make the decision for her.

Sarissa looked away.

"You risk your life," she said, her voice that of the young girl Tu'Pari, who had held him during the cold of the long desert night to keep him warm, had promised him help when the day came, and had never, in all their long lives, broken her word to him.

"I risk physical survival in favor of a full life, a life where we value our skills as more than a way of meeting quotas, where, even if we are imprisoned here, we learn what we can."

Solor flicked a glance at Serevan. "I daresay you could adapt our scanners so I could be monitored every step of the way. Think of the knowledge."

"Think of the risk," the engineer protested. A touch from Sarissa's hand silenced him.

I am dying here, Solor thought at her. *I must have something, or I will go out onto the ice with no purpose.*

"You want me to speak to our parents," Sarissa whispered.

"And back me before the council."

Her proud head drooped, then nodded.

She was not convinced, Solor realized. She merely loved.

The globe whirled in front of them, showing them ice, showing them fire, showing them shadow.

Showing them themselves.

THIRTEEN

PACIFICA

2377

"That was interesting," President Zife said to his chief of staff carefully. "The . . . Watraii, is it? Yes. The Watraii want to make demands on the Federation. A little arrogant of them, isn't it?"

"Premature, possibly," Koll Azernal replied. "Or that might be a bit of desperation." He checked the notes he'd made on his small padd. "Mr. President, you understand that whatever the situation, we can't simply dismiss their claims out of hand."

"No, I would guess not."

"And that a Starfleet ship . . ." Azernal checked the name on his padd. ". . . the *Alliance,* seems to have been involved in the situation adds a complication that we can't dismiss, either."

Zife blinked in surprise. "Oh well, surely that part of it is an issue for Starfleet alone to resolve."

"A Starfleet ship being involved in the situation, yes, certainly, particularly since its captain seems to have been acting without official orders. But, Mr. President, much as we might like it, we can't just turn the whole matter over to them."

Zife sighed. "No. Unfortunately, the Watraii did make their appeal directly to us. Tactless of them, wasn't it? But now, what are we to do, eh?"

"Puzzling out the true story in the middle of all this muddle is going to be the real problem for us, sir. But first and foremost, we need to know this: Are the Watraii speaking from a position of weakness—or of power?"

"There is that little issue." The President shook his head ruefully. "What do you think, Koll? Do we take them seriously, or not?"

Didn't you hear anything of what I just said? Azernal thought. *If they're speaking from a position of power, this could be their last communication before opening fire on someone. Don't you see that?*

It was never clear just how much the President was absorbing, and how much was wishful thinking on both their parts. But rather than say something so career-threatening, Azernal hesitated a second longer, organizing his thoughts into something safer. Maybe Zife wasn't the quickest of wits, but he made a very good presidential image, sitting there behind his grand presidential desk like a living holo of "The President," with his hands neatly folded, his suit neatly pressed, and that faint, meaningless smile on his face. A more cunning president would have been difficult to maneuver.

But even so, there was a great difference between an image and a president with full intelligence.

Look at that smile. Never a hint, the Zakdorn thought dourly, *that he couldn't manage a simple meeting with an ambassador without me. Let alone manage any type of political maneuverings and schemes.*

"I don't think we can afford *not* to take them seriously, Mr. President," Azernal replied. "But at the same time we can hardly be seen to be backing them, at least not openly. At least not until we hear what the Romulans have to say—particularly their Praetor."

"Ah yes. Strange that he should take such a radical step as leaving the Romulan Star Empire. I'd say that the Romulans, not the Watraii, must be the truly desperate ones for him to take that risk."

"Then again, Mr. President," Azernal prodded warily, "knowing what we do about the volatile Romulan temperament, he just might be angry enough not to care about the risk."

"I see. What do you advise?"

Azernal paused again, considering. There were always possible advantages to backing one side over the other, and even more possible advantages to backing both, as long as the backing was kept secret—but without further information about the Watraii, their strengths and weaknesses, and the validity or falsehood of their claims, it was best to simply play the waiting game for a time and hold both sides at bay.

"Wait and see what happens," he said at last. "Give the situation a little more time to develop."

And hope that we don't wait too long.

The antechamber's walls were painted a soothing tan-beige, their smoothness broken by regularly placed gold-framed images of Federation planets. The smooth tiles of the floor, laid out in a blue and tan geometric pattern that pleased the eye, were so finely polished they gleamed. The several chairs within the room were lushly cushioned in an equally soothing tan and pale blue fabric, and were softly flowing of shape, designed to be comfortable to many species and practically crying out to be lounged upon.

Neral had no intention of lounging, or even of sitting on those ridiculously luxurious chairs. He was the Praetor of the Romulan Star Empire, not some Federation sybarite to forget his mission in comfort, or some sniveling little underling to be kept waiting or cowering with anxiety—and he had not, Neral thought darkly, gotten to be Praetor by acting like either.

Enough of this.

He signaled curtly to his guards: Get that door open, get me into those offices.

The Romulans moved with warrior speed, one to each side of the door, disruptors drawn and ready.

But before they could fire, the door slid open and a thin, pale little human male hurried out. His neat, featureless blue uniform and studiously bland expression fairly screamed *bureaucrat*. He stopped dead at the sight of the armed guards, eyes widening, and Neral signaled to the Romulans: Back. They moved smoothly back to his side, weapons once again within their holsters, and the bureaucrat took a wary step forward, hands held out in a peaceful gesture—see, no weapons—and gave Neral a careful almost-smile.

"Our apologies, Praetor Neral, our sincerest apologies for having kept you waiting."

Neral said nothing.

The bureaucrat continued after that awkward half second of silence, "I'm sure that you, as a leader, will understand the reason, though, when I tell you that we had a sudden and totally unexpected diplomatic crisis on our hands, one that needed instant presidential resolution."

"I understand that you are about to have another crisis," Neral retorted coldly. "I will see President Min Zife, and I will see him now."

"Of course, Praetor Neral, of course. He is waiting for you even now. Please, follow me."

Had there actually been a crisis, as this idiot was claiming, or was this all just another one of the Federation's cursed delaying tactics? It was hardly likely that they would be so foolish as to try playing *him* for a fool—and yet, knowing their devious minds, such a concept was not completely impossible, either.

But either way, one did not waste time or lose honor by arguing with an underling.

More to the point, though, had the delay actually been due not to some diplomatic snag but to one of their agents picking up the message that *his* agent had just sent him from the *Alliance*? It was highly unlikely that they would have received any official word; Captain Saavik would hardly be advertising the results of a mission that had been borderline legal at best. But if she had somehow found out about the Tal Shiar agent aboard her ship—

Bah. Only fools worried about what might be. He was starting to let the false placidity of the place get to him.

Without a word, Neral, flanked by his guards, stalked after the underling, down a smooth beige and tan corridor hung with more of those neatly framed planetary images, to a pair of large, old-fashioned doors made out of what Neral suspected wasn't the seemingly realistic and elegantly carved natural wood—or Pacifican equivalent of wood—it seemed to be, but was actually a more durable and weapons-resistant imitation.

Two fully-armed Starfleet guards stood at full attention

on either side of the doors, the first jarring sight amid all the pretty tranquility. The guards eyed their Romulan counterparts uneasily, but at a nod from the bureaucrat, one of them turned to knock three times on a door.

"Enter," called a studiously cheerful voice, and the guards threw open the doors, then stood aside, still at full attention, to let Neral and his party enter.

There were times, Neral thought, when a human idiom was quite fitting. For there before him was none other than the Federation's blue-skinned "stuffed shirt" himself.

President Min Zife was seated behind a smooth tan desk at the far end of a large room with pale blue walls and tan and blue curtains, his hands neatly folded. The curtains behind him had been drawn back to reveal a sweep of white sands and rippling turquoise ocean. A pretty scene, this, Neral thought sourly, with the President's blue Bolian hue nearly blending in with his surroundings.

The President's chief of staff stood at his side. Neral recognized him at a glance: a burly, broad-shouldered Zakdorn named Koll Azernal, a brilliant strategist—but, Neral thought dourly, a proverbial thorn in his side by this point.

"Praetor Neral." Zife's smile meant absolutely nothing. "Please, do sit. Make yourself comfortable."

Neral toyed momentarily with a cold *I prefer to stand*. But that would be just too close to the stereotypical Federation image of a Romulan. Instead, he sat, but with the equally cold and utterly in control air of a leader taking the command chair of a warbird.

No use wasting time with the platitudes that the Federation bureaucrats favored. "You know why I am here," he said.

The President leaned forward slightly. "Perhaps you had better tell us so that there is no confusion."

That smug smile, those shallow eyes . . . what a small-minded, empty creature this was, Neral thought dourly, like most citizens of the pathetic Federation. And this was what he needed to convince. "President Zife, I should not need to remind you that it was the Federation that came to the Romulan Star Empire, not we to you, begging us to join your war."

"It was your war, too," Azernal commented.

Neral's glance flicked from Zife to Azernal, noting the cool expression and keen, cunning eyes. Ah yes, this one was almost certainly the real brain behind the meaningless blue smirk.

But even so, one did not ignore the higher-status being in an official communication. And so, although he would have liked to strike that smirk off the Bolian's face and get down to business with the Zakdorn instead, Neral's reply was all for President Zife.

"You all but begged the Romulan Star Empire to join you in battle. Yet now, after we have fought with you against a common foe, now, when we have been attacked without warning or provocation by an outside force, now, when our civilians have been murdered and our priceless relics have been stolen, you give us nothing in return but words."

"What do you expect from us?" the President asked. "Praetor Neral, we were all equally in peril during the Dominion War. We were all asked to make the same sacrifices. And surely you see the situation as it stands now: The privations and losses from the Dominion War have left us all, regardless of our planetary origins, in similar impoverished straits."

Without warning, a sharp flash of memory all but overwhelmed Neral. . . .

The Dominion War . . . and word drifting back to Ki Baratan from the battles far more slowly than anyone there would have wished . . .

The easy victories . . . the not-so-easy defeats . . .

Most terrible, the second battle of Chin'toka . . . three hundred twelve ships, Federation and Romulan together, advancing on the Dominion fleet, all those ships opening fire as one, keeping up one continuous massive volley . . . seeing the heavy damage to the Breen warships and the destruction of several of those ships . . . and feeling the dawning of hope in everyone, the thoughts of *this time we have them, this time we'll win*—

And then that sudden horrifying loss of all power, that massive energy-dampening field that left the allied ships floating powerless in space, deflector shields, cloaking devices, every means of defense or offense useless . . . leaving the ships easy targets for easy destruction . . . ship after ship exploding . . . crews slain as they waited helplessly, unable to fight back . . . no chance for any of the Romulan warriors to so much as take Final Honor . . .

With a great effort, Neral forced his mind back to the present.

"Indeed?" he said with great restraint. "Odd that I don't see that situation you describe at all. What I see instead is a United Federation of Planets, many of whose worlds suffered few or even no privations from the war at all. A United Federation of Planets that claims to defend and protect the rights of civilians, all civilians, regardless of shape, culture, or species. A United Federation of Planets that claims to stand for interplanetary justice—"

"Well, of course we—"

"—but a United Federation of Planets that now shows no interest at all in doing so much as helping the Romulan Star Empire to recover the priceless artifact that was stolen from us by those genocidal thieves."

Azernal glanced from Zife to Neral. "The Watraii are claiming that the artifact belongs to them."

"The Watraii lie!"

"Praetor Neral, I know that of course it seems that way to you, and I quite understand that it would. But as a representative of an unaffiliated third party, I—we—must ask if you have any proof of that."

"Other than my word?" Neral said very carefully.

"Ah," the President said.

"Believe me," Azernal continued, "we do not discredit your word. We would never dream to offer you such an insult."

"But . . . ?" Neral prodded.

"But surely you can see our problem. Without actual, physical proof, Praetor Neral, we cannot know which story is truth and which deception."

Neral stiffened in outrage. "If I had the artifact, do you think I would come here at all? Or—akhh, is that it? Do you dare to call me a *liar?*"

Zife flinched at the savage outburst, and Azernal said hastily, "Of course not! Please don't misunderstand us, we don't mean to insult you or doubt your honor! But we need to look at the clear, unbiased facts. You do not actually possess this artifact right now, do you?"

Damn you to Erebus, you small-souled bureaucrat! "Do you think I would have left the homeworlds and come here if we did?"

"Then, forgive me, but no matter how much we want to take your side, particularly since, as you remind us, the Romulan Star Empire did, indeed, fight with us in the Dominion War, I'm afraid that it does still remain a case of your word against that of the Watraii."

"This is outrageous!"

131

"I agree, I agree. I don't blame you for being angry. And believe me, the Federation would, as I say, much prefer to side with their ally."

"Ally." The word was knife-edged.

"It isn't as though we have simply turned a blind eye to the needs of the Romulans. I must beg to remind the Praetor that we did, indeed, send out a mission to aid you."

"A mission!" Neral echoed in contempt. "What you sent out to, as you claim, aid us was a farce! There was nothing but a token fleet of ships, and what's more, they were ships given no guidance, ships with captains who had no idea of where they were to go, no idea of how to find either the Watraii or the artifact. Ships, in short, that were in absolutely no danger of involving the Federation in any . . . inconvenience. All that nonsense had to have been deliberate! You cannot possibly expect me to believe that your people are that incompetent!"

"Your pardon, Praetor Neral," Azernal returned smoothly, "but can you in all honesty blame only the Federation for that confusion? Did the information—the misinformation, rather—as to the proper coordinates not come directly from Romulus itself?"

That brought Neral up short. Was that the truth? Charvanek had never mentioned any deliberate misinformation having been sent. Had it truly come from Romulan Security?

Charvanek, Neral thought grimly, *what games have you been playing? You have ever been Romulus's staunchest supporter, and I thought I surely could trust you above all.*

Or was it your doing after all? Could the traitor possibly have been Koval or one of his people? Has the Tal Shiar, perhaps, been up to its own little games?

The Praetor revealed nothing of his sudden disquiet.

But Neral knew he must not linger here for long. He must return as swiftly as possible to set things to rights on the homeworlds.

But he could hardly up and run like some child afraid that things were going wrong at home.

The debate continued on for some time. But Neral grew increasingly frustrated by his inability to convince the Federation President or that damned, too-clever Azernal to see things his way. He was also well aware by now of that ticking clock that warned that every moment spent away from Romulus meant another moment for would-be rivals to plot behind his back.

Can I trust Charvanek? Can I trust Koval? One or the other of them is being false to me, but which one is it?

Finally Neral gave up any hope of making progress with these Federation idiots, and got brusquely to his feet.

"It will be supremely ironic," the Praetor pointed out, ice dripping from every word, "that the very mission that was intended to solidify a Romulan-Federation alliance after the Dominion War turns out to be the thing that shattered it."

He turned and left the room with every bit of chill and outraged dignity he could muster.

Boarding the *Conquerer* once more, Neral curtly acknowledged the salutes of his officers and crew. From their wary expressions, he knew they understood exactly the waste of time he had just endured. No more. Almost before he had settled himself back in the command chair on the bridge, he ordered, "Set coordinates for Vulcan," and grimly (and with a great deal of private satisfaction) watched Pacifica fall away in the viewscreen.

To Erebus with that fool of a President Min Zife, that sly-

Josepha Sherman & Susan Shwartz

faced chief of staff, and that entire idiotic, infuriating, less-than-*werik*-slime entourage. The late Senator Vreenak had been right after all: Any alliances with the Federation were worse than useless; they were downright dishonorable!

We must get to Vulcan before Saavik and the Alliance *do, and then cut her off before she can land. Yes, and then we must find a way to convince her to give me the artifact—*

And if she refuses, then, if we must, we shall use force.

FOURTEEN

MEMORY

"I have heard the whispers I have been meant to hear: accusations that I squander resources on Solor's proposed exploration, not to attempt to meet the needs of the many, but to indulge the whims of the one—because he is my son. Untrue. Solor's surveys and flight tests have brought us new knowledge. Interest in his journey has broadened our focus from surviving to living once more. It is that focus upon life, not the routine of quotas and endurance, shift after shift, that will preserve us as a free people.

"I consider the effort worthwhile. It is an irony that I must also consider worthwhile the genetic manipulations of T'Olryn. On a more personal note, I note that her young son has begun to call me grandsire."

SOLOR'S STORY

Solor watched his father take his place in the gallery above the launch bay. For the occasion, his mother, T'Vysse, had ventured away from the archives she had been trying to create. Sarissa stood beside her. Serevan did not. He was making final adjustments to the prototype's engines.

Solor failed to suppress a second glance up at the gallery. T'Olryn was nowhere in sight. It was illogical to be disappointed.

Always parted, never touching and touched, he thought. *No longer.*

He took several deep breaths to regain his focus on his work.

This would be the final stage. This time, they would travel out as far as they had done the last time. Then, the ship's pilot would touch down by the shielded beacon that indicated the last supply cache they had dropped. Solor would leave the ship. Dragging a sledge of food and air behind him, he would attempt to struggle to the twilight region between fire and ice, then return.

His equipment consisted only of essentials—plus the ring of his broken bond and the blade N'Keth had willed him for keeping faith.

He had not yet activated the envirosuit's heater. Despite its insulation, he was cold in the launch bay. He nodded his head, an exaggerated movement to make sure that the pilot could see him, and started toward the craft.

"Let me join you," came a voice from the entrance.

Solor turned so fast he almost overbalanced.

What was Refas doing here? Solor had made no secret of his hostility to the man.

"You'd better clear the area," Solor said. "Once the gates open overhead, not even you could withstand the cold and the air, if you can call it that. . . ."

"There is room for another," said Refas. He wore what resembled the sand suits of Solor's youth and appeared perfectly comfortable in a level of cold that had frosted the bulkheads of the launch bay, making the metal of ship and controls dangerous to touch. "I require less food, less air than you. Let me make the trip. Or let me join you."

Solor stared into the face of . . . the father of his wife's child for the first time since T'Olryn had left him. Refas had become very thin, his temples sunken like those of a much older man, his eyes huge and lustrous. What hair he retained had receded until he was almost bald, and he was pale, paler even than Vulcans who never saw the sun.

That was a secret goal of Solor's: for the first time since landing, he would see sunlight.

Temptation burned behind his eyes. Refas wished to accompany him? By all means.

Two of them could go out upon the ice.

One of them would return.

Did Solor wish to revive Vulcan customs?

They could begin with the *Kal-if-fee.*

For that matter, why not begin now? Solor was armed. Refas was armed. These days, everyone carried knives. He even carried a te-Vikram honor blade with which to avenge his . . . not his marriage, but the breaking of it, and his heart, too.

Can you be certain that you would be the one to survive? he asked himself.

Did it truly matter?

Overhead, in the gallery, Karatek and the council watched. Even Solor's mother, T'Vysse, had come out. She stood beside Sarissa, bearing witness.

No, this was no time and place for a challenge.

If you consented, Solor thought. *Once we got to the ice . . .*

Refas shook his head. He chuckled, and Solor remembered just how strong a telepath his exposure to the extremo-philes—and to T'Olryn—had made him.

"You are in error. There is no challenge," Refas told Solor. "You have no need, because there is no bond. I am the biological parent of T'Olryn's son. You have refused to be a father to him. Shall I do the same? I have skills I can teach a child to let him thrive on this world."

"No one can thrive as a slave," Solor said.

Especially no son of T'Olryn's.

Refas's eerie dark eyes bored into Solor until a new temptation, to darken the visor of his helm, ate at him.

It would probably do no good.

At last, Solor said, "Rovalat taught me well."

"And me. Let me come with you. Together, we have a better chance of survival."

"Together, we have nothing!" Solor cried.

Overhead, he could see his father turning to speak to someone. Sarissa? No. He saw Refas look up into the gallery, too, saw the strange eyes fill with light.

So, it was T'Olryn with whom Karatek spoke. He had not expected her to come.

"Is she seeing *you* off?" Solor snarled.

"You are a fool. I wonder that I offer to accompany you, except that *she* wishes you to return safely."

Refas's appeal seemed to hover in the air between the two of them, an odd sense of kinship.

Solor turned toward the ship. If Refas refused to leave before the launch bay opened, on his own head be it.

Do what you will, you have lost this battle.

He had to perceive the logic of the situation.

T'Olryn's son had merely been the first of many children who would be born, their genes modified. He would require a mate, and he would find one, or several, among the daughters of the Vulcans who had been sent here, a second generation of prisoners and slaves who did what they must in order to survive.

Ultimately, Solor realized, generations from now, even those children whose genomes had not been modified would seek mates among the hybrids, who would be stronger both physically and telepathically. The race would continue, however altered, with T'Olryn as its mother.

Solor shook his head. He wanted no part of the emotions Refas was projecting at him: understanding, gratitude to T'Olryn, love for her.

Solor supposed he could hardly blame the man. The severance of his marriage bond ached like a phantom limb.

"Get out of here," he said. "If I do not return, marry T'Olryn yourself. If she is to be the mother of a new nation, her children should not be bastards as well as half bloods."

Solor clambered into the ship. Better than his word, he allowed Refas time to leave the launch bay before beginning the ignition sequence.

FIFTEEN

SOLOR'S STORY

As Solor neared Remus's twilight land, the wind picked up. It lashed about him, whipping the nitrogen pools and enveloping him with their spray. His sight was blocked! He raised his hands to his helm, breathing deeply—consuming more air!—to suppress panic.

Working by touch alone, he pushed the sledge into a crack in the ridge he had followed these last kilometers from the final supply cache and tethered himself to a spur of black rock that jutted clear of a tumble of blue-green ice. He turned up his suit temperature to compensate for the time he had wasted standing still, then smeared his gauntlet across the sealed visor of his helm, partially wiping it clean until the spume built up once more.

The wind picked up once again. It tore away the clouds of frozen vapor that limited his sight until, for one astonishing moment, when Solor looked up, he could see the stars. For many years he had not been able to take the time simply to look up at them and admire them as they deserved. Perhaps, one day, he would do so again as a free man.

Ice crackled underfoot, revealing dark rock. This close

to the twilight region, it was warmer by far. Perhaps Refas, wearing only a breather, could have endured this level of cold. Solor could not. That was why T'Olryn's young child was not his, he recalled with an anguish that pierced worse than the cold.

He shook his head in a pain he did not bother to suppress. Since T'Olryn left him, his control had raveled steadily. She had chosen Refas to father her son. But this journey belonged to him, not Refas. In this, at least, Solor would not be outdone.

His trek across the ice and rock had been even more difficult than anyone could have predicted. There had been the time he had approached one supply cache, and the ice had cracked. All that precious air, food, water, and even the survival bubble had simply plunged into a narrow crevasse too deep to attempt to plumb.

Another cache had been partially buried by a rockslide. Solor had squandered reserve air in digging it out because he knew he could not survive another sleep period out in the open; the survival bubble he carried on his sledge had to be reserved for the time he actually spent in the twilight.

He had become used to walking on ground that perpetually trembled. He had learned to thrust his sledge ahead of him to see if it tilted, breaking through thin or rotten ice. He had learned how to gauge the wind and lash himself at times when he sensed, as creatures of a world learn, that periods of the greatest turbulence would come.

Now, Solor leaned back against the rock and stared up at the stars.

Beautiful. But something was strange about them.

After a while, he identified the strangeness. The sky looked paler than he had seen it since they had landed. Much paler. He thought back to the nights he had spent sleeping on Vulcan's Forge when he had seen the stars that glinted above his birth world change in precisely this way just before dawn.

Perhaps, when he passed this ridge, or the next, or even the next beyond it, if he could cross the plain that scans told him lay ahead, he would actually be the first Vulcan to set foot in the tortured land between the fire and the ice.

He turned his mouth to his water tube and drank avidly, but forced himself to stop before he drank his fill. He must conserve his supply for the journey back. After all, what if another cache fell through the ice?

Once again, the wind erupted about him. It plucked at his tether, tugged at his sledge, and piled chunks of ice about him. If he remained here much longer, he would be buried. He had to seek what cover was available.

Solor backed into a crack in the rock and waited for this latest gust to subside. He shut his eyes. After a moment, he slept.

Instinct woke Solor. For once, it was blessedly silent. No rain of methane or nitrogen fell. Even the constant after-shocks appeared to have subsided.

Just for this moment.

Instinct told him that the final push was upon him.

He released his tethers and started forward, trudging up one ridge, then another, and a third.

For the first time in years, he realized he was being guided by natural light. Perhaps, if the area between ice and fire were narrow enough, he might see the sun at its horizon, might even gaze out onto a land so hot that it made Vulcan's Womb of Fire resemble the ice from which he had come.

At the final ridge, he leaned against an outcropping

that shadowed him and reared up three times his height. It blocked his view of the sky, but let him look down into the twilight. Here, the land was cracked and crevassed as the world twisted and shuddered in the perpetual struggle between fire and ice.

Could they build here? He must take careful readings and bring them back for the engineers to gloat over—assuming any Vulcan would admit to so ignoble an emotion.

Science would benefit, and that was all well and good. More to Solor's own point, his purpose was accomplished. Even if he failed to return, telemetry would record his accomplishment—for no other reason than it was Vulcan nature to seek, to strive, and not to yield.

Yet, even this success of Vulcan will and endurance was insufficient. Solor gazed down at his suit sensors. He had been right. Surface temperature was higher here. He had become so hardy on this world that this degree of cold was almost habitable. And ambient radiation levels were far lower than beneath the ice.

In that moment, Solor forgave Refas. He forgave T'Olryn. He forgave everything but the world he thought he would be able to see when he ventured onto the shadow plain.

He thought he could make it if he left the sledge behind. Lashing it to a stake he pounded deep within the ice, he packed up his tools, shouldered a reserve supply of air, and started down, keeping one shoulder against the rock ridge that protected him from the gales as it guided him toward the plain.

The wind subsided just as he came to the end of the ridge.

Don't count on it, he cautioned himself. He had seen weather on the ice change in a heartbeat. Logically, this region would be even more volatile.

Still tethered, Solor set one foot, then the next out into the twilight lands. As he emerged from behind the last bulk of rock, for the first time in years, he saw daylight. He gazed past the glowing orb of the oppressors' world, with its four low shimmering moons, past the shadow lands and onto the blazing anvil of the planet that always turned to face the sun. Then he flung up his hands and recoiled from the light.

The veils flashed down over his eyes and his helm darkened, but not in time to protect him from his first full-on glimpse of this system's star. Screaming in pain, Solor flung himself backward and toppled onto ground that trembled as it received him.

How his eyes burned! He could have fallen into a pool of liquid nitrogen and welcomed the cold the instant before it killed him if only his eyes would stop burning.

What a fool he had been. He would not have stood upon the peak of Mount Seleya and stared into Vulcan's sun. Why had he thought to stare full-on into sunlight here? Had he thought at all, or had he simply been so desperate for an achievement, any accomplishment at all to call his own?

He raised his gauntleted fists. He wanted to rub his eyes, but of course, he could not reach them through his helm. Lights leapt behind his eyelids, novae of pain from outraged optic nerves. Would they ever cease? Even blindness would be welcome now, even if he died in the next moment.

Telemetry was recording this, too, he reminded himself when he could think in the seconds between flashes of agony. And T'Olryn would see it.

There is no pain. He would *make* himself believe that. He forced his breathing to steadiness and waited until his mind believed his mantra.

The blazing hallucinations that exposure to the sun called

up subsided somewhat, and he forced himself back to his feet, retracing his way, by touch more than by sight.

One last, illogical thing he did before returning to the blessed shelter of the ridge: he shook his fist at the oppressors' star, the oppressors' world.

And then he started to fight for his life.

How prudent he had been to leave tethers and guideposts along his way. As he groped from one to another, he could hear himself panting with exertion now, as well as pain. He could hear himself whimper and was deeply ashamed of his loss of control. Nausea threatened, and he controlled that, breath by ragged breath, step by step, until he reached the sledge and sank down in its shadow.

Solor brushed away the rime that encrusted the sledge. It would not have taken long for it to be buried past his ability to dig it out, especially now. Working with desperate haste, a little mad from the pain in his eyes, he unpacked supplies. He forced himself to be methodical, although he longed simply to toss things here and there on the ice until he found what he sought. He did not. Instead, he identified his reserve survival bubble by touch, pulled it out, tugged the opening tab, and, as it inflated, scrambled within and let himself go limp.

The bubble's built-in air supply hissed, and gauges showed the buildup of an acceptable environment. Breathing heavily, Solor unhelmed. Freedom, finally, from the weight of that helmet on his shoulders, freedom to press his hands against his eyes brought pleasure beyond—or almost beyond—anything he had ever felt. Even with his wife.

In this welcome darkness, the veils over his eyes withdrew. Tears ran down his face. Finally, he could see, dimly, it was true, but accurately enough to find his medical supplies.

Yes, there were drops that would numb and soothe his eyes. Working by touch, he fumbled them out of the kit and applied them.

Panting, Solor sank down and waited for the pain to ease. When the burning subsided and he no longer felt tempted to claw at his face, he drank, but only a few sips for fear of setting off the nausea he had felt earlier.

The water stayed down. Safe enough, then. Solor sedated himself and sank into restless dreams of tiny glittering lights that coiled into helixes, then uncoiled and writhed across his tiny shelter, washing over him, seeping into his supplies, even into the tiny vial of drops.

Their brilliant colors—crimsons and blues, the purples of Vulcan's horizon, and the green of heart's blood—seemed to pool around him, welcoming and reassuring him, sending him deeper into sleep.

When Solor awoke, considerably to his surprise, he was refreshed. He was even able to see after a fashion. But he did not delude himself: his condition was serious. It was time to do triage. He had to abandon the sledge because he no longer had the strength to pull it. He barcly had the strength to move himself. His motions pained, laborious, like those of a much older and much sicker man, he dragged himself back to his last supply cache and hoped that the communications gear he had buried beneath it had survived.

He shut his eyes with relief as he heard the familiar, high-pitched sounds, felt the vibrations of well-maintained equipment. He triggered the distress signal and settled into what safety this cache's survival bubble, air supply, medications, food, and water might provide. He slept, and the dreams returned.

Vulcans were not meant to live in the twilight land. They

could no longer look upon the sun, and that was a failure they would have to live with.

But Solor's journey was far from a failure. Even if he had not found his people a new home on the surface, assuming he survived to make it back to the habitat, he could be the living reminder that there was more to life than survival. There was accomplishment.

One man can touch the future, he reminded himself. *I can. I have.*

It was time to summon the discipline of healing trance. Never mind the fact that T'Olryn had taught him how to refine his skill. That was false pride. It was logical and necessary for him to consume less air. He might even be healed by the time the ship came for him.

And if it did not come?

Improbable. If the ship could fly at all, it would come for him, to bring him back. Back home.

I can *touch the future,* he whispered before the trance engulfed him. *I* can.

The ground trembled as Solor struggled to wake. The air supply in the survival bubble was growing foul; it did not give him what he needed to fight the trance as he must. Panting for breath, he collapsed, then collected himself and began to fight again. Almost before the ship had steadied itself on a pallet of rapidly reforming ice, its pilot leapt out, ran over to the survival bubble, and clawed it free of the ice slick that covered it.

"Life signs," he reported. "Very faint. He's almost out of air. Be ready."

Unplugging his auxiliary tank, he attached it to the bubble and dragged it back toward the ship.

"Hatch is sealed. Prepare for takeoff," the pilot spoke into his wrist com. "On my mark. Now!"

Solor gasped and struggled once again as something slashed open the survival bubble that had all but been a death trap. He had to fight the healing trance, but he was weak, so weak.

He knew he was not alone. He had to wake, had to rise, had to tell them what he had discovered in the shadow lands.

"One man can touch the future. One man . . ."

"What's he saying?" demanded the pilot. "There isn't room for him to thrash about with four of us on board! He'll hit something."

"He needs help leaving the healing trance."

"Then help him or put him back under!"

Solor heard a murmur of controlled annoyance. Then, a hand slapped his face, again, and again.

"Central command is asking if he's fit to talk to them. What do I tell them?"

"Tell them we're trying to rise above gale winds and will contact them when we're through!"

"One man can touch the future," Solor muttered.

If they would only let him get up, he could explain what he had seen, what he still saw, what they could all be together. He could even help fly the ship.

He reached up to catch the hand that was guiding him back to the waking world. His fingers in their thick glove fumbled, but there was no mistaking the touch of that hand. That beloved, ringless hand.

It slipped from his grasp to brush his temples as if soothing old wounds.

"Parted," he muttered.

"Never parted," came T'Olryn's voice, as familiar and beloved as the touch of her fingers. "Never. Now, rest. Whatever you have to tell us can wait."

He opened his mouth to protest. She laid her fingers over it.

"Rest," she said. "They will hear you. I will make them understand."

SIXTEEN

U.S.S. ALLIANCE

2377

As the *U.S.S. Alliance* and its two Klingon escorts neared the Eridani system, the ten Romulan warbirds hung menacingly still in space, looking almost like ten predators hovering over their prey, staying just at the outer "edge" of the Eridani system, just out of legal Vulcan space. The warbirds were plainly aligned in a formation that could be easily changed to block any evasive moves that the *Alliance* and the two Klingon ships might make.

"Captain Saavik!" Captain JuB-Chal's voice sounded as suddenly and fiercely as a war horn. *"We could easily remove some or maybe all of those Romulan scum for you."*

Out of the corner of an eye, Spock saw Ruanek tense at the insult, then force himself to relax again.

"That will not be necessary," Saavik replied quickly.

"Captain Saavik!" Captain Tor'Ka added. *"The Vulcans are our friends and allies! We have never fought with them, and we don't want them harmed by those treacherous creatures."*

You merely wish an excuse, any excuse, to fight an old enemy, Spock thought but diplomatically refrained from saying.

"You will take no action," Saavik returned, in Klingon fashion demanding, not asking.

There was an awkward moment of silence, and then Tor'Ka all but growled, *"If you were not one of the heroes of the war and a gallant, proven leader, we would, I tell you, express ourselves more enthusiastically."*

Saavik raised an eyebrow. "Thank you for that vote of confidence, gentlemen. Lieutenant Suhur, kindly open hailing frequencies to Commander Tomalak's flagship."

"Hailing frequencies open, Captain."

"This is Captain Saavik of the *U.S.S. Alliance.*"

The figure of a tall, broad-shouldered, unctuously smiling Romulan formed on the viewscreen. *"Captain Saavik. You are in a perilous position."*

"I am on the verge of Vulcan space. That is hardly a perilous place for a law-abiding Starfleet vessel and two lawful allies."

Tomalak's smile was smooth and all but gloating. *"Ah, but are you truly law-abiding? I am very well aware that you have been acting without official orders, Captain Saavik. I also know what you carry aboard your ship."*

"Do you?"

"And as you see, we stand between you and those peaceful Vulcans. We have no wish to disturb them."

Saavik's voice still revealed nothing but Vulcan calmness. "Do you think they are not already disturbed by your presence?"

"There is a simple solution to this problem, Captain Saavik. Give us what you carry."

"Would you think to rob us?"

His smile hardened ever so slightly. *"Why, have you not already robbed another race?"*

"What is this? Have the Romulans now forgotten all honor? Have they turned pirate?"

Saavik, Spock thought, was doing an excellent job of the only recourse other than fight or flight: She was stalling the enemy. But for how long would Tomalak allow himself to be blocked?

Spock quickly moved to Lieutenant Suhur's communications station, and the younger Vulcan, only a glint of alarm showing in his eyes, stood aside. Of course Vulcan would be well aware of what was happening at its borders, and of course Vulcan Defense would already have been mobilized. It would take only one mistake on either side for Vulcan ships to be launched.

Spock keyed in secret codes, some known to him through the Vulcan Science Academy, others known to him through more devious means. And he sent a heavily encrypted message to Vulcan Defense and to the government itself:

Wait. Do not take action. It is Spock son of Sarek who sends this.

He added a private house signature to prove that it was, indeed, he.

The answer came with a swiftness that proved that Vulcan Defense was, indeed, at the ready.

We will wait.

Excellent.

Now Spock keyed in a new series of codes. If Admiral Uhura of Starfleet Intelligence had known that he knew these codes, she would, no doubt, have been surprised—but, being Uhura and knowing Spock as well as she did, she would not have stayed surprised for long. Spock quickly bypassed security screen after security screen, hunting with Vulcan speed and skill for what must, within an acceptably high percentage of probability be so . . .

Ah, yes. And what he found was amazingly ironic as well as precisely what was needed to solve this impasse.

But now, to see this through, Spock knew he must contact a man whom he found it difficult to trust. That was Admiral William Ross, the human who had proven himself to be allied with Sector 31, which was the closest that Starfleet came to its own ruthless version of the Tal Shiar, during the Dominion War. Ross might listen to Spock, but he might also well decide that the best action here would be no action: Let the *Alliance* and the troublesome artifact be destroyed by the Romulans, and then let Starfleet side against the Romulans once and for all.

But it was illogical to even try to predict what another sentient being might do, or to let something as utterly useless as worry enter his mind. Spock keyed in more codes, and sent his message. There was no immediate answer, but he expected none. The message would, of course, first be carefully scrutinized and analyzed, and presumably compared against what Starfleet Intelligence was also receiving from Vulcan and its own agents.

It would be as it would be. But a quick calculation of warp speed and distance told Spock that even were there a minimal delay on Ross's part, a certain amount of stalling would still be necessary.

Spock glanced at Saavik, whose face was still Vulcan-calm. But Tomalak was hardly going to be as patient. How long before his temper overcame him? Tomalak had a reputation as one who did not start a conflict, but Spock could not rely on that reputation to hold true today. The true danger was that Tomalak would open fire, destroying what he could not easily take.

Then Spock's glance stopped at Ruanek. Ruanek was standing absolutely motionless, his face so expressionless that he must surely be silently reciting every Vulcan discipline his Vulcan wife, T'Selis, had taught him to keep himself calm. Over the years of their friendship, Spock had come to know that Ruanek was not the sort to bear foolish grudges: If he disliked Tomalak so strongly, there was a good reason for that buried in the past.

"Ruanek," Spock asked softly, "would Tomalak remember you?"

The sideways glance that Ruanek shot him was as sharp as that of the warrior he'd once been. "Oh, without a doubt he would. Just as surely as I remember him."

"Excellent."

"I don't know if I want to know what you're planning, Spock."

"I believe that you will."

Quickly, Spock told both Ruanek and Saavik what must be done, and saw the coldness in Ruanek's eyes brighten to what was almost humor. Saavik, in true Vulcan fashion, expressed approval with the slightest nod and without the slightest change of expression.

"Can you manage this?" Spock asked Ruanek.

"Manage to make a fool of Tomalak?" Ruanek gave Spock his Vulcan-Romulan mix of an almost-smile. "Yes, Spock, I assure you that such a thing will be quite . . . acceptable."

With that, he moved forward to face the viewscreen directly, his posture that of a warrior more than a scholar, letting himself be seen clearly. "Tomalak. Do you recognize me?" He said it in Romulan.

Tomalak sat back, staring in blatant disbelief, then leaned forward again with a cold laugh. *"Why, I do, indeed!"* he said in the same language. *"I always wondered what happened to you after you fled the homeworlds. It is the cowardly little traitor himself!"*

"Never a traitor, Tomalak. I did what I had to do out of honor."

"Yet you are aboard a Starfleet ship."

"I am, indeed, and still without being a traitor to the homeworlds. For this ship has a truly honorable captain. A more honorable being than you will ever be able to imitate."

"You waste my time, Ruanek."

"Ah, he remembers my name!"

Tomalak frowned. *"Enough of this nonsense. What do you want of me?"*

Ruanek gave him a full Romulan grin, perhaps the first time he'd shown such a grin in over ten years. "Do you recognize me as a Romulan?"

"A traitor, yes, but of course you are a Romulan!"

"You call me both a traitor and a Romulan," Ruanek retorted almost cheerfully. "And that entitles me legally to the Right of Statement!"

"But—you can't—"

"Oh yes, I can. Take a look at the Romulan laws you claim that I broke. And, by the way, Tomalak, because you had this all on an open broadcast, your bridge crew—and maybe your entire fleet—has, of course, also heard me claim the Right of Statement, so you can't just try blowing us up to stop me."

"You can't hope to stall forever!"

"Oh, hardly. Just long enough."

"Long enough for your Federation friends to come to the rescue? That will never happen!"

"I'll take that wager, Tomalak. And win it.

"And now," Ruanek began with what was by this point undeniable glee, "I believe that I will begin my Right of Statement with the concept of honor, as seen both by the many worlds of the Federation and by the Romulan Star Empire from the earliest days. . . ."

SEVENTEEN

MEMORY

"*The twilight band between the ice and the zone of fire offers no refuge for us. To that extent, Solor's expedition proved to be a costly failure for which I had to answer, as did he.*

"*In a greater sense, however, I consider it a triumph. My son has, in essence, reinvented the* kahs-wan *and showed us that endurance itself can be a triumph. This may not be logical, but it is true, and it will allow us to derive some dignity from what we are forced to do.*

"*I would say this even if Solor were not my son, but I have already observed that my opinion is shared.*

"*Even though we know now that our time here has altered us physically, the years after Solor's return have seen positive changes. We are once again a people. True, we continue to work hard. But it has been not as much to satisfy our 'masters,' although we have met our quotas, but for our own reasons.*

"*Our network of tunnels grows. We have carved out a second launch bay. In it, a second ship nears completion. Solor has welcomed the new prisoners sent us. They follow him, giving me hope that we can integrate them fully into our*

157

community. It pleases me to see what a good leader he has become. It pleases me even more to see my son and his wife begin to glance at each other when each thinks the other does not see. Perhaps one day, they will speak, even reconcile. Regardless of the work T'Olryn does with our genome and the child she raises, I do not consider my hope to be wholly illog—"

A siren erupted through the habitat, echoing off the cold stone.

That particular shriek meant only one thing: someone had sealed the launch bay.

What fool would risk everything they had built for so long in such secrecy to make an unauthorized flight?

In haste to get to the command center, Karatek overbalanced and went sprawling. He hissed through his teeth at that sign of increasing weakness with which he had no time to concern himself and no patience to tolerate. As he fell, he ripped off the coronet. Why did the blood that trickled down his face not burn like ice? He knew, just as surely as if he had watched it on monitors, what had happened.

Solor had left.

And Karatek knew where he had gone.

Wadding frayed silks about the coronet, thrusting it back into its box, Karatek dashed out of his meditation chamber toward the launch bay.

His wife, T'Vysse, stood by the emergency exit, her eyes wide with shock. She held out both hands to Karatek. They were bloodied as if she had pounded uselessly on the access hatch, crying out to the boy she had raised since Karatek brought him out of the desert, long after the grown man had taken off in their laboriously built ship. When Karatek touched her fingers in greeting, T'Vysse struggled visibly not to collapse against his shoulder. She had grown so much weaker these past few years.

On her hand shone the sullen light of a bloodstone ring. It had been hers to wear before she passed it to T'Olryn. When T'Olryn had returned it to their son, Solor had worn it for reasons Karatek still could not understand. How had it returned to Karatek's wife?

"I found it in his quarters," she whispered.

That his wife, his refined, courteous T'Vysse, would intrude into her son's privacy . . . She rarely judged, but when she did, she had never been wrong.

"Why have you done this?" Karatek turned from her stricken face to the crowd that had gathered. His attempts at control made his voice a harsh whisper.

His eyes fell on the last group of prisoners. They looked away from him, then at each other.

And this is how you repay us? It was beneath him to ask that question. Let them ponder it, however. Let them ponder it for the rest of their lives.

The prisoners could have been left out on the ice to die, but instead, they had been rescued. Solor had reached out to them, and what did they do? They aided him in madness!

"Solor taught us that one man can summon the future," said Vejat. He had been one of the political prisoners abandoned here with the last shipment of supplies when he would not yield his lands to the ambitious daughter of a senator. "Now, he has gone to explain that to S'task. To ask again for a share of the green world, even the smallest and most desolate of its continents. To convince our captors to treat us as the brothers and sisters we were during the journey from Vulcan."

"Did he go alone?" Karatek demanded.

T'Vysse stepped closer, resting her face against his shoulder. How gray her long, sleek coils of hair had become. When had that happened?

"Your son took three of Vejat's friends with him," said T'Olryn. Her voice was pure ice.

The healer had come up behind Karatek so softly that he actually trembled from the shock. He began to apologize for his loss of control, but stopped when he turned to look at her. Her face betrayed no emotion, but she was disheveled, as if she had been picked up and carried against her will. As she stood before Karatek, she kept rubbing her hands and wrists. The nails on those skilled healer's hands were broken, and her delicate wrists were circled with livid green and blue bruises.

"I tried to sound the alarm," T'Olryn said. Her face twisted before, magnificently, her control reasserted itself. "When no one else would touch me, Solor bound my hands. He did apologize before they locked me up," she said in response to T'Vysse's exclamation. "Still, there is much that even he never learned about a healer's resources. I picked the lock."

Karatek opened his mouth—to do what? Apologize to his daughter-in-law? Beg her forgiveness?

She held up one of those injured hands. Beneath her composure, Karatek saw devastation.

"Apologies are futile," she said. Her face went completely expressionless again. Turning away from Karatek, she glanced up at the flight monitor. She did not even glance at T'Vysse's bleeding hands.

Solor's ship had already transited the dark side. It had left the ice and was heading straight toward those who had betrayed and enslaved them.

As Karatek stood amid the ruins of his family, voices erupted about him, blaming, second-guessing, fearing, even seeking to plan.

"Can you get through? Let his parents talk to him, try to call him back."

"We're being jammed! I can only get line-of-sight. Surely, he's reached the sunside by now."

If that was true, ships would soon rise from the green and golden world that had rejected them. Armed ships.

How long did Solor and those with him have to live?

There was no way Karatek could reach Solor now and undo the damage.

No way he could know why.

"I thought . . ." T'Olryn began, then turned toward the emergency access hatch.

T'Vysse stepped out of the circle of Karatek's arm and went over to her, to seek to comfort her. T'Olryn turned away, wrapping her arms about herself, as if she, who had spent so much time in the icy tunnels with Refas, was now cold, here in the warmest part of their habitat.

"I had had such hopes!" she whispered, and her voice actually broke.

"My daughter, if you could assist me . . ."

T'Vysse held out her hands for T'Olryn to see, letting the younger woman regain her control by tending an accessible injury.

Was there any hope that Solor could actually get through? Karatek thought. The odds—no, when it was a matter of his last son, his mathematics were uncertain. The people whom Solor planned to confront would never speak to him, never trust him because of the irreparable harm they had done in exiling other Vulcans to the ice. At one level, they might hate

161

and fear those they had made their slaves; at another, they hated and feared themselves far more.

If you cannot forgive yourself for what you have done, how, then, can you forgive your victim? Surak's *Third Analects.*

Solor would die to assuage their guilt. And it still would not be enough. The Vulcans on Romulus would punish them. This ice, this gray stone and metal that they sought to make habitable, might be the best they could hope for.

Sarissa ran in. Her face was terrible. From the first moment Karatek had ever seen her, she had been Solor's protector. Now she was as helpless as if her hands, as T'Olryn's had been, were tied past her ability to free them.

Her eyes blazed, restoring Karatek to his wits. He might be old, but that was no reason for surrender.

"We're not out of options," he interrupted the litany of what they could not do. "I want bay two opened. Prepare the ship for takeoff. I'll suit up."

"But it's untested!" T'Vysse screamed a protest.

Involuntarily, Karatek's eyes went to the sensors embedded in the wall, checking for zenite levels. Blue and green: nominal.

But his wife's loss of control was not the result of zenite contamination. She had lost too many children already. Compared with that, what were Surak's disciplines?

They were just another excuse for bad faith.

The sons and daughters who had died had been Karatek's children, too.

"I can do this," he told her. He went over to her to touch his fingers to hers. Then, despite the people crowding around them, he reached out to clasp the hand that T'Olryn had finished bandaging and press it up against his side so she could feel his heartbeat.

"That's what Varekat thought when he blew up his lab at the Vulcan Space Institute," T'Vysse reminded him. "Remember? When you came back to ShiKahr, you saw how the crater was still glowing. Most of us who were going to live had gotten over radiation sickness by then. But Varekat and his staff were ashes on the wind. Less than ashes."

I know that engine, Karatek wanted to plead. *I built it. It's just like the one in Solor's ship, but it's stronger and faster. If I leave now, I can catch him!*

A shudder of emotion went through him.

Why do you hold me back? he wanted to scream at T'Vysse. In all the long, long years of their marriage, he had never spoken to her with anything but the most tender courtesy.

"T'Kehr, we're getting a signal from a ship moving onto a landing vector. Cargo shuttle 80A. The engine flutter is unmistakable."

"Landing, not attack?" Karatek demanded. "You're quite sure?"

The woman who spoke to him was one of the most accomplished techs who had survived their first exile. She didn't even lift an eyebrow.

"The ship has crossed the terminator. Expected landing: thirty point nine minutes . . . correction, sir. The ship has leveled off. Its commander is demanding to speak with you." Disapproval chilled her voice to approximately the temperature of the nearest nitrogen pool.

"What's weapons status?" Sarissa demanded.

"Locked on us," the tech said.

"Father, if you even try to take that ship up, they'll fire. Remember. They've seen the prototype. They'll say we attacked, and they won't be taking any risks."

Her hands fastened about Karatek's arm, T'Vysse gazed at their daughter in sheer relief.

"Your logic is impeccable," he admitted. "I suppose I must listen to this message."

"Will you take it in private, sir?"

Karatek looked down. "What would be the use?"

The ship's commander appeared on a viewscreen. He was small for a Vulcan and unusually squat, his short hair curling tightly over a furrowed brow. *"Is Karatek there?"*

His voice was coarse, as if he had been granted no more education, no more cultivation, than he needed to do his job and assure his betters that it had been done.

"Speaking." No need to bother with petty courtesies. Karatek did not recognize this one, although his name, Paradaik, appeared on a badge he wore.

"Your people fought well even after we disabled their ship. That is quite a pretty piece of engineering. Fine workmanship. We see now we haven't pushed you hard enough, but all that is going to change. In token thereof, Karatek, you have ten point eight minutes to suit up and await us on the landing field."

Someone would have had to conclude that Karatek had designed the ship's engines. It might even have been S'task.

Solor's people had fought. Which of them had died first? Were *any* alive?

"You're not going alone!" cried T'Vysse. For the first time in all the years they had known each other, her voice belled like the hunting call of a hungry *shavokh*. Green lights from controls flashed across her face in a way that would have been ominous, if omens were not illogical.

Were they? Karatek had seen a sundweller the morning of the day he had met Surak.

Never mind that they had no privacy. Karatek put out a

hand and touched her face, fingers slipping to the meld point on her left temple. Their bonding was of such an age and depth that either's death might kill the other. Here, or on that other world of which they had been cheated: Karatek supposed it made no difference where they died.

Like his boys. Like all his daughters except Sarissa.

Like his ship.

They had destroyed *Shavokh*, too, scrapped it to build on the world that should have belonged to all of them, prisoners and captors alike. When so many people had died, how illogical it was to care for what were no more, really, than machines.

Machines that kept them alive all the long years of exile. Machines that brought his son and his friends to their death.

"You must come unarmed," said Commander Paradaik. *"If we detect even a utility knife, we will burn you."*

"And I would die warm," said Karatek. "There is no question that you could blast us all. You could do it now. What stops you?"

"Your fear is illogical," the ship commander said, rebuking a man at least one hundred years older than he. *"No one means your death. You are useful where you are, and we will return you. This is not a death sentence, but an invitation. Listen."*

The screen blanked. Instead of Paradaik's self-satisfied, sharp grin, Karatek saw a face almost as pale as a miner's. It was so heavily lined that the clever eyes were almost hidden beneath heavy brows and hair the color of the ice.

Night and day! S'task looked so old. Old and sick. And desperately sad.

S'task turned slightly. His motion was unfortunate, because he moved away from a window he had been blocking and let in slanting beams of light intense enough to make Karatek flinch from them, even in transmission.

"We have your son."

"Solor? He's safe?"

"Not safe, I regret to say, but in my keeping. I have prevailed upon T'Rehu"—his voice twisted, and people behind him murmured—*"to allow you to come here and take him home. Back to the ice, that is."*

S'task at least must have no delusions that a forced labor camp tunneled beneath ice and radioactive minerals could be called "home" in anything but the most bitter irony.

Karatek fell silent. The minutes passed.

At any time now, that impatient, arrogant shuttle commander was going to break in upon his thoughts. And it was vastly to be hoped he would not order his ship to fire. Karatek would give the man the count of three.

Three . . . two . . . one.

"Karatek?"

"What do you require?" he demanded.

"I was told that refusal was not an option. My duty is to bring you to S'task. For what it's worth, he calls you guest-friend. But do not press that bond too hard."

S'task was old enough that that bond was still sacred.

So where had he been when others of his people were betrayed?

No point in reproaches. S'task had Solor in his care and had summoned Karatek to retrieve him. He would go, and T'Vysse would go with him. All else was unknown.

"We will meet you at the appointed place," Karatek said.

S'task recoiled and signed off.

Even Paradaik winced at his sarcasm.

EIGHTEEN

MEMORY

"My coronet is in the *elassa*-wood box in my meditation chamber, wrapped in silk. You'll want to check the wires every year or so," Karatek said. "They've never needed repair, but . . . ask Serevan to look at them, if you prefer. Above all, take care of it. It holds my memories since the day I received it from Surak, the day we left Vulcan."

Sarissa knelt, testing the fastening of her mother's boots. T'Vysse wore envirosuits so seldom that Karatek had absolutely refused to risk her going to the surface without safety checks.

"Why are you telling me this?" Sarissa demanded. She unfastened T'Vysse's right gauntlet and secured it correctly over her bandaged hand.

"Rhetorical question, daughter. I hadn't wanted to burden you before, but you must be my heir in this, as in all . . ."

You are all I have left!

"I can do without this honor!" Sarissa's voice was low but heartfelt, as if she had heard Karatek's anguished thought.

She had stood with them before the adepts at Seleya when Surak had received the coronet from the high priestess. She had to remember.

"I told you before that the coronet was a burden," Karatek reminded her. "Others will covet it for its gems, its beauty. You must protect it for the knowledge it contains."

He set his helmet on his head, gave it the little twist that locked it into place, then double-secured it.

"Do you promise?" He regretted that what might be the last words his daughter would hear from him came out filtered, through the suit's communications units.

T'Vysse set a gauntleted hand on Sarissa's shoulder, pressing it. Her gentle touch compelled agreement where Karatek's words failed.

Sarissa inclined her head, obscuring her eyes, then led them to the airlock.

Control, Karatek whispered to himself. His suit's life support system was nominal. Nevertheless, he shuddered, not from cold, but from excitement and mortal dread.

He and T'Vysse stepped out of the access tunnel and onto the ice as if walking away from their lives. Their hands, in the articulated gauntlets of the envirosuits, met and clasped as they had on the grounds of *Koon-ut-kal-if-fee.* Then, as now, there was little need for words.

Now Karatek spoke the only word that needed saying. "Ready," he told the ship.

They remained hand in hand during the ship's descent. As it touched down in clouds of steam and ice melt, they separated, determined to show no emotion at all.

The ramp extended slowly. Guards marched out, weapons glowing the blood-green of full charges. Were so many guards truly needed to intimidate two elders?

Absurd.

This was no attempt at intimidation of Karatek and

T'Vysse, however. This was a simple, brutal show of force.

Karatek turned toward T'Vysse, inclining his head in a courteous half bow, before offering her his hand and formal escort up the ramp, which could have been, he saw, more skillfully maintained. He guided her over a broken plate in its surface.

The guards fell in behind them.

Once inside the ship, their suits' visors darkened in what was, to them, the painfully bright light of the ship's interior.

Instantly, the lights dimmed, a surprising courtesy.

"Take off your suits," came the order from Commander Paradaik, whose coarse face appeared on a small viewscreen built into the nearest bulkhead. He watched as his crew rifled through Karatek's and T'Vysse's packs. They contained little but the light hooded cloaks they would use on the other world, if they lived long enough to see it once more.

Not bothering to explain, Karatek held T'Vysse's cloak for her, then put on his own. They raised the hoods to cover their faces in case lights rose unexpectedly.

"Sit there, on those pull-down seats. Strap down. Do not move. Keep quiet." Paradaik instructed.

They complied. They had no need of movement because their fingers touched. They had no need of words, because they had said everything they needed. Parted and never parted. Never and always touching and touched.

The questions they wanted to ask were not those Paradaik would answer. *What had become of Solor? When would they see him?*

As if fearing obligation, none of the guards greeted them or offered fire, food, and water. Instead, they set down ration packs within reach. If Karatek or T'Vysse cared to take them up, well and good; if not, that was also no concern of theirs.

Courtesy had fallen a long, long way among the military since the days when Karatek's old friend Ivek commanded a detachment of guards outside the gates of ShiKahr.

But neither he nor T'Vysse deigned to accept the water that came without a welcome or assurances that it was not drugged or poisoned.

The ship emerged from the shadow of the ice and set course toward Romulus. Karatek caught a brief glimpse of the firefalls he had once observed from the surface.

The ship crossed the planet's terminator. They would be landing on the night side. Well enough; he would have enough to do maintaining composure without having to endure the sun.

The stars were fire enough. They were very beautiful. He tried to discern the distant sun that warmed lost Vulcan, but failed.

After the ship landed, Commander Paradaik returned.

"Up," he said.

Karatek inclined his head, then bent to assist T'Vysse.

The guards stepped closer, surrounding them and marching them to the landing ramp, then down it into the open air. Karatek heard T'Vysse, standing beside him, take in a deep breath, then another, as if gasping at the sensations of warmth, of comfort.

Of vertigo. They were no longer used to standing unprotected under an open sky.

For a moment, the stars reeled overhead. Karatek staggered as if he had slipped on black ice.

"My husband?" T'Vysse whispered, her hand going out to him.

The guards moved in, as if suspecting him of a feint. Karatek made himself regain control. He offered T'Vysse not just his paired fingers, but his arm, whether to give or gain support he refused to decide.

No ground transport waited. Instead, they were marched past a guard point, identified as prisoners, bound for S'task's house. Approval was given, grudgingly, as it seemed to Karatek.

Their own guards muttered, but took care not to do so loudly. Karatek glanced at his consort. One did not need to exercise emotions to be able to detect them in others. He sensed apprehension here, with anger simmering beneath fear.

"That way."

Now their guards led them toward a double line of torches. The veils of their eyes flicked down. As they became used to the natural light, the veils receded, letting them see a house much like the one that should have been built to receive them.

Who lived in that house now? Who harvested crops from what should have been' the land promised to Karatek and his family? There had been a view he had liked, of a stream, leading to a small waterfall: he had hoped to build a meditation chamber with a window facing it.

No matter, he told himself. Still, regret pierced him like the blade he had been forbidden to carry, a pinprick to distract him from the real pain.

Solor. My son, my son.

T'Vysse paused as they neared the house. Again, the guards loomed up around them.

Walk or be carried, was the obvious, unspoken threat.

After a moment, she shrugged and moved on, stepping onto a roadway that creaked with each step. Karatek raised an eyebrow at her. Even now during what might be their last moments alive, her historian's interest had been piqued by the revival of the old technique for detecting thieves.

The house had been built in the most ancient Vulcan style. It was walled, with a bridge leading to its main gate. On Vulcan, the walls would have been built of basalt. These walls were made of a translucent, white stone. On Vulcan, the ditch would have contained shards of obsidian and pointed stakes and could have been filled, at need, with combustibles. Here, the ditch was filled with water. About what might lie beneath the surface, glittering with reflected starlight and the occasional splash of some living creature, Karatek did not wish to speculate.

The entrance they approached was easily twice the height of a tall man. The gates were heavily reinforced and barred with metal that looked as if it had been torn from the hull of one of the great ships, perhaps even *Shavokh*. The gates opened as they approached—not just the small door used for casual comings and goings, as if such things could ever be casual in a house so well defended, but the main gates.

In the center of them stood the man who had been the author of their exile, who had stood by as his fellow travelers had been doomed to the ice: S'task.

Karatek peered out at S'task from beneath his hood. He squinted in the light of the torches thrust into holders on either side of the gate.

Why, he was even older than Karatek remembered!

Karatek remembered S'task as a zealot. During the fight to leave Vulcan, he had carried himself like a fire arrow, all passion and speed and brilliance. What faced them now was a narrow-shouldered, fragile man who moved cautiously, as if he expected his bones to break. His ship had suffered reactor leaks more than once, Karatek remembered. S'task's own response to radiation sickness had left him vulnerable to the epidemic that had wiped out his family and so much of his ship's complement that others had found it easy to wrest control from him.

"Be welcome," he said, and held out a hand that trembled slightly to T'Vysse.

"T'Kehr," began one of the guards. Both Karatek and S'task turned.

"These are my guests," he said in a ringing voice that belied the lung damage he had sustained. "If you do not hear me claim them as guest-friends, you cannot be blamed. Now, off with you. No doubt, you will know if I have need of protection."

His eyes flashed like the firebrand Karatek remembered.

He threw up his head proudly, exposing the stubborn jaw. And the vulnerable throat.

But the guards brought up their weapons in salute and marched smartly back across the creaking bridge.

S'task stood there for a moment longer, as if posing for a sculptor. Then, he seemed to sink in on himself.

"I had power enough to bid the council's guards bring you here. But I did not know whether I would be able to command them to leave us. Every day becomes a trifle more difficult. But come in, come in," he urged Karatek and T'Vysse.

He led them past the inner gate, a tunneled affair revealing the thickness of the protective wall, through an anteroom, and into a courtyard.

T'Vysse stopped short. Once again, S'task had reproduced ancient Vulcan in the design of his inner court, where, traditionally, the family met, and ate, preferably in the presence of running water. A stream ran into a pool whose natural rim was ornamented with fine stone carvings. An immense gray rock, whose craters and shadings and outcroppings lured the eye into one corner, while another stone ring, this one heaped with cushions, encircled a table from the center of which smoke rose.

It was Vulcan, yet not Vulcan. For one thing, the skies were alight with four moons plus the deadly bulk of Remus, the prison world. For another, the courtyard smelled not of the desert, but of growing things, herbs and ornamental trees. The air was thick and warm, almost too warm, with moisture.

S'task hobbled over to a low table. From a stone pitcher, he poured water into translucent cups and offered it to them.

"I name thee guest-friend," he said.

Karatek stared at S'task's shaking hand. Water was spilling from the cups he held. If S'task thought they were going to drop to their knees and thank him for their welcome, he could send them back to the ice right now!

T'Vysse threw back her hood. Gliding forward, she took one of the cups, drained it, and handed it back before giving the second cup to Karatek. Fresh water, not forced from icy rock, laden with minerals, and endlessly recycled: it was so pure it made his heart ache.

Oh my wife, far better than I, and so much more kind!

Spared the indignity of accepting friendship from the man who had betrayed him, Karatek drank. He had indeed been thirsty.

"Where is our son?" asked T'Vysse.

"I will take you to him," said S'task. "But first, I must prepare you. As I told Grand Councillor T'Rehu, I give no honor to brute force such as she wields. I must warn you, however, that there are many on this world, especially on this continent, who disagree. Since I walked out of council, there is much I do not hear and much, too, of which I am not told. It appears we remain in need of lessons in the art of casting out fear."

He coughed, almost doubling over. T'Vysse poured water quickly and handed him a cup, steadying his hand. He drained it, then thanked her with a bow as classic in its way as the motions she had regained the instant she stood again in a proper courtyard.

"I was standing in this courtyard when your son's ship appeared in the night sky. Instantly, I gathered a few of the sons and daughters of my old companions in exile and headed for the council chambers. By the time I arrived, they were washing blood off the stones. According to T'Rehu, in returning to this world after being exiled from it, your son's three companions had committed a capital offense. They have been executed. I grieve with thee."

"And their bodies?" Karatek's voice was as cold as the ice he ruled.

"Burned," S'task said.

What a people, carrying out their punishment past the body's death.

"What of our boy?" T'Vysse whispered. "How did my Solor die?"

S'task shook his head. "Long after he was surrounded by guards, your son fought. He fought until they brought him down.

"No," S'task assured T'Vysse, whose gasp made Karatek hurry to her side and ease her onto the waiting cushions. He knelt and chafed her limp hands. "He was captured unwounded."

Then S'task flinched from the expression of relief that made her young again. "Do not hope," he said in that beautiful mild voice that had changed three planets' fates. "Your son was interrogated. I could not stop it. He had defenses unlike any T'Rehu and her tame scientists had ever seen."

"He was . . . is . . . married to a healer," T'Vysse said. "She was a Seleyan priestess."

S'task bowed brief reverence. "That would explain his resistance. Even after mind-change failed and they strapped him to the mind-ripper, he told them that the only way to force access to his brain was by autopsy."

"My Solor," Karatek made himself remark. "Discretion was never his strong point."

"But he was very, very brave," S'task said. He bent over T'Vysse, who had sunk her head into her time-worn hands. "I suspect T'Rehu was gravely tempted to do just that. In fact, I know so. A guard made the mistake of laughing. It was the last mistake he made before his immediate execution. The young man had been impressed, you see, by Solor's courage. That and what influence I still have helped me carry my point. And bring your son to my home."

From within a fold of his overrobe, S'task produced a dagger, a wide triangle of gems, metal, and gilded leather sheath, that he handed, gemmed hilt first, to Karatek.

"Te-Vikram work, is it not?" he asked. "When they were finally unable to revive him, the guards appropriated it. I insisted they give it back."

Oh my son, my son! But N'Keth, who had given Solor his blade, would have understood.

He pointed. "He is in the chamber across the courtyard. I imagine, by now, the physicians are through with him. We have no healers on this world any longer: just engineers that tinker with body and mind, and follow our politicians in denying the existence of anything else."

T'Vysse rose from the cushions. "Take us to him!" she demanded.

"A moment more," S'task said. "You will find him much changed. But you would have been proud of him. When I took charge of him, I thought he was long beyond response, but he tried to rise, to greet me." He met Karatek's eyes. "It was clear who had the raising of him. I had him made as comfortable as I could. Once the engineers stopped prodding and poking at him, I sent them away, and he opened his mind to me. What was left of it."

T'Vysse gasped softly.

"He had asked the council for compassionate leave. Compassion, on a world that has abandoned that virtue as old-fashioned! He asked for us to treat you as brothers and sisters on a world where brothers and sisters daily fight each other to the death. He tried to wage peace, and when that failed, he fought like a warrior."

"That would explain the armed guards," Karatek said quietly.

"Yes. T'Rehu's people believe you have been turning yourself into a race of warriors up there." S'task sighed. "You will not, I fear, escape the consequences of that fear. Or of their shock at what you have become during your imprisonment. Some of them actually fear contagion."

Over the years, Karatek had grown used to their pallor, their thinness, their improved night sight. To their oppressors, however, Solor and his companions must have looked as alien as Refas's children did to Solor.

"At least," T'Vysse said, "my son's tormentors did not stay on Vulcan to abet wars on the Mother World. The means were flawed, and we reap the consequences."

S'task inclined his head. For a moment, they sat in silence, remembering.

Then, S'task led the way to the small, clean room in which Solor lay.

Their son's face and body were unmarked, but it was clear that he was dying, the link between body and mind mortally torn. Pale beyond the pallor of the ice caves, he lay on a traditional pallet beneath thin sleeping silks. He breathed so shallowly that Karatek paused in alarm, wondering if, truly, he breathed at all.

"Call the guards," said Karatek. "We will take him home."

Sounding shocked, S'task said, "Karatek, that is not a home, it's a prison camp!"

"It's ours. We bled for it. Every last tunnel."

"Every last ship, too, apparently. How many more of those craft have you built?" demanded the old man.

"Only the prototype."

No doubt his captors would seize it, dismantle it, and retro-engineer it. Karatek sighed. What had been the use of building ships if it had cost so many lives?

T'Vysse was leaning over Solor's bed, cradling his head in her long hands.

"My son," she whispered.

His eyes fluttered open. "Mother? Father? The raiders came. I thought . . . they killed Sivanon, but Sarissa is safe. You told me, 'Protect your sister' . . ."

Karatek shut his eyes in pure anguish, then took his son's hand. "This is Karatek, son. Remember, I brought you to Shi-Kahr and adopted you?"

Beneath the silks, Solor's body relaxed almost imperceptibly. He sighed with pure satisfaction and was almost able to return the pressure of Karatek's fingers.

"You've come to take me home?"

"Yes," T'Vysse assured him.

Solor's eyes went to the blade Karatek carried. He wrapped his son's fingers around the hilt, holding them there until he could make them grip it firmly.

"You are welcome to stay here," said S'task in a low, urgent voice. "You are my guest-friends. I may be a hostage in my own home, but you will be safe here with me. Solor can lie in the ground he fought to win. And I—I would be glad of the company."

"I will not trade one prison for another, less honest one," Karatek said. He saw a stretcher lying beside the bed and went over to it.

"No need to trouble the medics," he told S'task. "We will transfer him to the stretcher ourselves. Please, call the guards. There is not much time."

T'Vysse knew his mind. He wanted no more enemies touching his son.

Working as tenderly as if they bathed a feverish infant, Karatek and T'Vysse eased Solor from the bed onto the stretcher. They bent to pick it up.

"In thy honor and in thy service," S'task said as he reached for a handhold that might have overbalanced them all.

Karatek shook his head. "Thee could not carry him two steps before thy lungs gave out," he said in the beautiful Old High Vulcan of ceremony. "But I thank thee."

Could he and T'Vysse manage to bear their son back to the ship? The idea of collapsing, perhaps dropping Solor, killing him before what time he had left ran out, of guards having to take up the burden—all of the available options revolted him. His eyes met those of his consort, and she nodded reassurance.

Their time on the ice had left them very strong. Illogical as it seemed, this close to death, Solor seemed much lighter.

"You could ask to come with us," T'Vysse whispered to S'task.

He shook his head. "My fate is here. And soon will be upon me."

Then, to Karatek's surprise, S'task knelt before T'Vysse. The fragility of his bones must have made each movement agony, but he did not hesitate or falter as he bent his head to her. She touched his temple in forgiveness just as, before the exile, she had blessed Surak.

The old rebel had just made his life harder with the awareness that more than enemies lived on Romulus. Nevertheless, Karatek forgave S'task with all his heart.

After all, it was the only logical thing to do.

NINETEEN

SOLOR'S STORY

Starlight and the night wind flowed over Solor's face like a stream of pure water encountered in a wasteland. The last time he had been outside unsuited had been the hope-filled days when he had helped survey this world, before he and his family had been betrayed.

"Solor, hold on," came a soft voice. "We will get you home. Do you understand? Your family is waiting for you."

His family? His family was gone. Before the raid that had destroyed his home, when he and his agemates had stolen time from their studies and the chores of any desert-born child to act out "Gates of ShiKahr," he had spent his free time outdoors. He had been so happy to be alive then, even if his elders went armed and his sister, who was almost an adult, watched him the way a *shavokh* watches its first hatchling.

He heard whispers now, like adults worrying about a child. He recognized those voices. How could he have forgotten? He had won a second family, he and his sister Tu'Pari. No, that was not right. Tu'Pari called herself Sarissa now, and he was Solor, not a hero out of legend.

Just for a little while longer.

But it was "Gates of ShiKahr" all over again. At the end of the First Dynasty, Prince Ravanok had been betrayed. Then, his people rose against their enemies. They fought until the sand by the broken gates was green with blood. But they had come too late: in the end, all they could do was carry their dying prince into the city he had fought to win and set him in honor in its central square until his life and *katra* fled.

The boys had always taken turns playing the war leader and the prince. It had always been more exciting to play the war leader, Ravanok's brother-in-arms. You got to go on living. You led the dirge, and then you rebuilt gates and city until they were renowned across all Vulcan.

But the times you played the prince were the times you remembered, the times that made you shiver the way you did when the night wind brushed your face. If the boys drafted as bearers were strong enough and sufficiently sensible and did not snicker at the solemn parts of the story, you could lie on the crude stretcher they built to represent Ravanok's litter without having to worry that they would drop you and laugh about that, too.

If you were Ravanok, you got to hold the shard of obsidian that served as an improvised ceremonial sword. And you listened as they sang over you the dirge that had been the last song Ravanok's house bard ever made. If it made you shiver, that was the moment you knew you had brought the song to life again so strongly that even the youngest children who, like it or not, generally got pressed into service as torchbearers realized they were part of something special. Something eternally Vulcan.

Usually, about that time, they were caught and hauled inside. The last exception had come on that terrible day when the alarm screamed out and the settlement was overrun, almost at the same time. His sister had run out to find him. Sivanon, her betrothed, had followed, pushed them behind him, and died making sure they could run away. He had died like Prince Ravanok.

He had done better than Solor.

In sudden anguish of spirit, Solor called out for mother, father, sister. Gentle voices at his head and feet reassured him. Around him were torchbearers, and the wind flowed across his face.

But this time, it was not a game.

"Not long till we reach the ship, son," came T'Vysse's voice. "Hold on," it begged. "T'Olryn will be there. We will try . . ."

He turned his head on the pallet. The silks were softer than anything that had been his bed for years. They were almost as soft as T'Olryn's hair.

The old man pacing beside him reached down. Tentatively, he touched Solor's hand, which lay above the te-Vikram blade.

"You're getting tired," S'task called to Karatek and T'Vysse. "Why not let some of the others . . ."

Standing between him and the earnest, grieving faces marched a double file of guards. Some held torches, others *lirpa* or disruptors with full charges glowing a violent green.

"Bad enough you insist on coming out, S'task," said Karatek. "I will not expose your remaining people to more danger."

The air was so warm, so humid. It eased Solor's throat.

"Am I dead?" Solor whispered. He could not seem to shut his eyes. They were dazzled by starlight. *If this is the last thing I see . . .*

"Not dead," T'Vysse whispered. "Hold on. We're bringing you home."

He felt his feet rise higher than his head as his parents carried him up the ramp into the shuttle. They fastened straps to his stretcher, soothing away his weak protests at being bound again.

He felt the ship lift off. Not *his* ship; that one had been forced down. Not his friends; they were dead.

The guards stayed away from him, as if he carried some contagion.

Not death, Solor thought, but freedom. He would die free.

He did not even bother to look out at the firefalls as they gained altitude. They did not belong to him. They never had. Now, they never would. Still, he had tried.

His father, disdaining a safety harness, held Solor's hand as if he were a boy returning home after his *kahs-wan.* His ordeal had been a hard one, he recalled. Many had not returned. Old Rovalat, accompanied by one missing lad's *sehlat,* had plunged into the desert, hunting for survivors.

"Stay with us!" T'Vysse urged him. Her hands holding his head, fingertips pressing into his temples, trying to reach him, lend him her strength.

But Solor was so tired . . .

The guards' voices, muttering behind him, distracted him. He would listen. He would learn for as long as he had left. Just like his father.

"Just our luck," muttered one guard. "They've had the run of that place too long. Let the ice guard them, the Grand Council said. We'll give our orders and pick up our supplies. Easy. And now, who pays for their bad judgment? We do. The place is probably one trap after another."

"We've probably got better weapons than they."

"You saw that ship."

"So I did. Well, if T'Rehu's plans go right—"

"Quiet!"

"What difference does it make? He's dying and they're old. So, we stand guard until the next ship comes. Then, we rotate back home, and duty falls to the next unit of suffering bastards. Sooner or later, T'Rehu will set quotas so high that they'll have no choice but to turn some of their own people into guards. They can be hostages for one another. Clever, I call it. Logical."

My people. My poor, poor people. And I will not be there to help them, Solor mourned.

Not that his efforts had ever been that satisfactory.

He must have cried out, because his father was leaning over him again.

"Solor, my son. Never think you've failed. You gave us back our pride! Not much longer; we'll have you home soon."

Karatek was right. Not much longer. He could sense it, sense how his memories were beginning to swirl about a central spindle, like a glowing helix. . . .

"I'm sorry," came T'Vysse's voice. "We can't extend the ramp from the ship into the habitat. We'll have to put you in a survival bubble, son. It may hurt you to be jolted so we can get you inside. Please hold on."

He must have been drifting because his mother's face twisted.

"Please!" she repeated. In all these years, she had never needed to ask him for anything twice.

Solor felt his jaw set as they wrestled him into the bubble. It was too much, too many people tugging at him, pulling at him, as they had after he watched his last comrade die. Romar's neck had been broken by *tal-shaya.* N'Oblan and Awidat had been propped against a wall and used for target practice. They made Solor watch, hoping to frighten him so much that he would speak.

Finally, it had been Solor's turn. They had dragged him, snarling, biting, trying to lash out with hands or feet, to a cold black metal chair and strapped him in. Then, they had stood over him and applied blinking blue lights to his temples. They had asked questions. He had refused to answer. And he had felt his mind begin to tear until the old man, S'task himself, pushed past all the guards and commanded his release.

To think he'd believed S'task had all the power on Romulus, that he was their enemy.

How wrong Solor had been.

People were tugging at him again. Maybe that meant the questioning would start up again. He fought, twisting from side to side, trying not to listen to the cries, the questions his struggle provoked.

I breathed the way you showed me, T'Olryn. I set up the barriers, but it was hard, so hard. . . .

Voices woke Solor. He let his heavy eyelids fall open. The light was reddish, comforting. The air that brushed across his face, despite its warmth, smelled of rock and chemicals, not growing things. He could sense engines driving the flow of light and heat, not the wind and stars. He was back below-ground. Beneath the ice.

Home.

A familiar, beloved touch brushed Solor's mind, holding his thoughts.

He tried to fight free. This had to be a hallucination inflicted by his torturers. He longed to hear T'Olryn, he longed to escape, so they set before him the illusion of his estranged wife, his home. In a little while, the hallucinations would start to question him again in the hope that he would answer them as he had not answered those who had sentenced their own kind to the ice and killed his friends.

People were speaking behind him. He would listen to them. Perhaps he would learn how to escape, even now.

"The *veruul* have housed themselves in T'Zora's solarium." Sarissa's voice reported. "They said they didn't see why darkside scum needed that much light, seeing as we can't tolerate the daylight anymore."

Seravan, then: "T'Zora was so angry I thought she might walk out onto the ice. The cohort's leader was the one who killed her father. Not that he prospered from the murder, or he wouldn't be here. I suspect she'll live in hopes of finding him in the tunnels. What else has she got to live for now but vengeance?"

"Freedom!" Sarissa replied instantly. Though her voice was soft, it rang like a clash of blade upon blade.

"Freedom, indeed," said Seravan. "But they've raised our quotas, and now we have to maintain these . . . these slavemasters."

He almost spat out the words. Then, he sighed. "The ice may indeed be our best ally."

Not wise, Solor thought. *They'll kill ten of us for every one of them who dies.*

"I'm sorry, Father," Sarissa's voice came from behind Solor, someplace in the region where beeps and flashes of lights told him they had set medscanners on him. A waste of energy. "They've confiscated the second experimental ship and set up a guardpost in the launch bays. They want your research."

"Let them have it," Karatek whispered. "What choice do we have?"

"More options, perhaps, than they know," Sarissa replied. "From now on, they'll be using bigger ships to transport troops as well as cargo. I wonder how hard it would be to retrofit their engines."

"We'd have to reach a ship," said Karatek.

"Yes," Solor's sister almost purred. She would surrender only when she died and perhaps not even then.

"Later," whispered T'Vysse. "Solor went into convulsions when we had to get him into the bubble. We had to drug him."

"Will he wake up?" Sarissa demanded, uncertain for one of the few times in her life that Solor could remember. He wanted to rise, to reassure her, but what if she, too, were only a hallucination?

Soon it would no longer matter. Solor struggled for breath, felt a mask placed on his face.

"Breathe now. Long, deep breaths." Again, T'Olryn's voice. He would not have thought his enemies could create hallucinations this complete.

Something minty and astringent and cold had been infused into that air, restoring his senses.

"Is that a little better? Speak to him, Sarissa," T'Olryn said.

"Solor? Brother? I want you to know, it's all right." Even the night their parents were killed, their home destroyed, she had been strong. Now there were tears in her voice, and the hand he felt on his shoulder shook.

"You've done everything you can. I want you to know that. When you're ready . . ." Her voice broke.

Sarissa said he had done well? Solor had loved his parents, both sets of them, but his elder sister had always been the arbiter of what was right.

"No one could do more," she whispered. "T'Olryn, do you think he'll speak to us again?"

"The ethics of restraining a spirit that seeks to depart . . ." T'Olryn began.

"Ethics be damned!" Karatek snapped. "My son fought to stay alive this long. There is no logic in suffering for no purpose."

That was true. Solor had always suffered for a purpose he understood too well. He fought now to return to the waking world. He felt better now. It had hurt to be decanted from the bubble, like being born once more. When his *katra*'s wings grew strong enough, he would be born into a different sphere altogether.

But Sarissa had been wrong just this once. Solor did have just one more thing to do before he could rest.

Fingers brushed his temples. This time, he peered up into a grave and lovely face. It was T'Olryn, after all, not a hallucination. No hallucination would show her with tears on her cheeks. No hallucination would show her tired, aging, in despair. Illusions had been what estranged them, not this renewed oneness.

Parted and never parted. Never and always touching and touched.

"You came for me," he whispered. It felt strange to speak now. "Just as you did on the ice."

"Just so, husband."

He struggled to sit up. She lifted him against her shoulder. Once again he smelled it: cleanliness, incense, and flowers— T'Olryn's scent. Night and day, it had been so long.

And now night was on him, and it was too late.

"Time . . ."

Her arms tightened, sustaining him.

He felt her breath against his cheek. "Bring them," she told T'Vysse. "Quickly."

The door opened to admit their children. Grown. In no need of his care now. But they would want to say farewell to their father.

His *katra* beat against his waning consciousness. Soon, it would be time to seek the safety of a healthy mind. Which one should he choose? T'Olryn's nearness tempted him. She had suffered so much already, and she had years of work and life here, a life for which his mental "presence" would only hinder her.

He sighed, moving his head from side to side against her breast.

"Why is he fighting the journey?" asked T'Vysse.

"Where is the youngest?" he whispered, looking up into T'Olryn's eyes. *"Your* youngest."

Her eyes grew enormous, kindling with the expression she wore whenever anyone gave her an unexpected gift. She was not surprised, however. In all their years together and apart, Solor had never succeeded in surprising her all that much. She had always known him too well.

And so he was not surprised when Refas's child— T'Olryn's youngest—entered the medical ward in response to her gesture. He, too, had been waiting.

The boy was tall for his age, and very thin. His eyes were immense and almost bottomless in the pallor of his face, with its high, hairless brow and sunken temples.

Back on Vulcan, adaptive genetics had been regarded as scientific heresy, but Solor had followed this . . . project, this child's development even after he and T'Olryn separated, and he knew that extremophiles were mutating in the boy even now.

190

The child was still Vulcan, still recognizable. What his descendants would look like, think like . . .

Solor would have no time to find out.

He held out his hand to the child. They both watched it tremble. T'Olryn's arms tightened about his shoulders again, holding him in the world for the small time he had left.

"Come here, child," he whispered. "Will thee tell me thy name?"

The boy advanced gravely, silently.

"They call me Shadow," he said. His voice was deep for a child so young.

"The children—Shadow and the younger ones like him—do not like to disclose their names," T'Olryn explained. "Will you tell him your true name, my son?"

The boy leaned close to Solor. So young, yet already he had learned not to fear death. A brave child, a good boy. Solor had lost much in not knowing him better.

"I am called Rovalat," the child whispered. "That is because I am the eldest. I am guide for the others."

He was the prototype.

"I knew a Rovalat once," Solor said. "He was my teacher. Shall I tell you about him?"

It was getting hard to talk. Had Solor actually used words? *Yes, sir. Please.* The boy's lips did not move at all.

The child climbed deftly onto Solor's cot and took his hand in both of his. Their minds touched. A dazzle of helixes danced before Solor's eyes. Renewed well-being made him almost giddy. What strength the child had! He was a stronger telepath even now than T'Olryn, for all her years of study. What he would be in maturity . . .

Keeping those extraordinary dark eyes wide to prevent

tears or even a betraying flicker of veils, the boy leaned closer.

Solor opened his ravaged mind to the child who should have had his love and protection. He had denied him a name, a House, and an upbringing, but now at the end of all things, he gave him what he had to give: the memory of his *kahs-wan* on the Forge, Rovalat's training, and his sacrifice.

He showed young Rovalat the journey out from Vulcan and the betrayal which sent them to the ice and his own journey to the twilight.

I will never forget, the child assured him. *It will be a great epic of my people.*

Our people, Solor's mind whispered. *My son.*

He felt the boy's mind expand with joy, then felt anger, hatred of the murderer race.

"They are not all like that," he protested, and summoned to the forefront of his fading thoughts the image of S'task, of the faces of the other men and women who had wanted to help his parents bring him home, but feared to step forward.

Bloodshed had tainted the exile from Vulcan. Hatred and a desire for vengeance were no way to begin a new race.

The boy huddled against him, his pallid flesh strangely cool. The touch let Solor sense the child's love for the father he had wanted all his life to know.

True, Refas was his biological father. But his mother's longing for Solor had been too strong: Rovalat, too, reached out to him.

They were all clustered around him now, waiting to see who should receive his *katra.* Sarissa was closest, T'Olryn the best trained. But here was this son of an absent father. The child deserved some inheritance from Solor. And he had only two things to give. The te-Vikram dagger, which should go to his eldest, if it was not sent on with him. And his *katra*.

The decision was both just and logical.

Delight lit the boy's immense, eerie eyes.

That someone he had neglected, whose existence Solor had blamed for the ruin of his home, should be so glad of what little remained of him . . .

- The pain and the exhaustion seeped away. He looked up at T'Olryn. His wife shook her head minutely.

She had not been the one who had just touched his mind, easing the suffering of his passage. It had been Rovalat.

It is a great burden, he thought at the child.

It will be my honor—Father, the boy assured him.

Solor sighed. He could hear how his breaths had begun to rattle, halt, then start up, softer than before.

The others would understand. T'Olryn would make them. He heard his wife murmuring the invocation. His passing would be peaceful. That was more than he had expected to have.

His *katra* flew free.

Solor saw how Rovalat's eyes widened as he began to assimilate the years of his father's life, the passion of his memories, the pain of his final days, and, finally, this atonement.

It was done.

Solor lay staring into the huge wise eyes of what was, after all, really not alien to him.

After a while, the reddish light faded. The helixes lost their brightness.

It had been a long day. He was glad to rest.

TWENTY

IMPERIAL WARBIRD *CONQUEROR*

2377

The *Conqueror*, the Praetor's flagship, sped through space, flanked by its two escort ships, heading toward the Eridani system. All the while, Praetor Neral sat motionless in his command chair, refusing to show anything of the impatience surging through him. They had to reach *Alliance* before Saavik had a chance to turn over the artifact to the Vulcans.

But before they reached the Eridani system, while they were still in deep space, Kolora, the stern-faced woman at the tactical station, reported. "We are detecting other ships. They are of Romulan configuration, but are not broadcasting any identification signals."

Neral saw another warbird decloak, so suddenly that his crew had to take quick evasive action to avoid a collision. As they came about to confront the intruder, the Praetor's first thought was a purely indignant one: *Now, who in all the seven hells dares to interfere with the Praetor's business?*

"Open hailing frequencies," he said.

"Hailing frequencies open, my Praetor."

"This is Praetor Neral aboard the *Conqueror*. Identify yourself, and stand down."

Kolora suddenly said, "They're arming weapons! And four more ships are decloaking."

"What in Erebus are you doing out there?" Neral all but roared. "Identify yourself and stand down!"

"We are your nightmare come to life," said a cold voice.

On the *Conqueror*'s viewscreen formed the image of a faceless alien . . . no! It was a masked alien—

Watraii!

"Those ships have been taken over by Watraii!" Neral cried. "Shields up!"

In the next instant, the *Conqueror* shuddered under a direct hit.

"I said shields up!"

"My Praetor, the shields aren't holding! The Watraii are sending some unknown frequency that's jamming them."

A chill swept over Neral. The second battle of Chin'toka . . . the sudden horrifying loss of all power . . . deflector shields, cloaking devices, every means of defense or offense useless . . .

Damn them, no! "Identify the frequency!"

But after his frantic crew tried and tried to get a match, Neral heard a grim report: "Our computers can't identify the frequency of the Watraii weapons."

The Watraii had clearly had control of the warbirds long enough to alter and adapt them. Adept with all forms of energy, they had modified both the ships' cloaks and shields. One, then the other of Neral's escort ships erupted into fireballs, sending the *Conqueror* hurtling helplessly until the pilot finally brought them back under control.

The Watraii followed, still firing. "Fire at them!" Neral shouted.

Kolora obeyed his order, but in the next second, she reported, "No damage."

No damage? How could a direct hit have caused no damage?

But attack after attack on the Watraii proved the same thing: Romulan weapons had almost no effect.

This is impossible, this is impossible . . .

No. He would not allow himself to panic.

The closest aid . . . bah. Neral only briefly considered, then dismissed the idea of calling for help from the Federation. After that ridiculous encounter with President Zife and Koll Azernal, it would be the strongest dishonor to call to them for anything. At the same time, the Romulan ships surrounding Vulcan could not possibly come to his rescue in time.

A tremendous blow hit the *Conqueror,* nearly throwing Neral from the command chair. Fire erupted on the bridge. "Get those flames out," Neral said. "Damage report!"

The reports came flooding in, filling Neral with a renewed chill. So much damage done so quickly . . . and one by one, the choked voices doing the reports were dropping away, the crew, his crew, dying—

There was no avoiding the truth. His ship was now critically damaged, no longer spaceworthy. His escort was destroyed. There would be no escape.

So be it. He and his people would at least die with honor.

The crew knew what he had to do. They sat or stood in silence, watching him with eyes that said, *We do not blame you, we know we die with full honor.*

Grimly, Neral spoke the code words in the proper arrangement and ordered the Final Honor sequence activated, then waited with rigid dignity as the last second counted down—

But even as the ship suddenly burst into fiery shards around him, he felt a transporter beam catch him.

No! Damn them, no!

In that instant before he was pulled away into the unreality of transport, Neral knew that he, the leader of the Romulans, had just fallen into the hands of one of the enemy.

As their prisoner.

The blur of not-solid, not-real transport faded, and there was sudden solid footing under him once more. As soon as Neral's senses came back into sharp focus, he knew that he had materialized aboard a warship—no mistaking that general structure and lack of unessential ornamentation—but it was definitely not the warbird that the Watraii had captured.

Is this their flagship? Possibly. That's where I would have placed the Watraii leader had positions been reversed.

It was hardly an elegant bridge: wear showed around the edges of chairs and doorways, and the air was heavy with the smells of oil and what he assumed was Watraii sweat.

But this wasn't the time for analysis. Even as he found himself facing the row of grim, masked, featureless figures from out of a Romulan child's nightmares, his hand flew to his side for his Honor Blade. The Praetor of the Senate and the Romulan people should not remain alive in enemy hands.

But after that first moment of utter despair and desperation, Neral let his hand fall again, standing instead with a warrior's straight-backed pride, staring at his enemies with icy dignity.

I do not fear you, you masked cowards. And I will not give you the satisfaction of my suicide.

Oh yes, in the abstract, suicide rather than captivity would serve his honor. But Charvanek had been against this voyage,

Charvanek had been furious about his not listening to her, while it had been Koval who had assured him that it would be safe. It had been Koval, then, not Charvanek, who had betrayed him, deliberately or through incompetence brought on by his illness.

Either way, Neral thought grimly, he must live, at the very least to have his revenge. Koval must be removed—by the Praetor, deliberately and openly, before the disease could claim the traitor instead.

And too, a demonstration of how the Federation reacted in this situation would serve the Romulan Star Empire far better than his death.

If the Federation retrieved him, it would be proof that they not only valued the ongoing alliance with the Romulans, but that they were still willing to honor it, even in a first-contact situation.

If the Federation failed him, why then, the Empire would know that, too.

TWENTY-ONE

MEMORY

"Is there a worse fate than slavery?" Karatek spoke into his recorder. *"In his* Analects, *Surak writes that we blame no one so bitterly as those who made us act against the best dictates of our own hearts and minds."*

He paused. It had been, he thought, bad enough that the refugee Vulcans secure on a beautiful new homeworld had betrayed their companions. In turning them into slaves, they had turned themselves into slave masters. The consequences for their personalities and spirits were devastating. They had only worsened after Solor's rebellion. Now, guards were stationed throughout the labor camp beneath the ice.

"Our oppressors cannot reason away the impact of their actions," he added, *"because, to reason correctly, one must have self-knowledge, and that is the thing above all others that they cannot face.*

"We, too, have been transformed. Like te-Vikram on the Vulcan only some of us now remember, like people in the most ancient days, we go armed. Granted, our weapons are called tools, and the punishment for using them on our guards is severe enough that even the rashest of us is not tempted too

much. But if we cannot fight, we find honor in strength, in being prepared. That includes mental preparation."

Karatek broke off the flow of his narrative. The utility knives they wore had counterparts in many people's quarters, made, in their scarce spare time, of gems and the precious metals that were far from rare in their prison. Karatek's blade, however, was made of the most precious metal of all: scraps from the hull of one of the ships destroyed after they were banished here.

Thinking of his own blade helped him focus.

It was not true that honor lay only in preparedness. Since T'Rehu had slain S'task, leader of the exile, and become Ruling Queen, she had raised their quotas with every shipment. Therefore, it could hardly be considered surprising that the casualty rate among T'Rehu's guards here had spiked up. What was surprising, however, was that they had all died of natural causes.

Karatek had become used to explaining to newcomers how harsh the environment was on the ice and beneath it. He supposed that some casualties were inevitable, and had been since the first survey of this world when his own children had helped explore it. It was highly unlikely that T'Rehu sent anything but the dregs of her personal army and the sons and daughters of disgraced families to act as prison guards. So, it was a logical assumption that some among his children and grandchildren were not just mining, but killing, guard by guard, while mobilizing for a greater war that, like the exile itself, was intended to span generations. Because of the secrecy of the deaths, he suspected it was even more logical to assume that the people leading this silent violence could be the increasing number of children growing up with Refas's mutations.

He rose slowly. Although S'task's death, at the age of two hundred forty-eight, could hardly have been called unexpected, the manner of it—he had been struck down by a spear-dart in the Grand Council chambers—had shocked Karatek to his own heart.

He had overheard one guard telling another what the old rebel had said before he died. "The beginning is contaminated, and force will not avail you, or it." He had told that story to Sarissa in the hope that she would understand the lesson. But Sarissa had not seemed to listen. She had more important concerns than the judicial murder of an old, sickly, and almost forgotten man.

Karatek rubbed the small of his back. Old as he was, he ached when he sat too long. The ice itself seemed to invade his bones. If this kept up, he would become as frail as S'task had been before his death. But the ache down his spine was easier than the pain he felt when he looked across the table at meals every day.

T'Vysse was failing.

Karatek shut his eyes, remembering how, that night she had welcomed Surak, Skamandros, and Varen to their home, her dark hair had flowed down her slender, graceful back. Odd, wasn't it? Sometimes Karatek forgot the names of his great-grandchildren, but he remembered the names of Surak's two acolytes who had died on Vulcan. They had knelt at his wife's feet and accepted water from her hands. And then they had split Karatek's world asunder.

That long river of black hair she had never cut because it pleased him was brittle now, dull silver in color, and far too thin. As was T'Vysse herself. Karatek could not remember the last time he had seen her do more than pick at her food.

T'Olryn had examined her. When he dared ask about the

results, T'Vysse had looked away and down. T'Olryn had reminded him of her healer's oaths in a voice as chill as the ice. Sarissa had contrived to be elsewhere, taking out in action the sorrow that Karatek tried each day in his meditation chamber to master.

He thought he could guess what was killing his wife: small, slow cancers, scattered throughout her body, the result of radiation exposure; a weakness in her circulatory system that made her bruise easily and bleed too freely; overall exhaustion. Very little could be done. Medical care was triaged and rationed. Exemptions could be made in the case of people considered exceptionally valuable, but T'Vysse had refused all but palliative care. She preferred, she said, to abide by the system on which all had agreed: stronger medications must be saved for those who had a chance at longer life than she.

Someone else might have disappeared into the caverns or gone out onto the ice. But T'Vysse had always been stubborn. Her death was likely to take some time.

Karatek very much feared she remained alive because she knew how much he needed her. Well, he hoped he would not outlive her by long. He carried more years than S'task now, and in harsher conditions. Even though private quarters beneath the ice were better heated than *Shavokh* in those last desperate years before planetfall, the cold had long ago eaten into his bones. His capillaries had begun to break down, spilling livid bruises over his arms and body. Each day it was harder to rise, harder still to work.

He would try again tomorrow to meditate. Tonight he faced a harder task: coaxing T'Vysse into finishing her dinner.

Steam rose from the stone bowl of soup that T'Vysse raised to her lips. She sipped it, then set it aside in favor of tea. It didn't seem to Karatek that the level in the bowl had decreased noticeably. But she had eaten half of a flatbread and some of the vegetables that T'Zora's latest greenhouse had produced (and hidden from the guards).

She caught him watching her and raised an eyebrow, silver against the pallor of her skin in which he could see a fragile green network of broken capillaries. She knew. When she put out her hand to touch his fingers, however, the mind that brushed his was still strong. Still wise. Still loving.

Then the alarm went off.

Concentrating on T'Vysse's well-being, Karatek started and knocked over a bowl. It rolled off the table and shattered, a high, bright sound quickly overpowered by the pulsing screams of the sirens.

"Fourth shift," T'Vysse said.

Karatek made himself hurry to the door, unseal it, and, using it as a shield, lean out and listen.

"You won't hear anything from here," T'Vysse said. "If there's trouble, it'll be in the mine tunnels."

"I had better go," he said. He reached for his heaviest tabard, the one with the reinforced elbows and the patches at the knees. "Will you be all right?" he asked.

If he had not forgotten what shifts his children and grandchildren worked, he could have called one of them to sit with her.

"I'll have the best of care," T'Vysse promised him with the old, bewitching glint in her long black eyes. "I'm coming with you."

A becoming flush of green rose from her throat, and Karatek restrained himself—just barely—from smiling. He held a tabard for her, then, despite her protests, topped it with a cloak just as if they were back on Vulcan at an open-air concert, lying on capes warmed by the desert sand beneath them, looking up at the stars.

As they headed down, ever downward toward the seals blocking the colony's living quarters from the mines, a stream of much younger workers rushed past them.

Now the com system crackled, erupting from the command center. It had not been working well for the past seventy-three days, Karatek recalled. But the guards had diverted all engineers and technicians to shore up a new section of the mines instead.

The last cave-in had buried twelve guards, but no miners. Suspecting sabotage, Karatek had tried to spend more time with his daughter. If Sarissa wasn't responsible for it, she probably knew who was. He had been wrong. Sarissa also considered the cave-in a trap. Either she was making inquiries about it or trying very hard to warn the fiercest of the younger miners from similar attacks. The guard commander had threatened reprisals. Rumor had it that, in his last post, he had not hesitated to decimate a city that had refused to open its gates to the Ruling Queen.

As T'Rehu's quotas for resources and obedience grew more and more demanding, the guards' position worsened too until it was difficult to see who, prisoner or jailer, had the worse of the bargain. It was the logic of desperation.

"What are you doing here?" Serevan pounded past them, brought himself up short, then spun to confront them. "Pardon, Father. Lady Mother? You should go back." As he bowed, the heavy equipment harness he was struggling into jangled discordantly.

"We heard the alarm. Is it another cave-in?" Karatek demanded.

Serevan had each of them by an arm and was trying hard to make them retrace their footsteps.

He shook his head and took out a com.

"*. . . Rockfall! Never mind if we drill there, if more than two or three of us walk in at a time, the vibrations will set off another rockfall—get back, you fools!*"

"One or two people, working slowly and carefully, ought to be able to bring in support modules and expand them," Serevan said, pointing with his chin at his equipment belt. The support modules hanging from it were rods made of hyponeutronium. Once they were expanded, they would bite into solid rock, supporting the mineshafts against further collapse.

The ground shivered and rumbled underfoot. Serevan propped T'Vysse against the wall. A gust of cold, cold air made him place himself before Karatek and his mother-in-law.

"*Get in there!*" came the order from command. "*Use your bare hands if you have to!*"

They were near the seals to the mines now. Someone had propped open the seals, which accounted for the freezing air even here.

Now they could hear protests chanted against the guards for trying to force miners into an area they considered unsafe.

"I've got to run on ahead," Serevan said. "If I go in first, I can shore up the shaft. Then . . ."

He ran on ahead. Karatek and T'Vysse followed more slowly. The cold air rasped in his lungs, and he fought against the sort of coughs that could double him over and tear at his throat. Coughs such as used to afflict S'task. Poor man. He wondered if there had been time for anyone to receive his *katra*.

T'Vysse held his arm with one hand. The other, she cupped around her lips, prudently warming the air she breathed.

Karatek could hear the rasp of their breath, the pad of their boots—and something else. He stopped and turned around. A shadow vanished behind a retaining wall. Another shadow slipped into a side passage. Only chance let Karatek see a tall, pallid figure with immense eyes, its elongated fingers clutching what looked like a weapon. It seemed to stare back at him. Then it disappeared, leaving Karatek to wonder if he was losing his wits.

Faint, high-pitched calls echoed and reechoed ahead of them in the long corridor, glazed with rime.

Were those cries a new form of communications the mutants had developed?

Karatek raised an eyebrow at his wife.

"I suspect we have our answer," he murmured.

T'Vysse nodded.

The attacks were being carried out by the genetic changelings that T'Olryn had created, led by her own son, first of his kind.

She—and Refas, the boy's biological father—were the only Vulcans who had made the long journey from the Mother World who could influence this first generation of young people. For them, the cold beneath the ice was a natural habitat. Powerful in mind and body, they devoured any scrap of information T'Olryn could provide on medical care or the disciplines of the mind. They refused Surak's strictures about logic and self-control. And they hated the guards from what Karatek had once heard Sarissa call the murderer race for what they had been made to become.

They did not hate T'Olryn, however. She had equipped them to survive. And she was mother to Rovalat, their leader and protector.

T'Vysse's hand tightened on Karatek's arm.

"Do you hear that?" she whispered.

Shouts, disruptor fire, and eerie fluctuations in those high-pitched calls.

"You caught one of those freak *veruul?*" Central command asked. "Hold it till I get there. If it moves, don't kill it. Hurt it. Hurt it hard."

T'Vysse swayed.

"I've got to get you back to our quarters," Karatek told her. "Come on. I'm going to pass the word for T'Olryn."

His consort shook her head. "She's busy. You know she's busy. If you do not call for her, we at least leave her plausible deniability. She is coming to them. I know it. I have to be there!"

His wife set her head on one side as if seeking to listen: her mental powers had always been stronger than Karatek's. Then she tugged free of him. Before he could stop her, she set off at a stumbling run. Down, always down the corridor. Past the seals, into the mine shafts, guided by the shouts of their guards and the cries of their children.

TWENTY-TWO

MEMORY

T'Vysse kept her lead for two turns in the corridor, then faltered. Karatek found her leaning against the wall of the shaft, gasping for breath. Wishing for the days he had been strong enough to swing her up into his arms and carry her, he reached out to her. She warned him off with a glare.

Clutching at a rock outcropping, T'Vysse pushed herself back onto her feet. Step by faltering step, she forced herself to move forward. She even tried to move faster.

This section of the mines had been excavated only recently. The walls were still rough. The flooring was dangerously uneven, naked rock through which ran tiny veins of pergium. Equipment for laying down the tracks on which ore carts would carry unprocessed minerals lay stacked against the walls.

Raw dilithium crystals glittered in their blackish green matrix. Even the most flawed of the crystals, in their natural state, reflected the greenish white lights welded to the metal rods that shored up the excavation. Other crystals glinted with special fire. Those were the nanoblocs that captured and processed the radiation permeating the rocks.

"Hurry!" T'Vysse panted.

Now her hands were leaving green streaks on the icy rock. Karatek's heart ached in his side. He ran up to her and caught her, holding her until she was steady on her feet.

T'Vysse shook her head, her eyes enormous, filled with sorrow.

"You've made your point," he told her. "I'll go with you. Only on condition you allow me to help you."

Maybe he was too weak to carry her, but he still could take most of her weight. Just as well that their path lay down, always down, into the open pit where carloads of ore waited before the converters, three times the height of a tall Vulcan, that T'Rehu's tame engineers had installed. They were spotlighted by emergency lights that cast a dim, greenish glow across the pit.

Heat rose from the converters, but they were idle, with the workers who usually tended them pushed into a large rock alcove. In front of them stood guards, disruptor rifles held at the ready. Karatek saw glowing scars and scorch marks on the walls and floor of the pit and wondered who had already died.

T'Vysse gasped.

Standing in the center of the pit was the guard's commander. Before him, blood dripping in shocking green paths down his white face, stood one of T'Olryn's changelings, not Rovalat himself but one of the younger ones.

Young enough to be daring.

Young enough to be foolish.

Young enough to be caught.

The changeling staggered, blood dripping down one arm onto the rock as he grasped his other arm, which hung, cauterized, from his shoulder. The guards had obeyed the commander's order to hurt any captives only too well.

"Who helped you?" demanded the commander. Karatek had never seen him before. He had not been born during the exile, but on the new homeworld. His face might be pale from lack of sunlight, but it was contorted with rage. If he failed here, he would be as much a prisoner as the youth whose life he threatened.

The changeling simply watched him, his eyes wide and blank as if he concentrated on suppressing pain.

Now, those same shrill cries Karatek had heard rose again. They echoed off the corridors and fluted from tiny rock flaws, shrilling painfully all around the pit where ore was processing.

Realizing they were surrounded, the guards crouched back to back, as if poised to spring or be pounced on. They were armed, but here, in this place, in this task, among these people they hated and feared, they felt themselves under attack.

That put the prisoners in even more danger. Having no other recourse, they stood silently and watched. Some, Karatek suspected, were considering how many might die if they rushed their captors. How many of them had sufficient mental gifts to know what might be being "said"? Was it a rescue? Would T'Olryn come, escorted by her son and a host of mutants?

How many of the changelings had cooperated in creating this situation? And what aid had they gotten from Karatek's kin?

Karatek shook himself. He had to be having zenite hallucinations.

"You want more, little freak?" demanded the commander. "You're strong, I grant you that. I didn't know your kind had any endurance. We could use you. I've said so in my reports.

You'd make good guards back on the homeworld. So, let's see if we can't make a deal. You tell us where your leaders are, and I'll spare your life—and theirs. And I'll see you get medical attention. You could use it."

The high-pitched signals grew louder. The changeling raised his head, then shook it once in refusal.

"You're a fool!" spat the commander. "I've tried to strike a bargain with you. What's that you people talk about? Waging peace? You're like talking to the rock! Well, if I'm going to meet today's production quota, I've got to get these people back to work. Besides, I'm damned if I want to stay out here in the cold."

He raised his voice, amplified by his helmet com so Karatek could hear the uncertainty behind his bluster. "I know you're out there. Don't move. Watch this. It's what happens to bad workers and disobedient freaks. Don't think we won't hesitate to fire from now on, either!"

He raised his disruptor and aimed at the changeling, this time at his head.

"No!" cried T'Vysse.

Before Karatek could stop her, she hurled herself at the commander.

The disrupter blast only caught her in the arm, but even that was enough to throw her across the cavern, against one of the metal carts, glinting with raw dilithium crystals.

Bones snapped in the sudden silence as Karatek flung himself onto his knees beside her.

"Grandmother!" screamed the changeling, the first word anyone had heard from him.

T'Vysse's lips fluttered. "Run," she whispered. "Run!"

Karatek caught her, cradling her with one arm as he tried to dab away the green rivulet that trickled from one side of her mouth. She trembled, but the shivers that racked her grew weaker and weaker.

Guards ringed them, but they had lowered their weapons as if appalled by actions that, finally, they saw as having gone too far. Karatek had not known in what regard his wife was held among outsiders, changelings and guards alike: one of the survivors of the exile, ship commander's wife, and a very great and gracious lady.

The veils flicked out over his eyes, then retracted so he could treasure these last few moments of her life.

Behind him came orders of "Move them on out" and "You, get back to work." He even heard the subcommander relieve his superior of his responsibilities, urging him to rest. He would be resting soon enough, Karatek thought with bitter satisfaction. A struggle, a choked-off scream, and a blast of energy confirmed his hypothesis.

But he was wasting precious seconds. He turned back to T'Vysse. Her eyes glowed with love for him, the only thing about her now that was warm.

"Why?" he whispered.

"It seemed . . . like the logical thing to do," she answered. "That was one of Rovalat's children. I recognized him. He was so very young and I—"

Karatek bent to receive her *katra,* but she shook her head weakly. Only once, but he had known her since they were seven. Her mind was made up.

"I am ready," she told him. Her entire face lit with joy. For that last instant, she was as beautiful as she had seemed to him on the day that he had struck the gong at his family's ancestral grounds of *Koon-ut-kal-if-fee* and given himself to her forever.

"Freedom," she whispered.

Karatek laid his face against her silvered hair and wept. His tears felt like liberation, but they were not the liberation he sought, the freedom T'Vysse had achieved.

"Father?" It was Sarissa's voice, trembling as he had not heard it for years. She was pulling at his arm, trying to make him rise, to leave this place where his wife had died. But there was no escape from it, no escape for him, ever, from the ice or the memory of her murder.

"Father," she tried again. "I grieve with thee. We all do. But thee must leave this place before a riot starts. Logic requires—"

Holding his wife's body, Karatek surged to his feet with a strength he hadn't had since they were trapped beneath the ice.

"Logic?" he turned to Sarissa. Her eyes blazed like the sun his people could no longer bear to look upon.

But he did not flinch. His own eyes were dry now. Burned dry by the anguish that he allowed to consume him.

"Logic be *burnt!*" he hissed. "Damn logic, and damn Surak, too, to the deepest ice!"

TWENTY-THREE

U.S.S. ENTERPRISE

2377

"Ah, Captain Picard!"

Var Niebet's broad, pale tan face beamed at Jean-Luc Picard from the *Enterprise*'s viewscreen. Behind the Nar-a-Lethen leader, a quick swirling of music started up at that, as precisely structured as a Handel concerto, and he fell silent with a patient half smile on his face until, after a few awkward moments, it had ceased.

"So *pleased to see you,*" Var Niebet continued as cheerfully as though there'd been no interruption. "So *looking forward to meeting with you.*"

Another quick swirling of that precisely structured music began. As he'd been told was polite, Picard waited until it ceased once again, and only then dipped his head in courtesy. "And we, you."

The precisely structured music started up yet again. This was, it had been previously explained to the captain, merely a ritual greeting, one that was insisted upon by Nar-a-Lethen culture: the Greeting-Music-Before-Meeting-Music, as the translator insisted it was called. Picard and Riker would actually be beaming down in one planetary hour.

Such a slight delay is hardly a problem, Picard thought. Besides, the bit of extra time gave him the chance for one last look at the pertinent information.

Nar-a-Lethe was a Class-M world, the fourth planet from its sun. Its people were a small and sturdy humanoid species, not avian although some genetic quirk had given them feathers in place of hair. It covered their bodies with down and their heads with long, multicolored plumes that cascaded down their backs or stirred in colorful rainbows in the breeze. Var Niebet's face had been framed by dark blue and green feathers, and what would have been eyebrows in humans were in his case a ridge of dark blue down across his face over his beak of a nose.

"The Nar-a-Lethens seem to have an amazingly wide range of arts, theater, and music," Picard said as a murmured aside to a clearly skeptical Will Riker. "I imagine that there will be time to sample some of it."

"Ah."

Picard glanced at him. "What?"

"Remember S'ri Kurta?"

That forced a wry smile from Picard. "How could I forget?" That first contact had been friendly enough, but had involved five hours of a ritual epic recited by a tribesman with absolutely no sense of drama or style. "'We do what we must for the sake of peace,'" the captain quoted, the one line of the epic he actually remembered: an accurate quote, after all, in many Starfleet situations. "There's no guarantee that this will be as painful. The fragments of music we have already heard sounded quite interesting, in fact."

Riker merely smiled and gave the slightest of what Picard's French roots insisted was a *chacun à son goût* shrug: to each his own taste.

Cynic, Picard thought with a continued touch of reluctant amusement.

The Nar-a-Lethens had expressed a great interest in joining the Federation, and preliminary studies had shown them to be quite eligible for at least the first level of membership status—which was why the *Enterprise,* which happened to be the nearest representative of the Federation in this sector of space, was in orbit around Nar-a-Lethe right now.

It may not be the most dramatic role we have played, Picard thought, *especially not in recent years. But after all the trials and traumas of the Dominion War, a small, simple, peaceful mission like this is rather welcome.*

But then Riker leaned forward in his chair, frowning at the viewscreen, which was just then giving them a true-scale scan of the planet's surface. "Notice something odd, Captain?"

"Eh?"

Riker gestured at the viewscreen. "Their cities. All five of the ones on the screen right now seem to be completely alike."

True enough. The general city plan was attractive enough. Each city did seem to have been laid out with great attention to artistic detail, with each building placed so as not to disturb the overall design, with plenty of room left for the local greenery and flowers—but each city, as seen clearly from the *Enterprise*'s vantage point, had, indeed, been laid out in precisely the same pattern as the next, regardless of the terrain—one on a plain, one in a rocky region—or the climate—one in what the computer insisted was a temperate zone and another in what the computer insisted was a near-desert. One didn't need to be a Vulcan to see the lack of logic in that idea: an open plaza, for instance, worked well in a temperate climate, but was far less pleasant in a desert or a region swept by arctic gales.

Generally only a dictatorship imposed such utter regulation: Picard had a schoolboy memory of an antique photo of the Soviet Union on Earth, with similarities in its cities such as those wide plazas that had been decreed for both desert and arctic cities regardless of climate. But all the evidence about the Nar-a-Lethens indicated that this world had a freely elected government, not a dictatorship, one that seemed made up equally of politicians, artists, and musicians.

Maybe they just value the art of the overall design over its practicality. That has happened on other worlds, even on Earth.

He and Riker were still mildly debating the issue after they beamed down to the planet's surface and the specific coordinates they'd been given.

"We cannot judge another culture by our standards," Picard commented. He hadn't forgotten Dathon or the Tamarian people—and the unusual nature of their language, which was, unlike any others, based entirely on metaphors. "Perhaps the similarity of the Nar-a-Lethen cities is part of their culture, or perhaps it is merely a matter of architectural practicality."

"Oh, it is definitely both!" a cheerful voice exclaimed. "Cultural practicality, in fact!"

A small, stocky figure was hurrying to meet them—Var Niebet, without a doubt, his blue and green plumes bobbing about his face, his blue and green robes flowing in the mild breeze. Behind him was a small crowd of Nar-a-Lethen dignitaries, a colorful lot in blue, purple, and magenta plumes and robes. Interspaced with the crowd of dignitaries were musicians clutching horns and stringed instruments, and what might have been poets or other performers, judging from the books and scrolls they carried.

Var Niebet beamed. "They are all, each and every city on our world, laid out according to the design set forth in *Melia and Turib,* Surrin Garn's classic drama. I do hope that you enjoy a chance to see it."

Riker's raised eyebrow said volumes.

The government buildings of Nar-a-Lethe Prime, the capital, had one saving grace: they were handsome structures of the marbled white and gray stone Picard had been told was local. Swirling floral carvings and paintings ornamented the walls.

I should know. We've had time to count every leaf.

Negotiations had been going on for four days. Four interminable days.

Picard thought back to his hope that they would see some of the Nar-a-Lethen culture, and shook his head. Hadn't *that* been naïve of him? There was one ridiculous reason that everything to do with what should have been straightforward negotiating was taking so long—and that was that the Nar-a-Lethens were not merely culturally advanced, they were downright culturally obsessed.

It wasn't a case of failed communication, as it had been in the case of poor, doomed, heroic Dathon. Oh no, it was that every stage in the process, from opening remarks to discussions of each paragraph, had to be interrupted for a performance of poetry, music, or dramatic presentation.

Picard could accept cultural necessities. He could accept cultural differences. He could even understand cultural obsessions. But it was difficult to accept that none of this—not the poetry, not the music, and most certainly not the lengthy and seemingly pointless dramas—was comprehensible to outsiders.

Either that, Picard thought wryly, *or their arts really are every bit as tedious as they seem.*

They were now sitting in the great Conference Hall of Congress in the middle of act five of a six-act historical drama about two people—acted without much expression by a Nar-a-Lethen man with garish crimson plumes and a woman with lovely emerald green plumes—who apparently had done nothing at great length. The improvised stage was a simple platform. There was no scenery.

Beside him, Picard could practically feel Riker's eyes glazing over. . . .

But then, with a perfectly coordinated suddenness that said they'd rehearsed this, the actors turned as one to face the audience. "This is scene five of act five," the male actor announced.

"The scene wherein we learn the truth about them both," the female actor continued.

Around Picard, he heard indignant mutters starting up:

"This isn't right."

"You don't interrupt the play to explain it."

"What wrongness is this?"

But the male actor continued, his trained voice rising over the mutters, "This play has been performed for centuries! And in all that time, it has been performed unchanged, lifeless as stone. No more! Here is the scene as it should be played!"

The words of the scene were the same, but the actors' voices and movements spoke of passion, hot anger, hot lust, their characters all at once come alive, if a little too melodramatically so.

The Nar-a-Lethen dignitaries shouted them down in outrage, their plumes rising and flailing in waves of color. "Criminal! Criminal!"

"No! It cannot be changed!"

"It must not be changed!"

"Vandals! You are vandals!"

"Art is sacred!"

"Art is fixed, immobile, as it ever was!"

Var Niebet sprang to his feet, waving his hands at the others in dismay. "Please, be tranquil. We must not—we cannot—not in front of guests—please!"

"This is happening all over the city!" the female actor shouted.

"We are tearing off the shackles of the past!" the male actor shouted.

Then they had to run from the officials who were storming the stage. The rest of the acting troupe came rushing out to defend the two actors, but more officials were hurrying into the council hall.

What better time for a revolution? Picard thought wryly. *Federation guests, guaranteed worldwide publicity . . .*

Picard, on his feet, shouted with full command voice: "Stand down!"

That the words were military didn't matter; the sheer force of will and the trained volume of that commanding shout did. The Nar-a-Lethens stopped dead in a wildly colorful tangling of plumes.

"This is an unacceptable situation," Picard continued. "You wish to join a Federation dedicated to peace, and yet you cannot even get through one act of a play without fighting."

"But surely you understand that it is a crime to tamper with something as important—"

"It is a play! Yes," Picard continued before anyone could cut him off, "I understand how important your arts are to you. I understand that you may not wish classical works changed. But that is no excuse for attacking each other as though you were children!"

At that moment, with abysmal timing, Picard's combadge chimed in. *"Vale to Picard."*

He slapped it. "Not now, Lieutenant."

"But Captain—"

"Not now!"

"Now," said a cool voice. *"Sorry, Jean-Luc, but this takes priority over whatever you're doing."*

It was an unmistakable voice, Picard thought grimly, that of Admiral William Ross.

"Understood," Picard said. *"Enterprise.* Two to beam up." To the nearly hysterical Var Niebet, he added, "I'm very sorry."

"But—you can't—"

"I'm afraid that duty literally calls. I can assure you someone else from the Federation will be in touch with you, and that this matter has not yet been concluded. Good-bye for now."

But Riker managed to get in the last word. Just as the transporter beam caught them, he murmured to Picard, "Looks like we've just encountered another case of . . . culture shock."

Back aboard the *Enterprise,* the fuming Picard went straight to his ready room and had the communication patched through to him. What he received was now a heavily encoded message, top security, marked for his eyes only, and Picard raised a wary brow. Now what was Ross doing?

Frowning, he entered the proper coding, opening the secure channel.

"Very well, Admiral Ross. I am here in my ready room, I'm on a secure channel, and I'm listening. Sir, what is so important that we were dragged away from the middle of a riot—"

"Praetor Neral has just been taken prisoner."

"What?"

"This is not public knowledge, Jean-Luc."

"Understood."

"Praetor Neral left the homeworlds for a private meeting with President Zife on Pacifica."

Well, that was foolish, Picard thought. *Regardless of how desperate he was, surely there was someone he could trust to go in his stead.* Recalling what he knew about Romulan politics, including an undercover mission to Romulus nine years ago, he amended his thought: *Perhaps there wasn't such a person, after all.*

"But that meeting, not surprisingly, did not go well," Ross continued, *"and the Praetor left not long after, possibly en route to the Eridani system, though we cannot be certain of that. But wherever he was heading, his ship apparently flew right into the hands of a waiting Watraii fleet."*

"They wouldn't have killed him outright," Picard said. "A living Praetor of the Romulans would make too valuable a hostage for that."

"Exactly what we have been thinking." Ross leaned forward, staring coldly into the screen. *"I don't think I have to warn you that neither the Romulan Star Empire nor the Federation want this mishap made public. And I don't have to tell you the ramifications of the situation."*

"Hardly."

"Let us just say that Praetor Neral must be extricated from his predicament, and quickly."

"And?" Picard prodded warily. "Come, Admiral. There's more, isn't there? What haven't you told me?"

"Just to add to an already bad situation, we also have one very angry Romulan fleet just outside the Eridani system, led by Commander Tomalak."

What Picard thought about that was short, sharp, and very Gallic. What he said was simply a controlled, "I remember him."

Oh yes, he could almost hear that sardonic voice: *So, Captain, how long shall we stare at each other across the Neutral Zone?*

Tomalak had matched wits with him on several occasions over the years, usually in situations involving the Neutral Zone, and though Picard had come out ahead in all those encounters, he knew that while Commander Tomalak might be . . . reasonably honorable in his own way, he was hardly someone to be trusted. The Romulan enjoyed playing the role of a sneering, calculating diplomatic soldier, one whom experience had taught to be highly skeptical of anything he was told by anyone in the Federation. But not all of that was acting.

And Picard could not forget that tragic Romulan Admiral Jarok, who had lost all he loved through no fault of his own and who had been maneuvered by Tomalak into suicide. Picard also remembered Tomalak's sly, "You see, Picard, after we dissect your *Enterprise* for every precious bit of information, I intend to display its broken hull in the center of the Romulan capital as a symbol of our victory. It will inspire our armies for generations to come."

I'll see you in your Erebus first, Picard thought.

"I thought that you might remember him," Ross contin-

ued dryly. *"All right, Jean-Luc, the orders come directly from Starfleet: You and the* Enterprise *are to deal with this emergency."*

"Admiral, I must protest. While I agree that this mission is of great importance, we are also in the midst of delicate negotiations with the Nar-a-Lethens—negotiations that may have been scuttled by your interruption." Picard saw no reason not to let his disapproval show through. He'd never been comfortable with the military aspects of Starfleet, particularly now when the Federation wasn't actually at war with anyone. The *Enterprise* was a ship of exploration at heart, and he resented being taken away from that. "In addition," he added, "I'm short-staffed. Lieutenant Commander Data is on leave."

"I understand and sympathize, Jean-Luc, but for one thing, the Enterprise *happens to be the nearest starship to the Eridani system."*

"Convenient," Picard said flatly.

"Second, Starfleet wants you because you're the captain who has the most experience with matters both Vulcan and Romulan—including," Ross added almost sardonically, *"those encounters with your good friend, Commander Tomalak."*

"Very well," Picard said with a sigh. His objection had been noted and overruled, and while Jean-Luc Picard was willing to disobey Starfleet orders if the situation was grave enough—as he had done against the Borg and on the Ba'ku planet—this was not one of those situations.

"Get it done, Jean-Luc. Give Praetor Neral back to the Romulans before the news gets out and anyone starts shooting at anyone else. If anyone can do it, you and the Enterprise *can. Ross out."*

TWENTY-FOUR

MEMORY

"Sarissa is planning something," Karatek thought. Above his head glowed the coronet. These years, its crystals shone less brightly as his energy waned and he looked more toward the darkness than toward the light that, in any event, hurt his eyes.

He rubbed his temples where the wires prickled and wrapped his cloak in warmer folds about his shoulders. Last time he had bothered to look, he was as thin as S'task had been the last time he had seen him. Right before Solor died.

A year later, S'task was dead, too.

The comparison was disquieting. When had Karatek ceased to care about his life?

The answer to that was easy: T'Vysse's death had robbed him of his heart. What remained now was only an organic pump, old and worn past the possibility of repair.

Instant reprisals had accompanied the riot that followed T'Vysse's death and the assassination of the commander of the cohort guarding the prisoners. The guard who had killed his commander was thrown unsuited onto the ice, his body left as a warning to other guards until an avalanche had

225

buried it. Work quotas had become even stiffer as much to punish the miners as to meet the Ruling Queen's constantly escalating demands for crystals and rare metals to support her wars and her passion for architecture and personal adornment. A new generation of guards ran constant security sweeps that attempted to trap and control the mutants, but never caught anyone. Even T'Olryn, who might have proved a weak link, had disappeared, which meant that medical care was suffering.

These days, not even the very old could be exempted anymore from labor in the mines, and Karatek was weary. Even though Serevan had rigged a surprisingly effective contraband heater in his quarters, the cold had long since lodged in the marrow of his bones.

And there was one thing more. Karatek had cursed Surak. What else should an apostate be but heartsick? It was even logical. If controlling his sorrow meant distancing himself from his love for T'Vysse, he did not wish to control it. T'Vysse's memory was all he had left.

Not true, he reminded himself. There was Sarissa, last of his children.

For her sake, he wanted to reason this out. She was heir to all his memories.

"Ever since S'task was murdered and Grand Councillor T'Rehu declared herself Ruling Queen, Sarissa has been planning something. I thought then that it had been a highly illogical time for her to conceive a first child, then another, but asking a daughter 'why now?' is an impropriety I cannot commit. Even now."

He felt himself flush slightly and welcomed the warmth.

"Despite my misgivings, her son and daughter have grown tall and strong. On Vulcan, I would have taken great pleasure

in my newest grandchildren. They are practically agemates of some of my great-grandchildren. Here, however, I fear that they will be like the caged shavokh, *beating its wings against the bars until its heart bursts in its side. They have their mother's spirit.*

"They have learned some of the ways of the ice from their cousin Rovalat and his children, but have respected their mother's wishes and refused any of the genetic splicing that has helped many adapt themselves more effectively to our environment and enhance their mental powers.

"I have long suspected that Sarissa has been waiting until they were grown for—I do not know what she plans, and I will not risk further loss of life by asking before she is ready to tell me."

Karatek felt blood trickle down from his forehead. The radiation exposure he had sustained on Vulcan, on shipboard, and beneath the ice had weakened his circulatory system irreparably.

Enough for the day.

He took off the coronet, wrapped it in its fraying silk, and put it away, wondering, as he always did these days, whether he would ever find the moral resolution and the physical strength to take it up again.

Admit it, Karatek told himself. *You are afraid of the answer Sarissa might give you. You have no one to blame but yourself if she has learned from your example. You helped persuade people to leave Vulcan to save it from blowing itself up. And now you find yourself the patriarch of what is, once again, a warrior race, inventing and hiding weapons when it is not forced to tear deadly resources from the living rock of a prison planet.*

He let his chin fall onto the folds of fabric that shrouded

him, felt how they warmed his breath, comforting his worn-out lungs. Sighing, he drifted into the easy sleep of the very old.

Someone was shaking Karatek, shaking him from shallow, pleasant dreams in which he basked on a hot rock, the scent of the desert rising about him, as a sundweller flew high overhead.

"Bio-signs weak, but stable." That was Serevan's voice.

"His hands are so cold. Can't you get more heat out of that generator you gave him?" Where Serevan led, Sarissa followed. Or maybe it was the other way around: no matter.

"Not without registering a power drain in central command."

Warm, warm hands clasped Karatek's stiff fingers. "He's dehydrated," Sarissa mourned. "I don't think he's had a thing to eat or drink for days."

He heard heavy footsteps, then the sound of a massive figure kneeling beside his daughter. "Try the tea first. It's lighter, and he might accept it more easily than soup."

Karatek allowed his head to loll back against his daughter's shoulder in what he had to admit was an ironic reversal of their roles. He allowed her to tilt a steaming flask carefully against his lips. He sipped grudgingly, then more eagerly. As the warmth hit his system, the sundweller flew out of sight, his dream faded, and the waking world drifted closer.

Drifted closer, only for the present. The sundweller, he suspected, was simply a symbol of how his *katra*'s wings were growing, strengthening, for the day when it would be ready to abandon his weakening flesh.

He made himself look up into Sarissa's face. Because he was now an apostate to Surak's teachings, he even managed a faint smile. He was sorry she had heard him renounce Surak. She had been one of the earliest to hear his message and, unusual for a woman, had insisted on taking a name starting with *S* while she was still in her mid-teens.

Sarissa was so many things: wife, mother, an advanced student of the disciplines as well as of various scientific and, these days, military arts. Most important, she was his beloved daughter.

"I wish," he murmured, turning his face away from the tea, "you might have known no evil of anyone. You could have stayed on Seleya. . . ."

She shook her head. Her face was still fierce and as beautiful as he remembered it from her youth. "When the high priestess even hinted that I might remain, you took one look at the unbonded and couldn't wait to get me away to ShiKahr!"

Unlike Karatek, Sarissa did not smile, but her amusement gleamed in her eyes. She set aside the cup of tea and took both of his hands back into her own.

"You know," she said, "things cannot remain as they are. I disagree that you have completely renounced Surak's teachings. Granted, Surak said, 'What is, is.' But he never submitted to tyrants."

"Sarissa, why not let your father rest, perhaps eat the food you brought him?" Serevan asked. Karatek's quarters were so small that his son-in-law could simply reach over to his long-unused cooking unit on which soup, spiced as Karatek remembered preferring it back in the days when food still held any savor for him, had begun to steam.

"Believe me, if I could let him dream, I would. He's earned it," Sarissa said. "But you created the timetable, my husband. You know how tight it is."

Out of courtesy for Sarissa's beliefs, Karatek suppressed a chuckle. Just as he expected, Sarissa had a plan. She had always had plans and plots. He suspected this one would be her masterwork, assuming anyone survived it.

"Some of us are going to escape, Father," she said.

Serevan brought him soup. Karatek managed not to choke on the first mouthful. He sipped decorously, then set it aside to grow cold while his daughter poured out her words with the enthusiasm he had always loved in her.

Through her marriage to Serevan, Sarissa had joined the odd, almost inarticulate fellowship of engineers that Karatek remembered so well. Since the days of their second exile, she had also come to count among her friends some of the best fighters, weapons builders, and scientists who slaved and plotted beneath the ice. Karatek felt a moment's sorrow that she had named the fighters and weapons builders first, but what choice did she have?

The same choice as Varekat, back on Vulcan. Rather than fight, he had chosen to die.

But Varekat had been free, as Sarissa was not. And Sarissa was a warrior, not a builder of weapons.

He had to have spoken before he thought, because Sarissa's eyes turned to flame.

"We do not have to fight. We can leave!" she cried.

Karatek let his eyes drift toward Serevan.

"We have learned to irradiate dilithium crystals," his son-in-law said. "I wish I had time to go into the physics of it with you, but I've modified the engines from your old prototype ships. With these new crystals, I estimate an 86 percent probability that we can boost a ship's velocity almost to the speed of light. Pardon the imprecision—we haven't much time."

"Even with the plans they took from my lab after Solor died?" Karatek's eyes filled with the easy tears of old age.

Serevan nodded. "Even if they've adapted the engines of every ship in their home fleet to your specifications, we could outrun them. I've practiced on simulations. I believe I can retrofit a cargo vessel and get us offworld before they could bring weapons to bear on us."

"We've been saving up resources, building weapons, and now we're ready!" said Sarissa. "When the next ship lands . . ."

"My daughter, what are you thinking? Remember how big *Shavokh* was! We cannot all fit into one cargo ship, especially not for a prolonged journey. How can we abandon any of our people—let alone rob them of supplies that they, too, need?"

Sarissa flushed olive, and looked down.

"I've been talking to T'Olryn and the children of the ice," she admitted. "They do not wish to go. They've adapted here, and I think they believe that it is only a matter of time until everyone who remains here follows their example."

"What of those of us who've remained unmodified?" Karatek asked. "Surely, there are those with young children and those who simply do not wish to uproot themselves again." The old, the infirm, and those too brokenhearted to hope, he thought, but did not say.

Sarissa shook her head. "I've told them that the reprisals are likely to be worse than the ones we saw when Mother . . ."

She looked away.

"They know the risks. Especially, the people who have children. I have children of my own, and as I've watched them grow, I think we would be better off trying and failing than letting them live as slaves. And I've promised that, whenever it's possible, we will come to rescue them. If not we ourselves, then our descendants."

She let her hand drop to her utility knife as if taking oath on an Honor Blade.

Serevan let his hand drop onto her shoulder, cutting off her ardent flow of words. "Enough, my own. Let your father process what you've told him." He shook his head, looking rueful. "You know Sarissa, sir. Since, oh, long since before T'Rehu seized power on the other world, Sarissa has been waging peace practically across the entire compound."

"But why do you have to go *now?*" Karatek hated the old man's whine that his voice assumed.

Sarissa sat beside him, again taking his hands in hers. Karatek knew she was about to be especially persuasive and braced himself to resist.

"Father, there was a time—I remember it—when you knew every name and every rumor on board *Shavokh*. Even when we first came here, there wasn't an incident or a discovery you didn't know about, or a decision you didn't have a hand in making. Do you think I haven't noticed how much you've withdrawn since Mother died? So you probably didn't hear: T'Rehu's been overthrown. There was a battle outside her capital city, and someone cut her throat for her."

Sarissa thinned her lips. Karatek knew that only her allegiance to the disciplines prevented her from adding "and about time, too."

"I know you don't like the idea," Sarissa continued, the words tumbling out, "but I learned from S'lovan when he joined us on *Shavokh* that opportunity is given us to take or lose, and this is an opportunity we have to take."

"The thing has been decided. We're going to take the next

ship and leave, and we want you to go with us." That was his son-in-law: blunt, reliable, a hearth for Sarissa's fire.

"Next time Romulus sends a cargo ship," Serevan continued, "we will march onto it and offload its supplies like the obedient slaves they just wish we would become. Then, under the eyes of the guards themselves, we'll load it, not just with the crystals, ores, and processed metals they want, but with our own goods."

He paused as if aware he was about to say something that would displease his father-in-law. "With our own weapons. I've been experimenting."

Karatek managed not to flinch. "And once you've loaded the ship, what next?" Karatek watched his children closely.

They looked away.

Bloodshed.

Always bloodshed.

"I wish it could be otherwise," Sarissa said in a small voice Karatek remembered as belonging to a much younger girl caught in some minor transgression.

Karatek patted her hand, not in comfort but in understanding. What had to be, would be.

He did not doubt that Sarissa and her allies could seize the cargo ship. They were strong from the backbreaking labor in the mines. They were martial artists of no mean skill. They would not abandon their brothers and sisters, but they would go out—as Karatek himself had gone into exile—and return only when they were able to free the darksiders.

Perhaps it was time now for the coronet to pass to younger, stronger hands. It might travel to a new home, or it might be lost in the space between the stars.

Karatek braced himself with a hand on his daughter's shoulder until he could struggle to his feet. Slowly, he made his way over to the *elassa*-wood box that held the only heirloom he could give his daughter.

Sarissa was shaking her head.

"Do you think I would leave you behind?" she said. "You, too, will walk the new homeworld," she promised. "T'Olryn has given me the medical and genetic protocols for reducing our eyes' light sensitivity. So you will be able to walk in the sun once more. Come with us!" she urged.

Karatek shook his head. "Daughter, even assuming that Serevan can boost that ship's engines to nearly the speed of light in such a fashion that they don't tear the ship apart, I would, in all probability, not live to see yet another planetfall. I do not have to be a disciple of Surak to know that there is absolutely no logic in my occupying a place on that flight that properly should go to a younger man or woman. And you know it, too."

"No!" Sarissa said. "You may not be as strong as Serevan, but you're wise, you're our memory, our conscience . . ."

"Besides, you're still the best theoretical designer we've got, sir," Serevan added. "Even if you are slowing down a little."

Karatek met his son-in-law's eyes. Both of them knew that Sarissa might fall silent, might even say that she had accepted Karatek's reasoning, but that she would give up only after the ship had achieved liftoff.

"I will help you," Karatek said. "And I will consider going with you."

It was the only concession he could, in all honesty, give. And, just as he suspected, his daughter's face took on the "just wait till I reason with you" look he knew.

There were times, however, when even Sarissa had to yield to the logic of a situation.

TWENTY-FIVE

ROMULUS

2377

Hiding behind a placid smile and tranquil expression, Hiren stepped forward into the Romulan Senate's great Council Chamber in Ki Baratan. The room was in a building that was over two hundred years old—the pride of the architects (who, Hiren thought sardonically, had done so fine a job that they had not lived to build anything ever again).

He took a moment, as he always did, to admire the view. The Council Chamber was a huge, starkly elegant room with a high-arched ceiling from which hung long rows of lights, and its massive walls were vast sweeps of stone. Each of those walls was inset with its own red, blue, and blood-green mosaic images of past glories and metal trophies from various interstellar victories. A gleaming silver fragment of a Starfleet ship hull imbedded in one wall even commemorated one rare but spectacular victory against the Federation: a somewhat awkward trophy in these days of—Hiren thought in distaste—Romulan-Federation alliances. On the floor was emblazoned a circular star map showing both Romulan and Federation space, the Neutral Zone bisecting the circle.

The other senators were already seated along both sides of the long, dark green stone table. Nothing much had happened yet, since at the moment, at least, they were all still in their seats, not arguing or hurling themselves across the table at one another's throats. Hiren was used to such theatrics and ferocities, although he thought them rather useless when it came to actually getting anything done.

Hiren was, as always, precisely on time for the meeting. And as always, nobody looked up at his entrance. Nobody noticed him as other than reliable, predictable Senator Hiren.

Perfect.

This was not a major gathering of the Senate, just one of those that were necessary for the smooth day-to-day running of the Empire. *Very good,* Hiren thought. *For now, let it be just that. Let there be a normal meeting full of the daily minutiae of Senate business.*

There were going to be some interesting episodes for the Senate to discuss fairly soon.

Charvanek, her eyes cold and her expression grim, sat alone in her office, watching the current senatorial meeting from one of her secret viewscreens, knowing that the Tal Shiar was probably doing the same thing, and mulling over an assassination for the good of the Empire.

Hiren, now . . . Hiren was such a middle-of-the-line citizen, not the sort of fellow to—at least not in normal times—be making a grab for power.

But Charvanek, watching the screen thoughtfully, knew that appearances could be deceptive. As Hiren murmured to this senator and that, she mused that he was definitely sowing dissension in the Senate and quietly making allies. But that wasn't precisely unusual for a senator; many senators, after all, were ambitious. Was what she was observing merely the normal power hunger of a senator who was trying for a higher status among his fellows? Or was Hiren reaching for something more? Did he, perhaps, dream of being the leader of the Senate?

Or could Hiren be reaching even higher than that? Could he actually be trying for the praetorship?

Bah. He's not the only senator interested in that target. I could name half a dozen potential problems in that room.

It was both awkward and uncomfortable having to remain so unswervingly loyal to Neral, whom she neither liked nor, when it came right down to it, trusted. But he was honest enough where the Empire was involved. And there it was: He was the Praetor, quite legally, and as such, Neral must, as a matter of honor, have her support and the support of Romulan Security.

What the Tal Shiar thought about him . . . akhh, no one knew for sure what those slippery minds were thinking, possibly not even the agents of the Tal Shiar themselves. But so far, at least, they, too, seemed to be supporting Neral. After all, he had encouraged their restructuring after the debacle of their alliance with the Cardassian Obsidian Order that had resulted in the Founders' infiltration of the Tal Shiar and the annihilation of their fleet at the Battle of the Omarion Nebula. The Obsidian Order had not survived. The Tal Shiar had.

But what of Hiren, now? Should she simply eliminate him? What a lovely thought that was, and quite efficient as well. That would be getting rid of one potential troublemaker and sending a clear warning to the others at the same time.

Akhh, who am I trying to fool?

It was difficult enough holding her own against all comers as it was, without losing honor at the same time. Leave the secret murders to the Tal Shiar: they had the lack of morality for that. Their reorganization had left them more powerful and more devious than ever she could have expected. And with the treasury so depleted and with so much discontent in the air, who knew what would happen next?

Besides, she had as yet no real proof that Hiren had committed any crime. Ambition was hardly a crime.

Charvanek ran an impatient hand through her reddish-brown hair. There were times when she wished she could simply take a ship and leave for some more tranquil place. Some nice, peaceful, pretty colony world, maybe, someplace where no one was aiming at anyone else's back or analyzing every word for hidden meanings. But she could not abandon her duty, and such idle dreams were worse than foolish—they were dangerous.

There was this at the heart of it: Although the Empire might have done some truly dark things, especially during the Dominion War, Charvanek had never committed murder.

And I am not about to commit it now.

However, should Hiren, or anyone else, for that matter, step out of line even slightly, commit even the smallest of wrongs, she would bring the wrath of Romulan Security down on their heads.

Senator Rokonik brushed back his graying hair with one hand, and then strode out boldly over the rocky region of Gal Gath'thong, headed overland for a peaceful tour of the firefalls. He had been one of the most outspoken and prominent critics of a Romulan-Federation alliance. But the aging senator, no fool, had soon come to terms with the need for that alliance, and had reversed position to become a staunch supporter of Praetor Neral and his politics.

Now, though, with the Praetor away on a mission that was well meant but, alas, sure to fail, and with so much dissension tearing the Senate apart, Rokonik had decided, for the state of his health—mental as well as physical—that it was time to take a brief vacation from politics. He might not be young anymore, but he was certainly still fit enough for a good hike.

Rokonik stopped to admire the flight of a flock of wide-winged *mogai*. Ah yes, almost there. Those birds never flew in such large flocks anywhere else on the planet. And it was wonderful to get away from the arguments—and from the gentle murmurings of Senator Hiren, with his constant hinting that Neral might not be right for the job of postwar restoration.

Maybe Neral is and maybe he is not, but he is still the Praetor! And I will . . . I . . .

I . . .

Something was wrong. Without warning, Rokonik couldn't seem to catch his breath. Suddenly his heart seemed to be beating at twice its normal rate, and pain was shooting through him. This was impossible, he was in perfect health, and . . . and he . . . was falling. . . .

"I truly hate to be the one to announce such tragic news," Hiren said sadly, "but I have just chanced to hear this directly from Senator Rokonik's aide, Sanra, who ran into me in the hallway. The senator is . . . dead."

He waited for the startled murmurings to die down, and then continued. "No need to look so alarmed, colleagues. It wasn't assassination. The poor man was no longer young, as we all know, and according to his physician, Rokonik's heart simply gave out while he was hiking, presumably a bit too strenuously for someone his age. So it was, and so it is. Now we must honor his memory. I vote a posthumous award for service for the late senator's family."

There were shouts of approval at that, and Hiren dipped his head in feigned respect and just barely hid a smile as he did so. *Well done, Rehaek, very well done, indeed. You said that it would look like nothing more alarming than a death from heart failure, and it did.*

And, in a way, it was. Heart failure from a subtle dose of melanth. *So convenient a plant,* melanth, *growing as it does so conveniently near the firefalls, where Rokonik was heading. The senator, poor fellow, must have, all unknowingly, inhaled its toxic pollen.*

But of course this would be the first and last "tragic death" Hiren planned to report. One such report could be quite by chance. Two or, Elements help him, more than two? No. No need to generate even a germ of suspicion with anyone.

Charvanek looked up grimly from the data on her desk to the man standing nervously before her. "Well, Dr. Terali? *Was* it heart failure that killed Senator Rokonik?"

The physician, a stout, middle-aged man with short-cropped dark hair, tried his best not to meet her steady stare. "So it would seem."

"That is not an answer. Was it heart failure or was it not?"

"I . . . so declared it."

Charvanek frowned. "In other words, you either weren't sure or are afraid to tell the whole story." She paused, studying him. "You are safe from the Tal Shiar in here, Doctor. And I assure you there are no telltales or other security breaches in this office. Whatever you say will reach no other ears. Now, which was it? Heart failure or something else?"

"I, uh, there, uh, might have been a few grains of *melanth* pollen in the late senator's lungs."

"And you're not sure?"

"Ah, no, I fear that I am not."

"Why not?" Charvanek asked very, very carefully.

The doctor swallowed dryly. "If that was truly *melanth,* the samples were far too few for any accurate analysis."

"Hah."

"B-But even so, even if there were such grains in his lungs, that would be unfortunate for the poor senator, but hardly unusual given the time and place of his hike. The fact is that the unfortunate man had chosen to hike near the firefalls, and that is, of course, the region in which *melanth* grows. The senator was not a botanist, so it would have been unlikely for him to have known that it was also almost precisely the time of year when the *melanth* plants tend to release their most toxic pollen."

"Melanth," Charvanek commented without expression, "is a rare plant, even in that region."

"True. But it is, indeed, as I say, native there."

Charvanek said nothing, only waited in icy silence.

The physician added, after a nervous moment, "There were no signs of physical trauma on the body."

Charvanek sighed soundlessly. "In other words, it really might have been an accidental inhalation of the pollen, or a case of true heart failure. Or maybe," she added dourly, "someone used a simple tube to blow the pollen at him so that the late senator would inhale it without even knowing what had happened to him."

"That, I cannot answer."

"No. I don't expect you to start inventing possibilities."
That, she thought, *is my job.*

Charvanek released him from her stare. "Go back to your work, Dr. Terali. And if you're wise, you will say nothing to anyone about anything other than medicine for some time to come."

Hiren, Rehaek thought, was a pedantic fool. An ambitious fool, though, as well. One who should prove quite useful and malleable as a praetor. Assuming that he actually survived long enough to get that far.

"Torath," Rehaek said thoughtfully, "I think that it's time for us to do a little productive weeding."

The bigger man blinked. "Weeding of what? I don't know of any gardens that we—"

"People, Torath, not plants."

Torath straightened in embarrassment. "Ah. Of course. Which people do you have in mind?"

"Let us see now . . . yes. Here's one who should be neatly removed. Do you know Lithani? The third undersecretary for our dear Praetor?"

"I think so. She's the slim, pretty one with the black eyes and the longish brown hair?"

"That's the one. It's a shame, really. But the young woman is unfortunately being a bit of a nuisance for us, Torath, since she is so very unswervingly loyal to Neral." Rehaek smirked up at his aide. "So much so, in fact, that one might think that it just could be more than mere loyalty on her part. *Such* a shame that word will get out about her extracurricular work. And that of course the poor thing will be so ashamed by her dishonor being made public that she'll just have to put an end to it."

"Is she really the Praetor's mistress?"

242

"Torath, my loyal but less than quick friend, I neither know nor care."

"Ah. Understood. And if the young woman is stubborn about, uh, doing the right thing?"

Rehaek's smirk of a smile thinned ever so slightly. "I look to you, Torath, to see that she's not."

Charvanek let out her breath in a silent sigh. Only two days after the death, possibly by accident, of Senator Rokonik, and now here was another governmental death.

Yet this one seemed, at least on the surface, to be absolutely unrelated to the first. Neral's third undersecretary, who had hardly been an important political figure, had just been found in her quarters with a communications tablet clutched in one hand and enough medication in her system to kill a squadron of warriors, let alone one slender young woman.

A copy of the message from that tablet was on Charvanek's desk right now, and she had to admit that it looked like an almost stereotypical suicide note from an overwrought youngster. Too much so?

She claims to have been Neral's mistress . . . shaming the family, too dishonored to live. . . .

Oh, I sincerely doubt that. Whatever else he may be, our Neral is no fool. Any mistress he might have is hardly going to be anyone as easily reachable as a member of his staff.

Had someone fed the unfortunate Lithani that medication? Or was it the suicidal act of a genuinely disturbed young woman who'd been fatally frustrated over not being able to seduce the Praetor? Lithani had been just young enough and emotional enough for that scenario to be credible. And with no signs of violence on her body, no signs of her having been force-fed the medication . . .

"Damn it to Erebus!" Charvanek erupted.

There was more to this unfortunate death, she was sure of it. But the suspects could be anyone from the public or secret government with an eye toward disgracing Neral's praetorship—or even some frustrated would-be lover. Without further evidence—*and why am I so sure there will be none?*—it wasn't even a case for Romulan Security to handle.

Charvanek opened a secure communications channel. "The suicide note is not to reach the media," she said succinctly to her agent at the other end of the connection. "Out."

Damage control, as she'd heard Starfleet call it, and she hoped it would prove sufficient.

At least for now.

TWENTY-SIX

MEMORY

Sarissa had been extremely clever in her plans. So soon
after the downfall of the Ruling Queen, the outgoing guards
showed logical apprehension at meeting and being replaced
by guards of differing factions. There would be tension, confusion, and opportunity in the transfer of supplies and command. But their masters needed supplies. Thus, the cargo ship
that they sent was the largest vessel that could touch down on
the ice with any degree of safety.

Karatek and his daughter had been ordered to stand in the
corridor that led to the final locks between the habitat and the
uninhabitable surface in what people called a "show of good
faith."

In truth, it was a show of further submission by the laborers. Not only were the prisoners being used as a buffer between warring parties, but their leaders were held hostage for
their obedience.

"Quite the irony, is it not, that we stand as protectors to our
oppressors?" Sarissa observed as she checked the last fastenings on Karatek's envirosuit.

Her eyes flashed. It was as well for her ongoing mental

health that she finally had the opportunity to implement her plans to attack and capture the cargo ship.

One squad at a time, the entire guard cohort was changed. How interesting it was to watch them march in, wearing the livery of the various states on Romulus now at war, always at war, it seemed, with one another. All of them seemed to agree on only two things. They needed the resources that slave labor provided, and they needed, at least for now, not to shoot at each other lest their governments be unable to keep on amassing stockpiles of ores, rare metals, and crystals.

Seeing the canisters of supplies dragged in, one after the other, Sarissa shifted only once from foot to foot. Karatek understood her reasoning. The travelers could indeed have used that food, those medical supplies, but she had had to concede that the labor camp had a prior claim. Besides, the plan had been made: changes at this stage of events might result in confusion and failure.

As planned, the laborers had managed to time the unloading and reloading of the cargo ship to correspond with a change in their work shift. So it was logical for the area to be filled with workers. And if some of them moved as slowly as Karatek, while others were a little small, the quotas were onerous, and designed to be so. Exhausted slaves could not be rebellious ones. If filling the quotas required the labor of the very young as well as the very old, it was the guards' concern only to keep order and to see the quotas filled, not to protect the weakest of what were, after all, slave laborers.

It had been a major task, and not an easy one, to ensure that every one of the people who had agreed to attempt to escape with Sarissa had a functioning envirosuit. And that they were not spotted as the guard cohorts swaggered into their new responsibilities, which would be their last.

The guards shifted their disruptor rifles from hand to shoulder and back again, glancing upward as though unnerved by how noisy the habitat was. The clamor of unloading masked the high-pitched signals that passed throughout it as T'Olryn's people leagued with the Vulcans who had chosen to remain.

What sort of life would they have? Karatek thought. What sort of life could there be here once Sarissa escaped? He would have pitied them, but all of these problems now seemed so remote.

Inside the colony, the labor gangs moved slowly, as the guards expected slaves would do. Karatek pretended not to listen to promises of how lazy darksiders could be smartened up.

"Serevan's crews will have to move twice as fast. We can use some of the components we were supposed to deliver ourselves. And we could only move our own supplies up at the last minute," Sarissa whispered to Karatek.

The last work gang to reenter the habitat—composed entirely of people who had elected to stay on Remus—cycled through the locks into the corridor in which Karatek stood.

"Shift is changing," Sarissa observed.

Customarily, changes in work shift were accompanied by announcements, warning sirens, and bells. As the sirens blared, Sarissa took a deep breath. She reached for a weapon she had concealed within a pouch shielded against scanners.

"Now!" she cried, the belling of a *shavokh* before it strikes. "For freedom!"

"For freedom!"

Others took up the cry. The mutants' voices shrieked painfully up until they reached a register that only they could hear. As the very old, the very young, and the infirm assumed their helms and crowded into the airlocks, the workers rushed their guards.

The duranium plates of the passageway became slick with blood. In the cold created by so many transits in and out of the colony, each one draining warmth from the air, it froze almost instantly to a repellent, slippery greenish slush.

"Go, go, *go!*" cried Sarissa. She fired at a guard who had brought down a straggler until he vanished in fire, then whirled to check again on the progress of the evacuation.

The high-pitched screams died. In the sudden relative silence, Karatek turned.

There stood T'Olryn. The children she and Solor had raised—and their children—clustered around her. As the youngest knelt for her blessing, she touched his temple with infinite tenderness. Every one of them wore envirosuits. T'Olryn, however, wore a heavy cape over her priestess's robe.

"Did you change your mind? Are you coming after all?" Sarissa demanded.

In that case, it would take precious moments for her to suit up.

The healer's eyes were enormous, glistening in the lights set in the ceiling with emotion that even a healer with an adept's training could not suppress. She cast one last, desperate look at her adult children and their families, then shook her head.

"My other children need me more," she said.

It was logical. Of all of the Vulcans on this accursed world, T'Olryn was the best trained, the best suited to teach a clutch of nearly feral telepaths. She might fail, but she was their matriarch.

From behind her emerged the looming, pallid figures of

the mutants and one other: Refas. He put a hand on T'Olryn's arm as if to draw her back into hiding.

Her regret reached out, striking grief into their hearts.

"I made them," T'Olryn said. "Solor understood. He foresaw this."

Already, Vulcan's strangest children were tugging her back toward the secret lairs that no guards had ever been able to find. "They will protect me. Now, go!"

The veils flicked over Karatek's eyes as his family was sundered once more. He preferred not to think of what, if all went well, was happening on board the cargo ship. He tried not to think of the screams, the explosions, and the fires as the slaves who had obediently filled the ship's holds transformed themselves into warriors. They would overrun the vessel, determined to overpower as many of the hated guards as possible and expel them and the ship's crew onto the ice.

To minimize reprisals, they had been told to disable, not kill. This restraint would raise the number and severity of their own casualties.

What was, was. They would heal where they could and mourn where they must.

Sarissa tilted her head, listening to a message from the ship. "It's secure. The rest of you, out *now!*"

One hand on Karatek's arm, she tugged him toward the airlock.

Shrieks rose from the lower caverns. Sarissa hissed under her breath.

"Some of these new guards are no fools," she muttered. "They're trying to regroup and charge us. Now, assuming our plan worked, Serevan should be discharging survivors from the ship's crew onto the ice. The plan was to deplete their suits' air supplies, leaving them sufficient oxygen to reach the habitat, but no more."

Karatek's blood chilled. If the guards on the ice chose suicide rather than refuge, the remaining escapees could find themselves trapped between two hostile forces.

Sarissa's face went expressionless. Turning to the last twelve people whom she had selected to surround her and Karatek as they made their escape, she said, "Get *T'Kehr* Karatek to the ship. I will stay behind to hold the airlocks. No, I need none of you to join me. There will be few enough of us as it is to go into exile. But"—her voice went a little rough— "speak of me, please, to my mate. Tell him to lead with honor and to remember me to our children."

Her followers met her eyes, then looked away. She was the leader. This was her duty as well as her right. Karatek knew that the time Sarissa could survive in a crossfire could be counted in minutes, if that. He also knew she was fierce and wily. Possibly, just possibly, she could give them the time they needed to escape.

Do you see, T'Vysse? Pride is an emotion, but . . . oh, it is such a logical *reaction when one has raised a daughter like this.*

He drew a deep breath and set his jaw. Possibly, just possibly, there was another, better way that would spare Karatek's last surviving child.

"You go, my own," Karatek said. "I will stay."

"No!" Sarissa shouted. "You! T'Zora! Get my father out of here. He'll be slow on the ice. Don't let him fall. Help him."

Her personal guard glanced from daughter to father and back again. Karatek knew what they saw. He was nearly three hundred years old. His years had not been the easy ones of city, home, research, and meditation. Instead, he had been hammered out on a forge of deserts, ships, exile, and revolution until he had become something that Vulcan might shrink from recognizing, much less embracing as kin. His body was feeble, but his will was stronger than it had ever been. It was a weapon his daughter could use.

"Sarissa," Karatek said. "There isn't time to argue. I can't make the run, and I don't want to hold up two people, or even the ship, assuming Serevan's logic is as defective as yours."

She shook her head, stubborn as always.

Karatek set gloved hands on her slender shoulders. At least, this was one responsibility he could lift off them. "Thee is the one who must go, daughter. Thee is the Vulcan heart. Thee is the Vulcan soul. And thee is my beloved child. I would have thee live long and prosper, even if I do not see it.

"Besides," he said in a much more matter-of-fact voice, "I have a plan. It means depriving you of an heirloom, but I cannot say this particular ornament has been an easy one to bear. Yours will be a new people. You must learn to keep your memories in a different way."

His meager personal effects had been carried onto the ship, but he had tucked the coronet in its silk wrappings into his pouch for safekeeping.

Now, he took it out. He let its tattered silk wrappings flutter to the blood-slick floor. They no longer mattered.

"At least, take my sidearm," Sarissa begged.

"I don't need it," Karatek said, letting her see the smile in his eyes for the last time.

He set the coronet onto his head. The wires pierced his brow for the last time.

Yes, he thought. *I am ready now.*

For all these years, he had transmitted his thoughts, his

memory, his life force into the crystals that glowed above his head. Now, he sent his *katra* into the recorder's central gem.

Fascinating. It was as if he had gained an entirely new sensorium, as if his consciousness took wing and overflew the entire habitat.

"The guards are coming," he told Sarissa. "Go now."

He brushed her temple in blessing, then turned his back on her, her followers, the promise of a new start on life that he had, quite logically, to refuse.

He barely heard the airlocks slam, the cycle of decompression beginning for the last time, as he mustered the energy he found. Light bloomed over his head, enveloping him, then expanding: golden light, paling to white, with lightning at the core. Sparks played along his nerves, as exhilarating as the Forge before the sand fires struck.

For his daughter's sake, Karatek had to last as long as possible. He drew on what life force remained in his physical body and poured it into the crown.

About him rose the cries of the mutants: his other children. Were those wails a warning or a tribute to him?

No time to wonder. Here came the guards.

Suited and helmed, they crept up the ramps, trying not to slip in that terrible green slush. Their weapons were live, their motions cautious as they fanned out.

The first sight of the guards almost made Karatek's knees buckle. He was growing cold, so desperately cold. And so much weaker.

Not yet, he commanded himself. *You cannot die yet.*

He made his voice resonate through the light that drained and sustained him.

"Go no further," he ordered. Drawing on what remained of his energy, he drew himself up. Ahhhh, that was it. He was warm, so very warm, filled with a vitality he had not known since leaving the Mother World.

The guards paused.

What did they see? Did they see a civilized old man, standing in their path, or a godling—perhaps one of the god-brothers of Vulcan legend—crowned in flames, prepared to bar their way and blast them to the Womb of Fire?

The cold struck him again. The light above him faded.

Hurry, he wished his daughter and her friends. *I cannot hold this.*

Energy was starting to seep out of him the way ice crumbles before a flood of liquid nitrogen pouring onto the rippled plain over their heads. He backed up against the control panel, shielded from the airlock by a narrow metal barrier.

You see, daughter? I, too, can fight.

His plan had been to wait until the guards rushed him, then open the hatch and vent them, unprotected, onto the ice.

As he laid a shaking hand on the controls, he heard the high-pitched hunting calls of T'Olryn's people.

Were they coming to claim him for their own?

If he opened the airlocks, they too would be sucked out onto the ice, and, mutated though they were, even they could not survive on the surface yet.

Besides, what had been, was. He had had a long life. It had been longer than enough. And even if the end of it was not what he might have hoped, it had nonetheless been a life that was . . . eventful. Satisfactory in many ways, he saw that now—especially now that his daughter had pledged to regain the honor they had lost in slavery to their kin.

This close to the airlocks, the cold grew even more cruel. Karatek's face grew numb past aching. By now, frostbite must have claimed his ears. His fingers would be next. He was old and would weaken fast, even if the guards took their time. Either way, he would not live long enough to suffer.

He could feel the ground rumble underfoot and overhead. It was the ship, taking off, abandoning these newcomers just as they and their families had once marooned him.

They shouted with rage, then collected themselves and prepared to fire. No use wasting energy charming one old man. At least this lot had discipline. He preferred not to die at the hands of savages.

The mutants screamed and charged them.

"No!" he cried. "Get back!"

To his astonishment, they obeyed.

The guards came on, sensing an advantage. They would want to take him prisoner. T'Olryn's children would want to preserve him, and he . . . After all these years, what did he want?

He could not achieve an accurate count of the years since he had laughed. He thought it had been that night in his home when Surak had sat at his table. He laughed again now.

As the hearthworlders reached out, eager to seize the brief, cheap vengeance of murdering an old man, Karatek drew his Honor Blade. The metal sizzled as it touched the lightning that still shot from the coronet.

As he raised his blade, the lightning stung it out of Karatek's hand before he could accept Final Honor. It clattered against the smoothed rock wall. He did not hear or see it fall.

Nor did he feel anything when he collapsed on the cold, bloody ground before the guards could rush him and snatch the coronet, still glowing, where it had fallen from his head.

TWENTY-SEVEN

U.S.S. ALLIANCE

2377

". . . and so," Ruanek continued steadily and at a slow, careful, measured pace, "as cannot be doubted from the linguistic evidence I have just related, the relatively modern Romulan term of 'Honor Blade' comes down to the modern Romulan language directly from Late Pre-Surak Vulcan through the time of the Sundering, and just as clearly referred originally not to the blade that is currently worn by all Romulans of rank, but to one of the many knives that were used by the te-Vikram priests to grant quick and merciful death to injured foes or slower death to ritual victims."

"Are you finished yet?" Tomalak all but snarled at him.

Ruanek merely held up a hand for silence, his face as tranquil as that of a true Vulcan. Or, Spock thought, as that of a lecturer who was used to the demands of the Vulcan Science Academy—which, of course, in addition to being a martial arts instructor, Ruanek was.

"And that usage in turn," Ruanek continued, showing no

apparent signs of fatigue or vocal strain even though he had been speaking—or lecturing, rather, Spock corrected silently—for several shipboard hours by now, "leads us logically to the use of the term 'Manil Arek,' as it is said in archaic Vulcan. The term is no longer to be found in the modern Vulcan language, although a consensus of linguistic historians states that the term can best be translated as the 'Swift Death.'

"However, that archaic term must logically still have been in use at the time of the Sundering, since a form of it does appear in modern Romulan, although over the centuries it has, in modern street Romulan, become 'Ma'l Arik,' which is, of course, a slang term for murder, and as such has lost its ritual status."

"What has all this linguistic nonsense to do with the subject of honor?" Tomalak asked impatiently.

But Ruanek merely held up a hand for silence once more, with the air of a patient but determined lecturer who was being forced to deal with an unruly student (sending the slightest ripple of amusement through Spock, who knew Ruanek to be many things, patient not being one of them).

"And that, in turn," Ruanek continued, "leads us to the concept of the ritual death that was once, if the records are correct, delivered to the ancient Vulcan criminals and still lingers in the form of the modern Romulan penalties for such crimes as high treason—"

"Which you will face," Tomalak cut in, *"if you continue to keep up this ridiculous flow of words rather than providing a logical Right of Statement and—"*

"Captain Saavik," Lieutenant Suhur said suddenly, "a Starfleet communication is coming in, ship-to-ship."

"On-screen," Saavik ordered.

First the image of a very familiar ship formed on the viewscreen: It was none other than the current incarnation of the *Enterprise* itself. Then that sight faded and an equally familiar image formed as an equally familiar voice announced, *"This is Captain Jean-Luc Picard of the U.S.S. Enterprise."*

Saavik gave Spock a quick sideways glance, as if to say, *You knew he was coming, didn't you?* It was true enough, so Spock merely dipped his head slightly to her in agreement. Saavik said, "Greetings, Captain Picard. This is Captain Saavik of the *U.S.S. Alliance*. It is quite agreeable to see you again."

"*Alliance, we see that you're caught in something of an awkward situation.*"

"As you say," Saavik replied tranquilly to that deliberate understatement.

"Good timing," Ruanek murmured to Spock. "I was beginning to get heartily sick of my lecture."

"I'm sure that Commander Tomalak feels the same," Spock returned without expression, and caught a hint of Ruanek's customary almost-grin.

"Picard," Tomalak exclaimed, sarcasm fairly dripping from his words. "*Just what this situation needed to make it perfect. I might have known that there would be a greater Starfleet presence here to interfere with legitimate Romulan concerns—and that it would be* you *who would turn up again to bother me.*"

"*I could say the same about you, Tomalak,*" Picard answered without rancor. "*I'm sure we could debate that you have come with 'legitimate Romulan concerns,' since you are here not in Romulan territory but on the edge of Vulcan space. However, that is not the main issue just now.*" His voice sharpened, turning suddenly cold and crisp, the voice of the true leader. *"I assure you, Commander, that the* Enterprise *is not here by chance. You and Captain Saavik both need to know this: an emergency condition now exists for the Romulan Star Empire."*

"What foolishness is this?" Tomalak asked sharply.

"No foolishness at all, Tomalak. Praetor Neral has been taken prisoner."

Numerous explosions of disbelief interrupted him, from Ruanek, from the Romulans, even from the two Klingon privateers.

"Impossible!"

"This can't be true!"

"Who would dare—"

"How was it done?"

"It was done by Federation treachery!" Tomalak's savage shout cut in through the noise.

"Watraii treachery, actually," Picard said calmly, and there was sudden tense silence. *"Of course you—all of you—know that the Praetor visited the Federation world of Pacifica for unofficial Romulan-Federation negotiations. But what at least some of you may not know is that those negotiations broke off without warning, and Praetor Neral left suddenly. His intentions remain somewhat unclear, since Praetor Neral's course seems to have been taking him toward the Eridani sector of space rather than back toward Romulan territory."*

"Just a coincidence, of course," Ruanek murmured sardonically to Spock, who raised an eyebrow at him.

"What is known for certain," Picard continued, *"is that before the Praetor could reach his intended destination, whatever it might have been, his flagship and entourage were intercepted by Watraii ships in a surprise attack. Apparently the Praetor's flagship and guard ships were destroyed in that*

attack before they could fully defend themselves. But Starfleet has learned that Praetor Neral himself was, indeed, beamed aboard a Watraii ship."

How Starfleet had received that information was obvious, Spock thought: There must have been a Starfleet agent aboard one of the Romulan ships, possibly aboard the Praetor's flagship itself. Politics as usual, as he'd heard humans put it, in the post-Dominion age.

Picard paused ever so briefly. *"The news has not been made public, either to the Federation or to the Romulan Star Empire, and I'm sure you can see why it has not. I'm also sure that you both, Captain Saavik and Commander Tomalak, see the need for a swift, secret rescue."*

"We *see* it," Captain Tor'Ka cut in with a roar of a laugh. *"Romulan he may be, but a leader of his people, even a Romulan leader, deserves something more honorable than a cowardly kidnapping!"*

"This all sounds just a little too convenient," Commander Tomalak snapped, ignoring the Klingon outburst. *"How do we know that this story is true and isn't some Federation trick?"*

"You do not," Spock answered. "But logically, Commander, you have only two choices. Either you accompany us now to rescue Praetor Neral, or you stay here and risk both a war with the Federation and the abrupt ending of your career when the Romulan Star Empire learns that you abandoned your Praetor to the Watraii."

There was a long pause during which, presumably, Tomalak was picturing his career going down in the flames of disgrace and himself named as a traitor. Then the Romulan said grudgingly, *"You argue convincingly, Vulcan. We shall accompany you. But if this is, indeed, a trick, you shall not survive it."*

Josepha Sherman & Susan Shwartz

"Threats," Spock blandly stated, "are illogical."

Ruanek, who had, after all, served as Sarek's aide on Earth and knew almost as much about the late ambassador as Spock himself, finished wryly, "And payment is usually expensive."

This time he ignored Spock's raised eyebrow.

The irony to both Captain Picard and Commander Tomalak that after so many years and so many encounters they were now, for the first time, actually going to be working on the same side could not have been lost on either of them.

"Ah, Captain Picard?" said Lieutenant Commander Data, who had been quietly staying at an aft science station. "Permission to come aboard."

Picard must have been wondering what the android had been doing aboard the *Alliance,* but all he said was a very carefully neutral, *"Granted. It will be good to have you back on board, Commander."*

Data rose from his seat. "My leave can now be said to be officially over. Thank you, Captain Saavik, and everyone else on board the *Alliance* for the hospitality."

"You are quite welcome," Saavik returned as calmly as though there never had been that covert operation to recover the artifact and Admiral Chekov. But to Picard she said, "Unfortunately, Captain Picard, we have a few problems. Aboard the *Alliance* just now are both Admiral Pavel Chekov and Captain Montgomery Scott, names you undoubtedly recognize."

"Indeed," Picard said with surprise.

"Admiral Chekov may be a strong man regardless of his age, but he is surely in no shape for another mission, not so soon after his time as a Watraii prisoner. If you do not know about that issue, I fear I cannot enlighten you about it just now. In addition, though, after all that the *Alliance* and its crew have just undergone," she added, just barely keeping the proper Vulcan self-control in her voice and on her face, "I now have a tired crew and a ship that is without a doubt in need of overhaul."

Spock could hardly fault his wife for her barely controlled burst of frustration, nor for her very clear concern for her crew and ship. "There is a very logical solution," Spock said. "With Captain Picard's permission, Ruanek and I will join Mr. Data in beaming aboard the *Enterprise,* together with the artifact," Spock added for Tomalak's benefit, "so that there can be no accusations of trickery. The *Alliance* will then be free to continue on to Vulcan. And the *Enterprise,* with its greater size and, should such become necessary, its greater firepower, shall aid you, Commander Tomalak, in rescuing Praetor Neral."

"We are not going to allow this," Tomalak said stubbornly, *"not with all that is at stake—not without, at the very least, a Romulan observer aboard the* Enterprise.*"*

"What did you think we were going to do?" Ruanek asked sardonically. "Hand the artifact over to the Watraii?"

Tomalak glowered at that, but before he could answer, Saavik cut in, "It seems only logical that there is already a Tal Shiar agent aboard my ship."

"That is hardly the—"

"Please, Commander. Don't even try to deny it. How else but through a spy would you have known that we had changed course for Vulcan? But I make no accusations, since the times are as they are."

"It seems to me," Picard cut in, *"that you have no choice, Tomalak, nor any real bargaining power. We have the artifact, and you don't know where to find Praetor Neral. Every moment spent here means that the Watraii have had that*

much more time to get safely away. So come, be sensible, take back the agent, and I will accept one *observer on my vessel.*"

That the observer would also be a Tal Shiar agent seemed almost certain to all—but this would at least be an overt, not covert one, an agent who could be watched.

"So be it," Tomalak muttered, and echoed with a sardonic half smile, *"One observer only."*

"Attention," Saavik announced to the entire crew. "One of you is not of Starfleet. I offer you this: You shall neither be harmed nor imprisoned, and you shall be transported aboard Commander Tomalak's ship. You are to report to the transporter room at once. I repeat: Report to the transporter room at once."

Getting to her feet, she said, "Lieutenant Abrams, you have the bridge. Spock, Ruanek, Mr. Data?"

Together, they all headed to the transporter room. Ruanek, as seemed only proper, held the artifact in reverent arms. On the way, Saavik ordered security to meet them there.

The one who stood straight-backed and cold-eyed was hardly a likely choice for "Tal Shiar agent." She was, or seemed to be, young, blonde, and human.

"Ensign Tara Keel," Saavik said, and Spock caught the faintest hint of surprise in her voice. "I must say that I did not think you to be the agent."

"I am not Tara Keel," the Romulan agent said with clear distaste. "I am T'Gara, loyal agent of the Romulan Star Empire, and my mission here is complete."

No doubt, Spock considered, there would be some quiet investigations on both sides as to the fate of the genuine ensign, and some efficient cover-ups of the facts for the sake of keeping smooth Romulan-Federation relations.

I trust that someone will at least notify her family, Spock thought, *and possibly even be relatively humane about it.*

He made a mental note to make certain that it had been done after this mission was completed.

Spock and Saavik could make no emotional parting, of course, but as he and Ruanek stepped onto the transporter plates, he heard her murmur to him, "Parted and never parted. Go safely, my husband."

"Go safely, my wife."

In the next instant, the familiar shimmering and sense of nowhere, nothing engulfed him. When that second of non-reality was done, Spock, Data, and Ruanek stepped off the transporter platform onto the *Enterprise.*

Along with a security detail led by the *Enterprise*'s security chief, a blonde lieutenant, Jean-Luc Picard was waiting to greet Spock. "Mr. Ambassador."

"Captain Picard. It is agreeable to see you again."

Turning to the android, the captain said, "Mr. Data, welcome home."

"Thank you, sir," the android said with a smile.

But now Picard was staring past his second officer. "Ruanek?"

Ruanek, who had been reluctantly handing over the Romulan artifact to the security chief, turned to face the captain with his almost-smile.

"Indeed. Captain Picard, we do seem to run into each other at some very odd times."

Spock recalled that he and Ruanek had been rescued by Picard and his then-command, the *Stargazer,* as "Romulan refugees," a time Spock remembered not at all.

At that moment, though, a new figure beamed aboard. This new arrival, looking utterly unperturbed about now being on a Starfleet vessel, was clearly the Romulan "observer," a tall, lean, narrow-faced, cold-eyed man who identified himself curtly: "Laratos."

"That may, indeed, be your name," Spock commented. "I doubt, however, that as such it is your entire rank."

Laratos gave him a keen, sharp, calculating glance. Spock looked back at him just as steadily but without hostility and continued. "I note, for instance, that your bearing lacks the proper rigidity of a member of the standard Romulan military, and your uniform, while perfectly fitted to you, is not quite a second skin to you and therefore not that which you are accustomed to wear. You may be honest with us, sir. I assure you that we shall not betray you to your agency."

"You are Spock," the Romulan said coldly.

"I am."

The Romulan dipped his head ever so slightly in acknowledgment of one clever agent to another. "No other Vulcan but you would possibly be at the same time so observant and so knowledgeable of Romulan ways and behaviors. Very well, Ambassador Spock, I will admit this much to you. I am *Colonel* Laratos."

He didn't add, "Of the Tal Shiar." Such a detail as that was hardly necessary; they already knew what he was.

On the *Enterprise*'s bridge, Spock was invited to sit at the captain's left—a seat normally taken by the ship's counselor—while Commander William Riker sat at Picard's right. Ruanek took up position next to the tactical station alongside the security chief, whose name, Spock learned, was Christine Vale.

"I must confess to a certain uncertainty about our chances of overtaking the Watraii," Spock began.

"I feel the same way." Picard frowned. "They do, after all,

have quite a head start. And they do have full warp speed capability."

"They were able to keep up with us at nearly warp eight," Ruanek added, "although they could not quite overtake us."

Spock noted with the faintest touch of wry humor that Picard did not ask either of them for numerical advice about their chances.

Presumably, Spock thought, *he does not want to hear the odds against us figured down to the power of ten.*

But the fears of not overtaking the Watraii vanished in an instant.

"There is a Watraii fleet dead ahead," Data announced. "Fifteen ships."

Fascinating, Spock thought. *Why didn't the Watraii ship holding Praetor Neral simply flee? But . . . there is that intriguing fact that they never were able to quite overtake us during our flight from their planet.*

Can they, perhaps, achieve such extreme speed only for brief bursts? And are they now, as they did once before, focusing all their power on defense rather than on flight?

It seemed highly probable. Whatever their situation, though, the Watraii fleet could hardly have been placed where it was by chance. The ships were clearly positioned in a three-dimensional format that put them, no matter what moves the *Enterprise* and its allies might make, between them and the ship that was holding the Praetor.

The implication was obvious: If they were going to be able to get close enough to Neral to rescue him by any means, without the danger of interference literally scrambling his atoms, they were going to have to fight the Watraii.

"Another battle!" Captain JuB-Chal shouted gleefully.

Captain Tor'Ka added, *"Captain Picard, you are a brave war leader, and we honor you!"*

Picard's mouth tightened ever so slightly at that "war leader," but he said only a neutral, "We shall do what must be done."

But Spock warned, "Morality aside, there is a clear danger if we do fight, and not merely to us. We must ask ourselves this: If we open fire, will the Watraii kill Praetor Neral?"

"He is the most valuable hostage they could hope to hold," Picard said. "It would hardly make sense for them to kill him."

"They may decide that a hostage is not as important to them as the artifact," Spock countered.

"It is a gamble," Commander Tomalak agreed grimly. *"But it is one that, no matter the outcome, must be taken. The Watraii cannot be allowed to hold Praetor Neral a prisoner. So be it. We must fight."*

"Wait," Spock ordered. "There is always another option."

"Such as what? Talk?"

"Negotiate."

Picard said, "It's worth a try. Lieutenant Vale, open a channel to—"

"This is nonsense!" Commander Tomalak snarled. *"There can be no negotiations with those creatures!"*

In a double burst of energy, his flagship opened fire on the Watraii.

TWENTY-EIGHT

SARISSA'S STORY

The hatches slammed shut on what Sarissa knew would soon be a battleground, her father's last fight.

She raced toward the cargo ship, driving the spikes on the soles of her heavy boots into the ice with the skill of long practice. There had been a storm the "day" before. The footing would be treacherous.

At least, this would be the last time she would have to come this way! She would be free, or she would be dead.

The need to choose the safest footing, to seek the trail marks her people had created in their years of slavery, proved to be a mercy. It all but crowded out the final, unbearable moment when she realized her father had decided to remain behind and trade his life for her people's. For hers.

By now, she knew, he was probably dead, killed protecting his children from the murderer race, just like her mother. At last, they were together as Karatek had wanted more than anything else.

But all the logic in the universe could not make it easy for her to bear.

The veils fluttered over Sarissa's eyes, but she mastered

them. The surface was too treacherous to allow herself the self-indulgence of tears. Mourning would come later, and after that, remembrance.

And vengeance.

Over her head, her helmet lights glowed the somber red of the Forge, illuminating the hazards that remained between her and the ship. Sometimes, even after all these years, she still saw Vulcan in her dreams. Now, the image was mingled with a blood-green rage she had neither the time nor the desire to suppress.

Sarissa could see the cargo ship's lights, turned into a greenish white blur by the wind-driven, poisonous sleet. She could see no name, only a number. Even the ships the murderers sent were like convicts shipped off to the ice to be worked to death. They had no names, and therefore no meaning. Their value lay only in what they carried.

But this ship had immense meaning now. If Serevan had not managed to secure it, their escape attempt could be measured in minutes, not years.

Its ramp was down, and figures were stumbling toward her. She recognized their suit markings as belonging to the murderer race. Any guards who had survived the revolt had been cast out onto the ice. Serevan had succeeded, but his wife had no time for exultation.

Without breaking stride, Sarissa watched contemptuously as they struggled through winds that were scarcely gale force. They would use up their air before they reached the airlocks.

Was it her concern if they were incompetent and weak?

The wind was picking up. Even if the engineers had completed initial thruster modifications, takeoff would be rough. The people trapped outside would burn, and she would be responsible.

It was one thing if the planet to which the guards' masters had consigned their brothers and sisters killed them. But Sarissa did not want her people to be responsible for their deaths. Beginnings, as Surak said, were important. Even S'task had agreed.

Activating her suit's com system, which Serevan had boosted to command grade, she shouted. "Run, you *veruul!* Get below with the other murderers or we'll burn you where you stand, assuming you last that long!"

As wind buffeted her, she crouched, lowering her center of gravity, but keeping her pace. Not too far to the left was ice. Below it, she knew, was a pool. The ice would be thin. If she were blown off her feet, she would land there, and she would break through.

Look! Someone had tumbled, was rolling on the ice toward the fog that meant an open pool of liquefied gas. Would his fellows come to his aid? She doubted that any of the murderers had that sort of unit cohesion. Slave-driving, yes. Bloody-mindedness, politics, greed—but not honor enough to risk themselves rescuing a comrade.

If she gave the fallen guard a hand, he might pull her down along with him. The ice was treacherous here, ridged and thin, with old cracks slicked over. They could both wind up flash frozen in the nitrogen pool that steamed through fissures in the snow.

She didn't want to save them.

Let them *die,* she thought.

Then she thought of her father. Karatek had sacrificed the last of his life to give her people their chance at freedom. He would have taken the risk of helping an enemy. Wasn't that how he had spent his entire life?

Ducking hail that fell thick, hard, and fast enough to damage her suit if it hit a critical point, Sarissa drew her disruptor, ran over to the fallen guard, and reached out a hand to grab his gauntlet.

"Get below!" she ordered again. She pointed with her chin at the lights above the entryway.

"Don't leave us here!" the hearthworlder demanded. He looked around, desperation obvious even in eyes shadowed by his helm. Sarissa looked up at the frost plumes rising from the ground, the eruptions of nitrogen geysers, the cracking ice. An avalanche grumbled down from the ridge at the horizon. It seemed to take forever to fall, landing in billows of frozen nitrogen that drifted in the frigid air, producing pale billows and giant floating crystal formations.

Overhead, the tiny moons that orbited the unseen murderers' world shone distant and cold, bright in the eternal night of the dark side.

"Don't leave us. We'll die if we stay here!"

"Then pray you die quickly," Sarissa told the man she had steadied. She glanced at the oxygen gauge prominently displayed on his tank. Less than two minutes. "If freedom is as dead in your heart as honor, run. Run, if you can, and live. If you can call that life!"

The man screamed a war cry at her and lunged, grabbing for her hand, determined, if he must die, to take her with him. Murderers, all of them. There was no point in showing them decency. Karatek had never understood.

"Sarissa! They're pulling in the ramp!" one of her companions shouted.

Sarissa chopped her hand down upon her attacker's wrist. She twisted free, then tugged, sending her would-be killer staggering onto the thinnest part of the ice. It shattered, plunging him half in, half out of the pool of freezing, deadly gas.

He had less than a minute to know what was going to happen. Definitely not long enough to suffocate before he froze. If the others ventured out, and sooner or later, they would have to, let them see his twisted, frozen body lying alongside their path.

Perhaps the Romulans would turn *them* into slaves. How else could their precious quotas be met?

"Sarissa!"

Serevan's voice. Her consort. He could call her back from the Womb of Fire, and she would answer.

Her heart pounding in her side until it was one agonized thrum of effort, she ran. Could she reach the ship in time?

"Sarissa, run!"

She had given strict orders for the ship not to delay. The storm was building up, she couldn't make the speed she needed . . . there!

Just as the ramp was being drawn back into the ship, she leapt for it. As it withdrew, she hit it, fell, and slid inside the airlock.

Serevan was waiting for her as it cycled open. Catching her hand, tugging off her helm, he pulled her out of the darkness into what felt like incredible warmth, drawing her up against him with that extraordinary strength of his. She permitted herself to rest against him for a precious, wasted instant that he could have been using to retrofit some instrument. When he did not recoil from the coldness of her envirosuit, she pushed away; no need for her consort to risk frostbite.

"Secure for takeoff!" she shouted into the com set into a bulkhead. Then, as she struggled out of her envirosuit, she demanded of Serevan, "Why did you not leave me?"

"Your question is illogical," Serevan replied with a flash of

271

mischief. "I have become too used to your company after all these years to sacrifice it now."

Sacrifice.

That reminded them both.

"I grieve with thee," Serevan murmured. His hands went out toward her shoulders, then fell. Now was not the time.

She blinked furiously. On Vulcan, tears were a waste of the body's moisture; on the ice, they froze the skin. And they clouded her vision at precisely the time she needed to be most alert to escape. They had to assume that the murderer race would send ships to retake them.

Karatek had been old. He had lived an eventful and honorable life. She had become too used to his company to sacrifice it, yet sacrifice it she had.

But Serevan was right. Now was not the time.

"Did you get it safe on board?" she demanded.

They both knew what "it" was. Sarissa might have been cheated of her father's coronet, but T'Olryn's gift, a sphere containing the Vulcan genetic code, was a greater treasure by far if their race were to continue on a new world.

The stolen ship was creaking and groaning up off the ice.

"Grab a handhold and wait till we're out of the atmosphere before you go to the controls!" Serevan ordered.

"What about you?"

"I must get to engineering."

"My place . . ." Always keeping one hand for the ship, Sarissa made what haste she could toward the ship's command center, banging against bulkheads, staggering, as the ship struggled to gain altitude in the high winds of the upper atmosphere. Then, they had passed the worst of it. The ship's course smoothed so quickly that she slammed into one more bulkhead.

By the time she reached the command center, the ship had crossed the terminator dividing the ice from the sun. She flinched, then forced herself to look at the light. Her eyes were dazzled at its beauty.

She was unused to naked sunlight. Logically, that had to be the reason for the tears that poured down her face.

They had buried Solor's Honor Blade with him. Karatek's crown had fallen into the hands of the murderers. But Sarissa had Vulcan's genetic legacy.

Perhaps T'Olryn had not been able to come herself. But she had sent a great gift in her place.

"Commander!" cried T'Mirek, sitting in the communications officer's chair that Sarissa had once occupied on board *Shavokh*. "They must have signaled for help."

"We'll help them," Sarissa murmured. "All the way to the ice."

During the long voyage out from Vulcan, the peerless engineers who had built the generation ships had mechanized them so they could be run by minimal crew. Though they had held thousands, several hundred trained individuals could serve one of the ships as crew—even one in as bad condition as this one. It was smaller. It had proved easier to win, and it could be crewed with far fewer.

The battle to take the ship had waged from compartment to compartment, deck to deck. Even as they won an area, they began to refit it. After all, they were used to hard labor, and they had had years to refine their plans.

"What of ship's weapons?"

"Adequate. Barely," said N'Livek, their newly constituted weapons officer.

"Are any of the new weapons operational?" she called down to engineering.

"Disruptors and torpedoes," came Serevan's voice. *"I am unsure about the plasma. And I am still installing the experimental—no, no, not like that!"*

She palmed intraship communications off. This was not a time to talk, but to fight.

Their eyes were fire. Their blood was fire.

After all those years, all those deaths, their vengeance was only logical.

No matter how long it took.

"Let the murderers think we have only what weapons we took from them," Sarissa said. "How many ships did they send after us?"

"One cargo transport, now coming into range," said N'Livek. "Two . . . three . . . five shuttle-class vessels, and three of those single fighters."

They would have their work cut out for them.

"Wait until the first ship is in range."

The enemy cargo ship turned fighter turned and sped toward them. It was newer and in far better condition than their own vessel, poor nameless slave that it had been.

Well, the murderers only thought they had turned their cousins into a race of slaves. Slaves they had been, but they were slaves who could fight. And they had desperation and blood oaths on their side.

"Ship within range now."

"Fire at will."

Serevan had done his work well. Fire lanced out from the weapons ports, impaling their enemy until it burned through to critical installations and the ship exploded.

N'Livek shouted in victory, a cry as old as Vulcan's Forge.

"Silence!" Sarissa demanded.

"Commander!"

Odd to hear that title and know it had to mean her.

"More ships. Those solo fighters can move!"

"Head for the edge of the planetary system. Maximum speed."

They had loaded this stolen ship with immense reserves of crystals, of fuel. They could outlast their enemies. But heavily laden as they were, they could not outrun them.

"They're overtaking us! We'll be within range in ten seconds . . . nine . . ."

"Kroykah! Come about," Sarissa ordered. "Ships on visual. Extreme magnification."

That was, she saw almost instantly, a mistake. Each of the ships coming to kill them or force them back to the ice bore a sigil she remembered from her earliest days. A *sehlat.* A *lematya.* A *s'gagerat* with waving, deadly tendrils. A *kylin'the* in bloom.

Some symbols made N'Livek catch his breath, while others were new to them all, possibly drawn from the murderers' stolen world.

There was even a *shavokh.* How could she bear to fire on that?

Then she saw the different House signs each ship also bore. For all she knew, these were warring parties, united only in their determination not to lose their slaves.

Karatek might have repudiated Surak, but he had still refused to fight until the very last. Illogical. Her father had been a great and good man, but he was not always right. Logic, they had found, was a bad master. But it would make a very good servant now.

Inspiration struck, or, perhaps, a deadly sort of logic that was new to her.

"We'll try to divide them, get them to turn on each other,"

Sarissa said. "Each of you, open a channel to a different ship. Call out to it, tell each one you're authorized to strike a bargain, but only with that ship's government. Let's see if they'll attack each other!"

And then, because the most terrible thing had to be said and might have to be done, she added, "Hold off. If any ship tries to flee, destroy it."

As her crew flinched from the firefight, Sarissa made herself watch. She must become accustomed to the brightness.

Now, only one ship remained undamaged. It seemed to be moving fast.

That was only because it was so immense.

Day and night! Those murderers had pulled one of the generation ships out of orbit around Romulus and sent it after them.

The murderers might mean nothing to her but an opportunity for vengeance, but how could she fire on one of the ships of their exile?

Very easily indeed, she found.

"Fire at will," Sarissa ordered, her voice toneless. She had to set an example.

That ship was fast. Clearly, engineers had retrofitted its engines, using her father's designs. Murderers, thieves who stole only the best.

"Serevan!" she cried. "Can we fire the plasma bombs?"

"If we come to a full stop," he said. *"Otherwise, the power drain . . ."*

"Can we survive it?"

A pause. Serevan was calculating the odds. No time to wait for his slower, more careful thought processes to tell her the wisest course.

"Fire!" Even Sarissa heard the warbird's fury in her voice.

Their ship lurched, staggered like a guard on the ice, then came to a full stop. The lights darkened. Below, the children must be screaming in fear, but they were still Vulcan children and would swiftly master themselves.

"Do we have power?" she demanded.

Her navigator shrugged.

"Divert from life support." They were used to cold, to thin air. She hit intraship communications again. "Take hold, my own."

Even gravity could be sacrificed for a time.

She could feel the engines shuddering through the deckplates, hear the grind and whine of their struggle to build up speed. The noise built up and up, and the ship trembled, yet seemed fixed in this part of space as if caught, itself, in a *s'gagerat*'s web.

Sarissa didn't need to know that if this went on, they faced a choice: shut the engines down or let them go critical and explode.

Wait until that ship is in range. At least we can take it with us, she told herself.

Better dead than enslaved. If they returned to the ice this time, it would be because they had surrendered, not because they were betrayed.

A cry of victory echoed through intraship communications. Never, in all their years together, had Sarissa heard Serevan shout that way. She pressed her lips together lest she smile, as the engines lurched one final time before sending them smoothly on their way to the system's edge. At this rate, their stolen ship might even earn itself a name.

"That power surge boosted our speed, Commander," said navigation. "We're making . . . no . . . dropping back. And that ship is coming up on us again."

"Which ship?" Sarissa demanded.

"Rea's Helm."

S'task's own; flagship of the exile. Damn it to the ice. It stood to reason that they would send the flagship after them now that their own *Shavokh* had been cut to scrap.

"It's firing on us!"

Superfluous, Sarissa thought.

She fought not to be flung from her chair. Others were not so fortunate.

Sarissa had not, it seemed, factored all available variables into her calculations. For example, she had not expected that the murderers would send one of the ancient generation ships against them. Her own ship, likely to remain nameless given the probable brevity of its life, could outlast any other ship sent against them if it was properly fueled and kept repaired. But as it flew now, it was no match for *Rea's Helm.*

"Evasive," she ordered.

Further strain on the engines, but perhaps they could lose the other ship.

"Leaving the system, Commander."

Navigation's voice was heavy. Was T'Aloren old enough to remember the relief and joy with which they had entered the system? No knife could cut deeper.

Rea's Helm sent massed disruptor fire against them.

Mercifully, it missed. But its weapons officer would soon get their range.

"Message coming through from *Rea's Helm,* Sarissa," T'Mirek said.

Sarissa knew what that meant. It was the order to stand down, to prepare to be boarded.

The time had come to decide whether to blow up the ship

as well as *Rea's Helm,* with all its history. It seemed logical to get as many as possible within range.

"Ship's opening fire!" N'Livek reported.

"Evasive!" Sarissa ordered.

They lurched from side to side. Ship's gravity fluttered. If they had had time to retrofit the entire ship, they might have been able to sustain fire from *Rea's Helm,* but they hadn't had the time. They were out of time.

Nevertheless, Sarissa ordered the ship to alter heading slightly, avoiding an area of space that looked—there was no other way to describe it—strange. If it were cloth, she would have said it was fraying.

From outside the compartment came pounding, then a grating sound as someone struggled with the doors. Grudgingly, they slid apart. It took only two steps in the light gravity for Serevan to propel himself to Sarissa's side and take hold of the back of her chair.

He should have remained at his post, she thought. But his first loyalty had always been to her. They would die together.

But there was no sorrow, no resignation in her consort's eyes, only the curiosity, even the mischief, with which he approached any new technical challenge.

"Do you remember from the exile," he asked Sarissa, "the stories about how you could create a wormhole? How whole ships could disappear into one and be translated to another region of the galaxy?"

Sarissa simply looked at her mate. Had he gone mad? She remembered the loss of seven ships.

"Signal coming through from *Rea's Helm.* As we expected. Stand down and prepare to be boarded," T'Mirek said.

"Shall I open the self-destruct?" asked N'Livek.

"I came up here to tell you"—Serevan's voice, so close to

her ear, was almost tender—"that we have two of the experimental verteron torpedoes on board. I loaded them before I came up here."

"You told me those things would probably implode upon launch," Sarissa whispered.

"Our tests were in atmosphere," Serevan said. "The atmosphere of our prison, at that. Launched into hard vacuum, however, and into space where the space-time fabric looks ready to tear . . ."

His eyes warmed as they always had when he was hatching a plot. "At any rate, what do we have to lose?" He pushed over to navigation, displacing T'Aloren, his big hands moving on controls as if on a lytherette as he set their new course.

"Rea's Helm on final approach, Sarissa," T'Aloren leaned across him to report. "Its disruptor ports are open. All of them."

Whoever captained that ship had to know that she would not surrender, would not go back. Now *Rea's Helm* sought only to kill and to kill quickly. That was, she supposed, honor of a sort.

Very well. In return, she would try not to kill him with this final attempt at escape.

"Alter heading," she ordered. Remarkable how composed her voice sounded.

Her screens showed the shifting colors, the distorted starview of this part of space.

Would *Rea's Helm* follow them? She had a nightmare image of their enemy pursuing them forever, locked in the time-bind of a wormhole. She couldn't let the ship get that close!

"Fire verteron torpedoes," Sarissa commanded.

It was the last throw of the dice. Her tormented ship

lurched again. As the verteron torpedoes streaked out into the long night of this second exile, Sarissa leaned forward. More than anything but their freedom, she would have liked to lean against Serevan's shoulder in that moment, but her mate's attention was glued to ship's instruments and the viewscreen that showed twin streaks of white light plunging into the rent in space.

They exploded into a conflagration she could not look at.

When the veils retracted from her eyes, she saw it: ribbons of iridescence, twisting out of the rip they had created in the fabric of space.

One gamble had worked. Now, the final one remained to be tried.

"Rea's Helm is retreating," T'Aloren reported. Her voice barely trembled.

"Want me to fire?" N'Livek asked.

It was a waste of energy they might need.

"Ahead," Sarissa whispered. "Full speed."

Now Serevan was by her side. She put out two fingers to brush his wrist, then his hand, which reached out and covered hers. For this instant, at least, she was warm.

The wormhole twisted, showing purplish white streaks of light that gaped wide to receive them.

TWENTY-NINE

ROMULUS

2377

Hiren looked about at the other four members of the senatorial fact-finding committee: Erona, the youngest of the five, looking more like a sullen girl than a politician; Turan, heavy-set and dull as rock; Serik, a sleek, pampered-looking career politician out for the easiest way to a wealthy retirement; and Muratik, solid and middle-aged, a former military man and still as fit as someone in active service. All four looked more resigned than interested or enthusiastic.

But then, the subject of this meeting was hardly a complex or controversial one, simply a matter of resolving some problems in the transport of various items of food from Xanitla, Ralatak, and Virinat to Romulus. Hardly the stuff of which heroic sagas were composed. But, Hiren thought with an inner smile, any subject, no matter how trivial, could be carefully subverted to his own purposes.

"Senators," he said, looking around the room again, "I believe that we are all in agreement. Since the end of the Dominion War, we have all become a different people, more suspicious, more wary, even, I dare say it, more fearful."

"We are not afraid," young Senator Erona cut in indignantly.

Hiren smiled paternally at her. "Ah, the fires of youth!"

"I am hardly a child!"

"No, of course you are not." *By about five years, perhaps, oh daughter of another senator and child of nepotism.* "My apologies, Senator. No insult was meant. And perhaps 'fearful' was too strong a word. But then, you are too young to remember how matters were before everything changed."

"I repeat, I am not a child! I certainly do know what things were like under the previous administration, yes, and the one before that."

"Ah, then you can understand my argument. And you, all of you, have been angry with the way the Romulan role in the Dominion War was handled." Hiren stopped just short of mentioning that it had been Neral who'd roused that anger. Let them draw their own conclusions. "We have also, all of us, been harboring a great deal of anger about the alliances that were made with the Federation. After all, now that the war is over, what has the Federation done for us?"

"You know the answer to that, Hiren," Muratik said. "I won't say that things were better under the late Praetor Narviat, who was far too liberal in his views for my taste, or under his predecessor, the unlamented Dralath, who did more to harm Romulan honor than any Praetor I can recall. But at least in both of those administrations we were not forced into the wrong side of a war we never wanted."

"Indeed we were not," Hiren agreed amiably. "Had I been in charge of the matter—which, of course, none of us here were—had I been in charge, I assure you things would have been far better."

"If you were Praetor?" Serik asked warily.

Hiren waved that off. "Oh, it is merely a theoretical question. But if I were, indeed, Praetor, let me assure you, all of you, that I would have seen to it that both the Dominion and the Federation wooed us, brought us advantages, and made it worth our while not to join either side. I would have made sure that both sides paid us, and would have kept the Empire prosperous and, with our enemies fighting each other and ending up weakened, even more powerful."

Muratik sighed gustily. "Excellent points, Hiren. Unfortunately, the current administration was not so forward-thinking."

Ah, yes, Hiren thought. *You are hooked, Muratik. And I think you may be, too, Serik and Erona.* Never mind the fact that Neral had done precisely that with the Dominion; the Romulans had signed a nonaggression pact, one the Empire broke when it was decided that the risk of Dominion invasion of Romulus was too great.

"Administrations do change," was all he said aloud.

Hiren could afford to move slowly. He had already pulled several other senators to his way of thinking. Not enough of them yet for what he planned, but they would come around soon enough. There was enough dissatisfaction in the Senate to assure that. And he had begun gently testing the military as well. Judging from what he'd seen and heard from officers and lesser nobles alike, a great many of them would come around to his way of thinking as well.

And those who would not? Akhh, he would simply leave to Rehaek the elimination of those who would not play along with him.

Levak looked even grimmer than he usually did, Charvanek thought, studying him. The young double agent still held himself with his usual straight-backed posture. But his eyes were deeply shadowed.

Charvanek fought back the urge to snap at him as though he were an erring child, *"Now* what's wrong?" No use taking out her frustrations on Levak, not when he played so dangerous a role for her. Instead, she contented herself with simply ordering, "Report."

"Commander. It has been an . . . interesting time for the Tal Shiar. Someone, and I cannot yet prove that it is Rehaek and his cohort Torath, has been carefully eliminating all those members who have shown themselves to be too closely allied to the current Praetor."

"I trust that you are being properly wary," Charvanek commented. Then she wryly balanced that moment of caring with, "I would hate to have to find another such agent. Now, give me some details."

She listened without showing the slightest expression to the list of "accidents" and more deliberate challenges and killings. Oh yes, there was no doubt about it. Rehaek, and she was fairly sure it was he, was definitely working overtime to remove all weaknesses from the Tal Shiar, which was hardly surprising for someone who almost certainly wanted to replace Koval as its chairman. That Rehaek hadn't actually assassinated Koval . . . akhh, that implied that he wasn't ready yet to make his move—or else that Koval's guards were too strong and too loyal.

But was Rehaek in league with anyone else, besides, of course, that hulking aide-cum-bodyguard, Torath? Was he working in tandem with any of the senators? Ambitious ones, of course, dissatisfied with their current status—ambitious senators such as, perhaps, Hiren?

The idea of selective assassination raised its ugly head

again. Charvanek stifled an impatient sigh. Hiren, damn his devious soul to Erebus, had still done absolutely nothing that could be defined as a crime. One could hardly have a man slain for talking to others.

Honor could be useful in its place, but right now she was finding it to be a definite problem.

I will not *murder.*

But it might not truly be murder if one were to remove a clear danger to the Empire.

Make a mistake, she silently goaded Hiren. *Make just one small, irrevocable, undeniable mistake. Give me the excuse I need to remove you from the field of play once and for all.*

As for Rehaek, whatever murders he might have committed and might still be committing within the confines of the Tal Shiar were not her concern. The more their agents died, and never mind how that happened, the less of a problem the Tal Shiar created for Romulan Security in general and herself in particular.

What Rehaek might be working outside the Tal Shiar's figurative borders, she could not say for certain. So far, he'd been very careful, but even the most careful of *zdonek* could slip. She could wait. And Rehaek was not so highly placed that he couldn't be removed.

One way or another.

She found the first surveillance device in her office so easily that Charvanek knew it had to be a false one, a distraction deliberately placed for her to find. She also knew that the thing was meant to inspire a time-wasting hunt throughout her office for the others that were surely also there.

I have aides for that. And then I can finish up with my own search.

That someone had gotten into her office to plant the device—or devices—wasn't as alarming as it might have been. Perfectly ordinary people from various branches of the Romulan government came to see her every day with honest questions or requests, and in the process of entering or leaving, someone might not even realize that he or she had been carrying someone's device that had been programmed to detach itself from an article of clothing and attach itself to, say, the underside of a desk. Charvanek had, after all, used that technique not a few times herself.

But what is Rehaek, or whoever is behind this, trying to accomplish with this? It is such a primitive form of annoyance. It can't possibly be meant as a serious form of surveillance. Is he, Rehaek or whoever, trying to distract me from something more important?

Such as what?

Something to do with Neral?

Yes. That seemed the most likely. Distract the chief of security so that you could do . . . what?

Was it something about bugging his office as well . . . no, that was too simple, and utterly useless, since his staff would routinely sweep his office for such devices before he returned. . . .

His office, though . . . what about it? What would they want her not to realize until it was too late . . . ?

Damnation!

There was no way to prove her sudden hunch but to act. A secret passage linked her office to that of the Praetor, dating from the time of Narviat, when it had, Charvanek thought with an unexpected spike of nostalgia, sometimes been used for more than affairs of state. In these later days, since Charvanek and Neral knew that neither would ever attempt to assassinate the other—not when it was far more valuable to the Empire to keep them both alive—the passage had not been blocked up. It was too convenient, since there were still those times when there were deeply urgent matters of state that needed to be conducted in secrecy.

Such as now.

Silent and careful as a stalking *rorenik,* her weapon in hand, Charvanek stole through the passage and out into Neral's office, which was a somberly elegant room of deep brown walls and blood-green draperies. Very determinedly masculine, and as free of excess ornamentation as the man himself.

But it was empty.

Good. If her hunch was correct, she was in time to stop . . . whatever was going to happen.

Charvanek seated herself at Neral's desk, which hadn't even the smallest personal item on it, and waited.

Ah, yes . . . she had guessed correctly after all. Someone was, indeed, at the door, working so softly and efficiently that she almost couldn't make out the hints that he or she was managing to override the lock.

I told you to upgrade your security, Neral. I told you that anyone with any skills at all could get in when you and your guards weren't here. Now maybe you'll actually listen to my advice.

The would-be burglar was a small, slight, and wiry man, dressed in the plain blue tunic and trousers of a Class 3 office worker—someone with the clearance to be in this part of the complex. He made his way carefully into the office, then stopped short at the sight of Charvanek—and of the disruptor that she was casually and quite steadily leveling at him.

"Jolan tru," she drawled. "I take it that you know who I am, and why I'm here to meet you."

He didn't act the way she'd expected. His eyes widened, but instead of running or trying to attack, he simply . . . bit down and swallowed.

Erebus!

Charvanek rushed to his side, but the telltale pungent aroma of *turath* told her it was already too late. *Turath* was a foolproof, almost instantaneous poison, rarely used by assassins since it was so easily scented, usually saved for merciful deaths or quiet executions. Or for suicides.

Isn't this just wonderful? she thought dryly. *Now, who were you working for, you poor fool?*

The body had conveniently fallen outside of the office. She didn't have to move it and risk disturbing any evidence. It was no surprise to her that the body gave up no obvious clues.

Charvanek first made sure that Neral's door was secure once more, and then tapped her com device once.

"Charvanek here. I want a forensics team here, just outside the Praetor's office—and I want them here now."

She knew that they would be there as quickly as they could run. She also knew that they would scan the body down to its component atoms, and if there was any evidence to be found, they would find it.

So far, there had been nothing but minor annoyances, a suicidal would-be burglar, and two deaths that might or might not have been natural. But it was time, Charvanek thought grimly, to raise the stakes. Time to hit both Rehaek and Hiren themselves with a few annoyances, and then to sit back and watch what happened.

THIRTY

SARISSA'S STORY

The ship plummeted into the wormhole. Instantly, it shuddered, buckled, and yawed in at least three dimensions at once. Decks and bulkheads groaned, and the discordant rumble of the engines pitched up to a wail that tortured Sarissa's ears. At this rate, the ship would be crushed in the void before it had even been named.

And they would be annihilated with it.

She had an instant of regret for the people on board, the dreams they still cherished, the lives they had led, even for what might be the useless torment to which her will and her will alone now subjected this ship and its passengers and crew.

Not alone. Never alone.

Serevan's mental "voice" had never sounded so clearly.

Sarissa might wish to be with all her people, but it was riches past counting that her consort was here at her side in these moments wrenched out of time and space.

She made a supreme effort to turn her head, to look at him. He was distorted, phasing in and out of shape, in and out of her consciousness. She looked down at her hand, still resting in his. At times it seemed suffused with a white light. At other times, it vanished, while at still others, she could see the blood pulsing green around dark bone and flimsy living flesh.

If you could call this life.

She tore her gaze away from her mate. Now, she could see twisted lips move. She knew people were trying to cry out, protest, restore order, at least mentally, but none of that was possible.

Was the ship operating? She still perceived; she had to assume it was, at least for now.

Her gaze blurred. It was like looking on the face of madness, with past, present, and what had to be the future or a host of alternate futures locked in mortal battle with time and space as a weapon.

She saw T'Olryn and her second brood of children, saw how their faces whitened, their temples sank in, and their eyes bulged. Their teeth sharpened, and their nails turned to claws, as savage as she felt. She saw the murderer race, her enemies who wore a face like her own, a face that, from now on, she would be ashamed to present to the universe.

She saw, yes, those were her parents, both Karatek and T'Vysse and the parents she had lost long ago on Vulcan's Forge. She had not seen their faces so clearly, even in dreams, since exile began.

Was this what the seven ships lost at the beginning of exile had encountered? Could it be that even they were still alive beyond some unimaginable event horizon? Or had their ships' engines exploded, mercifully hurling them into oblivion? Was any of this possible or even remotely sane? And how long could it last?

Terror threatened to engulf her. She could see it on the faces of her crew, turning them as pallid as the mutated Vulcans who remained beneath the ice. She could not hear herself speak, but she made herself subvocalize, think, even, a mantra of control she had learned from Surak himself.

It was not enough.

She forced her will to rekindle, as if she faced a mortal enemy and drew from the braids of her hair a tiny dagger to serve as a final weapon.

She had will, family, comrades, and—for as long as it held together—a ship.

Those things would be enough; she would *make* it so.

She felt Serevan's touch on her hand. No matter how distorted her fingers were, or his, she felt his touch.

I think we may be emerging. Serevan's "voice" worked its way through the tumult of fear, hope, and sorrow that had threatened to devour Sarissa.

Do you see?

She bent to her instruments. Chronometer and other readings were beginning to make sense once more. Her hand on the controls was honest flesh once more, of a size and shape she recognized, not transparent, compressed, or attenuated into a spectral horror.

Around her, she began to hear voices. At first, they were simultaneously fast and shrill, or booming and long-drawn-out. Even as she listened, however, they returned to their normal pitches. Her crew. Her crew's voices.

Questions and damage-control reports crackled over the main speakers. And complaints. *Very* definitely, complaints.

Her mouth was almost too dry to speak. She swallowed once, then again.

"Navigation, report."

"We're out, Sarissa. We're definitely out."

"Where are we?" she asked.

The navigator turned to Sarissa.

"I don't know," she admitted. "The stars are completely unfamiliar."

"What do you mean, you don't know?" Sarissa demanded. "At least, you can provide our relative position."

Her demand faded away as she met the navigator's eyes.

"We have no records for this sector of space. I cannot even see Vulcan from here or . . ." Even now, the navigator refused to honor the two worlds' sun with the name the murderers had given it.

"Never mind that," Serevan interrupted, turning from the control console to which he had anchored himself the instant that the ship seemed to have reached normal space. "We're breaking up!"

If only Sarissa were not so new to command.

"Damage control, report!" should have been her first thought upon reentry.

All too fast, the reports came in. Two decks reported hull breaches. Seventeen of her crew had died. Fifteen had been vented into space—and might eternal peace welcome their *katra*s! Two had died with spines snapped from the force of the ship's exit from the wormhole. The medical technicians—for they had no healers—reported finding numbers of people curled into fetal balls, rejecting the sensory chaos induced by the wormhole.

The engines were going critical, and even the restricted life support that was all the ship could muster was faltering.

So close to freedom.

There was still one thing she could do, and do better than any others of her people.

She could fight to live. She could warm them with her mind and spirit.

"Even if all of these stars are unfamiliar," she said, "you can still identify stellar classes. Look for ones that are relatively near. Try to see whether any possess planetary systems."

"System point-seven light-years from here. It's a G-type star, newer on the main sequence than . . ."

Let the name of the star they fled be blotted out, she told herself. We will start anew.

"How long till we reach it?" Sarissa asked.

"Assuming engines don't blow?"

"Assume that and that the upgrades hold up," Sarissa said, as firmly as if she could force deteriorating systems to obey her.

"You're not going to get those upgrades working, not unless you want to risk the engines going critical in three point eight days," Serevan told her.

In the months it would take to reach that system, they could die fast of an explosion or slowly of radiation, but they would die fighting.

Her eyes lit.

"It's not as if we're not used to long rides," she commented. "I want repair crews suited up, trying to patch those hull breaches. Hull integrity and engines are our chief priority, followed by astrometrics. I'll be down with the medics."

They might blow up in the next instant or survive to make planetfall.

And as long as the ship held up, it mattered not at all whether they made planetfall seven months from now or ten.

What mattered was that they try.

No, that was wrong: what mattered was that they do. The murderers had betrayed them. The people who had remained behind were no longer like them. And who knew if the people on the Mother World even survived?

What mattered was that they succeed.

And then return to mete out vengeance.

As leader, it was her duty to look in on the casualties, to sit with the injured, watch over those who had curled in on themselves, rejecting the ambiguity of the wormhole in favor of a fugue state, and to ease the dying. She was much afraid they would need *katra* bearers. Every survivor's experience was now priceless.

Above all, she had to see for herself that T'Olryn's gift, which meant the difference between a viable colony and lingering death by inbreeding, had survived the wormhole transit.

And then, her real work would begin. It hadn't proved easy to destroy or wreck or steal a ship. It would be even harder to master a new world.

THIRTY-ONE

SARISSA'S STORY

Even the dim, reddish light in the command center made Sarissa's eyes ache. She steepled work-roughened hands over her eyes, shading them. Assuming her crew of refugees could find a suitable planetary system, how would they become used to sunlight again if they could not even bear the light of the stars?

The ship was dark. Unlike the planet they had escaped, it lacked an unlimited supply of power that could be mined from the sterile rock. The ship was cold, too, as cold as the prison colony in its nightmarish first days when lying down and dying had at times seemed like the most logical alternative. The air was dry and thin, the gravity sporadic.

Even when they had been slaves of the murderers, they had not worked this hard. Work shifts had disappeared: work ended when an engineer or scientist was too tired to go on and stretched out for a few, begrudged moments of rest before another installation broke down or burned out. Children who should have been studying had been drafted to cook or to scrub the grime off dented, battered bulkheads and decks in an attempt to make the ship a reasonably healthy environment. If they lived, this journey would stand as a sort of collective *kahs-wan.*

Sarissa had seen beauty, occasionally, in the fall of snow, the formations of crystals, even the glow of the extremophiles in their volcanic or frigid habitats. She had seen beauty in the starlight over the barrier range that separated their prison from the wilderness beyond. There was nothing remotely appealing about this ship, the worst, no doubt, of the fleet and therefore the most sensible choice to ferry prisoners and cargo to a slave mining operation. At least *Shavokh,* before the murderers destroyed it, had glowed with mosaics and murals, the creative efforts of the exile.

This ship had borne only a number, not a name. It had not proved worthy of a name.

Have I made a mistake? Have I cost us all our lives?

Sarissa tightened her fingers over her eyes until light brighter than starlight exploded behind them.

There was not even a proper astrometrics laboratory. Two astronomers shared one station in the command center, studying the unfamiliar stars in this region of space. Looking for planets. Looking for a new life.

Were they wasting their time?

Where is your courage? she asked herself. *You said better dead than a slave. You planned for years to escape. You sacrificed lives, including your own father. Was all that planning necessary, or was it cowardice in the hope of avoiding this day?*

Her father had renounced Surak, Sarissa remembered. But he had never renounced logic. A civilized man living through savage times, Karatek had always resisted, even when it seemed as if he were no more than a slave driving other slaves.

That had been the difference between Karatek and S'task. S'task had crumbled, dying at the last because he had turned his back on a murderer who had proved too haughty even for a race of killers. But Karatek had always preserved a proud, independent core.

Always, when Karatek had grown weary or disheartened, he had withdrawn, either to meditate or to record his people's history in the glowing crystals of the coronet Sarissa herself had seen Surak receive upon Mount Seleya.

It should have been mine!

And yet, at the last, her father had turned even that coronet into a weapon. He had not hesitated to use it to set his children free, although it had cost him his life. Of all the insults, Sarissa thought, that was one of the smallest and hardest for her to bear. The murderers possessed the coronet that should have been hers. They controlled her people's history.

Rage washed over her, more powerful than any anger she had felt since the night when Surak knelt at her feet, requesting entry to the poor shelter that was all the home she and her brother had. Of all the people who had survived that terrible night after her first family had fallen to raiders, she was the only one who survived now.

The rage warmed her. It was, after all, logical. How many times had she rebuilt her world from the time she had been an innocent girl betrothed to Sivanon? She couldn't even remember his face now. She barely remembered the faces of the parents whose places Karatek and T'Vysse had taken. Even her own name was different.

A tech rose from the deck by navigation, stretching out muscle cramps and taking over his station once more.

Sarissa nodded acknowledgment and reached for the personal electronic slate built into the command chair. She might not have the coronet, but as long as anyone on board this ship lived—and longer still—the murderer race would not control her people's history. She began to write.

"In the escape from our prison and our passage through the wormhole into uncharted stars, we have lost track of time. We shall not do so again.

"I am Sarissa, daughter of Karatek. I command here. And I will remember."

The constant subliminal vibrations of engines and life support seemed to be running more smoothly now. So, when the doors to the command center grated open and the medical technician Syrilius entered, Sarissa set down the slate quickly.

Too quickly and with insufficient control.

She stood, steadying herself almost instantly, and leaned over to check on the astronomers' progress.

"I want to examine you," Syrilius said. "Please come below."

She ignored him.

"Please come now," he repeated.

Sarissa would have obeyed T'Olryn, if not without question, then at least promptly. But T'Olryn had remained behind with her own second family, and this young man lacked her training.

Syrilius had had the potential, though. T'Olryn had spoken well of the strength of his mind. But there had been no time and not enough adepts to raise him to healer status, and now there never would be.

Sarissa glared death, cold as the ice, at him: another sign that her control was faltering.

"Some of those who withdrew are beginning to stir," Syrilius added. "You might be able to help us rouse them."

Yes, a strong mind indeed, and a manipulative one. No wonder T'Olryn had trusted him.

"I will come," she said.

The doors grated, shutting off the barren compartment, her empty chair, the vacant screens, and her exhausted crew from her aching eyes.

The first thing Sarissa saw as she entered the cramped medical center was equipment: an ordered confusion of medical technicians and willing hands working to make an inadequate facility at least usable. The second thing was the number of her people still coiled in rejection of the impossible wormhole environment through which they had plunged.

She wandered among them, touching a hand here, a brow there, recognizing friends, extended family, reminding herself.

These are your charges, she told herself. *And if they die, their lives are on your soul.*

Syrilius trailed her, insisting she lie down, sit down, at least eat this bar of concentrate or even drink this mug of tea, and that, no, they were for her, and her alone and that she was *not* to pass this wretched excuse for a meal along to the children, who had already eaten, or the techs, who were being fed.

Then, she caught sight of the tiny, precious sphere that held the Vulcan genetic legacy preserved for them by T'Olryn. How the lights on it glowed, brighter even than her father's coronet.

This was all the inheritance that any of them needed.

But to use it properly, she must be fit.

She turned, startling Syrilius with her sudden obedience,

and stretched herself out on the pallet that he indicated. She ignored the lights and the prodding and let, at least briefly, the burden of worlds slip from her shoulders, so she might be better able to bear it when she took up her duty again.

Once again, Sarissa nodded obediently to Syrilius, who had come hunting her at her duty station.

Yes, she agreed with him. She could do no good for her people if she collapsed.

He stood over her. Once again, he watched as she ate and drank. Finally, he nodded grudging assent, and she could stop.

She gained additional approval by asking for more tea, then squandered it by standing up.

"Where do you think you're going?" Syrilius demanded. "You're off-shift until I say you're back on."

Even a healer could presume upon his status at times. Sarissa raised an eyebrow in rebuke.

Besides, where did he think she would go? She was headed for the rock and bone of the ship, the very foundations of her own existence. To engineering and her mate Serevan.

At least, she would find out from Serevan how repairs progressed, notwithstanding Syrilius's foolish statement that she had been temporarily relieved of duty. Leaders were never relieved of duty until they were dead. She would share a mug of tea with Serevan, and she would draw on his strength.

And if Syrilius wanted to call that being off duty, he could justify it any way he cared to.

It was warmer in engineering than anywhere else on the ship. Sarissa stepped to an intraship com and instructed child-care workers to shift the ship's crèche to a nearby storage facility—once it had been thoroughly scrubbed.

She basked in the warmth, then looked for her husband in the crowded installation.

Finally, she saw long, long legs stretched out beneath an installation that ticked and lit sporadically.

Had Serevan married the wrong person? If he had married a . . . less volatile woman with a less politically sensitive family, perhaps he would have been safe.

Safe where? Among the murderers? They'd have sent him to the ice within months. Besides, Sarissa would have challenged anyone who looked at him, and she knew it.

Sensing her presence, Serevan apparently gave the installation he was working beneath one last tweak, because lights fountained from it, then settled into an agreeable and symmetrical pattern. He extracted himself from beneath the console, wiped his hand on his stained tunic, and extended it, first to touch her fingers, then to enfold her hand in his and draw her down to sit beside him.

She gave him the tea. He took a ritual sip and handed it back to her to finish.

"You still need more rest," he told her.

"So you know Syrilius all but pulled me off the command deck. Were you the one who sent him after me?"

Serevan raised an eyebrow, his eyes glowing at her.

"He's capable enough to figure out for himself that we all warm ourselves at your fire. Especially me." His fingers coiled around hers and brushed the inside of her wrist, quickly, secretly. She looked down and away.

He ignored her silent protest, took the mug out of her hand and set it on the deck beside him before he began to rub the tension from her shoulders.

"Does acupressure work on engines, too?" she asked. She could feel a yawn starting.

"Indubitably. Stay where you are. I checked on the children, too. They will assist in setting up that crèche you ordered even though you have been, allegedly, relieved of duty. There is nothing else for you to do, for the moment. Rest."

The warmth, the relaxation, were like a healing trance. She could hear voices rising and fading over her head, and Serevan's voice rumbling beneath them all, lulling her. She had had her rest. She should get back . . .

"Sarissa to command center!" erupted from the bulkhead unit.

"Can it wait?" protested Serevan's voice.

"Sarissa to command center!" So much for waiting.

Sarissa pushed herself to her feet. The empty mug went rolling away. Serevan secured it before rising, in turn, more deliberately from the deckplates.

Gravity felt more stable as she headed for the com. Progress on one front.

"Sarissa to command. What is it?" She asked.

The astronomer's voice rose in excitement.

"It's planets!"

She remembered how, when the Twin Worlds were discovered, S'task had had to lean against his chief astronomer lest he collapse from the epidemic that had killed his family, much of his ship's population, and devastated him.

Sarissa, however, was able to run.

She ran, Serevan following.

It was not often a race was granted a second chance. Or a third. Or fourth.

THIRTY-TWO

U.S.S. ENTERPRISE

2377

With twin bursts of flame, Commander Tomalak's ship opened fire on the Watraii. The battle had begun.

The Watraii ships instantly retaliated. Eerie blasts of green engulfed one Romulan ship, outlining it starkly against the blackness of space. Shields held . . . but not quite long enough.

"Evasive action!" Picard told the Trill conn officer hastily.

The *Enterprise* swerved violently to one side as the Romulan vessel exploded into a yellow-white fireball.

At almost precisely the same moment, when the Watraii ship's shields were still down, the two Klingon privateers hit it from both sides. A second fireball, even more enormous than the first, sent shock waves that shook the *Enterprise* again and sent some of the smaller ships tumbling.

"This is insane," Picard said. "Lieutenant Perim! Get us out of this tangle. We are in far greater danger from those out-of-control ships hitting us than from any weaponry."

As Perim carefully maneuvered the *Enterprise* out of immediate danger, Ruanek muttered something under his breath in Romulan—Vulcan apparently lacking the rougher vocabulary he wanted—about Tomalak and lack of common sense. What bits Spock overheard were decidedly uncomplimentary.

Old feuds are not the issue, Spock thought. *Watraii motives are.*

Which was particularly true just now. Why would the Watraii be so reckless, so downright suicidal, as this when their species' numbers were already so low? Why would they risk even one precious life in combat, let alone fifteen crews' worth of Watraii?

All that he knew about the Watraii flooded Spock's mind. He put the data into order—and suddenly the answer struck Spock almost with the force of a mental blow:

This was not merely reckless behavior that the Watraii were revealing. What he was witnessing was despair, a deep and utter ingrained despair so heavy it all but overrode the will to live. These were the actions of a people who could no longer think logically about their actions, a people who had been driven to the edge of existence—but as much by themselves and their bleak discipline as by any outside source. They were a people who, as a result of what they had done to themselves, were seeing their own culture, their own reason for existing, on the verge of extinction.

And they do not know what to do to save themselves. We should not *be fighting them. We never should have fought them. Yes, they committed a terrible deed when they annihilated a Romulan colony—but that, too, could well have been the act not of a fiercely vengeful race but of one grown so desperate that morality was not even an issue.*

The Romulans, then, whatever the truth of the past, had become a symbol of all that was destroying the Watraii people.

We must do our best to help them understand both sides' points of view, to accept that both sides have a legitimate point of view, and to realize there is still hope for peace and mutual survival—or we may well see a species commit racial suicide as we watch.

As another of his ships opened fire on the Watraii—and made no impact—Commander Tomalak, in a savage burst of what Spock assumed was an overblown form of Romulan honor rather than human self-sacrifice, sent, *"Go on,* Enterprise. *Get out of here. Go get Praetor Neral back. Go, curse it! We shall hold them here."*

Spock turned to his right. "Captain Picard?"

"He's right," Picard said reluctantly. "The quarters *are* too close. And if we open fire, we could well hit an ally by accident."

"We serve a better cause by rescuing Praetor Neral," Spock said. "Tomalak made his choice."

As the *Enterprise* left the battle, Ruanek merely shrugged. Spock stared at him. It was not typical of him to be callous.

Catching Spock's glance, Ruanek said flatly, "He'll survive."

"You cannot be certain of that."

"Oh, yes I can. I know a deliberate grab for glory when I see it. And I knew Tomalak back before either of us held much rank. Trust me, Spock, Tomalak has no intention of dying or losing too many ships in such a small battle—particularly when he has two Klingon ships stealing some of that glory. Our valiant commander will manage either to destroy the enemy or to make a skillful retreat so that either way he winds up a true hero. And no, Spock," Ruanek added with the faintest touch of irony in his voice, "before you say anything else, I am not letting personal grudges get in the way of logic."

"The issue is no longer Commander Tomalak," Spock agreed. *Certainly not,* he added to himself. *There is something more important than a commander seeking glory—if Ruanek is, indeed, right: Where is the Watraii-stolen warbird? Where is Praetor Neral?* "Colonel Laratos," Spock said to the Romulan observer, "I have some difficult questions for you."

Laratos frowned ever so slightly. "Speak."

"This concerns the Watraii and stolen Romulan warbirds."

"There have been no stolen warbirds!"

"Yes," Spock replied, "I am certain that such is the official Tal Shiar statement. But if we are to find Praetor Neral, I cannot make use of political protestations, and neither can the *Enterprise* personnel. We already know that not every warbird that was attacked by Watraii raids was destroyed."

"I cannot agree."

Spock fought down a very non-Vulcan urge to shake sense into the agent. Violence was illogical, and the Tal Shiar was as it was, down to making its agents excellent at saying much and nothing in one, and there was little that could change it.

"Colonel Laratos," Spock said smoothly, "I assure you, I do not seek to dishonor the Empire. I *do* wish to save Praetor Neral's life."

It took more precious time, and more absolutely steady words and a level, fully ambassadorial gaze—the gaze that had broken down reluctant diplomats of many species before this—but at last the Tal Shiar agent's fierce stare faltered.

"Yes," Colonel Laratos admitted grudgingly, clearly hating every word he had to say, "the Watraii on occasion have, indeed, managed to steal a few Romulan ships and made it impossible for their crews to choose the Final Honor."

"I do not believe that I need to remind anyone of this," Data commented, "namely, the fact that the Watraii have already revealed themselves to be expert engineers. They have surely had sufficient time to learn all of a captured warbird's systems—including the full operations of its cloaking device."

"We must learn more as well," Spock said. Abandoning the glowering Laratos for the moment, he moved to where Geordi La Forge sat at the bridge engineering console. "May I join you, Commander?"

"Of course, Mr. Ambassador."

The two settled down to work. After a moment, Ruanek moved to Spock's side, curiosity roused, watching what they did with great interest.

"Are you a scientist?" Laratos asked in surprise at his sudden intensity.

"Hardly!" Ruanek returned honestly. "I know this much about what they're doing, though. When a ship is cloaked, it can only be detected via tachyon detection. A tachyon—"

"I know what a tachyon is," Laratos retorted. "And I know that is how one detects a cloaked ship. But this . . ." After silently watching Spock at work for a time, the Tal Shiar agent challenged him, "The *Enterprise* is but one ship. How do you plan to detect a cloaked warbird without a fleet to back you up?"

"We have no intention of doing so," Spock replied calmly. But then he pointed out on the console's screen, "There. Do you see that?"

"What?"

"There are almost infinitesimal perturbations in the deep

space 'noise' of micrometeorites, radio waves, and solar winds."

It took a few moments for Laratos to puzzle out what Spock was indicating. But then he gave the softest of comprehending hisses. "Indeed I do see it. Something is out there. Something . . . yes, something cloaked."

"Precisely," Spock said. "That 'something,' which we can safely assume is a warbird, presumably the warbird of mention, is blocking the radiation levels that are normal for that area of space."

It vanished. A distortion turned up elsewhere in the spectrum of light and sound observations. And elsewhere. And elsewhere.

"Fascinating," Spock murmured. "Clearly, the Watraii have not only analyzed the captured warbird's systems, but have begun to modify them, in the process making them more efficient."

"And more difficult for us to fight," Ruanek noted. "I mean, look at that: The vessel is obviously cloaked, but the cloaking frequency keeps shifting . . . without any clear pattern, for that matter."

"In a manner quite analogous to Borg adaptation," Spock agreed, "making detection difficult and piercing the shield almost impossible—"

"*Almost* impossible," Ruanek corrected with a hint of his Vulcan-Romulan almost-grin. "Unless, of course, one has a scientific team like you, Spock, and you, Commander Data, ah yes, and you, Commander La Forge."

"Your confidence in our abilities is flattering," Data replied, giving Ruanek an answering smile.

"Flattery," Ruanek said with great relish, "is illogical."

Spock permitted himself an instant's bemusement. During the time that Ruanek and Data had spent together stealing back the Romulan artifact, they seemed to have struck up a friendship.

That was not of importance just now. Spock returned his full consciousness to the problem at hand.

As Spock worked with Data and La Forge to, at the least, decrypt the pattern of phase sequences or, at the best, nullify the Watraii version of a cloaking device, Spock wondered aloud, "The very fact that the Watraii are still here at all, rather than having already entered their own sector, is not logical. Instead, it indicates something fascinating indeed."

"Oh, it does indeed," Ruanek agreed. "Namely, that their ship may not be functioning properly."

"Precisely."

Spock, Data, and La Forge murmured together once more, pressing controls and pointing at the console's screen.

"What are they doing now?" Laratos asked Ruanek impatiently.

"I couldn't tell you," Ruanek said with cheerful honesty. "They've gone far beyond my lay knowledge."

"Yes, but—"

"I'm a linguist, Colonel Laratos, not a physicist."

"It seems evident," Spock said suddenly, and both Ruanek and Laratos started and looked sharply at him.

"At least within a 97.58887 percent degree of accuracy," Data agreed.

Spock nodded approval. "Precisely the degree of accuracy that I was about to state, Commander."

"*What* seems evident?" Laratos said with great restraint, looking from Vulcan to android and back again.

Spock turned to look not so much at Laratos as at Picard.

"It would seem that the Watraii's ship cannot manage warp drive right now."

"That solves one problem," Picard answered. "But I assume it still does have full shield and weapons capacity."

"Unfortunately, the shields do seem to be up and functioning, apparently at full strength. Although we cannot prove this, the same can be logically extrapolated about the state of their weapons."

Spock paused, suddenly remembering something . . . something about shields . . . something from the days of the original *Enterprise* . . . something about a code . . . a prefix code . . . yes!

"There was a time, back when I served aboard James T. Kirk's *Enterprise,* when he and I used the *Reliant*'s prefix code to make it drop its shields and keep its weapons inoperative long enough for the *Enterprise* to attack."

With that, Spock looked directly, pointedly, and unblinkingly at the Tal Shiar agent.

After a stubborn moment, Colonel Laratos begrudgingly admitted, "Warbirds do have similar codes."

"And you're not precisely thrilled about admitting it, are you?" Ruanek commented. "But thrilled or not, you are going to release the prefix code of that captured warbird."

"I seem to have no choice," Laratos muttered.

"For the sake of Praetor Neral, no, not really."

With poorly concealed irony, Laratos added, "So far, for the sake of the alliance with the Federation, the Romulans have allowed the Federation to attempt to rescue our Praetor. But you are running out of time and we are running out of patience. If the Federation fails in this attempt, I will have no choice but to pass a recommendation on to the Continuing Committee to prepare for a military buildup!"

Spock, an ambassador recognizing bluster when he saw it, simply asked calmly, "Are you, then, Colonel Laratos, going to take responsibility for announcing the facts of your Praetor's capture to the Romulan people?"

Colonel Laratos, like most Romulans, Spock thought, was nothing if not pragmatic. "No, of course I am not. Very well, then." In a tone that made it sound as though he was offering them all a gift, he continued. "No more threats. I will grant you this much: What you propose, Ambassador Spock, is not only logical, but sensible and honorable. A quick attack will return our Praetor to us while making the Watraii ridiculous in death."

Picard told Colonel Laratos coolly, "We're not about to attack. Just because we are able to fight—and fight effectively—doesn't mean that we must."

Spock added thoughtfully, "And is fighting the most logical use of the knowledge we have gained? There is always another way to recover a stolen object. . . ."

It was Picard's turn to raise a brow, this time in definite confusion. "I'm sorry, Ambassador Spock, but I don't think that I'm following your train of thought."

"I am," Ruanek cut in with a touch of very non-Vulcan impatience before Spock could add anything. "Simply put: Ambassador Spock keeps them talking long enough for our people to get in, get Neral, and get out."

"That *is* the gist of it," Spock said.

He turned back to Data. "I believe that you are the best person aboard this ship to find a way of penetrating the modified cloaking effect."

Data blinked, considering. "Indeed I would seem to be, sir," the android said without false modesty.

"You need to penetrate the cloaking effect only long enough to access the ship's prefix code."

"Ah, yes, I quite understand. And with that, I shall be able to force the ship to drop its cloak, lower its shields, and lose the ability to bring its weapons online."

"Precisely," Spock said. "Once the warbird's cloak and shields are down, it should not be difficult for the *Enterprise*'s personnel to identify one Romulan amid a crew of Watraii."

Data nodded enthusiastically. "And beam him aboard—swiftly."

THIRTY-THREE

SARISSA'S STORY

"We were indeed fortunate in emerging from that wormhole near a star system containing the sort of sun that might possess planets that are at least marginally Minshara-class, and even more fortunate in the fact that it does indeed possess at least one such world. As a result, I decided that we would divert course into this system.

"We might well have made it to the next star system, but even without this diversion, it would take us 4.6 years, with no promise of habitable worlds. Serevan does not think this ship's engines can hold together 4.6 years. In fact, he projects that the strain on life support of so many more passengers than the ship was built for will cause an irrevocable breakdown of critical systems in 1.2 years and possibly much less. Chief Medical Technician Syrilius is equally discouraging. Less concerned with ship's systems than with our well-being, he says he expects crowd psychosis in a third of that time.

"Once this decision was made, our good fortune diminished considerably. Our initial survey of this planetary system indicates that the only planet in the system that is even *marginally* Minshara-*class possesses animal and vegetable life. We have seen no evidence of artifacts, but we have not yet examined this world from orbit. Our mineral assay indicates substantial deposits of light metals only. Once our supplies of crystals and ores are exhausted, that will pose a considerable challenge to our engineers, one I suspect they will appreciate.*

"Of more concern: we can indeed breathe this world's atmosphere unassisted, although Syrilius warns that our children's children will face respiratory difficulties. It is likely, however, that a cure or a genetic modification may be found. We will be able to move about on this world's surface, even live there, assuming that we can surmount its greatest challenge: violent storm systems. We think these storms result from an interaction of the world's minerals with peculiarities in its atmosphere: they should be possible to predict and, at some time in the future, to control.

"For now, however, we can only hope to withstand them. Because our shuttles are unlikely to survive entry into this world's atmosphere, we are bracing the ship's hull and reinforcing its engines in preparation for landing. Once we have actually landed, however, I do not know whether we will be able to take off again."

Immense swirls of cloud, lit by fire from within, engulfed the dorsal ridge of sharp young mountains on the continent on which Sarissa's navigators planned to land.

She thinned her lips before "Can we divert?" escaped from them. The continent they had chosen had the largest concentrations of minerals, the best sources of water, and—despite current conditions—the least devastating storm conditions anywhere on the planet.

As they continued in orbit around the planet, the storms—those storms, at any rate—disappeared. Now they saw immense, turbulent seas, smaller continents, ice caps all too reminiscent of the world from which they had fled.

"Have you been able to identify any sort of pattern to the storms?" Sarissa asked instead.

"N'Livek and I have worked out a preliminary algorithm," replied T'Mirek. The ship lurched in low orbit, then steadied as the navigator adjusted course.

"Could the storms be affecting the planet's magnetic field, causing turbulence even high above the atmosphere?" Serevan had posed the question to Sarissa the watch before. It seemed quite logical to him: after all, what was a planet but an engine that generated a magnetic field?

"Quite possibly. And the electrical discharges could be exacerbated by exposed mineral deposits."

Would they never be done with mining?

"It would be prudent," the scientist added, "to observe several more storms over our proposed landing site before we attempt to land. I could refine our algorithms, perhaps improve the probability of an uneventful planetfall."

It was the "fall" in that word that troubled Sarissa.

Sarissa began to nod, to grant the scientists the time they had requested, when engineering signaled. She shut her eyes, awaiting word that she immediately suspected would be bad.

"Life support is breaking down!" came the voice of Serevan's assistant.

"Can you make repairs?"

"I can hook it to the ship's engines," came Serevan's voice, muffled as if he were crouching beneath an installation, fighting to restore it to operation. "If I do that, we'll have no margin for error when we land."

"Projections?" she asked.

"Systems will reach critical within six hours. Of course, if I could switch off the generators, I could make repairs, but then we have no backups." Serevan paused for a long, long moment.

The eyes of the crew in the command center returned to their consoles, leaving Sarissa isolated. The decision was hers. Had to be hers.

She took a deep breath, already aware of a change in the thin, noisome air.

"Coming in to optimal range to begin descent," warned the navigator.

"Begin descent," Sarissa said.

She activated intraship communication. "We are leaving orbit," she said. "Make certain every system is secured, any breakables packed away. All children and invalids should be strapped down. Landing will be difficult, so be prepared for considerable turbulence."

Days before, Syrilius had secured the Vulcan genetic material in the most secure part of the ship. Sarissa regretted that she had had to reject his suggestion that all but essential members of the crew be sedated. If they had to evacuate upon landing, there would be too many to revive or remove in time.

She whispered a mantra of control, one of the first she had ever learned, then turned to her duties.

"Take us down," she ordered.

As the ship left orbit and began to descend into the violent atmosphere, its engines groaned, then rose to a roar.

"Screens on," Sarissa ordered.

Whatever came, she preferred to meet it with her eyes open.

Light and fire wreathed the ship as its hull temperature rose.

"As soon as we reach the thicker layers of the atmosphere, the storm will hit us," the navigator said.

"Hull charge," said Sarissa. It might serve to deflect some of the lightning they would encounter. Or it might magnify its effect. They had had limited time to build and test a model.

As the engines' roar intensified to a shriek, the ship began to shake. Engines and hull were only patched together, Sarissa thought. They had never been intended for the sorts of winds that now battered them, seeking to toss them out of the sky.

"Activate all scans," Sarissa ordered. It took every bit of control she had ever learned to keep her voice level.

As they struggled to land, scans showed them the world that would be their refuge and the home base of their vengeance in the years to come, if they survived. Its peaks were higher and sharper than either Vulcan or the Two Worlds that they had fled. They seemed to rush up toward the ship like a volley of spears.

No, it was not a beautiful world.

But it would be enough if it were not instantly deadly. Once they landed, after a time, they would no doubt find aspects of this new world that they could appreciate.

"We're taking lightning strikes," warned the navigator. "Hull charge will be neutralized in—"

Circuits exploded, a stink of fire and black smoke, quickly contained.

Sarissa snatched a breath. From now on, their lives would depend both on the skill of their navigators and how thoroughly their engineers had reinforced engines and hull.

As the ship yawed from side to side, it began to shake violently. System after system went off-line. Now, all but emergency lights went dark. Still, they plunged downward, fighting to wrestle their ship into an attitude that would allow them to land rather than crash.

Call it a controlled crash. Sarissa went flying from her chair, crashed against the viewscreen, then caught herself with arms outflung. The impact of the cargo ship with the surface of their new world crumpled bulkheads and destroyed systems.

She smelled smoke, fused circuits, and a new smell, she thought with a dull wonder, that might be the air of their new world.

They were down.

Remarkable. The viewscreen showed the smoke and fog of their landing. They had—no, she could not say they had "touched down." If they had hit any harder, they would have been smashed against the side of the mountains she saw less than a thousand meters away. High and stark those mountains might be, but they were pockmarked with caves that would make satisfactory housing, at least for the present.

"We're getting rain through a hull breach," came a cry from one of the outermost compartments. "Lightning just struck twenty-five meters away."

"Engines are gone," reported Serevan. "I can use stored power to recharge the hull. But the ship's the tallest thing in the area except for the mountains."

"Prepare to evacuate," Sarissa decided.

Crippled as the ship was, emergency systems fed off stored power. Sirens whooped and lights flashed. All over the ship, medical and security personnel began to search out those too injured to move and assist them—all except Syrilius, who had made T'Olryn's gift his personal charge. Each person carried a survival kit.

Should the ship not explode, critical supplies could be offloaded later. But for now, the most logical thing to do was to get the refugees out, reunite families, head for the high ground, and set up an armed camp in which they could last out the storm.

Sarissa had been last to enter the ship back on the ice. Now she was the last to leave it. As she struggled down a ramp knocked askew by the violence of their landing, wind and rain hit, drenching her and sending her tumbling onto the ground.

Her first impression of this new world was that its ground was rocky; its sky, although overcast, was too bright for her to look at for long; and its air reeked of smoke and ozone. Lightning seethed within the heavy cloud cover, whipped about by more than wind. The clouds opened, and bursts of red and blue fire erupted in their midst, reaching toward the upper atmosphere faster than disruptor fire.

Night and day! How had they survived that landing?

Now the thunder hit, an almost palpable wave of sound, followed by strike upon strike, from the clouds to the grounds, as if lightning sprang up like stalks of deadly grain.

Sarissa ripped a strip of cloth from her overtunic and used it to shield her eyes. A faint purple glow played about her hand.

Another peal of thunder, more terrible than the rolling waves of sound that fought with the wind and the driving rain. For an instant, she reeled from sensory overload.

Familiar, reassuring hands caught and held her. Then, Serevan set her back on her feet.

"I sent the children on ahead!" he shouted over the storm's fury.

For an instant, she allowed herself to meet his eyes and cling to him.

Tell me I have done right! she pleaded silently, and, as always, was answered.

What if this world wasn't a welcoming hearth, but an enemy with ferocious weather?

They would meet it as they had met and mastered every other hardship in their lives, his touch seemed to tell her.

And if not they, then their children.

But if there was a time for satisfaction, this wasn't it. Now, another danger faced them in the lightning that had crippled the ship as it descended.

Narrowing her eyes, Sarissa looked out across the plain. The purple glow she had seen above her hand haloed many of the people who streamed across the open ground toward the mountains.

Lightning struck again. The mountains would attract most of the strikes. The downed ship might take some of the others. But lightning was unpredictable. It might strike anywhere. And this much lightning had to hit something.

Her people were exposed.

Another set of lightning strikes. Now, she could see ball lightning form: round, slow-moving, but quick enough to hit a struggling figure and consume it before moving on to strike another.

"Get down!" Sarissa screamed. "No, don't lie down, just make yourself smaller targets. Move, move, move!"

Others took up the cry.

The globe lightning seemed to veer toward one group, then another, people scattering before it until, finally, it exploded with a crack that turned the ambient thunder into a mere whisper.

She looked at Serevan, struck by a new and terrible idea.

What if the lightning were to strike Syrilius and destroy what he carried?

Knowing her mind, Serevan whipped distance lenses out of his tunic.

"I see him! T'Zora's down. He's stopped to attend her. Syrilius!" Serevan roared. "Get yourself out of there!"

Only Serevan's voice could have been heard across the storm.

The medical technician stood up, gesturing vehemently. He knew what he bore, but clearly, his conflicting duties toward the woman before him and the lives that were yet to come tore at him. A lightning strike might be the easiest way out of his dilemma for him, Sarissa realized. And every second he waited increased the chances of his being hit.

"I said, I'll tend to her!" Serevan said. "Now, *move!*"

"No!" she cried. "I'll go."

If anyone could build a civilization from scratch, it was Serevan. Having made the plan that had brought her people here, Sarissa was now expendable and could not allow him to assume that risk.

Crouching low, Sarissa set off across the plain. She would not have thought it possible to get any wetter. Her boots splashed through puddles on slippery ground. Lightning was reflected in them, and that deadly purple glow that heralded yet another—she hurled herself forward, ozone acrid in her nostrils.

Rolling into a ball, she pulled herself back to her feet and pushed Syrilius away from the botanist. "I'll get her to shelter," she said.

"I don't know if I managed to start her heart. Let me examine . . ."

Sarissa touched the other woman's side. "Heartbeat's faint. Some minor fluttering. We have to risk it. We can't risk you, and not what you carry. Move it, man, run, run!"

Serevan would be coming up behind her, she knew that as surely as she knew the laws of gravity. Too many of them together, she thought. They would be a target.

She began to drag T'Zora toward shelter.

The purple glow began to build up around her. Hoisting T'Zora to her shoulders, she dodged, this way and that, summoning all the energy she possessed.

Thunder pealed behind her.

"Sarissa, jump!"

She felt Serevan tackle her, sending her sprawling. Then a crack of lightning threw her against a rock.

No rain poured down on Sarissa's face. The thunder seemed to have diminished. Aching in every bone and muscle, she found herself stretched out on a thin ground-pad, warmly covered. Somehow, they had reached the caves.

How many of them had survived?

She made herself look up at Serevan and Syrilius, crouching beside her.

"The genetic code?" she whispered.

It seemed to take as much effort to force the words out as it had to drag T'Zora across the plain. She feared the answer.

"Safe," Syrilius said.

She could feel her heartbeat subside to a less damaging speed.

"T'Zora?" she asked the next question. "The others?"

"We lost three to lightning," Syrilius answered. "T'Zora survives. No thanks to me."

"Thee did thy duty," Sarissa told him. "I grieve . . ." She

coughed, almost gagging from the dryness in her throat, and was glad of the water that Serevan held to her lips. "I grieve with thee."

She tried to force herself to her feet, then fell back.

"You do no good attending me," she told both men. "I will be satisfactory."

"You took a considerable shock. I should put you into a healing trance," Syrilius said.

"I will consider it—consider it, mind you—when I have seen my people settled!" she snarled.

Pure rage let her force herself to her feet on this try. She reeled, and had to lean against her consort, who had duties, surely, that he should be attending to rather than coddling her.

Serevan gestured, and the crew who had held off until they saw how she did came up. Now, they provided her with another sort of storm, this one of information.

They had lost 10 percent of their company, including two people who panicked, ran out onto the plain, and were consumed by ball lightning.

The survivors had made for the caverns that pocked the foothills and set up camps. Thus far, they had found no natural enemies other than the savage environment, but they had armed guards out and were scanning the area. The storm seemed to be lifting, but it was possible that another would strike soon.

In the days to come, they would have to take the risk of stripping the ship if they were to turn this world of devastating storms and lightning into even a temporary home.

Best not to think of it as temporary, or even as home.

It was a fortress. In it, they would build homes and factories, hidden from the eyes of any oppressors. And they would forget *nothing,* not the world that had cast them out, not the world that had enslaved them, nor the world that had tested them, proved them, and given them the strength to escape.

And when they were fully prepared, in every detail of mind, body, and matériel, they would return to free the descendants of the people they had left behind and avenge their kinfolk's slavery, though it might take two thousand years. In the end, all debts would be repaid. This would be their start.

She said as much.

"My wife," Serevan addressed her, using the intimate, rather than the public mode, "do you recall how your father used to quote Surak, who said that beginnings were as important as means."

She nodded. What was Serevan driving at?

"I am Serevan," he said. "You are Sarissa. But we were not born with those names."

Now, she saw it. When Karatek had adopted her, she had chosen a new name, one that reflected not just her new life as daughter to him and T'Vysse but her moral allegiance to Surak.

Now her people were making a new beginning.

"You think we need a new name?" she asked her mate.

He inclined his head.

Sarissa looked about the people surrounding her and saw agreement in their eyes.

Names speak truth, she reminded herself. It was one of the axioms of Surak's *First Analects.* With that awareness came an understanding of one's nature and, hence, of one's proper name.

"If we need a new name, will you trust me to give us one?" she asked.

"We shall call ourselves," she told the people clustering

about their leader, reassured that she was already on her feet, "the Watraii."

The name came from the Old High Vulcan word that meant *betrayed*.

They nodded solemnly. They were the Watraii. They would remember.

Sarissa forced herself to the opening of the cave. The storm was clearing. Light—not lightning, but sunlight—pierced the cloud cover like a beacon. It hurt her eyes.

She found the strip of cloth she had used in the wreck to protect her eyes and drew it across her face, masking it and easing her sight.

It might be that she would become accustomed to natural daylight. If she did not, her children would. Meanwhile, concealment of her face, so like that of every member of the murderer race, seemed not only logical, but desirable. Until they were ready to return and repay their betrayal, no one but their friends would look on their faces and know them for who they were.

THIRTY-FOUR

U.S.S. ENTERPRISE

2377

While he watched Data at work, Spock did a swift mental analysis of all the facts that he had learned about the Watraii—in addition, that was, to the near-suicidal desperation and despair that they had just revealed.

There were his firsthand observations from his time on their planet. Those had shown him a people grimly struggling with the double handicaps of a damaged genome and an exceedingly hostile planetary environment, but a people who were gifted with a leader who cared about his people's survival and well-being.

There was the evidence of Pavel Chekov's survival there, the prisoner of an undeclared war. Chekov had been kept unharmed out of respect for his advanced age, advanced age being something that was, tragically, almost impossible for the Watraii to achieve.

And there was the evidence that the Watraii could be dealt with only if they were convinced that they were dealing with people whom they considered worthy.

Their leader did come to consider me worthy when I was his captive. Let us see if that fact remains the same.

"Captain Picard, I believe that my speaking directly to the Watraii might be useful."

"I'll take you at your word, Ambassador Spock. Lieutenant Vale, open a direct channel to the Watraii."

The tactical officer said, "Channel open, Captain."

"I am Ambassador Spock," Spock began. "You have met me before this. I wish to speak to the Watraii leader, as I did on your home planet."

He waited, face tranquil but mind busily multitracking thoughts, two subjects at a time without losing track of anything, as Vulcans could do, considering both what the next step should be in a potential Federation-Watraii relationship if the Watraii would not speak with him now and how they could most safely recover Praetor Neral without completely destroying all chances for future negotiations.

Then a masked face appeared on the viewscreen and a cold but familiar voice said, *"I will speak with you, but not on an open channel with the potentially unworthy listening to us. You must come aboard my ship."*

"I understand," Spock said tranquilly, aware of the others' sudden alarm around him. "But you surely understand that I must have some time to consider this offer."

"Do not take overly long to do so," the Watraii leader returned coldly, and cut the signal.

"Spock," Ruanek said urgently, "you can't mean to do this!"

"I can."

"Ambassador Spock," Picard announced, "my ready room. Now."

It was definitely not a request. The captain was already on

his feet and on the move, adding over his shoulder, "Commander Riker, you have the bridge."

"You can't really believe this is a wise move," Picard began the moment they were seated in the captain's ready room.

"I do."

"Mr. Ambassador, please! You will be giving the Watraii two bargaining chips, not one. And there is no guarantee that you won't be slain before we can beam you back on board."

"I am quite aware of the risk," Spock said calmly.

"You are gambling that you can win them over."

"I do not gamble. Nor am I seeking glory, as Ruanek has assured us Commander Tomalak is doing. And arrogance is an emotion, so I can certainly assure you that I am not arrogantly thinking I alone can turn war into peace."

"Then what *are* you doing?"

"Simply this: attempting to create an opening for negotiation."

"Do you really think that you can negotiate with a people who wiped out a defenseless colony?"

"Captain Picard, you are a man of reason. You must agree with me that the course of making peace requires the taking of certain risks."

"Yes, but—"

"But I assure you that I have not become suddenly suicidal or utterly naïve. I have already met once with the Watraii leader, and seen something of the terrible conditions under which his people live. And I am fully aware that he really does wish the best for his people, and is not a blind fool, regardless of his people's seemingly irrational and mindless hate of the Romulans."

"He knows, I take it, that you aren't a Romulan despite the genetic resemblance."

"Indeed he does."

Picard let out his breath in a silent sigh. "I could, as captain of this ship, keep you from taking what I see as a highly perilous move."

"You could, indeed. You could even have me confined to quarters or, at the worst, placed in your ship's brig. But I doubt that you will do anything so radical."

"Ah?"

"Captain Picard, we both know that you are a man of peace and thought, and as such, you surely know that this may be our best chance for opening true negotiations with the Watraii. By my remaining on board the Watraii ship, I give them assurance that you will not attack."

"Remaining!"

"Indeed. I assure you, the Watraii leader knows that a diplomat is a noncombatant; he logically will not harm me."

"Assuming," Picard said dryly, "that he's thinking logically, which is something I strongly doubt you can prove."

"There is always a risk, as I've stated. But at any rate, no matter what happens, you will still have the chance to rescue Praetor Neral and prevent an all-out war between the Romulans and the Watraii."

That won him Picard's wry grimace of a smile. "In other words, you aren't giving me much of a choice. Very well, Ambassador Spock, while I'm preventing all-out war between the Romulans and the Watraii, can you assure me I won't have the Vulcans coming down on my head?"

"I fail to see why you would even consider that. It would not be at all logical for them to blame you for my actions."

"You are a good negotiator, Mr. Ambassador, but I knew that already."

Spock waited.

"Very well," Picard said, getting to his feet. "If you are willing to take the risk, who am I to deny you the chance to do so? Let us at least try for peace."

As soon as the blur of transport cleared, Spock saw that he did, indeed, stand on the deck of what had been a Romulan warbird. The basic shape of the bridge was unchanged, but a scorched, empty wall marked where the Romulan insignia had been forcibly removed, and the entire layout of instruments, seating, and even what looked like a network of Borg wires was changed, fairly shouting *alien*.

So did the line of masked Watraii facing him. Their masks were a wall of green-black emptiness, even though he could pick out differences in individual height and body type. But Spock, after all, had seen such a display before, on their homeworld; it did not disconcert him now.

"I am Spock of Vulcan," he said, raising one hand in the standard split-fingered Vulcan greeting. An odd flash of memory . . . ancient Earth motion pictures . . . there was no real way around saying it, but at least this time the clichéd line would be true. And so he added, "Take me to your leader."

The Watraii, of course, could not know the irony in that statement. "I am here," a familiar cold voice said, and the line of figures moved aside to let their leader pass.

Excellent! "Thank you for agreeing to speak with me." Spock paused. "Perhaps there is a room in which we could talk in private?"

"There are no secrets here."

And of course you do not wish to do anything as soft as sit around a table. So be it.

"Then there shall be none," Spock agreed.

"I . . . do not understand you," the Watraii leader said after a moment of studying Spock's apparently total tranquility. "You were our prisoner, and yet you spoke of honor and betterment for the Watraii."

"Indeed I did."

"And now, you put yourself willingly into our hands and again say that there may yet be restitution for my people. What manner of being are you?"

"An ambassador. A Vulcan." Spock stared at him with calm, unblinking eyes. "And someone who does not take pleasure in seeing a species, any species, forced to the verge of extinction."

"Smooth words. I could almost believe them."

"I have no reason to lie. I am certain," Spock continued, "that you remember what we discussed planetside."

"I do. But I cannot ignore the fact that you came after us just now aboard a warship."

"I came this far aboard a Federation Starfleet vessel—yes, a warship, if you prefer to call it such—but you have surely noted that it has made no threat to your own ship. As I mentioned to you when we were planetside, the Federation has no fight with you or your people."

"Then why have you pursued us?"

"It was necessary, as you surely can understand."

"Explain."

"Sir, you know why. The prisoner you have on board could create a war far wider than one between your people and the Romulans—a war with hundreds of other worlds, the members of the Federation, one that would lead to disaster for your people." Spock continued into the sudden stunned silence. "I do not offer this as a threat. Threats are not logical. But I do offer it because I never could wish for such horror to happen to any sentient beings, regardless of species. And I believe I know why you have taken so great a risk as this, leaving the security of your planet. I understand the desperation you must be feeling for the sake of your people."

"Do you?"

It was, as Ruanek might say, worth a new gamble. "Let me tell you a story of one people who became two," Spock began, "one half of them remaining on the homeworld to follow a new path of peace, the other half leaving in the great Sundering to find their own way. It was despair such as your own people feel that made them make so terrible and final a decision."

The Watraii leader stiffened in sudden comprehension. "You speak of the Vulcans! Are you saying that your people and the Romulans are one and the same?"

"I will not deny it."

"You . . . did not need to tell me that. If I were truly a leader, I would be forced to instantly name you a deadly foe."

"You are a true leader, sir. You think of your people before all else, including your own desires. And logically, I did need to tell you of the Sundering. I know I must be truthful with you if you are to accept anything that I say. And yes, as you can see, I do understand something of the desperation you feel for the sake of your people. But surely you must agree that kidnapping another race's leader, as you have done, cannot be the way to peace."

"The one we have taken is the leader of the murderer race." The Watraii leader stopped short, as if realizing for the first time the ramifications of what he had just said. "I do not mean to challenge the Vulcans with that statement."

"Understood."

"But they, those who are now the Romulans, they are the ones who fled your race. They are not anything that the Watraii consider worthy."

Very, very carefully, Spock said, "They fled because they saw no other hope for survival." It was, after all, what the Watraii claimed they had done.

For a long while, there was silence, the Watraii hiding his emotions behind his mask, Spock behind Vulcan training. Then the Watraii said, "I am Suwarin."

Spock understood the value of the gift he had just been granted. "I am Spock, son of Sarek, and I honor the name you have revealed."

"Still," Suwarin continued, "the Romulans chose to flee. We fled that we might live."

"Yet you have not slain their leader."

"So valuable a prize? Of course we have not."

"I suspect that there is more to it than cold calculation," Spock countered. "I challenge you that you have not so much as harmed Praetor Neral, because I have met you both, and I know that you both carry yourselves with courage."

The Watraii leader paused at that, and Spock thought, *He doesn't believe what I say—not yet.*

Predictably enough, Suwarin retorted, "We have not harmed our prisoner because we wish to take him back to Watraii space for the public execution of so notorious a war criminal."

"I must counter, though, that civilized people do not kill when there is a more logical option, especially when the well-being of the Watraii people is at stake, as indeed it is."

"You speak with grace. I will show you our captive to prove to you that we are, indeed, civilized."

At a quick command, two masked figures left the bridge. In just a short time, they returned with the defiant, furious, but clearly unharmed figure of Praetor Neral. The sudden surge of violent emotion filling the bridge, emanating from Neral, from the Watraii—hatred, fury, sheer primitive terror of the Other—was so powerful that even a touch telepath could feel it. Spock nearly staggered and hurriedly slammed in place every mental barrier he could summon.

This will be even more difficult than I expected.

"Commander," Data said abruptly, "I have isolated Praetor Neral's signature pattern. He can be beamed aboard."

"Finally," Riker said, getting up from the captain's chair. "What took so long, Data?"

"It has been difficult to isolate the individual life signs. At first, I believed it to be an interference pattern run by the Watraii, but I believe the difficulty is more fundamental than that." The android looked up. "The Watraii life signs are very similar to those of Romulans and Vulcans."

Stepping over to look at the readouts, Ruanek said, "Incredible. I know that there are other Vulcanoid life-forms in this region of space—Rigelians, Mintakans—but the Watraii are, also?"

"So it would seem," Data said. "However, I have isolated both the Praetor and the ambassador. We can beam either or both of them on board."

Ruanek started. "Not both of them, surely. Spock said that he wants to stay on the Watraii ship, at least for the time being."

Riker frowned slightly at him. "I'd think you of all people would want him safely back on the *Enterprise,* Ruanek."

"I would, and I do. But being who and what I am—and we

335

won't go into that right now, I trust—I can also appreciate the gamble that he's taking. And if anyone can win that gamble, it is Spock." Ruanek paused, staring at Riker. "You *are* going to follow his wishes, aren't you?"

"That's up to Captain Picard," Riker said.

And there is a nice, evasive answer, Ruanek thought.

But he knew it was useless to argue.

Neral stopped short, staring at Spock in astonishment. "You!"

"Yes," Spock said. "You do, indeed, recognize me." Since it was possible that Neral might blurt out some unfortunate pseudonym dating from earlier visits to Romulus, now, when truthfulness was most important, he added, "I am Ambassador Spock of Vulcan."

"What in all the seven hells of Erebus are you doing here? Are you in league with *these?*"

"I am in league with neither side, Praetor Neral. Say rather that I am in league with logic. And peace."

"Easy words!"

"Perhaps. They also happen to be the truth. As I have been discussing with the Watraii leader, the Federation does have the missing artifact. The information it contains—" Neral's start and stare said clearly that the Praetor had not known it contained anything. "The information," Spock continued levelly, "will be studied and translated by a neutral source."

"The Vulcans, I assume," Neral said with a sneer.

"You must admit that there can be no more unbiased source." Spock glanced at Suwarin. "And you, sir, must see in the Praetor's very reaction that what I say is the truth."

"Perhaps."

Then Suwarin did something Spock did not expect: he removed his mask.

The action revealed a gaunt visage, as one might expect from the living conditions on the Watraii homeworld.

But for the first time, Spock noticed something else: pointed ears.

The Watraii were of Vulcanoid stock.

And then the memories cascaded downward, from eleven years earlier, to the last time Spock had held the artifact, felt the words and thoughts of Karatek, before returning it to Charvanek, understood the truth of the rift between his people and the Romulans, and the fateful decision to dedicate his life to reuniting his father's people with their Sundered cousins.

One other memory now came to the fore: Karatek's daughter, Sarissa, and those who left Remus with her, never to be heard from again.

Until now.

Spock realized that the Watraii's claim on Romulan territory was greater than any of them had ever known, and he cursed himself for not seeing it sooner.

But before he could speak, a too-familiar shimmering took Neral and him together.

No! Not now! Captain Picard, what have you done?

"Got them!" Ruanek heard Commander La Forge exclaim.

In the next instant, Neral and Spock both appeared on the bridge of the *Enterprise*. Neral gave his rescuers an ironic salute. "Thank you," the Praetor said sarcastically, "for delivering the artifact."

But Spock whirled to the viewscreen. "I have not played you false," he said to Suwarin.

Too late. The Watraii instantly attempted to open fire.

"They cannot," Data assured everyone. "Right now, the *Enterprise* has their ship paralyzed in space. It is deprived of cloak, shields, and weapons capability."

"Suwarin," Spock said urgently, "there is still time for us to continue our talk."

Suwarin drew himself proudly erect. He was all too clearly considering honorable suicide.

No. From what I have seen of them, the Watraii are not suicidal if there is any other honorable way out.

To Spock's surprise, Picard leaned forward in his command chair and said, "Sir, I take full responsibility for interrupting your negotiations. I believed that I was acting for the best. There was no treachery on the part of Ambassador Spock, who remains as he was, a highly honorable man."

It was precisely what Spock could have wished. He continued to Suwarin. "You have a choice, sir. Die without a point. Or talk. Dying without making one's death count is not only illogical, it is unworthy of a commander of his people."

The Watraii commander's face remained as empty of expression as it did when masked. But then he said, *"I am listening."*

"My message is simply this . . ."

Spock chose his words carefully. His own clandestine use of the artifact eleven years ago needed to remain a secret. "The Federation does, indeed, have the artifact. We will not argue over which race has the right to claim it. The message that it carries will be translated with unbiased care by my father's people, by the Vulcans, and no other. Should you wish it, a representative from your people may be present— as may be a representative of the Romulans. We shall learn at last the truth, untouched, unaltered by wishes, old fears and hatreds, or folktales."

"Continue."

"What this means, sir, is that the Watraii, like the Romulans, have now been given a second chance for peace. For life. You will be able to choose again and this time to make a truly worthy choice. And this time, you may know and understand that neither you nor the Romulans will be making it alone."

THIRTY-FIVE

EARTH

2377

It hardly seemed possible, Spock thought, even allowing for the variability of time and space created by various voyages at various warp speeds, that only two short Terran months had passed since he'd last been here on Earth, in the city of Paris—and in the Palais de la Concorde.

It was, ironically enough, even the same room in which he'd last met with other Federation ambassadors—a meeting the Romulans had departed early because, as it came out, they'd been busy attempting to fight off the Watraii.

The Watraii, in fact, who had just stolen that extremely important artifact.

The room was large, rectangular and soothingly, simply, furnished in warm reddish wood paneling and deep blue carpeting. The curtains that half covered the tall windows were still that slightly lighter shade known as Federation blue—the same hue as the beautifully enameled Federation emblem on the far wall. Not surprising that this room had been chosen,

Spock thought, since it was the largest of the meeting rooms, here on the third floor of the Palais, the seat of the Federation government. The room's main furnishing was one long, rectangular table of the same reddish wood as the paneling, with terminals placed in front of every seat—and this time around, every seat was filled.

Spock looked about at the assembled crowd of many species. Federation species, such as humans, Bolians, Vulcans, Damiani, and Trill. Allies, both Romulan and Klingon—not the two privateer captains, of course, who were hardly officially sanctioned by their government, though they had sent Saavik a message that both they and Commander Tomalak (brave, as they said reluctantly, for a Romulan) had survived the recent battle. Perhaps most amazingly, considering past and recent history, there were also several Watraii officials, including Suwarin himself.

It was surely the most impressive gathering of Federation and non-Federation personnel since before the first Watraii attack on the Romulans had been so suddenly and horrifyingly announced.

Delay, Spock reminded himself sternly, was decidedly not logical. He began, "Gentlebeings all: The truth is so improbable that I am forced to adapt the words of the human who first invented communications satellites. 'The history we have believed is false . . . so false we have not yet been able to reconcile it with the truth.'"

Quickly, he brought them all up to date on the subject of the artifact—though not on every detail about the awkward story of its recovery from the Watraii, nor of his own secret exposure to the artifact—and the unraveling of the secrets that it had been hiding for millennia.

"But that point, fascinating though it may be, is but a peripheral fact. The most important issue among all others," Spock continued, "is that the artifact has given us, the Federation, the Vulcans, the Romulans, and the Watraii, all of us, the *true* story—the story that neither the Vulcans nor the Romulans have reason for separation, that the Watraii have only a partial claim to the truth, that the Romulans were desperate, and that the Watraii attacked and were attacked.

"Both sides, therefore, were in the right, and both sides were in the wrong. Both sides nursed their grudge and false memories, as have the Vulcans and Romulans themselves."

As he spoke, Spock glanced subtly at two of those nearest to him. Praetor Neral, for all his fierce self-control, was clearly still shaken. He had experienced the artifact's influence firsthand—at his request, to do him some justice—and was now convinced of the actual truth, or at least as convinced as a Romulan Praetor was ever going to get. Suwarin, his Watraii counterpart, was hiding his emotions behind his mask, but Spock had no doubt that he was feeling much the same.

Neral cleared his throat. "I must state that, of course, I have been influenced by the way that the Federation came after me while at the same time giving up none of its principles or the opportunity to deal with the Watraii. It would seem that much discussion awaits me on the homeworlds, but I will say now that I shall cast my vote that they are desirable allies in peace as well as in war." Then, clearly trying to save face as much as possible, he added, "My test has proven that the Federation can, indeed, be trusted."

Ruanek had stayed behind on Vulcan, both because he had told Spock frankly that he and T'Selis really needed some time together, and because his status as former Romulan might have raised some awkward questions with the Federation and the Romulan representatives both. But Spock could almost hear Ruanek's sardonic echo, *"My* test. As though the kidnapping had been his idea!"

Ah well, Neral was as he was, and even kidnapping by the Watraii was unlikely to change him.

"And what Ambassador Spock has proposed," Neral continued, "is, after all, simply a different sort of unification from the one that I tried unsuccessfully—a military takeover of the Mother World."

There were a few angry murmurs at that, but Spock held up a hand for silence. "Peace, gentlebeings. Let our guest finish."

Neral dipped his head to Spock in courtesy, and then continued. "It is only logical to keep good allies. But I will not move too fast. Too much haste was the fatal flaw of my late predecessor. I will, however, agree to the release of the true story—at least to selected members of the Senate, perhaps to the Continuing Committee.

"Oh, and lastly, I will not object to the fact that the Watraii have made a claim on the Federation—especially if Vulcan assumes some responsibility for partial payment."

"In other words," Saavik murmured to her husband, "there is no peace—but one day there may be."

Spock retorted, just as softly, allowing the very faintest hint of satisfaction in his voice, "And Vulcans and Romulans will attempt at least the preliminaries of discussions about unification."

Aloud, he said, "Now, with the permission of the Watraii, Admiral Chekov will now speak of the Watraii homeworld."

Chekov had completely recovered from his ordeal. In fact, Spock thought, he looked—were such a thought not the essence of illogic—younger than he had when they'd first headed after the Watraii.

"Picture a world with savage weather, never-ending storms of gale force winds and perilous lightning strikes," he said. "Picture a world covered with knife-edged rocks, sand, and gravel, a world with almost no surface water and almost no vegetation, with perpetually gray skies and that endless howling of the winds. Not a place to go for a stroll, or raise your crops, or let your children play. Not a place to even stand outside for long, because one of those terrible lightning bolts might strike you without warning.

"That, gentlebeings, is the place the Watraii, perforce, call home. I am no geologist or agronomist or any other type of 'ist,' but I have to believe that the Federation, with all its scientists and wiser minds than mine, can provide those poor people—their poor children, too!—with technical and humanitarian assistance."

"We are not asking for charity," Suwarin cut in suddenly, voice cold and flat.

"No," Spock agreed. "We would not so insult you. But nor are we offering it. If friendship is a concept that you are now prepared to consider—possibly, given the history we have uncovered, for the first time—then why not also consider assistance among friends?"

"I fail to see your point, Ambassador."

"There is a great deal of trading of scientific and other advances that goes on throughout the Federation. It is quite possible that the Watraii might have something that the Federation would want. I suggest, for example, your phase-shifting shields. In addition, the Watraii's skill in manipulating power currents would be useful both in peacetime construction projects and in weapons systems, such as in defense against the fatal adaptability of the Borg, should they ever return. At the very least, the Federation is prepared to listen."

There was a long silence in the room, as though no one was willing to be the first to break it. And then, in token of that unprecedented level of trust, all of the members of the Watraii delegation removed their ceremonial masks, meeting aliens' eyes, meeting face-to-face, for the first time in their troubled, paranoid history.

Praetor Neral suddenly broke the silence. "It is the Romulans' turn now to meet the challenge created by so much trust." There was just a touch of sarcasm in his voice. "That will require, to start with, an explanation on the homeworlds and, to go on with, the years necessary to come to terms with the lies that have been taught instead of the truth. The time has come for truth, or as much truth," Neral added sardonically, "as the Empire can stand. But first," he finished, getting to his feet, "other matters must be attended to. I must return to the Empire."

"So be it," Spock said.

And, for the sake of unification, I could wish you the traditional "Live long and prosper." But, alas, that is seldom true of Romulan Praetors.

THIRTY-SIX

ROMULUS

2377

Neral knew almost from the moment he left the ship at the spaceport in Ki Baratan. When no one would quite meet his eyes, he was certain that he had, indeed, been gone from the Empire too long. And when he demanded to meet with Charvanek, she was strangely "unavailable." Koval, of course, was genuinely sick, too far gone in illness to be questioned.

The accidents began soon after his first open speech to the Romulan Senate.

Security refused to swear on their families' hearths that no *remat* detonators had been attached to Neral's clothing or his skin after the last reception, when at least twelve senators had rushed to greet him. Because even one of the tiny devices could reduce its victim to scorched and writhing flesh as he emerged from a transporter beam, Neral had chosen instead to ride in a groundcar convoy to his mountain retreat high above the Vale of Chula.

The convoy had actually reached its destination without

346

suffering breakdown, bomb, or any other lethal incident. Its safe arrival meant simply a respite between attempts to kill him. They were growing more frequent. Sooner or later, one would succeed.

It was endgame, and Neral knew it.

Get on with it. He didn't know whether his thought was addressed to himself or to his enemies.

Not waiting for his guards, Neral opened the groundcar's door and stepped out.

"Sir!" Neral's driver, a wizened, clever centurion, dared one last protest.

"You already lost this fight, Vorat," Neral told him. "Let's say I threw a legion into Chula during Four Moons Rising. How could I ever face my neighbors again? No, I don't even want an armed escort to my gates, man. You have done your duty, and I thank you. Dismissed."

Obedient even in the face of what Vorat clearly suspected was some strange version of Final Honor, the centurion drove off. Neral brought fist to chest in salute. The gods grant Vorat no lethal surprises on his way back to Ki Baratan and (on the remote chance that the veteran survived the return trip) what he would find to be an unexpected and surprisingly lucrative retirement.

Neral's outer perimeter guards had been beamed into place around the house before dawn. Guards, unlike a Praetor, were beneath the more creative forms of assassination, although, in the endgame, they were preliminary targets. Dralath had died fleeing and insane. Narviat had died surprised. With his enemies tightening their nets about him, if Neral had to die, he would do it on his own terms, in his own time, and in his own house.

Raising his head so the proximity sensors could scan his

retinas, Neral started across the bridge toward the main gate, embedded in a palisade of spearwood beyond a narrow bridge across a ravine. The bridge, creaking underfoot in the best archaic fashion, was a primitive defense, unlike the sensors and proximity detectors of his real house security systems. It shook slightly as he crossed. This close to the time when all four of the homeworld's moons would shine full in the night sky, quakes were as much to be expected as spectacular tides in the Apnex Sea.

That, too, was a sight Neral would have enjoyed. Unfortunately, what official reports called a severe quake had taken out his retreat in the high black basalt peaks overlooking the sea. He missed the place, but he missed the longtime staff who had been stationed there even more.

Torath's attempt at initiative, Neral suspected. Rehaek's methods ran more to torture and imagination: hence, Neral's rational concerns about transporter failure. But how did Hiren kill? That remained to be seen.

By coming here to the peace above the Vale of Chula, Neral gave enemies a chance to take their best shot at him. If they succeeded, the task of rebuilding an empire exhausted by yet another "last imaginable" war would fall to them. That would serve them right—until their own enemies served them as they had served him.

And there was always the chance—admittedly remote—that Neral would survive to be stalked yet another day.

The strong spring winds scoured the clouds from the gold and green dawn sky, bringing him the scents of the day. When the moons rose tonight, the night blooms would open, scenting the entire valley. If the winds were right, they would waft the delicate fragrance upward, through the house shields, so he could savor it for what might be the last time.

This place had been in Neral's family since planetfall, and he loved it. As a boy, he and his brothers—many years dead now, all of them—had always come back here when they were on leave. They had spent years chipping the gaudy viridian stone facing from the house walls, peeling them back to their ship-metal beginnings, then refacing them with wood in the very oldest style.

Neral suppressed the impulse to whistle for Pyncho, the *setlet* he had chosen from his last pet's final litter and raised by hand. Perfect Romulan hunters, his father had called the *setlet*s the old man had made a hobby of breeding: silent, quick, deadly, and loyal.

After the quake in the mountains, Neral had sent Pyncho off with a family that had served his House for seven generations. He had placed Pyncho in the eldest grandson's arms, then nodded harshly and turned to go. The *setlet* had promptly coiled his tail about the boy's waist and rested his head against his shoulder in apparent contentment. However, as Neral strode from the room, suppressing emotion unworthy of a Praetor of the Romulan people, Pyncho had let out a desolate howl, disgracing his training and almost breaking Neral's self-control.

But Pyncho would be safe now. So would his surviving clients. Neral had transferred funds sufficient to enable them to live anywhere. They could even emigrate to the Federation, assuming they wanted to be talked to death by humans, who talked more and said less than even Cardassians.

Touching his signet to the gate to unlock it, Neral entered his house. It was small and rustic, ostentatiously so, but it possessed broad terraces and a spectacular view.

Spectacularly indefensible, Charvanek had called the place the one time she had agreed to visit.

He walked through the great hall and the atrium and out onto the terrace that overlooked the Vale of Chula. On misty nights, all you could see below was clouds. He hoped tonight would be clear so he could see the moons rise and the night blooms open.

The house was empty, but not neglected: superb automatic systems were the one modern luxury Neral installed when he had inherited the place. Retreating to his room, he tugged off the polished boots and somber suit with its stiffly padded shoulders *and* the body armor beneath it that were senatorial wear in favor of a country nobleman's: worn, far more comfortable boots that sagged at calves and ankles, loose breeches, and shabby tunic. More out of habit than caution, he ran a hand scanner over the garments: no poisons, no darts, and no spy sensors. He left off the body armor: if it came to a fair fight, he could never take on Torath. He might have given Rehaek, at least a generation younger than he, a good fight, and he was more than a match for Hiren.

In the days before Neral had come to power, he had valued the privacy for him and his family. In more recent days— well, suffice it to say, he had pensioned off the old retainers for their own protection and dismissed the newer servants, even the ones whose integrity Charvanek could vouch for.

There was no place here, either, for Neral's Reman cohorts. Although they had fought well for their Romulan masters during the Dominion War, their grumblings that they deserved better than a simple return to things as they were called their loyalty into question. He could not allow the Senate to think he had developed a distaste for being served by soldier-slaves.

Again, he suppressed the impulse to whistle for Pyncho.

Animals knew. Animals knew when the hunt was ending and led their hunters away from their lairs to protect the innocent.

Charvanek had rescued innocents, or what passed for them on the homeworld, several times. Neral had seen her do it with that under-officer, a pleasant fellow, never quite as successful as people would have expected, who had disappeared about the same time Narviat came to power. She'd pulled off the same trick with Neral's own agemate and bitter enemy, the traitor M'ret. It was good form among the noble-born, and Charvanek wasn't just noble, but imperial.

Neral, too, had done what he could. As he sensed the tide of this silent, covert battle for power turning against him, he had sent his Honor Blade to the Hallows. Because most civilians no longer carried them in ordinary life, the move might have been noted, but was not commented upon. If Hiren—or Rehaek—succeeded in killing him, the priests would send the Blade to his heir, a distant cousin. If the Klingons had not killed Neral's wife and children, the man wouldn't have inherited a single crystal: now he inherited the headship of a House Major, and all the risks that went with it. Lucky him.

Neral drew a deep breath as the familiar pain, undimmed by time, struck again. He had done many hard things in his life: allying with Klingons after the death of his family had probably been his hardest victory over his own heart.

He wandered about the house, idly straightening a hanging here, a chair there, rubbing at a tarnish spot on an arms display against a wall. Without loyal staff, things went so quickly to rack and ruin. After his wife's murder, because that was all it was, there had been other women, but no one he cared about for long. He thinned his lips as a recent, painful memory struck him. If he had truly thought Lithani cared about him, he would have found her a position other than his third undersecretary, one far from him. Charvanek, who could not avoid reading the autopsy report, had muttered imprecations about a long-dead enemy and Narendra III before she wished for Rehaek's head on a pike and a more gruesome disposition of some of Torath's other body parts.

Neral could have ordered her to take both men out. He knew she was tempted, but she had never murdered in her life, and she was too old to start. Besides, what if she had not obeyed him? They neither liked nor trusted one another, but they had always maintained the chain of command: faith kept, in their own fashion.

The house was quiet. When would the strike come?

More aftershocks. A glance at the screen told him what had just happened to his outer perimeter defenses. There might just be time to burn incense in their memory before his would-be assassins moved in.

The suspense is killing me. It was a phrase, typically human and inaccurate, that had always made Charvanek grin.

Suspense did not kill: wars and assassins killed. He knew Charvanek dreamed of being out of the game. Had her contacts with humans made her too soft? Humans were a bad influence on Romulans. They had just as much passion, were just as likely to express it, but had an unfortunate tendency toward sentiment that could be disastrously seductive. Neral had observed humans for years. Take that conference on Romulus when a young human doctor had corrupted a senator and Koval had escaped a quick death, only to endure the slower one that had been waiting for him all along.

You should have come to me, he had told Kimora. He had had such hopes of her, too, until the moment when he had to order her arrest.

Typically, the humans' Federation—Neral did not delude

himself about who ran what in that chaos that called itself a government—had issued a protest. He had sentenced the woman to prison, however, if not for treason, then for catastrophically bad judgment. Despite the Federation's attempt to intervene, his sentence stood.

Was that his own sentimentality at work? Dralath would have had her killed. Slowly. Narviat would probably have let her off with a reprimand, which was why Narviat had died so quickly. But one day, Kimora Cretak's cell was empty. Charvanek had met Neral's eyes blandly, then disappeared offworld.

Humans bent everywhere, but rarely broke. Romulans never bent, but there came a time when they reached breaking point. Then, you saw judicial assassinations. Senators were sent constituents' Honor Blades. You saw Final Honor, or the sort of intervention that could bring even an emperor down.

Was Charvanek as near to breaking as Neral himself?

She was, after all, a predator, and there was always a time with predators when you had to free them or kill them. Humans negotiated terms. Romulans fought.

He remembered the first times Charvanek had flared across his horizon, attracting his attention. He had been an uhlan, all calculation and lust for power. He looked at her and wondered how she had not just recovered from disgrace, but solidified her power base. How she had glittered in the Central Court, pursued by Narviat and shadowed by a tall, dour academician called Symmakhos. How chagrined Neral had been to learn too long afterward that the scholar had been none other than the infamous Spock of Vulcan.

The Vulcan was again in hiding somewhere in the Empire. Neral knew better than to ask if Charvanek knew where. She had had many loyalties in her long life, not all of them connected to him. Besides, he had always known he could not trust her, and she could not trust him.

Time to make that call to the Hallows at Gal Gath'thong. Anyone skilled enough to eavesdrop would only hear a conversation about his will, a subject that could be expected to render any ambitious enemy overconfident. He thanked the archpriest, a new one in whose selection he had had a hand, then made another call to a tall, thin young man with a face so disciplined he could almost be Vulcan. In this young operative's position, that was a good thing, Neral had to remind himself.

Hard to believe the boy could stiffen even further to attention.

"Sir! How may I serve the Praetor?" he asked, just as if he probably had not run simulations on ways that Neral could be taken out and calculated the odds of success for each.

Not wasting words, Neral told him.

The young man's eyes lit. He even grinned, a loss of control that made Neral's heart warm to him. How cold-blooded he must have become to be pleased by such a small thing.

"With my life!" Charvanek's double agent vowed enthusiastically. He struck his chest with his fist and bowed deeply. On him, the move seemed somehow appropriate.

"We will hope it does not come to that," Neral drawled. "One more thing, Levak."

"Lord Praetor?"

"I recommend you request sanctuary for yourself as well. Just stay out of her way."

Trapped in sanctuary by the firefalls, Charvanek would no doubt be furious. She would say she had been right neither to like nor to trust Neral. But there was no logical reason for one of her own operatives to suffer unnecessarily for respecting the chain of command. A Praetor outranked his chief of security.

Today would have been a good day to spend in the kennels, but he had closed the kennels in the days immediately after he was named Praetor. The dark corners where litters were whelped, the training runs, the equipment sheds—his guards had given him lists of the grisly surprises that could erupt from such places. Over the course of years, the words "We cannot recommend the security risk, sir" had eroded much of his life.

It was time and past time to regain it, now that he suspected so little time remained.

"Music," Neral told the house systems. "File Neral 2032." Franjhot's delicate fourth ballade echoed in the still air of his study. The light filtering through the clouds seemed to brighten, dancing with the music. It had been years since he had allowed himself to listen to music composed by the family disgrace, who had exiled himself from the Romulan Star Empire three generations ago.

Drawing the heavily carved chair of a Head of House up to his worktable, Neral sat. He had letters to write, and he wanted them to be real letters, not just transmissions. He took his time over them, with attention to phrasing as well as to calligraphy. He had been carefully instructed as a boy; now, it gave him a distant pleasure that he remembered his lessons.

Finishing his last letter, he stamped his signet on the blood-green wax and set the stack of correspondence aside.

He glanced out. The sun was high, and the wind was eating away at the clouds that still covered the valley. Time for him to eat, too, but he stood for precious moments longer. As a child, he had watched from the outermost terrace, guarded by his family and their clients. When he and his brothers were older, they had camped in the Vale. In the early years of his marriage, he and his wife had wandered, arms about each other's waists, through the deepest glades—no, he would not think of that. He did not want to break, not yet.

Since he had actually lived until midday, he rather thought that it would be Hiren who would, ultimately, accomplish his defeat. Without Rehaek, Torath was nothing but a thug, notwithstanding the miasma of other rumors about them. Rehaek, who made Koval seem sane in comparison, might take pleasure in his skill at prolonging suspense, but Rehaek was also cruel enough not to have allowed Neral this last precious day to make the final arrangements any gentleman needed to make.

Hiren, though, so moderate, so civilized, a man of Neral's own class, actually understood such niceties. It was even, in a perverse way, a bond between the two of them.

Neral thought he would put his crystals on Hiren.

After the noon meal, Neral occupied his time packing up a few small treasures and labeling them so that they would not be corrupted by endless litigation should he not survive the night.

When he finished the last of his tasks, he decided he could venture—not safely, perhaps, but with the sense of having earned a reward—out into the gardens. Lacking regular attendants, they were running wild. What had once been carefully cut shrubs arched now over the stone pathways, and the flower beds, too high for the luminous white night blooms to flourish, were tangles of rich color. But there were no orchids. Neral had grown them until a senator had been assassinated by orchids.

Not wanting to risk the lives of his gardeners, he had ordered the orchids in his own gardens to be plowed under by machines, then had the area covered over by a mosaic on which stood a small pavilion containing an altar.

He burnt his incense there and watched the smoke rise in the waning light, sunlight, motes, and incense dancing against the almost imperceptible flicker of the screens protecting his property. The hillside trembled, then shook more strongly, dislodging rocks that ricocheted down the valley walls. The shields sparked and buzzed, then subsided. Gradually, the dust settled, blown away by the wind.

It was going to be a beautiful night.

Neral flung an old jacket, worn as his other clothes, over his shoulders and strode across the atrium toward the outermost terrace, poised just where the cliffs jutted out farthest above the Vale of Chula. He set a decanter and glass down on the stonework, which made a fine table, and dragged up a bench.

The music of Franjhot still rang out from the house. Neral silenced it with a gesture. Pouring himself a glass of Saurian brandy from the last of his prewar private stock, he saluted the landscape, then gazed up into the sky and waited for the moons to rise.

The brandy warmed him as the wind drove away the last clouds. He drained his glass, considered hurling it against the flagstones in ironic celebration, then set it down so carefully that it did not even click.

Now, the moons had risen fully. Even Remus, the largest, possessed a kind of spectral beauty. In bygone years, Neral's family had competed to see who could write the best poems praising the night; his mother had chosen the literary form each year, and she never picked easy ones. Now, however, Neral was alone. Safer thus: he had already lost more people than he could bear.

Flattening his palms against the retaining wall of the terrace, he leaned out over the valley. Now, he could see the white blossoms open, like so many cups to catch the moonlight. They reflected it back into the sky. The wind rose again, allowing the flowers' fragrance to rise. The night's breath, Neral had heard it called. Closing his eyes, he drew a deep breath of the perfume-laden air.

The *neiirrh*'s wings whirred, a second's warning before it struck. Instinct made Neral fling out an arm and dash the tiny avian with its brilliant plumage and its deadly poison spur away from him onto the pavement. His hand stung. A glance down showed the streak of dark blood where the creature had marked him.

Those quakes must have weakened the shields that surrounded the terraces, he thought. And remembered, in the next instant, that Hiren possessed an aviary. When that had first become known, it had been regarded as laughable. Who would have guessed that the damned birds would prove as deadly as the old Emperor's fish?

How wise Neral's physician had been to treat him prophylactically for common poisons. He could survive this attack, with little more than . . . the effects would not be pleasant, but he would survive.

It was a pity that he would have to miss the rest of the festival, but prudence demanded that he hunt out his medkit as quickly as possible. A little unsteadily, Neral strode toward the house.

Birdsong warned him: an entire flock of the tiny creatures had managed to break through the shields. He could flail his arms about, possibly killing most of them as he ran to the house, but Hiren could easily have fitted some of the *neiirrh* with subdermal spy-eyes. How he would laugh to see the

Praetor of the Romulan Star Empire try to fight off a flock of tiny birds, then run like a coward, dripping blood through the house, before he collapsed. He might even be taking bets with his associates on how long it would take Neral to die.

This was grotesque. This was unacceptable. This spoke of such surveillance that he could never escape without appearing to place his life above his honor. *This,* Neral realized, was where humans and Romulans differed. A human might run and flail for his life, but not a Romulan, especially not a Praetor. If life could be had only on these terms, it was not worth it.

Let Hiren sink to this level of squalid dishonor in his lust for Neral's position. If this was what he was prepared to do for power, he was welcome to it, just as he would be welcome to whatever revenge might, one day, be exacted upon him by someone equally ambitious and unscrupulous.

Birdsong and the drumming of his rapid pulse thrummed in Neral's temples. As his breath came more rapidly, the odor of the blossoms in the Vale of Chula had never smelled sweeter.

Neral fought to steady his breathing. He knew that if he went motionless, *neiirrh* were easily distracted. Sooner or later, they would flit away. But he had already taken several stings, and his knees were buckling. Another *neiirrh*'s wings fanned his cheek as he fell. It struck, and even though he had taken a full hit from its poison spur, it did not burn as painfully as the first, the second, or even the third.

Neral felt himself falling and flung out an arm to catch himself before he hit the stone. Two more *neiirrh* struck.

He accepted that he would never reach his house and the waiting antidotes. He accepted that here was an enemy he could not fight. What he could do, however, was deny his enemy the sight of his fear, of a mortal struggle that could not help but be ludicrous.

Neral's side ached, and it was getting harder to breathe. Colors swirled before his eyes, like a wormhole with his own death at the other end of it. But Neral refused to die tumbled in an ungainly heap or toppling from the terrace into the valley below.

Reaching out almost blindly, Neral grabbed the bench where he had sat, savoring brandy, moonrise, and the beauty of the Vale of Chula.

For a merciful instant, the cold stone revived him. With his last strength, he dragged himself back onto it and let himself fall flat. Folding his gashed hands on his breast, Neral gazed up into the sky, watching the full moons dance in the night sky through dimming eyes. At the very least, he had turned defeat into dignity.

That might not be much of a victory, but until his personal night fell and his eyes shone only with the light of the moons, he honored it.

THIRTY-SEVEN

VULCAN

2366

Spock raised the coronet from his head. The tiny wounds on his brow stung, then closed almost instantly. As he held the gleaming coronet in both hands, they scarcely shook at all. His touch was as gentle on the intricate filigree of wires binding the glowing central crystals as they would have been on the strings of his lytherette—or his wife's lips.

At the last, Karatek had used his crown as a weapon, but it had not struck Spock down. It had not so much as scorched his graying hair. He was very tired now. But it had been worth any degree of exhaustion to make Karatek's acquaintance. Not since the discovery of the *Kir'Shara* had Vulcan learned so much about the life and times of Surak. And never before had anyone obtained so much information about the exile itself.

In the days to come, the full story that the coronet held— Karatek's full story that Spock now knew as intimately as if he'd lived through those violent, valiant, and supremely illogical days—would have to be relayed to his distant kin. He had promised that to the people who had sent it to him. All of the people whose valor, betrayals, vengeance, and struggles toward atonement Karatek's story chronicled needed to hear it.

Vulcans and Romulans had long spoken of the Sundering. By that, most people had understood that the race had been split in two: the Vulcans who remained on the Mother World and those who left and became the Romulans. The Remans, however, had never had a voice.

Now, it appeared that yet another offshoot of the Sundered remained to be found, the people whom Karatek's daughter Sarissa had led away from Remus. That clan would have bitter and legitimate grievances against the Romulan Star Empire and, very possibly, against everyone else it met. Assuming they still lived, which was an assumption that Spock personally considered highly logical. Whatever else these fugitives were, they had once been Vulcans. So, they were probably out there, remembering, searching, planning, and preparing to strike.

The four-way sundering of his race reminded Spock unpleasantly of that story from Earth's early history of how the people of its Eastern steppes punished traitors. They were stretched out on the ground. Each of their limbs were tied to a spirited horse. Then, warriors whipped the animals into a frenzy so that each horse ran in a different direction and the traitor was torn apart.

When Vulcans had first unearthed that story, there had been debate about whether even minimal contact with Earth should be maintained. Even when the decision was made to continue relations, technology transfer had been drastically slowed.

The Sundering had been far worse. Even now, Spock

suspected, its consequences had not fully manifested themselves. It was easy to say that Vulcan had not committed these crimes, but that was a rationalization. As Spock saw it, his duty was clear: to bind up what was wounded, mend what was torn, create harmony where there had been only rage.

First, the Romulans. Then, the Remans. Then, assuming they turned up, the descendants of Sarissa's fugitives.

There was, however, no use in what Dr. McCoy had always called borrowing trouble. Spock knew he would face enough trouble persuading his father that the task of reunification was logically his and that it was worthwhile. His consort Saavik's reaction would indubitably be even more vehement.

But Spock had always managed to hold his own with them. None of them would have had it otherwise.

At some point, he realized, Karatek's history would have to be shared with the other members of the Federation, too. The days when the Vulcans could hold themselves aloof from the less advanced and the less logical were days that had to end, or they might as well not have left the Mother World or struggled not to destroy themselves.

And then Karatek's legacy would have to be returned to Romulus. That had been one of the prime conditions that Charvanek and her former eaglet, now Vice Proconsul M'ret, had set on the artifact when they realized that the ancient, disused coronet, spoils of Remus, was more than an impressive piece of jewelry. With Charvanek's usual pragmatism, she had smuggled it out of the Empire at considerable personal and political risk. It must have been a tremendous loss of face for her to admit that the Vulcan disciplines could succeed where Romulan force had failed.

They would have to discuss that. They would have the time.

If Spock had wanted confirmation of the rightness of

his choice to seek reunification of Romulus and Vulcan, Karatek's history provided it. It compelled Spock to return to the Romulan Star Empire. Anyone could bring back the coronet as he had pledged, but only he, as he saw it, saw reunification as his duty. As several humans had told him throughout his life, he was a very stubborn man. That was just as well, now that he realized how much more complicated the problem was than he had originally estimated. He would have to think of it like chess: the hard games were the most worthwhile.

It would not be the first time that Spock had put his life and *katra* in jeopardy—but better risk both of them than his integrity. Or the honor of his family, which Surak had once headed.

But before Spock returned the coronet to the Romulan Star Empire, he faced one additional task. More than Karatek's memories lay embedded in its gems. Its central gem, in which a halo shimmered beneath its facets, held his *katra*. Spock understood Karatek's mind. His spirit needed to be returned to its beginning point and released.

Knowing that, Spock knew what he must do.

Nevasa rose, brilliant and sudden, over the Forge on the Fifth of Tasmeen. These days, the ceremonies commemorating the departure of the generation ships from Vulcan were subdued, so sparsely attended that some questioned the logic of holding them at all.

Spock would have to miss the ceremonies again this year. Rising, he ignored the weapons, the uniforms, and the gemmed robes to which he was entitled as a Starfleet captain, an ambassador, and the heir of Surak's own House. Instead, he put on pilgrim's robes. They were homespun, rougher and cruder than those he had worn as a postulant of *Kolinahr* or when he had been restored to life in the *fal-tor-pan*.

Barefoot, Spock left ShiKahr by the very same gate where Karatek had first seen Surak. The gate was ruined now, its columns tumbled and half covered by grit. In another thousand years or so, it would be gone, unless Vulcans decided to continue to preserve it from the encroaching desert.

Waterless and fasting, Spock took the pilgrim road toward Mount Seleya. Along the way, he chanted the songs and performed the meditations that had been old well before Karatek's birth. Nevasa rose in the crimson sky toward zenith. It beat down upon the Forge, its harsh light piercing the hood of his robe until he was forced to lower his eyes to the desert floor, where ruddy grit was interspersed with flecks of obsidian and slivers of polished bone.

The wind threatened to sweep the desert clear, hiding the path from sight. But Spock—and Karatek—remembered the path to the holy mountain on whose peak lightning danced amid the eternal snows.

Reaching Seleya's base in the late afternoon 3.7 days later, Spock knelt before the ablution pools, cleansing himself. He healed his feet in the ancient way, anointing them with sap from the broken leaves of the *kylin'the* that flourished at their edge. This was their blooming season. Their white and purple blossoms, like so many chalices, cast heavy sweetness over the pools. He whispered thanks to them.

Purified and refreshed, Spock climbed the thousand steps of Mount Seleya where his life had been renewed. By midafternoon, he had reached the plateau where Seleya's peaks divided. He passed through the narrow tunnel between mountain and sky, then crossed the narrow bridge that arched through the hot, thin air and led to the amphitheater where

T'Lar and T'Pau had gifted him with a sword when he was a boy. He bowed deeply to the altar, then turned toward the Hall of Ancient Thought where he bowed even more deeply, this time to the *Kir'Shara* enthroned on the dais, the light playing down upon it. Behind it, in a niche carved deep in the ancient stone, was the vessel that contained Surak's *katra*. Light pulsed behind the curves of its clay, the gem that crowned but did not seal it.

After all these years, Surak's *katra* still had not sought its freedom. That majestic spirit remained on Vulcan. In saying, "I come to serve," Surak had made a commitment that stretched, like Karatek's memories, beyond the bounds of his own life.

But Spock had not come to commune with Surak. He had met him, or a simulacrum, once; and though the experience would no doubt be fascinating, this pilgrimage was not for him, but for Karatek.

Spock bowed a last time and left the hall. Taking the coronet from beneath his robes, he held it up to catch and refract Nevasa's light.

Do you see, T'Kehr? *You are finally home. The desert is very beautiful today.*

Spock walked without hesitation to the lip of the cliff. He let his memories mingle with those of Karatek and drift, simply drift, out over the immense, clear horizon.

The day Spock had been honored for the *kahs-wan,* he had seen a *shavokh.* It was illogical to stand and hope to see a spirit guide, as if he were an ancient tribesman on a vision quest.

Nevertheless, Spock waited.

What flew past the platform on which he stood was not a *shavokh,* but a sundweller. Nevasa's light struck rainbows from its wings.

As it passed Spock, it turned, then headed higher. He had seen one only once before, when he was a boy. He had cried out in wonder, and Sarek had rebuked him, not even for the first time that day. Spock remembered each reprimand as if he had just heard it.

The day Karatek had met Surak and his life had changed, he had seen a sundweller, too. Spock sensed the *katra*'s awareness—almost a mental sigh—of satisfaction. Although the concept was sentimental to the point of illogic, Spock was certain now that Karatek realized he was home.

What need was there now for the rituals of incense, bell-banners, or *systra?* The spirit was prepared and willing to go. It would be impropriety verging on the blasphemous to restrain it.

Spock let Karatek's *katra* fly free. Perhaps it would join the sundweller as it flew upward, always upward, until it was too bright to watch. Or perhaps the thing that dazzled his sight was the *katra* itself.

Spock's eyes veiled. He sank to his knees. For 35.9 minutes, his concentration was engulfed in profound meditation.

The sky had darkened by the time Spock returned to the waking world. He could see every light on or above the Forge for a distance of several hundred kilometers.

The wind whipped about him as he rose to his feet and turned back toward the bridge. He remembered how his mother Amanda had feared it and how she had worked to master that. Karatek and his children had been similarly apprehensive. They too had prevailed. But that did not mean that the risk was not genuine.

As sunset approached, Seleya's thermals grew strong

enough to push a full-grown man off the bridge if he was not watchful. Spock knew he was tired.

If he was to cross back today, it must be now.

He knew he could command a pallet as austere as those of the indwellers in the Hall of Ancient Thought. Once he had no greater wish than to become an adept, although his own path had taken him to Gol.

If Spock elected to remain for the night, he could join the adepts for the evening meal and meditation, then rise before dawn to join the chant saluting the sun. The idea possessed the logic of closure, of coming full circle. It even had good sense to recommend it. It was not wise to travel on Vulcan at night. Granted, no wild *sehlat*s or *le-matya* had been observed near Mount Seleya for 233.56 years, but the ones seen before that had devoured three pilgrims.

He was unarmed.

But Saavik would be waiting for him at the base of the mountain. Throughout the years of their marriage, they had had very little time together. If he followed through on his plans, they faced even greater separations.

That decided him to attempt the descent now. He would spend no more time apart from her than logic—and his forthcoming mission—absolutely required.

Balancing against the gusts that buffeted him, Spock crossed the bridge in one swift motion. He glanced back at the altar, one of his first memories after his life was renewed. He had looked up then and seen oddly familiar faces. Some were Vulcan. Others were alien, blazing with an emotion he had had to learn again to call welcome. Saavik had looked down and away. Years later, he had understood her sudden flush and her downcast eyes, too.

Down the thousand stairs he walked as the last ragged banners of sunset faded. The wind sang in the turns of the steep ancient spiral. He heard *myrmidex* rustling along the path, the jump of a sand toad, the triumphant hunting cry of a *shavokh*.

The steps twisted again. He was nearing the bottom now; and in the lights that glistened off the bubbling fountain, he saw a tall shadow. Saavik. All alone. Waiting for him.

He remembered her words from the call with which she had summoned him: *I shall await you at the appointed place.*

She was nothing if not a woman of her word.

Spock quickened his steps toward all he desired of home.

THIRTY-EIGHT

ROMULUS

2380

The caverns trembled from their nearness to the firefalls. Inside the shrine, the rumbling of the lava pouring off the lip of the flawed volcano into the sea battled with the shrill jangle of the *systra* and the boom of ancient, ship-metal gongs.

Each time the gongs rang out, a rhythmic torrent of sound, the congregants cast incense into a firepit. Aboveground in the Hallows prayed the mourners, bowing before the main altar in an immense shrine, paneled with mosaics. Light poured in through the windows right below a dome that seemed almost to float on a circlet of glowing windows.

Belowground was where the penitents came. They, too, bowed and hurled incense. Then, in expiation of their sins, they slashed their hands or wrists with Honor Blades. Stepping closer to the fire, they held their wounded hands or arms over it until the priests determined they had atoned sufficiently. If atonement was judged impossible, they would be left standing. Some toppled into the flames. The rest fell where they had stood and were dragged off to aristocratic tombs.

Then, the rock floor was cleansed, ready for the next congregation.

A figure in acolyte's robes stepped forward to refill the incense bowls. Today's expensively robed penitents had consumed an entire bowl of incense, but had shed very little blood. These days on Romulus, ritual blood-letting was not much in fashion. Those whose social and political standing admitted them to the Hallows preferred to shed other people's blood, for other reasons.

Fire erupted in the pit below, hurling a cascade of sparks toward the roof of the cave. The acolyte wiped flecks of ash and sulfur off the altar. She flung back her hood in mute reaction to the heat. The priests flicked warning gazes from the pilgrims' backs to her too-recognizable face but, at her glare, bowed apology. Suppressing a hiss of frustration, she turned back toward the altar and made a display of ordering the ritual objects on its polished surface.

Liviana, called Charvanek, once a commander in Grand Fleet and consort to a Praetor, let her fingers brush the sacrificial knife that so few penitents used these days; a coronet restored some years back to imperial care; and an Honor Blade that had belonged to her consort, sadly enough, last of his line.

The shrine's priests had constituted themselves her protectors. She, however, considered them her captors. What kind of fool did they think she was? No one knew the Empire's senators and aristocrats better than she. The only ones with the imagination to even speculate that the altar might be tended by a woman they counted as safely dead were all dead, too.

It had been a close call, more than once. After her consort

Narviat's assassination, Charvanek had all but bled out before that very altar. It did not matter that she had been offworld: she had been chief of security and should have protected him better.

Nor had that been the first time she had stood in this place and drawn knife blade across her wrists. There had been the small matter, several wars back, of a cloaking device stolen from her, not to mention her part in firing on the Empire's ships in a revolution against a madman.

She certainly had led an eventful life.

Each time, though, she had been pulled back from death before the altar. She had been out patrolling the borders against the Dominion, whose treaty of nonaggression she had trusted not at all. It was one of her major regrets that she had not gotten to take a hand in N'Gathan's death.

Charvanek set her late consort's Honor Blade down. She bowed from the waist and cast incense into the flames. Then, picking up the sacrificial knife, she slashed it across her palm, let the blood drip into the pit in ongoing sorrow.

If no pilgrims remained in the Hallows, she decided, she would go out and cleanse the sulfur dust off Narviat's tomb and place another crystal upon it. If the pilgrims lingered, she would prowl the caves once more. Her explorations reminded her of holidays when she, like other promising children of the imperial line, had been dressed in tiny replicas of House livery and sent off for audience with the Emperor.

Show proper respect to the Emperor, or he'll feed you to his fish! The noble-born children whispered to each other in gleeful attempts to terrify each other, the beginnings of what would become the next generation of psychological wars among the clans. Charvanek's own family had simply reminded her of her duty. Not that they had needed to.

She remembered her own first audience. As a very apprehensive file of "eaglets" lined up to salute the Emperor as he walked in, Charvanek had not been impressed by her first sight of what seemed like only an impossibly old man in shabby robes. Then, she had seen his eyes: keen, wise, and alight with a wicked, subtle humor.

Shiarkiek had apparently recognized something in the tense, gifted child who caught his gaze. Quick to rebuke ambition or flattery in a bold child, the scholar in him could spot ability and nourish it. And he had no direct heir, which accounted for the presence of children like her, Narviat, the twin sisters T'Revana, betrothed to Narviat since childhood, and T'Lyris, the mother of Charvanek's own protégé M'ret, now in exile on Vulcan.

All the eaglets had agreed that His Majesty had always liked Narviat best of all. Nevertheless, the devious old man had always put off naming him as heir. Perhaps that had been a way of keeping Narviat under control. Perhaps it had even been a way of keeping assassins at bay—for all the good that had ultimately done.

But Shiarkiek had liked her, too. He had spared her life. Even during her years in disgrace, he had received her. First, he would insist on showing her the newest in his collection of fish, each specimen more bloodthirsty than the last. Then, they would explore the libraries or the treasuries of Romulus. As M'ret grew up and proved intelligent, they invited him along.

That was how they had found the coronet. The cracked *elassa*-wood box had not been prepossessing. Neither, when Shiarkiek pried open the lock, were the few stained rags of silk that covered what looked like an armature of metal wires. Shiarkiek, however, had unwrapped it and smiled as M'ret gasped in shock, then ducked his head in apology, no doubt thinking of the Emperor's fish and their sharp little teeth.

The way the light pulsed in the great central crystal, wrapped in intricate twists of precious wire, instantly drew and held Charvanek's gaze. Smiling to see one of the fiercest fighting commanders in the Fleet enthralled by a piece of jewelry, Shiarkiek handed it to her.

Power seemed to shoot out from the coronet and run up her arms. Lights exploded behind her eyes and almost made her drop it. She covered her own surprise by bowing thanks and handing the lovely, dangerous thing back.

"Do you think the Ruling Queen wore that crown, Majesty?" M'ret had asked. His voice had not even started to break.

Humor warmed the old man's tired eyes.

"I think it predates T'Rehu, do you not?" he asked Charvanek.

So he had them all back at school, did he? Charvanek smiled, inclined her head, and gave the dates of the Ruling Queen's accession and death in battle. Her eyes met the Emperor's in perfect understanding. The artifact was not Romulan in origin. It had been crafted on Vulcan, and the energy Charvanek sensed had been mental.

Shiarkiek was old, Shiarkiek was bored, and Shiarkiek was curious. Shiarkiek was quite aware that Charvanek maintained contact with Vulcans, who preserved the disciplines of the mind that Romulans needed equipment to perform and used only for interrogation. For that matter, His Majesty had even met one of those Vulcans himself. Anything as old as that coronet might shed some light on the origins of their race. If he had to use the Vulcans to find out, well, learning was learning, and Shiarkiek had always been more scholar than emperor.

Probably, the old wizard had planned for her and M'ret to smuggle the thing off Romulus all along. That, no doubt, accounted for the ease with which the deed had been accomplished. Shiarkiek would probably have made it similarly easy to smuggle the coronet back in, if Spock had not saved them the effort.

Now it lay upon the altar of their greatest shrine. Romulus, too, had a great deal to atone for.

But Charvanek had had enough of shrines, chanting, and incense for the day. She headed for the path that led to the upper air. Priests blocked her way—no surprises there. There was no point in trying to fight her way to the surface. In the desperate boredom induced by her status as, essentially, a state prisoner, she had sparred with some of them. The best of the priests were as good in hand-to-hand as any warriors in the Fleet, and she was, she had to admit, no longer in her first youth.

It was beneath Charvanek's dignity to admit defeat. She turned on her heel and started down into the caves. She knew another way out. If the priests knew that she had found that one, they owed her a few indulgences as well as their "protection."

Not that their protection was worth anything these days.

These days, "to the strongest" was the rule of the game they had once run. Not all the strongest were Romulan. Federation ships crossed the Neutral Zone into the Empire, bearing assistance. Even less acceptable: *Klingons* had made the Remans a protectorate. Temporary, they called it, but no Klingon grasping a prize that rich would loosen his fist.

In less degenerate days, that would have been cause for war. Narviat had attacked Khitomer for far less. The attack and its repercussions had weakened his position so that he fell at the next crisis. Her fault, her fault.

So was Neral's destruction. "The time has come for truth," he had said when he learned the story of Karatek, contained in the coronet that lay glinting on the altar. After the costs of the Dominion War, the Empire—or at least Senator Hiren and his backers—had not been in a mood for truth. That story and the Watraii attack a year after the Dominion War had precipitated Neral's "replacement" by Hiren. Then Hiren had died in the Reman revolt. Another death Charvanek regretted not having had a hand in.

Narviat and Hiren had been surprised. But Neral had seen his fate approaching. She should have guessed when he gave away his pet *setlet,* Pyncho. It was not that he was so busy he could not take proper care of the creature. After all, he had a houseful of servants who could have tended it. Instead, Neral had found the poor beast a new home so that it could live out its remaining years in safety. Perhaps, if he had shown signs of spiriting away his family—but, then, Neral had no family to worry about. They had died years before, killed by Klingons. Apparently, however, he had had another person whom he wished to protect: Charvanek herself.

She had been astonished when she went to bed in her own home. She had taken all security precautions, but she woke to find herself held in protective custody by the priests. Since then, she had been virtually a state prisoner, held by the priests in deference to her imperial blood.

Worse yet, they had kept her ignorant! It had taken her—her!—far too long to find ways of reaching her old sources of intelligence. She had learned one hundred five days after her abduction how Neral's servants had found him lying in his garden. Curious, wasn't it, how poisonous birds could have gotten past his force shields?

She and Neral had not been friends. Certainly, despite the usual rumors, they had not been lovers. Neral had been scarcely older than M'ret. They had been associates who worked well together. She honestly regretted his loss.

Charvanek smiled, but there was ice in it. They had not even told her that a battle involving Romulans, Remans, the Federation, and Klingons had been fought practically over her head.

They should never have allowed me access to a computer.

She might owe her life to the priests' connivance with Neral, but they had slain her Emperor. They had captured her. They had kept her ignorant. They owed *her*.

Charvanek slipped out of the priests' line of sight toward the passage that led to the tombs of the Houses Major and her temporary freedom.

His Imperial Majesty always said a Praetor's life had room for about three good crises before the assassins came. How many Praetors, he would ask, had died at home, of old age? The first one—grand- or great-grandchildren, nephews, nieces, whatever—to get them all right won a prize. Being quick, Charvanek had often won those games, especially when the answer was the name of a famous warrior.

"There you go, Charvanek!" His Majesty would say. The last time they'd played before she entered the war college, he'd given her her Honor Blade.

But it was not just Praetors: it was any member of a Romulan House Major. Any Head of House who felt himself losing control did one of two things: either he committed atrocities like Dralath's raid on Narendra III, or he began to protect those closest to him, especially the innocents. Of course that assumed anyone on Romulus was ever innocent.

Charvanek knew what it was to get innocents of her own to

safety. During the revolution that brought Narviat to power, she had gotten Spock back into the Federation. He was incapacitated, so it was no fair fight. Just as well she had used that Commander Ruanek anyway. Disastrously blunt of speech as he was, he probably would have gotten himself killed before the year was out.

Years later, she had smuggled out M'ret and his aides. Some whispered that M'ret had been her son. His father was rumored to be anyone from Narviat in the years before their marriage to the Vulcan who was her dearest enemy.

M'ret had paid dearly for his freedom. He was called M'ret the Traitor now, and farewell to any hopes Charvanek had had that he might rule one day as Emperor. But M'ret sent her reliable information by his allies, the unificationists.

Charvanek was certain she did not approve of unification. She had been appalled to learn she shared that view with Spock's consort, Captain Saavik. That woman! She had taken severe wounds during the Dominion War, but recovered and returned to battle. Romulan blood, as the saying went, bled green on either side of the Neutral Zone.

Ah, Charvanek saw light coming from the exit from the caves. Not a priest in sight, either. Victory! Charvanek raised her hood once again and stepped outside.

The rush of the firefalls grew louder as the cave mouth opened onto bent, skeletal trees and tombs coated with yellowish dust. Her path took her by Neral's tomb, an impressively carved statue etched with the secret name he had never shared with her. The man had deserved to go down fighting. She left for remembrance not a crystal, but a fragment of obsidian shaped like a dagger.

She headed for Narviat's tomb, one among a row of monumental basalt slabs marked with names she had known since childhood. She brushed her consort's name briefly clean of the drifting dust, ash, and glass filaments that filled the air. She traced the names "Narviat" and "Devoras" on the warm stone before laying her wounded palm against it. She was surprised some fool hadn't suggested they inscribe her names on the tombstone, too.

The suggestion had probably been raised and adroitly sidestepped by the priests, who kept their secrets—and their prisoners—far too well.

She, too, hoarded secrets, brought her once again by the techs who had helped Narviat become Praetor when they were little more than feral children with a talent for computer sabotage. After Narviat's accession, he had found posts for them in his government, posts they had lost after his death. Just as well; they had joined Spock's underground and were an unceasing source of information.

How else would she have obtained copies of Surak's *Analects,* the *Kir'Shara,* Karatek's history, or, most recently, the Watraii rationale for their strike at Nemor, A little scheming that alleviated the boredom of her days had brought Charvanek an account of the first mission to the Watraii homeworld.

Apparently, the healer priestess T'Selis who led it had been trained in the old ways on Mount Seleya. From reading Karatek's account of the healer T'Olryn, who had married Solor, Karatek's tragic firebrand of a son, she had some notion what this entailed.

What made Charvanek smile each time she thought of it was that *this* healer had actually married Ruanek! And to think that in sending Ruanek to Vulcan, Charvanek had wished him peace and long life. With a wife like that, Ruanek might actually achieve the long life. The peace, however . . .

well, Vulcans could lie about it as much as they wanted, they were no more peaceful than Romulans.

Or Remans.

"Only think, husband," she whispered, "your Commander Ruanek's wife actually confronted the Watraii. You are well revenged for his insolence."

Charvanek drew a deep breath. At least she had been able to have this hour alone with all she had left of Narviat. She had not loved him, but they had had . . . *something.* Leaning her head against her husband's gravestone, she basked in the firefalls' warmth.

Who knew when she might be able to come this way again?

Charvanek looked up at the sky, dominated by Remus. It was time to emerge and rebuild her life once more.

"I do not want to do what I must do," she admitted. She pressed her cheek against the place where her husband's secret name was carved into the stone.

Narviat would have brushed her hand, then her lips, with his fingers. She could almost hear his voice saying, "Hardly for the first time. And not the last, either, if I know you."

He had always known her better than she realized.

She was going to have to go to Remus, back to the ice, the darkness, and the hatred. For an instant of pure self-indulgence, she wanted very much instead to be back in the Fleet, even as the least of its officers on the most battered of its ships. If she could not escape back into service, she thought death might be preferable.

That thought was unworthy. She had wished to die before and mastered the impulse after the debacle of her first encounter with the *Enterprise* a century ago, again during her imprisonment by Dralath, and yet again when she returned to the homeworld to find herself a widow. Her wishes did not matter. Besides, she had destroyed her Honor Blade at Narendra III.

"There is no point in renewing your life if you only relive your errors."

That was not the voice of her dead husband, but of her living nemesis. Spock. She could hardly believe that her choices had narrowed to only one: joining Spock on Remus.

It was not as if she was unfamiliar with Reman mercenaries. Dralath had kept an entire Reman legion to unleash on rebel provinces. They had probably enjoyed being ordered to kill Romulans.

After her disastrous first encounter with the *Enterprise,* the Senate had sent her to Remus on punishment detail. Narviat, who had risked speaking for her when she had found nothing to say in her Right of Statement, later told her she was damned lucky to live, much less retain her commission.

She had not thought so at the time. Remus was cold and dangerous, the Remans pallid, violent grotesques. The fact that her ancestors' treachery had made them what they were did not make her like them more.

Years later, after her marriage to Narviat, she had had to have Reman guards of her own. Her own honor required her to provide for them decently. So she had ordered her house steward to transform remote storerooms into clean barracks that could be appropriately chilled and darkened until "her" Remans lived in the bleak level of comfort that was all they would accept from her. She had never even learned their names.

She supposed Spock would consider that a failure of compassion.

Isn't compassion an emotion, Spock?

No, Commander. She would always be "Commander" to him except for the rare, dangerous moments when she was "Liviana." *Compassion is a logical response to what the Remans have endured at the Empire's hands.*

The worst of it was that Charvanek had to agree.

Sarissa's account of the flight from Remus had convinced her of the truth of the Watraii story. Their ancestress was as alike in mind to Charvanek as any sister. Admittedly, Charvanek had always been strange in her choice of "sisters." Rachel Garrett, who fell with another damnable *Enterprise* at Narendra III. That Saavik, now living in the Federation the life of valor and honor that the Empire had denied her. And now, Sarissa.

"I am honor bound to go, Devoras," she confessed at Narviat's tomb. He would not have been pleased. But he would have understood Spock's statement in his last message to her: "We have much work ahead if you want to help right an ancient wrong."

For Spock, the matter of the Remans was an issue of basic rights. Because Charvanek refused to be shamed by a Vulcan, she had made the calls she knew she must. Tonight she would leave the Hallows, leave Romulus, possibly for all time, and go to Remus.

A pity she could not see the priests' faces when they found her missing.

The Remans might kill her. No doubt, they would try. They might even be justified. She suspected, though, that Spock would hold up a hand and forbid it, whereupon even the Remans would bow and agree.

"I come to serve," he always said, but he always turned out, instead, to lead.

Charvanek had once offered to "make a place" for him

in the Romulan Star Empire. Now, he made a place for her on Remus. The Klingons and their Reman Protectorate had no idea what was about to hit them. And if Spock's precious Federation thought they could restrict her movements any more than her own priests, she would disappoint them, too.

The situation possessed an irony that appealed to her. It was, in a word, only logical.

After all, Spock had expanded his theories on unification to include Romulus and Remus. She knew the time was coming, if it had not already arrived, when he would expand them still further to take in the Watraii. Just let there be one person, one person alone, among the Watraii who still possessed the courage and resolve of Sarissa. Just let that one person unmask and face her, honestly, across a conference table or the viewscreen of a fighting ship, and Charvanek would stake her life that she could *make* that person listen to reason.

Another "challenge of a lifetime." Night and day! When did it *stop?*

Not now, that was for certain.

The Empire had wronged the Remans. So it stood to reason amends must be made. If the Empire had wronged the Watraii, as they claimed, Charvanek would want proof. If their grievances were legitimate, she would see that the Empire made amends, even if she had to kill the leader of each faction in it herself and take the throne *herself* to do it. Not because of Spock's theories, not for her own goals, not even for the sake of the Empire itself.

But because honor demanded.

About the Authors

JOSEPHA SHERMAN is a fantasy novelist, folklorist, and the owner of Sherman Editorial Services. She has written everything from *Star Trek* novels *Vulcan's Forge, Vulcan's Heart, Vulcan's Soul, Book I: Exodus,* and *Vulcan's Soul, Book II: Exiles* with co-author Susan Shwartz, to biographies of Bill Gates and Jeff Bezos (founder of Amazon.com), folklore titles such as *Mythology for Storytellers* (from M. E. Sharpe) and *Trickster Tales* (August House), and fantasy novels such as the forthcoming *Stoned Souls* (Baen Books) with Mercedes Lackey. She is the winner of the Compton Crook Award for best fantasy novel, and has had many titles on the New York Public Library Books for the Teen Reader list.

As of this writing, Sherman is editing *The Encylopedia of Storytelling* for M. E. Sharpe. For her editorial projects, you can check out www.ShermanEditorialServices.com. When she isn't busy writing, editing, or gathering folklore, Sherman loves to travel, knows how to do horse whispering, and has had a newborn foal fall asleep on her foot. You can visit her at www.JosephaSherman.com.

SUSAN SHWARTZ's most recent books are *Second Chances*, a retelling of *Lord Jim*; a collection of short fiction called *Suppose They Gave a Peace and Other Stories, Shards of Empire* (Tor) and *Cross and Crescent* (Tor), set in Byzantium; along with the *Star Trek* novels (written with Josepha Sherman) *Vulcan's Forge, Vulcan's Heart,* and *Vulcan's Soul, Book I: Exodus,* and *Vulcan's Soul, Book II: Exiles.* Other works include *The Grail of Hearts*, a revisionist retelling of Wagner's *Parsifal*, and over 70 pieces of short fiction. She has been nominated for the Hugo twice, the Nebula five times, the Edgar and World Fantasy Award once, and has won the HOMer, an award for science fiction given by Compuserve.

Her next novel will be *Hostile Takeovers,* also from Tor. It draws on over twenty years of writing science fiction and almost twenty years of working in various Wall Street firms; it combines enemy aliens, mergers and acquisitions, insider trading, and the asteroid belt.

She received her B.A., *magna cum laude* and Phi Beta Kappa from Mount Holyoke and earned her doctorate in English from Harvard University. She has also attended summer school at Trinity College, Oxford, and has held a National Endowment for the Humanities grant for postdoctoral study in conjuction with Dartmouth College.

For three years, she taught at Ithaca College in upstate New York, but, for the past twenty years, she's worked on Wall Street at various brokerages, a leading bond-rating agency, and an asset management firm. She is now Vice President of Communications at an alternative investments firm in New York.

Her nonfiction has appeared in *Vogue, The New York Times, Analog, Amazing,* various encyclopedias, and collections of critical work. She is a frequent public speaker, most recently at the NSA, but also at Harvard, Princeton, Mount Holyoke, the University of Connecticut, the State University of New York at Binghamton, Smith College, the Naval War College, and the United States Military Academy.

Some time back, you may have seen her on TV selling Borg dolls for IBM, a gig for which she actually got paid. She lives in Forest Hills, New York.